SECRET SALVATION

CHAD JOSEY

Copyright

SECRET SALVATION
Copyright © 2017 by Chad Josey

https://ChadJosey.com

Biblical scriptures from the Public Doman (Bible in Basic English), http://www.o-bible.com/bbe.html

Published by Hicks Creek Press

First Edition, 2017

ISBN-10:   0-9994959-0-9 (paperback)
ISBN-13:   978-0-9994959-0-2 (paperback)
ISBN-10:   0-9994959-1-7 (e-book)
ISBN-13:   978-0-9994959-1-9 (e-book)

For my wife, Amanda. Thank you for your love and support through this creative endeavor with your words of encouragement. You give me strength.

PROLOGUE

E LI BISHOP stood in the shadows of the House Chamber inside the Capitol Building. A sly grin appeared when he heard his words he had penned as the President spoke before the Joint Session of Congress. The Eden Foundation's plans to save humanity were underway... to reach Salvation.

Now it is time to take longer strides—time for a great new American enterprise—time for this nation to take a clearly leading role in space achievement, which in many ways may hold the key to our future on Earth.

I believe we possess all the resources and talents necessary. But, the facts of the matter are that we have never made the national decisions or marshaled the national resources required for such leadership.

... No single space project in this period will be more impressive to mankind or more important for the long-range exploration of space, and none will be so difficult or expensive to accomplish.... in the very real sense, it will not be one man going to the Moon. If we make this judgment affirmatively, it will be an entire nation...

... Perhaps beyond the Moon. Perhaps to the very end of the solar system itself... let it be clear that I am asking the Congress and the country to accept a firm commitment to a new course of action—a course, which will last for many years, and carry very heavy costs...

- John F. Kennedy, President of the United States
May 25, 1961

PROLOGUE

1 - EDEN

TORRENTS OF BROWN DUST spun in the air trailing the limo as it sped into the darkening canopy of pine trees blocking out the sunlight; a thick and dusty reminder they were on a road less traveled. An hour had elapsed since Dr. Joseph Bishop had passed any signs of civilization from his back-seat vantage point.

The cityscape of Denver had long left the limo's rearview mirror. Glorious snow-capped mountains rose before the car as it turned off the main road to a hidden dirt path paralleled by a small stream meandering through the thick evergreen forest.

The tinted privacy window inside the limo slid down behind the driver's shoulder. The driver was immaculate. He wore a crisp, white dress shirt under his black suit and tie, topped off with a plain, black driving cap. An oddly familiar red, metal lapel pin with a white outline of a circle within a triangle stood out against his black jacket.

His leather-gloved hands clenched the steering wheel tight wrangling the car down the gravel path. The driver made eye contact through his mirror with his passenger.

"Dr. Bishop, we will be at the Eden Foundation in fifteen minutes."

"Thank you, Thomas."

Vibrations filled the car from the pebbled road as the privacy window hummed closed. The announcement gave Dr. Joseph Bishop, Joe to his closest friends, the opportunity to review his notes and make last-minute annotations.

Joe had met Thomas only two days earlier at Joe's house in Stony Brook, New York. The Eden Foundation had provided Thomas as Joe's personal driver to JFK, his escort onboard the Foundation's private jet, and his driver upon their arrival in Colorado.

The two men had spoken few words. It was not for lack of trying on Joe's part. Thomas maintained a serious appearance, not once cracking a smile. Joe imagined Thomas as his personal bodyguard given his muscular build.

Joe placed his notes into his backpack, twisted the top of his Mont Blanc pen given to him by his wife Mary, and slid it into the liner pocket of his blazer. Joe sighed and peered out the window admiring the landscape. Feeling a ping of nervousness, a bead of sweat formed below his hairline.

A promising benefactor, the Eden Foundation had offered a large sum of money for Joe's presentation, today. His goal is to parlay the success of his speech to receive full funding for his continued research identifying the genetic markers of certain cancers, which will someday help advance a cure. This goal drove Joe through university as he had made a promise to his deceased mother, Rachel, who had passed due to a brain tumor when Joe was only ten.

The winding stream paralleling the limousine expanded, stretching the distance between the roadside and the opposite shoreline. White foam raced over the smooth, black rocks drawn out between the banks of the forming river. A light drizzle peppered the windows as the sun disappeared behind billowing clouds. Darkness from the thicket of pine trees above them hid away the remaining light.

Joe rubbed the underside of his wedding ring with his thumb. A nervous habit he had developed over the past fourteen years.

A tall metal fence suddenly eclipsed his view of the river. Razor wire curled and danced along the top of the solid wall with the passing speed of the limo.

Joe peered ahead through the rear passenger window. A small building protruded from the metal fence. Thomas slowed the limo coming to a stop. A figure of a security guard dressed in a black uniform approached the driver's window, humming as it lowered. A red lapel pin matched Thomas's and was noticeable against the guard's black clothes.

"I have Dr. Bishop, here," Thomas said.

The guard attempted to peek into the back of the stretch limousine. The tinted windows prevented him from seeing Joe.

Satisfied, the guard spoke into a microphone affixed to his shoulder. A large, rusting pulley spun above the metal fence sliding open the wall. Thomas drove the limo inside the gate.

The dirt path continued to a bland, one-story building. Tall pine trees speckled the land between the road and the structure; perfect protection and cover to keep the facility secret.

The limo parked parallel to the curb in front of the barren building. Silence filled the inside of the car. Thomas opened the back door.

"Dr. Bishop, Mr. D'Angelo will meet you inside the building."

"Okay. Thank you, Thomas."

Joe stepped out of the limo and placed his backpack over his shoulder as he approached the building. The exterior was pale brown absent any windows or signs. Only Thomas and Joe stood outside.

The drizzle collected on the lens of Joe's wire-rimmed glasses. As the droplets grew larger, he wiped his left hand across clearing his view as the door to the building opened.

A tall man wearing a white linen suit with a bright-blue dress shirt and dark-blue tie approached Joe. His muscular shoulders wanted to burst through the form-fitting Italian clothes. The white suit contrasted against the stark, desolate backdrop of the compound and especially flaunted his red lapel pin.

The two men only had limited contact through email and one phone call. Today, was their first meeting; a day changing Joe's life forever.

"Good morning, Dr. Bishop. I'm Gabriel. Welcome to the Eden Foundation. I hope you had a good flight and enjoyed the hotel last night."

"Like I said over the phone last week, call me Joseph or Joe." They shook hands as they greeted each other. Joe's hand crushed inside of Gabriel's fist.

"Okay then, Joe it is. And, your flight—"

"I've never flown in a private jet. It was great, and the hotel was the best I've ever stayed."

Gabriel held open the door for Joe as they entered the building with the door closing behind them. They were alone inside a dimly lit lobby absent any pictures, plants, or furnishing. One lone, metal chair sat next to a closed door opposite the entrance.

"So, what do you think?"

"About this place or my presentation this afternoon?"

Joe scanned around the inside of the building. The vacant lobby, the echo of their footsteps indicated they were alone in the spacious building.

"Both." Gabriel did not let Joe answer. "Here, let's take a short tour of our facility."

"When do the other guests for the presentation arrive?"

Gabriel opened the door beside the metal chair and led Joe into a hallway. Fluorescent lights flickered overhead as they passed several closed, white doors along both sides.

"There's plenty of time to talk about your work. But, I know what you must think?"

"Yeah, what's that?"

"Our building doesn't look that impressive, does it?"

"Well, um, it's not that…" Joe found his right words, "it's just when we spoke on the phone, you mentioned the Eden Foundation is 'doing exciting things.' That an audience had interest in my research."

"Yes, Joe, that is all true. We are doing otherworldly things. And, many have an interest in your work."

Disbelief crept into Joe. This place seemed like a prison, not a world-class research facility, which further fed his skeptical belief in the Foundation.

"This facility is one of our many locations. We focus more on our work and the knowledge we share rather than fancy furnishings. Let's go *in here*."

Gabriel opened a door and led Joe into a small room with a single table and chair. Another chair sat in front of a large, flat-panel television screen on the opposite wall. Uneasiness rumbled from Joe's gut.

"Take a seat, and I will start with a short introduction video. Can I get you some water?"

"No, I'm fine, thanks."

The lights in the room dimmed. In the center of the screen, the television came alive with a picture of Earth spinning taken from a satellite. Mathematical equations and coordinates radiated to the right side. On the left, four images of an elongated, black object appeared. The top image dated 1957 was small and fuzzy. The bottom one dated 2012 was larger and crystal clear. As the pictures appeared, Gabriel walked between Joe and the screen.

"What if I told you we know the exact moment the world will end? Even with this knowledge, nothing will save Earth. Everyone and everything here will be gone in an instant." Gabriel snapped his fingers; the sound bounced off the cold, empty walls.

The perpetual smile Gabriel had worn since Joe had arrived vanished. Gabriel stood stern and serious. A curiosity consumed Joe forcing his attention to Gabriel, not the screen.

"Life on Earth will vanish. But, what if I also told you that your research holds the key to sustaining the future of humanity?"

Gabriel's question provided truth to Joe's theory. "That explains this place. It's a cult. What's my cancer research have to do with this?" Joe stood. "I knew it was too good to be true. This whole damn thing is a joke, right?"

"If only I were crazy, then everything would be okay. But, please, Dr. Bishop… Joe, sit down. I will explain why Eden has asked you to join Project Salvation."

Joe remained standing and turned away from Gabriel backing from his chair. The morning had become a blur. Long gone was the comfort of breakfast in the five-star hotel in Denver.

In the quietness of no response to Gabriel, Joe heard his departed Grandma Liz's voice in his head with her thick Texas accent reminding Joe he had made a promise to Gabriel to present his work. Liz had assumed custody of Joe after Rachel's death since he was an orphan. His father, Jacob, had died before Joe was born. Liz was no stranger to sadness after losing her husband, Eli, to an accident one Thanksgiving Day many years ago.

A promise is a promise. Joe stopped short of bolting from the room and turned back to Gabriel returning to the chair.

"You flew me out here. You put me up in a very nice hotel last night and promised me a lot of money for my presentation. I'm still getting paid, right?"

"Yes, *here* is your fifty-thousand, now." Gabriel handed him two white envelopes. "In fact, *here* is another one."

Joe's eyes grew wide as he fingered through a thousand, one-hundred-dollar bills.

"Joe, the money does not matter anyway. The Eden Foundation has faith that your work is valuable in sustaining the future of human life. That's why we chose you for our program. As I share this information with you, I think you will be happy to join us. The alternative is to die with everyone else."

"Um, okay. So, tell me… how does the world end?"

Gabriel slid a metal chair across the floor next to Joe. A piercing, scratching sound echoed through the cold room. Joe focused his attention back to the screen as Gabriel sat beside him. The spinning Earth with its mathematical equations and fuzzy pictures intrigued Joe.

"What you see *here* is an image into space captured by the Hale Telescope at the Palomar Observatory in California in 1957. Unfortunately, the quality of the picture is not that great. But, we can compare this to the same picture taken from the Hubble Space Telescope in 2012."

"Sure, there is color, and I see more detail."

Gabriel held a wireless clicker and pointed it to the screen. Each of the four progressively more clear pictures zoomed out. Numerous white dots provided a backdrop to the elongated object in each frame.

"Look at the pictures." Gabriel stood to point to a black smudge on the 1957 photo.

"Okay, in the bottom picture the smudge is clear and... a little larger... and?"

"Yes, this newer picture is more clear, but shouldn't most things closer to a camera be that way?"

"You mean, just because the Hubble Telescope is in orbit and higher up, the object is more clear and larger?"

"Yes, but it's not that, this object is much closer to Earth in the last picture."

"The object? What the hell is it?"

"We have identified *this* as CIE.57.20"

"Ooh," Joe said mocking back.

"The 57 is for 1957, the year of discovery. And, the 20 is when the event will occur in 2020—"

"And, CIE?" Joe interrupted. He enjoyed riddles, but Gabriel had tested his patience.

After a long pause and a deep breath, Gabriel spoke his words in a slow manner. "CIE stands for Confirmed Impact Event."

"Impact Event? Impact of what? A meteor? A comet?"

"CIE.57.20 is larger than what we think of as a meteor. We have identified this as a planetoid, larger than our Moon, but smaller than Earth."

"A planetoid?"

"They are leftover fragments when the universes were created. As planets were forming and colliding, large chunks of debris merged. Based on collisions and gravitational pulls from planets in our solar system, planetoids are pushed along different orbits around our Sun."

Joe understood Gabriel's description of a planetoid. Growing up in a Houston suburb where many families had involvement with NASA, his high school offered many astronomy classes, which had been Joe's favorite subject.

"Okay, so you are saying this planetoid will hit Earth? And, you've known about this since 1957? Where will it hit? What kind of damage? What has anyone tried to do to stop it? And, why hasn't this information been made public?"

"Lots of great questions, and over the next two days I will provide the answers. After the first observations in the '60s, the calculations confirmed a collision is certain. It doesn't matter where. Unfortunately, given its size, material make-up, speed… where it hits… nothing will be left."

Gabriel gave Joe a red binder with pictures and calculations. Joe flipped through the pages. "After sixty years, there must be a plan to destroy it or push it away from Earth?"

"The Moon race in the '60s… well, this was a cover story by us and the Soviets to get to the Moon. Ours are the only governments aware of CIE.57.20. Once we got to the Moon, we established monitoring systems to collect more data."

"Wait, you are telling me the Russians know about this, and the Moon was nothing more than a fact-finding mission?"

"Yes, that was the initial purpose, but there's more."

"That's one helluva conspiracy then?"

"Oh, we are only beginning." Gabriel walked behind his chair to the table by the door. His calm demeanor vanished as he lifted a pitcher from the table. His hand developed a noticeable shake as water poured into a glass.

"Back to your earlier question about plans to destroy it."

"Yes, because after knowing about this thing for so long, surely there must be a plan in place?" Joe asked.

"From our readings, CIE.57.20 is composed of ninety-percent iron and nickel. It is traveling at an estimated speed of seventy-five thousand miles per hour."

Joe attempted a rough-cut estimate in his head of his own calculations.

"It is four-thousand miles in diameter, twice the size of our Moon. And, it is on a direct collision course. Now, you're a scientist, just by those statistics alone, I am sure you can imagine the outcome?"

Joe shifted his eyes to the upper-right performing calculations in his head. After a few seconds, his gaze fell back to the screen. Joe stood and slowly walked toward the image touching the newer image. He turned his head toward Gabriel who stood beside him.

"The energy of this impact will..." Joe paused for a moment not believing what he was about to say next, "cause the Earth to explode on impact."

"Yes, explode. We have ran the simulations many times, and we get the same results. CIE.57.20 is just too big, too fast, and too dense to destroy. Even if we detonated every nuclear weapon ever built, CIE.57.20 is still coming toward us."

"And exploding nuclear bombs near it won't nudge its orbit so it misses us? I mean, given the distance, nudging it even an inch would cause it to miss Earth entirely given the geometry."

"From our calculations, the gravitational pull from the planets as CIE.57.20 enters our solar system keeps it in-line with impacting Earth."

"But, so that's it. Simulations say this, and we won't try?"

"That's just it, Joe. We have tried. Entities in our governments have been building and testing larger nuclear bombs for decades for this purpose."

"What? You're telling me all the nuclear bomb testing is part of this too?"

Gabriel grasped Joe's shoulder. "The Cold War... we staged this. It was our cloak-and-dagger way to confuse the Public, because of all the nuclear testing we needed."

Joe stepped away from Gabriel in disbelief pushing Gabriel's hand off his shoulder and returned to his chair.

"We even sent missions to intercept other known meteors with similar characteristics to test our detonations. The results were all the same... our weapons will be useless."

Joe sat in silence. His eyes darted between the screen and Gabriel.

"So, you're telling me that all the nuclear testing and scare tactics of the Cold War were nothing more than an excuse to test weapons to blow this thing away?"

"Exactly... I know it is hard to understand. This isn't some science-fiction movie where we have a powerful laser that can blow this thing up. We have only the weapons we have been able to develop so far."

"So, even if all this is true, and I'm not saying I believe any of this... then, why in the hell are you telling me this? Why am I here?"

"Joe, your research holds the key for the human race survive—"

Joe stood from his chair and interrupted Gabriel. "Survive? How the hell does my genetic biological research for cancer treatments go about trying to stop this son-of-a-bitch?"

"It won't... your research will help us to sustain human life on Mars."

Disbelief and rage overcame Joe. He leaned forward placing his head into his hands with his elbows on his knees. After a few seconds, Joe leapt from the chair and grabbed his backpack from the table. "Okay, that's it, I am out of here. I entertained your crazy shit out of respect. But, you, my friend, are officially nuts."

He turned from Gabriel to leave the room and grabbed the doorknob. Gabriel advanced the picture on the television.

"Joe, what you see *here* is our facility on Mars. We call it *Salvation*. This is where we are moving a selected sector of the population. Salvation is our only chance for the human race to survive."

Joe stopped. His curiosity increased. He released his grip on the doorknob and turned back toward the screen.

"So, you're telling me this place will be built and people will go there to live?"

"Joe... we have already built *Salvation*... it's operational now."

Joe inched his way down in the chair. His mouth was open in disbelief. "This place is on Mars... that means we have already landed on—"

"Yes, Joe, we have been going to Mars since the mid-'80s."

"But... why me? Why my research?"

A ping of excitement aroused Joe with the possibilities of Mars. Gabriel's voice murmured in Joe's brain as childhood memories rushed back to Joe from the first time he had watched the Moon landing as a child.

2 - RACHEL

"HOUSTON. You're 'Go' for landing. Over."

Voices cracked over the television speakers in the corner of the living room. They had belonged to Ed Aldrin, the Lunar Module pilot on Apollo 11, and Mission Control from 1969 on the twentieth anniversary of the Moon landing.

"Roger. Understand. Go for landing... Kicking up some dust... Drifting to the right a little... Contact light... Okay, engine stop."

"We copy you down Eagle."

"Houston. Tranquility Base, here. The Eagle has landed."

A faint cheer erupted from Joseph. He sat on the floor, his face a foot away from the television screen, the smell of warm dust seeping from inside the gigantic Zenith wafted through the faux-wood, plastic cabinet. Grainy, black-and-white images filled his eyes from the old television standing on four, short metal legs. The twenty-year-old events captured his imagination blocking the sadness around him.

"Bless his heart. Liz, look at Joseph sitting on the floor watching that program," Martha said.

Liz Bishop and Martha Unger stood under the archway separating the kitchen from the living room. They had been best friends since Liz and her husband, Eli, had moved to the Houston suburb of Pasadena, Texas in 1961. Their closeness was obvious based on their matching black dresses and bouffant hairstyles.

"It's so sad to think about it. I asked Joseph why he was sitting so close to the screen. And, do you know what he said?" Liz asked.

"Uh-huh." Martha's response echoed from her glass as she sipped the last drops of her southern sweet tea.

"He said he turned the sound down not to disturb anybody." Liz held her empty glass with its clanging ice by her side.

"Disturb anyone. Oh, my. It's us who are disturbing him. When my mama died, I didn't want anyone around me at all. Heck, I was twenty then. With Rachel gone, I can't imagine what it must be like for him being only ten-years-old." Martha finished her tea and took Liz's empty glass to the sink. "And, not to mention an orphan now with Jacob passing just before Joseph was born."

"It hurt me when my son was killed, but, now with Rachel…" Liz's thoughts lingered as she watched her grandson. "Huh, Joseph is closer to his parents watching that program about the Moon landing than sitting out there with a bunch of strangers."

Piercing handclaps interrupted their conversation. This happiness contrasted against the somber mood of the twenty people inside Joseph's house for his mama's wake. A house now left to him and his grandma, Liz.

"What are you watching?" a young girl asked. She had walked over to Joseph from the front door after hearing his excitement. She was the same age as Joseph.

"We're landing on the Moon." Joseph sat his bowl of macaroni-and-cheese beside him on the floor. "You wanna watch?"

"Okay." She knelt and joined Joseph making sure not to step on the bottom of her black skirt. Joseph's bowl sat between them. Both stared at the images on the television screen. After a long quiet moment, she whispered, "I'm sorry about your mama."

"Thanks." Joseph stole a quick glance over to her and back to the television. Her wavy, auburn hair hid her light-green eyes. "What's your name?"

"Mary."

Joseph smiled and hummed; *Mary had a little lamb.*

"Is this happening now on the Moon?"

"Nope, this is like old or something." Black-and-white images flickered off their faces as they continued watching the television.

Martha had left Liz to wash the overflowing kitchen sink of dirty dishes after meals of ham, green beans, and cornbread. From behind her, Liz whispered into her ear, "Martha, you have to come see this."

Martha rinsed her hands in the lukewarm water from the faucet and placed the clean, wet glasses into the holder beside the sink. She followed Liz back to the archway.

"Awe, that's so cute. Who is she?" Martha asked, clasping her hands together under her chin.

"I think her name is, Mary. She's Bob's new foster kid." They smiled watching Mary and Joseph.

The two kids sat in amazement on the floor sharing the same bowl of macaroni-and-cheese. It was a surreal sight given the sadness-filled living room as others shared their memories of Rachel.

"What happened to the little boy Bob used to foster?" Martha asked.

"I'm not sure. I heard he takes in foster kids so he can get money from the State," Liz said. The pleasant sight of Mary and Joseph broke through their shared disdain for Bob Warner. "Don't they look so cute together?"

"Liz, I can see it now, *Mary and Joseph.* Those will be the roles they will play in the church Christmas play."

"Yes!" A scream came in unison from the living room.

"Excuse me, Martha. I should go tell them to be quiet." Liz gave Martha a quick touch on her shoulder, leaving her standing under the archway.

"Why are y'all so excited?" Liz asked.

"Look, we did it. We stepped on the Moon," Joseph said. Bob had joined the three of them from the opposite corner of the living room upon hearing Mary scream.

"Liz, it was such a beautiful service." Bob took her hand in his. His rough callouses rubbed against her as if she held a piece of sandpaper.

"Thanks. Minister Greene gave a lovely service don't you think?"

As Liz spoke, Bob knelt behind Joseph and Mary. "Joseph, I'm so sorry about your mama." Bob paused for a moment. "If you ever need anything, you let us know, Son." Joseph shook his head to acknowledge Bob; his eyes never leaving the screen.

"Well, Mary, we should go."

"Mary, thank you for coming. I hope to see you at church." Liz hugged her as Mary stood beside Joseph.

"Thanks." Mary's voice was no louder than a whisper, smiling as she walked away with Bob.

Liz prepared to kneel behind Joseph when Mary returned. A smudge of yellow-powered cheese remained in the corner of her lips. Mary placed her arms around Joseph's shoulders.

"Sorry again about your mama," Mary said.

Liz sighed watching Mary hug her grandson. She released Joseph and rejoined Bob who had been waiting by the front door to leave. Liz sat beside Joseph on the hideously upholstered footstool her daughter-in-law had adored.

"So, people will leave soon. Do you want to tell anyone good-bye?"

"That's okay. I don't wanna miss anything... *this* is so amazing—"

"The Moon landing was amazing when it happened." A proud smile cracked through the layers of her makeup, while runny-mascara tracks streaked from her eyes.

Liz placed her arm around Joseph and whispered in his ear. "In fact, I bet your daddy and mama are watching you right now."

Joseph's earlier excitement of watching the landing escaped his body. His shoulders slumped closer to the floor.

"Your mama loved you. And, she'll always be with you."

"Just like Daddy was supposed to be?" Joseph focused his attention away from the television and stared at his grandma.

"Your daddy will always be with you. My son would have loved to have seen you when you were born. Jacob was taken away from us so young. You know what?"

"What?"

"He gave your mama and the rest of the world a miracle gift in you before he died." She hugged Joseph tight.

"But, I pray every night to see Daddy. He never appears. Now, I need to pray to see Mama. That ain't fair."

Large tears formed in his eyes, barely clinging on to the edge of his eyelashes. As soon as he glanced up at his grandma, the teardrops could no longer hold on as they fell to his shirt.

"It's not fair. When we got the call about your daddy's accident, your mama was so brave. And, when the doctors told her about the brain cancer, she was so strong. Now, you need to be brave and strong too."

"It's still ain't fair." He turned his attention back toward the images of the Moon.

Her grandson's breathing had become shallow. The flickering images on the screen from Mission Control broadcasted across the world in July 1969 caught her attention.

"Look. Maybe your prayers are being answered," Liz said with a higher pitched voice.

"Huh?"

She grabbed his tear-soaked hand and placed it on the television screen. "You see all those people *there?*"

"Yeah?"

"Well, I remember watching this same broadcast with your daddy twenty-years ago. Jacob sat in the same spot you're sitting in now. He was touching the screen *at this point*... did you know Grandpa Eli was in *that* room?"

"Grandpa used to work on rockets, right?" he responded.

"Not exactly. He worked with NASA and was on the Mission Control Team. And, I remember your daddy wanted to be with your grandpa so much. Back then we hardly ever saw him."

She rubbed the back of Joseph's shoulders as she continued. "Your daddy was about the same age as you are now. I remember him touching the screen and saying, 'I miss you, Daddy.' So, see, you're connecting with your daddy now by watching this program."

Pride overwhelmed Joseph. He felt the swelling within him, lifting his shoulders upward.

"Wow, Daddy was watching this too, just like me?" he replied with amazement.

"Yeah, we tried to find your grandpa, Eli, but never saw him on TV."

Joseph turned away from his grandma. His eyes darted around the screen attempting to find a familiar face.

"But, that's just it. Now, with your mama, you must find these same kinds of moments to be with her too."

With some effort, Liz stood. Her knees cracked and pins pricked the bottom of her left foot. "I'll let you sit here and watch more. If you need anything, just let me know." She kissed the top of his head and hobbled to the kitchen.

Joseph remained fixated on the broadcast. Walter Cronkite's voice from that day in 1969 narrated.

"Since the earliest time, Man has imagined this moment... the moment when his fellow Man would make the first journey to the Moon. Now the time had come. In the sixth decade of the Twentieth Century, the ancient dream was to become a reality."

The voice from the television describing the amazing events twenty-years ago drew Joseph closer to the images. He blocked out the conversations happening around him in the room where Rachel's friends remained. Their conversations provided color commentary of the earlier funeral service.

"It was a lovely funeral."

"Her dress looked so beautiful."

"Did you see how her hair looked? She never wore curls like that?"

"I know. She looked like a totally different person lying there."

"What will happen with Joseph now that his parents have died?"

Hours had passed. Various people, strangers to Joseph, had leaned over to hug and offer their condolences. He whispered *thank you* each time someone told him *good-bye*.

He remained entrapped by the images of the Moon, his eyes transfixed by grainy image projections. This was his way to escape his sadness, his opportunity to connect with his daddy in this moment.

After everyone had left, Liz came back to Joseph, who had fallen asleep. She lifted his lifeless body off the carpeted floor and walked him upstairs to his bedroom.

He got into his blue pajamas covered with yellow stars and the planets of the Milky Way. Joseph scanned his bedroom and placed a toy car, a picture of his mama, and a belt on a table beside his bed.

"Why did you put those things *there* just now?" Liz brushed his hair from his eyes as his head lay on his pillow.

Joseph smiled. "These were the last few things Mama gave me. And, I wanna connect with her like I did with Daddy, today."

With a gulp under her breath, she patted the top of his head. "That's so sweet. You get some sleep, and I will see you in the morning."

Her knees cracked as she stood from his bedside and stepped to his bedroom door, turning off the lights. She closed the door behind her leaning against it. Tears rolled down her cheeks.

She whispered, "Oh Rachel, I miss you so much. Lord, give me the strength to take care of Joseph."

After composing herself, she stood back up, reached and turned off the hall lights. The hardwood floor creaked as she walked through the hallway to Rachel's bedroom.

The light coming from underneath the door disappeared stealing Joe's sight of the items he had placed on his bedside table. He rolled onto his back staring at the black ceiling overhead. Memories of his mama when she was last healthy flashed into his dreams as he fell asleep.

MARCH 26, 1989
PASADENA, TEXAS, *EASTER SUNDAY*

THE DARK-GREEN OLDSMOBILE glistened in the bright sunlight. Reflections of white, billowing clouds passed over the hood as the car toured through the neighborhood on its way to Middle Creek Baptist Church of Pasadena a few miles from Joseph's house. It was a glorious morning for a drive in southeast Texas; but the afternoon forecast was calling for approaching storms.

Joseph sat in the expansive backseat on the white upholstered leather. In his unbuckled seat, he leaned forward and propped up his arms and head on the middle of the front, high-back bench seat. He could not help but notice how pretty his mama looked as she drove him and Grandma Liz to church.

Sunday mornings were Joseph's favorite. This was the only day Rachel allowed him to wear his nice clothes. He liked the attention from the older church women his pressed black pants and white, long-sleeved dress shirt brought.

His mama had a special glow about her. This was the first time she could show off her new car to her church friends. Joseph could tell how proud she was this morning, as lately smiles from her had been hard to discover.

Rachel and Liz held their usual Sunday morning gossip session during the drive to church. This gave Joseph the perfect opportunity to inch his right hand into his pocket. Success. He pulled out a small, chocolate peanut butter cup. The crinkling candy wrapper pierced through their conversation, easily getting Rachel's attention.

"Joseph, I told you no candy until we get home." Rachel gave Joseph the *you're in trouble* look through the rearview mirror.

"Mama, I know. But, I love peanut butter cups so much." He pleaded his case. "The Easter Bunny was extra good to me this year and brought me a lot."

"If you get any chocolate on your clothes or my new car, I will be very upset."

"Rachel, your car rides very nice, and there's so much room." Liz rubbed her hands across the front bench seat between her and Rachel.

"It's so much better than Jacob's old car. That car had seen better days that's for sure."

Rachel glimpsed at herself in the rearview mirror. An unforced smile stared back to her. "I'm happy I could save enough money to finally get a new one."

"Mama, what are we having for lunch?" This was Joseph's second favorite part about Sunday mornings; his anticipation of having a wonderfully cooked dinner. It was this anticipation of a special meal, which made the long church service bearable.

"Since it's Easter, when we get home we will have a nice ham dinner with all the fixins." Liz spoke first before her daughter-in-law could answer.

"Are we having macaroni-and-cheese?" Joseph jumped from the back of his seat and leaned on the front to look at his grandma.

"Yes, we are having macaroni-and-cheese," Rachel said as Joseph turned his stare to her. She gently snatched his left shoulder as she drove. "Now, sit back, and get ready to go inside. We're here."

They drove through the overflowing church parking lot. Dozens of people entered through the front door of the church built during the Sixties, a time when every suburb in Houston experienced tremendous population growth due to the NASA programs. The church was a nondescript, brick building with a tall, white steeple; it was a cookie-cutter church in a cookie-cutter neighborhood.

Joseph opened his passenger-side back door first and got out, looking down at his pants and his seat. "Mama, it's all good. No chocolate, nowhere."

"That's good, Dear." She checked herself one last time in the mirror applying another pass of lipstick before getting out of the car.

"Why Liz, you're looking as beautiful as a June bug," James Unger said as he opened Liz's front, passenger door.

Liz smiled and said, "James, you always say the nicest things. Happy Easter."

Martha's husband loved to flirt with Liz. But, then again, James loved anything in a skirt.

"Happy Easter, Liz... Happy Easter, Rachel," Martha said between hugs to them both. Joseph made his way to the front of the car to everyone. "And, Happy Easter to you, too, Joseph. Was the Easter Bunny good to you this morning?"

Joseph stood with his cheeks puffed out. "Yeah, real good." He muffled a reply due to a mouth full of chocolate peanut butter cups, which he had smuggled from his pocket. He was careful to avoid his mama's eye contact.

"Nice car. What year is it?" James asked Rachel, placing his left hand on the top of the car while looking inside the window.

"Thanks. It's an '87. I got it yesterday at Mr. Young's Used Cars. I couldn't take our old one breaking down any longer."

The pleasant, deep clang of a church bell broke through the crisp morning air, interrupting them. "Time to go inside, Joseph," Rachel called out as the Ungers started toward the church door ahead of them.

"That James is something else, isn't he?" Liz whispered into Rachel's ear.

"Hush. They've been happily married for thirty years; you home wrecker." Rachel loved joking with her mother-in-law about James's obvious advances to Liz.

"He's always flirting with me," Liz said as Joseph stepped in front of them inside the church.

The Ungers held hands. "Weren't they adorable," Martha said to James as they waived to another couple already sitting in a front pew.

"Rachel looked pretty good… considering," James said as they took a seat in a middle pew.

"She sure did. I will say a special prayer for her." Martha bowed her head as she sat.

"Where do you want to sit, Mama?" Joseph asked.

"There's empty seats there," Rachel said pointing to the third row from the back.

Liz entered the pew first followed by Rachel with Joseph sitting on the end. Rachel leaned over to him and whispered in a stern voice in his ear. "Joseph Jacob Bishop, do not open any more of that candy." Joseph's full name emphasized the seriousness of her command.

"Okay, I promise." He tapped on his front pocket with three more peanut butter cups fighting his temptation.

The sanctuary filled with people. Organ music reverberated across the pews. The choir entered behind the front altar of the church. Minister Samuel Greene followed.

Joseph liked Minister Greene. For such a quiet, reserved man, halfway during his sermons, his face always turned bright red. He paced as he preached in front of the congregation. It mesmerized Joseph.

A packed sanctuary of people reached for their hymnals to sing-along with the choir. Everyone stood. Joseph fidgeted in his space; the candy in his pockets called to him, but he remembered his promise to his mama.

With the blaring organ music providing cover, Joseph reached into his pocket, slipping out the small, orange-wrapped piece of candy. The music stopped. Crinkling candy paper echoed throughout the church. It was enough to make Rachel grab his hand and give him *the stare*. He felt six inches tall. "Joseph, shh!"

Joseph realized he was in trouble and sat while everyone stood. The backsides of the men in their light-colored suit jackets and women in their paisley dresses filled his view. He sulked and swung his legs back-and-forth with his head down.

Minister Greene welcomed everyone to this morning's Easter service. The congregation sat. Rachel leaned over to his right ear and whispered, "Joseph, do not get any more of that candy. Pay attention and listen to Minister Greene. He will explain why we celebrate Easter."

Joseph lifted his head and looked around. Everyone in the congregation gave Minister Greene their full attention.

Offering envelopes sat in a holder in the pew in front of Joseph at his eye level. Twenty minutes of flipping pages in the hymnal and then the *Bible*, Joseph grew bored. He took the envelopes and drew images of birds, rabbits, and Easter baskets in the white spaces.

He listened to Minister Greene preach. "And, on the third day, Jesus arose from the dead. It is this promise that Jesus lives that gives us *salvation* today."

Doodles of a rabbit carrying baskets overflowing with candy and birds flying above stretched across the envelope. Joseph smiled at his work.

"It was forty days after his resurrection that Jesus ascended into heaven. Now, the promise is one day Jesus will return. We will not know when, but all us believers will leave with him. We will join him in heaven where we will be with our friends and families once again." Minister Greene paused a few seconds and then said, "Let us pray."

As Minister Greene led everyone in prayer, Joseph tapped on his mama's right knee. Rachel opened her right eye and peeked down at him. Joseph looked up to her. His eyes filled with tears.

"Amen," the entire congregation said. Minister Greene continued speaking in the background.

"Why are you crying?"

"Mama, I can't wait for Jesus to come back." A single tear fell across his cheek, hanging at the bottom of his chin.

"Oh, Joseph…" She positioned her right arm around him pulling him closer.

"Because that means, I will see Daddy again." He buried his face into his mama's dress. She wiped away the tears from his face.

The congregation stood to sing the last song of the service, while Joseph and Rachel sat in the pew hugging each other. Even though Joseph never had the opportunity to meet his father, there are times a little boy needs his daddy. Liz placed her right hand on Rachel's shoulder having overheard the conversation.

With the sermon over, everyone filed out of their pews. The eagerness to go home to finish preparing Easter dinners made the church empty fast.

Rachel pulled at Joseph's hand leading him out of their seats. Liz followed. Minister Greene stood in the doorway greeting everyone as they left.

"Oh, Minister Greene, we loved the service," Liz said shaking his hand as she passed.

"And, Joseph, how did you like my message?" Minister Greene patted the top of Joseph's head much to Joseph's annoyance.

"I liked it, but I never learned about the Easter Bunny," Joseph said with a serious look on his face.

"Bless you, Rachel. I hope you enjoyed the service," Minister Greene said taking both of her hands. "I see I was not the only one hot inside here, today." The minister looked down at her hands glistening with sweat.

"Sorry, yeah... uh... um... I started to not feel too well during the..." Rachel said stuttering her speech. She swayed side-to-side.

"Are you okay?" Minister Greene asked, releasing her hands and grabbing her shoulders.

"Um... what? Huh..." Rachel's face became pale in an instant. Sweat rolled through her makeup as her eyes lifted into the back of her head.

Minister Greene stepped closer to her; her body fell limp in his hands. "Rachel? Rachel?" Minister Greene attempted to get her attention. "Grab her. Grab..." He yelled out to James Unger, who stood behind her.

Joseph was oblivious to what was happening behind him. He walked toward the car, his last two peanut butter cups crammed in his mouth.

A chorus of gasps behind him caused Joseph to look ahead at his grandma. Liz turned around to the church and screamed, "Rachel!" as she hurried by Joseph.

Joseph's eyes followed his grandma as she ran by him toward the church. After Liz had cleared his view, he saw his mama sitting on the ground in the arms of Minister Greene and James Unger.

"Mama? Mama? ... Mama!" Joseph shouted in a panic and shouldered his way through the people crowding around Rachel. "... Mama?"

3 - GRADUATION

"HURRY UP. You're going to be late."

"I'll be down in a minute, Grandma. I can't find my..." Joseph's response grew faint.

Liz stood in the living room, holding a video camera in one-hand and car keys dangling in the other. A Hard Rock Café-Dallas key chain spun from her French-tipped nails. Raising her grandson had given Liz a purpose in her life. She dedicated her time in the gym and made healthy choices in her meals. Liz often received compliments by people amazed that she was fifty-nine-years-old when she could easily pass as ten years younger.

Liz held her camera pointed up the stairs waiting to capture every moment of this special day. While she was happy for Joseph, a touch of sadness crept inside her. Joseph soon would leave for college.

Joseph bouncing down the stairs drowned away the clanging of her keys. "Okay, I'm ready."

"What are you looking for? I have your graduation cap."

"Mom's college pin... I wanted to wear it today to honor her." Joseph took his graduation cap from Liz as he placed the red pin on his gown.

"She'd be so proud of you. Her Baby, graduating and going off to the same college she attended." A beaming smile appeared under Liz's video camera, hiding her eyes from his view. "All right, well, we need to go. You need to be at the school in fifteen minutes." She turned off the video camera and pushed Joseph out the front door, closing it behind them.

Inside the car, all was quiet in stark contrast to the chaos earlier before they had left. The faded-green Oldsmobile rumbled through the neighborhood to the football stadium. Reflection was the reason for the silence: about the day… the events of the past few years… and the longing for his mama to see him graduate.

"I bet you wish she could be here with you now?" Liz asked.

Startled as if his grandma had read his mind, Joseph replied, "Uh… yeah? Oh, you mean Mama?"

"Of course, who else?"

"For a moment, I thought you were talking about Mary."

"Who's coming to see her graduate?"

"Her dad's coming. He told me I'll be able to hear him when they call her name." Joseph sat daydreaming out the window about Mary. "Can I have the car tonight?"

"Sure. I'll ask Bob if he wouldn't mind bringing me back home afterward." Liz and Joseph continued through the neighborhood. "Big plans tonight after graduation?"

"A few parties with friends. We aren't sure which ones we're going to yet, though."

Hundreds of teenagers ran through the parking lot in excitement. Heat from the sweltering Texas sun stirred a light breeze through the stadium. Their blue, polyester graduation gowns ruffled in the wind.

"Hey, let me out here, please. There's Tommy." Joseph jumped out of the car before waiting for it to stop.

Liz found a parking place and walked over to Joseph. "Take our picture, Grandma," Joseph said as he placed his arm around his friend.

She reached into her purse and pulled out a small thirty-five-millimeter camera. "Okay, say graduation."

"Graduation!" they screamed at the same time. The camera flashed unnoticed as Joseph and his friend gave each other a high-five.

"Okay, I'll come find you after the ceremony. Have a good time," Liz said, placing the camera back into her purse.

As she turned around to walk to the stadium, Liz felt a hand grab her shoulder. Joseph spun Liz around and gave her a huge bear hug and whispered in her ear. "Grandma, I love you. Thank you for everything."

Liz pulled back and kissed his cheek. "It was all I could do. I did it all for Rachel, and I am so very proud of you."

Joseph released Liz allowing her to catch her breath. "Okay, I'll see you in a few hours."

Liz turned away and wiped away a single tear falling to her chin. She whispered a prayer. "Rachel, he did it. And, he will make you very proud."

The blistering sun on this early June day sat behind the horizon. The graduation theme blared through the stadium. Two hundred seniors marched in front of their proud friends and families. An air of happiness enveloped all in attendance.

Joseph found his seat and joined his classmates. Everyone scanned the crowd to find their loved ones. From a distance, Joseph saw his grandma sitting in the stands beside Mary's father, Bob. Her joyful smile was obvious from behind her video camera she held to her face.

Joseph found Mary in the blue sea of gowns sitting in the back row. He made eye contact with her and mouthed the words 'I love you' as she repeated the same to him.

An hour had passed. Sunset turned to night. Lightning flashed in the distance. The ceremony continued. Then, the big moment arrived. It was time for the graduates to walk across the stage.

Joseph anticipated hearing his name. His heart pounded. He stepped closer to the side of the stage.

"Joseph Jacob Bishop," the principal said, her voice reverberating across the stadium.

Upon hearing his name, his chest expanded, his shoulders lifted as he stepped up to the platform and over to the principal shaking her hand. With his diploma in his right hand, Joseph rubbed his Mom's college pin affixed on his gown at his collarbone. He felt his mama's presence with him.

Joseph continued across the stage and stepped to the ground. An elderly looking man walked in front of him wearing a gray jacket and a frayed, black New York Yankees cap. In an instant, the man snapped a quick picture of Joseph. The flash caused Joseph to look away. Joseph ignored the cameraman as his friends laughed, teasing him after hearing his middle name, Jacob, after his father.

The elderly man was quick to walk out of Joseph's way as Joseph rejoined his classmates. He gripped tight his diploma inside its blue, leather folder in his lap. Screams of joy filled the stadium. The principal continued with the roll call of names.

The last row of students stood and made their way to the stage. This was Mary's group, and Joseph watched smiling as she walked up for her turn.

Mary smiled at Joe when their eyes met. Her name was next. "Mary Alisha Warner," the principal said.

Joseph stood and yelled, "Mary, I love you."

Mary looked at him from the stage. Her face was bright red with embarrassment hearing Joseph's professed love. Their eyes locked until she sat, lost again in the sea of blue gowns. As he searched for her, he noticed his grandma standing on the field beside his classmates.

Joseph refused to make eye contact with Liz embarrassed she would get too close for his picture. The principal's voice came over the speakers. It was time for the graduates to stand and turn their tassels on their caps.

The instruction resulted in a blizzard of blue, graduation caps filling the air. Joyous yells from the students matched the loudness of cheers from the stands.

Blue caps fell everywhere. The new graduates hugged each other and slammed high-fives across the rows. Happy chaos.

Joseph broke a rule. Instead of marching out in the same alphabetical order, he pushed through the hugging graduates to find his Mary. As he got to her, Joseph picked Mary up in his arms and spun her around kissing her.

The graduation march again played signaling the graduates to file back out of the football stadium. Their friends and families in the stands waved and yelled as everyone passed. Joseph attempted to find his grandma, but the maddening crowd hid Liz from his view.

Several minutes had passed after the ceremony. The graduates searched for their families; their families searched for their graduates. During the happy reunions, Joseph and Mary became separated for a few moments.

"There you are," Mary said with a burst of happiness and the biggest smile Joseph had ever seen from her. She ran to him screaming, "Joe! Joe, I love you."

A camera flashed from behind them. It captured the perfect moment. Mary had jumped into Joseph's arms, wrapping her legs around his body. In the sudden attack, his graduation cap had fallen from his head. Liz had taken the perfect picture of pure happiness between them.

Mary unwrapped her legs from around his waist and slid down his gown standing. "I can't believe we've finally graduated," she said.

"So, where are you two headed off tonight?" Liz asked in an approving way.

"Don't worry. We'll be home sometime tonight." Joseph laughed as Mary pinched his ass out of Liz's view.

"Okay, well, if you need anything call me. You both have fun, tonight," Liz said as she gave them a hug together at one time.

As the crowd thinned, they walked back to the faded-green Oldsmobile. Their graduation gowns and diplomas held like prizes in their hands. Joseph placed their things in the backseat and pulled the car out of the parking space. As he backed out, a brilliant flash of lightning blinded them.

"Wow!" They both yelled together as the booming crack of thunder muffled their voices. The sudden clasp caused her to leap over from her seat onto his shoulder.

Joseph looked at her startled face and stopped the car leaning to kiss Mary. But unlike the thousands of other kisses over the past four years, this kiss felt different. Intense.

Large raindrops exploded on the windshield as if they were under attack by small water balloons. The innocent kiss became more passionate as Joe placed both his hands around the bottom of Mary's petite face. Joe pulled away from Mary, her eyes still closed. "I've got an idea. Let's drive around behind the elementary school and wait this storm out there."

"Um, okay," she said back in a soft whisper, opening her eyes to him.

Joseph again started the car and left the parking lot. Everyone else turned right to go into town. Joseph turned left and into the parking lot of the elementary school. The rain became blinding.

They parked out-of-sight behind the back of the school building. The fading stadium lights became blurry. Heavy rain pelted the windshield creating a kaleidoscope of light shining into the car.

Joseph turned off the car's engine and unbuckled his seatbelt sliding closer to her. His right hand caressed her hair.

Mary had not taken her eyes away from him since leaving the stadium parking lot. She closed her eyes and tilted her head back, resting it in his hands. Mary opened her eyes and turned toward him kissing his wrist supporting her head.

He leaned closer and reached across her waist to unbuckle her seatbelt. As the belt slid across her t-shirt, he caught the buckle in front of her, pressing his hand into her chest. Joseph released the buckle, causing it to bounce off the side of the door, slamming into the window. He massaged her chest, leaning to kiss the side of her exposed neck.

His lips moved upward meeting her cheek. Mary turned her head away from his wrist and kissed his lips with a hunger building for years. The pounding of the rain hitting the car's roof provided a rhythm to the kissing and caressing.

For the next half hour, wind and rain bombarded the parked car, hidden by the darkness of the building. The rocking of the car back-and-forth from the wind assisted the passion.

It was as if Mother Nature had provided a soundtrack to their desire for each other. The pelting rain subsided. Blue gowns covered their heaving naked bodies. Joseph and Mary held each other tight. Rolling thunder matched their heartbeats.

"I love you so much," she whispered into his ear.

Joe hugged her closer.

"I cannot believe what happened? It was like something came over us from out of nowhere?" Mary said brushing her hair away from her eyes.

"Uh, I know. I mean, we've talked about it before. We always said we would know the right time, but I didn't see that coming?"

"Well, it's been building for so long," she said smiling.

Joseph stroked his fingers back-and-forth across her naked arms wrapped around him. She squirmed. The sensation tickled.

"Mary, I have been in love with you since the day we met. And, I promise you this. I'll always love you, and we'll always be together."

"Joe," she said holding back tears in her eyes, "I love you, too."

4-Destiny

"SHIT!" JOE YELLED as he bolted from the Number 4 bus as it rumbled into the stop at the Student Quad. He threw his black backpack over his shoulder and darted between the students on their way to class. Joe felt like he was the starting running back for his University of Stony Brook football team darting to his left, then right, avoiding the people in his way.

Brookings Hall... Room 411...

Joe wiped the sweat from his forehead walking into the four-story, brick classroom building. Green ivy climbed across the façade. As a junior, he felt the pressure to decide on a major narrowing his choice between biology and chemistry. Late, on his first day of class, only added to his pressure.

Joe made it inside the classroom as the door closed catching his backpack on the handle. The noise from the students talking muffled the snap coming from the door. He slid his backpack off his shoulder to remove it from the handle.

The classroom had a similar arrangement as his freshman chemistry class. It had a comfortable familiarity. A large wooden desk and podium sat at the bottom of the lecture hall. A green chalkboard behind the desk spanned across the entire width of the room. Rows of seats cascaded upward from the floor, like a small stadium.

His preference was to sit near the back, in the middle of the class. But, being late, the only seat available to him was in the center of the first row. Joe hurried to the seat, removing a notebook and pencil from his backpack.

As he tried to close the tear, he heard his new professor say, "Good morning, class. My name is Professor John Baptiste. And, yes, my parents had a sense of humor with my name."

Professor Baptiste stood before the class welcoming his fifty new students for the semester. The overhead fluorescent light reflected off his glowing baldhead catching Joe's attention from the front row.

As the professor scanned his new audience, he removed his black-rimmed reading glasses snagged by a silvery, metal-linked necklace around his neck. "Welcome to Genetic Biology 401."

Professor Baptiste turned his back to the students. He stepped up on his toes to reach the small cord hanging from a rolled-up projector screen. Joe smiled taking amusement at the professor's short stature.

The screen lowered with a zipping sound releasing streams of dust particles into the air highlighted by the projector beam coming from the back of the lecture hall. Professor Baptiste faced his students holding a wireless clicker he had removed from his front shirt pocket hidden underneath his pale-brown sweater with its dark-brown, leather elbow patches.

The professor wasted little time as he jumped into his opening speech he had delivered twenty times in the past. The professor's words intrigued Joe as he had expected the usual routine of reviewing a course syllabus and learning about office hours.

"My class is very challenging. Not in the subject matter itself, but in the work you will need to put into this class and in the lab. Our field of study is expanding exponentially every year. It potentially holds the key to solving some of humanities biggest challenges, determining how genetics influences the human biology."

With each passing statement, the professor advanced the slides projected behind him. Images of people suffering with various epidemics throughout human history appeared with magnified views of the responsible bacteria or virus.

"Ebola… the plagues that ravaged Europe in the Middle Ages… fear of Avian Flu… on and on." The slides advanced with each grotesque disease mentioned with small snippets of history.

"Researchers believe in the Fourteenth Century the Black Death reduced the world population from about four-hundred-fifty-million to three-hundred-million in only seven years—"

A voice beside Joe interrupted the professor. "But, Professor, I thought rats carried the plague to Europe?"

Professor Baptiste broke his rehearsed cadence and turned to the students. "Technically, the rats carried fleas—"

"And, the fleas infected the people," the voice said interrupting him again lost in the crowd of students.

The professor pointed his clicker in the air as a Y-shaped image zoomed-in behind him on the screen. "No. The *Yersinia pestis* bacterium is the culprit, which the fleas carried via the rats."

The voice fell silent. Professor Baptiste held everyone's attention.

"But, what about the diseases of today? AIDS… Tuberculosis… the Swine Flu… What about future diseases? What about the bacteria or viruses unknown to us which may even be worse than what humanity has already seen?"

Joe attempted to keep pace with the professor in his notes. The names of the diseases and hand-sketches of the matching responsible bacteria or virus scribbled across the pages of his red notebook.

"In this class, we will learn how genetics play a role in the evolution of bacteria and viruses. How the human biology adapts in positive ways to fight these infections. And, the negative ways the body succumbs to them."

Professor Baptiste paced in front of his students. His pacing reminded Joe of Minister Greene back home in Texas. The only things missing from Baptiste's sermon were the damnations to Hell and a chorus of amen echoing from the classroom.

"From this understanding, scientists will learn how to prevent or cure these diseases and the ones not even yet known. Who knows, maybe one day even leading to a cure for various cancers that humanity has had to endure."

Joe again paused his note taking. He wrote the word 'cancer' in capital letters as he tapped the eraser end of his pencil on his notebook. His tapping caused his Mom's metal, *University of Stony Brook* pin to fall from his shirt pocket. His earlier encounter with the door had loosened it.

He had worn her small, red pin with the school's mascot inside a white triangle and circle for good luck on the first day of class and during his exams. The anguish he felt was too much as he watched it bounce off his desk, spin on the floor, and come to rest to the left of the professor's foot.

Professor Baptiste saw the rolling pin and gave it back to Joe without pausing his lecture. "So, this is my challenge to you. Whatever your major... whatever your chosen career after college... find your passion and follow it. You will be successful in life. And, if your passion is genetics and biology, then you are in the right class."

Joe snapped his pin back onto his shirt, giving it an extra push to make sure it was not falling off again. The professor's challenge to the class caused Joe to write simple questions across his notebook without answers. *What is my passion? Mama. Cancer. Cure???*

The class continued for the next forty-five minutes. Professor Baptiste presented the course syllabus, his office location, and office hours. Joe took more notes than he remembered. The words the professor spoke resonated, today.

Maybe it was the direct and straight approach the professor delivered? Or, maybe the challenge Baptiste made in finding one's passion triggered the answer Joe already had known of what his true purpose in life was to be?

While he had always excelled in math and science, deciding on his major was a difficult decision for Joe. He switched many times between chemistry, biology, and engineering with accounting as a backup.

As the class ended, the students gathered their belongings. Joe collected his notes, placing them inside of his backpack. Halfway to the door, he stopped and turned back to the professor, who sat behind the desk.

"Professor Baptiste, thank you for handing me my pin back. It was my mom's."

"No problem. I didn't want you to disturb the class to get it." Baptiste sat shuffling together his lecture notes.

"Professor?"

"Yes?"

"I am looking forward to your class this semester. Your opening speech to us hit me. I've been debating on my major for some time now, and—"

"Hold that thought, Son. Don't let one lecture decide your fate or your major. Do the work. In a few weeks, make an appointment, and we can talk further."

"Thank you, Professor Baptiste. I will definitely schedule a visit. See you Wednesday."

Joe left the classroom to walk back across the Quad to his next class, Statistics 201. He took his time since he had twenty minutes. An open bench outside Edwards Hall welcomed him to sit and watch various groups mulling about on the Quad.

Thoughts of the professor's introduction to the class raced through his mind. Joe unzipped the top of his backpack and pulled out his red notebook opening it to his notes from Professor Baptiste's class.

Joe read the various bullet points of facts the professor presented and reviewed the course syllabus. But, his eyes kept going back again to the words he had written at the top of the page: *What is my passion? Mama. Cancer. Cure???*

"Hey, Joe… How was your summer?" came a loud voice from a large guy running to Joe.

"Charlie! Hey, great to see you, Man." Charlie's greeting made Joe realize he had missed his best friend during the past three months. "My summer was good… the best it can be I guess since I had summer school and all. How was yours?"

Joe and Charlie were roommates in one of the freshman apartments off campus. It did not take long for them to develop a close friendship. Neither had a brother, and it was their shared bond of being from the South with Joe from Texas and Charlie from Georgia, which had developed their brotherhood. Their inside joke was they needed to stick together up in Yankee Country.

"Dude, my summer was awesome. Couple of friends and me, we rented a house at the Shore and had a blast," Charlie said.

Charlie had invited Joe at the end of last semester to join him this summer. Charlie had promised Joe that after one last summer filled with parties, he would get serious about college.

"Beer and bitches everywhere." Charlie had a devilish grin visible through his unshaven, chubby face.

Joe admired Charlie's carefree spirit while hoping he would get serious about his studies.

"How's Mary doing?"

"Mary? She's doing okay. She's decided to go into teaching."

"Awesome, that's great. Man, too bad y'all are still together. You would've loved spending the summer with us."

"What class do you have next?"

"Hell, I don't know. I think it's biology with Baptiste." Charlie turned his body following a six-foot-tall blond girl passing between them. "Damn, Dude." Charlie tapped Joe's shoulder. "That ass."

"I just got out of a biology class with Baptiste. I really like him, but his class sounds hard."

"I tell you what's getting hard…. Hey, I'll check ya later, Dude." Charlie left Joe sitting on the bench as he watched Charlie catch up to the blond in the center of the Quad.

Joe checked his watch and closed his notebook, slipping it inside his backpack. He stood in time to see the aftermath of Charlie's meeting with the blond girl. The sound of her hand slapping against his face bounced off the ivy-clad buildings.

Charlie turned back to Joe and yelled across the Quad. "I freakin' love college, Man."

"Damn, he's crazy," Joe said as he shook his head leaving for his next class.

Hours had passed. Joe walked home to his apartment he shared with Mary. Professor Baptiste's words still reverberated in Joe's thoughts, as he opened his apartment door.

"Joe? Joe, are you home?" Mary asked from the kitchen. Joe entered their first-floor apartment above the used college bookstore on Ninth Street near campus. "How was your first day of class?"

Mary stood behind their small kitchen table with its two, mismatched wooden chairs. Dinner and wine sat on the table.

Joe appreciated the dinner, as Mary had made it a habit to surprise him occasionally. At most, he expected a take-out pizza since Mary had her first-day also starting community college.

"It was great, Mary." His excitement was obvious to Mary as he kissed her.

"Whoa, you missed me, didn't you?" she asked as he held her closer.

"Of course, I did. I always miss you. But, the extra kiss is for this dinner." He leaned over to kiss her again.

"It's nothing special. I wanted to make something nice for us since it was our first day back to class. The chicken, that's takeout. I made your favorite mac-n-cheese. And, the wine... well, the wine is from a bottle and not our normal box. I guess you can say that's fancy, huh?" She laughed at herself.

"Thanks, Sweetie, it looks great. Let me go change, and I'll be back in a couple of minutes." He kissed her one last time before going to the bedroom.

A few moments later, he came back into the kitchen. "I saw Charlie today. He wanted me to tell you, hey."

"How's he doing? I can't believe he's not been kicked out of school, already?" Her tone was sarcastic as she poured wine into the glasses.

"He's good. Charlie is well... Charlie. The food looks great. Thanks for doing this, Sweetie."

"So, how were your classes, today?" Mary asked, passing the chicken to him. The scent of the Italian seasonings made his mouth water.

"Great. I think I've decided on my major."

"Really, after the first day? You still have other classes tomorrow."

"I do, but those tomorrow, I've already had the first level."

"So, what are you thinking about majoring in?"

"Biology."

"Biology? Just like your mother and be a teacher?"

"Well, not because Mama majored in biology. It has to do more with what I learned about a specific field of biology." Joe bit into the chicken breast. Steam escaped his mouth; grease stuck to his lips.

"My class today was about genetics and how it impacts biology." He sipped from his wine glass between bites of chicken and macaroni.

"Sounds interesting. You must have had a good professor, today? Because you've never seemed too interested in biology before?"

"Professor Baptiste is great. He looks like a mad scientist that's for sure. But, what he was telling us about biology, genetics, viruses and stuff... I felt so connected." Joe took another sip of wine. "Damn, this is the good stuff."

"Good in that it was ten bucks," Mary said. Her voice echoed inside her glass.

"Mary, my professor talked about helping people. Possibly finding cures for things, even maybe someday for cancer." Joe froze and looked at her as he held his empty wine glass.

Mary squeezed his hand showing she understood what he meant by finding a cure. "Well, if anyone can, that's you, Babe. I believe in you." She leaned across the table to kiss his cheek.

"Thanks." Joe finished eating his chicken and macaroni. He poured another glass of wine. "Did I tell you? Some girl slapped the hell out of Charlie's face today? Funniest shit I've seen in a while.

5-PARIS

DARKNESS FILLED THE ROOM. Heavy, thick-fabric curtains draped over the bedroom window with a closed door. Quick, sharp chirps from Joe's alarm clock pierced the silence.

"Ugh, mmm."

Grunting noises came from Joe as he reached for the snooze button. His eyes remained closed while drifting back to sleep. In a shock, brilliant-bright sunlight rushed into the room as Mary threw open the curtains.

"Wake up, Mr. Sleepy Head." She sang, "Good morning. You gotta get up. You're gonna be late."

Joe lay motionless hoping Mary would stop and let his sleep last another few minutes. Mary shook Joe's lone, exposed foot sticking out from under the cover.

"Ugh, it's too early," he said stretching, reaching for the pillow to cover his eyes. Joe wanted to drown out her way too cheerful singing this morning.

"Today's the big day. You've got two hours to get ready before your limo is here."

Joe released a lengthy moan as he turned over to his side away from the sun and his morning cheerleader.

"I wonder what the neighbors will say when the limo shows up," she said snatching the pillow away from his face.

"Come, here." Joe stretched out his arms to her grabbing her waist. "Have I told you how much I love you?"

"Yeah, but tell me, again."

"I love you…" he said pulling her onto the bed, "… this much." Joe tickled Mary as her punishment for waking him, as they giggled rolling on the mattress.

After a long-exaggerated kiss, Mary pulled away from Joe. "I'll go make us breakfast, while you shower. I want to make sure you're not rushed before going off to Denver."

With one last sigh, Joe threw the blanket off his legs and sat on the side of the bed rubbing his eyes. After a shower, he joined Mary downstairs in their kitchen.

"Is that bacon I smell? I thought that was off limits because of my last doctor visit?"

"Well, I know how much you love it, and heck, why not, Mr. Speaker." Mary smiled preparing their plates. "So, are you ready for your presentation?"

"Yeah, I mean, no one knows this topic more in the world than me, so it will be an easy talk. What I'm not too sure of are the questions the audience will ask, 'cause I'm not even sure who all will be there?"

"Well, you'll be wonderful. Who knows who you might meet there? You may even get someone interested to fund more of your research?"

"In all honesty, that's what I'm hoping comes out of this. They said the Eden Foundation wanted to change the world."

The breakfast food disappeared from his plate as Joe excused himself from the table. He kissed Mary before going back upstairs, while she cleaned the kitchen.

With the last glass emptied from the sink, Mary yelled upstairs. "Sweetie, your ride is here. You will not believe it when you see it."

Joe came downstairs with his suitcase in hand and backpack over his shoulder. As the doorbell rang, Joe opened the door. The driver stood in the doorway dressed in a black suit with black sunglasses and a flat, black driver's hat. Only the driver's red lapel pin stood out.

"Good morning, Dr. Bishop, my name is Thomas. I am here to take you to the airport and accompany you to Denver."

"Great, I'll be out there in a couple of minutes." Joe held back his true excitement as he handed his bag to Thomas.

Mary came out of the kitchen. Joe hugged and kissed her goodbye, whispering in her ear. "Can you believe it… a stretch limo?"

"I love you and am so proud of you," Mary whispered back to Joe.

"I love you too. I'll call you tonight when I get to the hotel."

Mary watched Joe walk down the sidewalk toward the car. Thomas already had the back door of the limo open waiting for Joe.

"Such a beautiful day," Joe said as he entered his ride.

"Yep, but I think storms are coming later tonight."

Joe sat in the back-seat as Thomas closed the door. A bottle of champagne on ice welcomed him.

"What kind of conference am I going to?"

The limo backed out of the driveway. Joe reached for the champagne and popped open the top of the bottle. Bubbles raced to Joe's hand as he poured himself a glass.

"Cheers to me," Joe said lifting his glass in the air.

He sipped from the glass as the Stony Brook campus passed. "I deserve this. It sure has been a long journey."

He sat his glass on the small table protruding from the sidewall by the rear door. His hands were cold and wet from pouring the champagne.

Joe leaned back in the plush leather seat. With his thumb, he rubbed the underside of his wedding ring as he closed his eyes recalling distant memories the last time he had received the same type of treatment from an organization. A nervous smile crept across his face.

AUGUST 3, 2001
STONY BROOK, NEW YORK

FOR JOE, RUNNING through campus was his way to relieve stress. He ran by the stately brick buildings around the Student Quad at Stony Brook. Most of his route took him along trails following the winding stream flowing through campus. This made a natural border between the academic and student dormitory sections.

His 5K route relaxed him, surprising given his mix CD of heavy-metal music blaring in his ears. This was his alone time. Time away from exams, student loan dues, and having to pay the mounting bills collecting in their apartment.

Today's run, he reflected on his latest telephone interview with *Sauvage Enterprises.* A start-up pharmaceutical company in Paris, France, *Sauvage* specializes in human genome research. Their mission is to identify causes of various cancers in hopes to find a cure.

Alone, listening to Metallica, thoughts about the interview raced through his mind.

I think it went well… I hope I explained my research work okay… Dammit.

He stopped along the stream to tie his right shoelace. His Sony CD Walkman slipped out of the front pocket of his shorts. With ninja-like reflexes, Joe caught it in mid-air.

"That would've sucked."

He continued his run. His thoughts returned.

Paris… Mary said she wanted an adventure when she moved with me from Texas. I hope she was serious?

His thoughts trailed off as he jumped over a small, mud puddle created from last night's rain.

I can't believe they contacted me out-of-the-blue. The first thing I need to do is learn how to pronounce it correctly. I wonder what Sauvage means in French anyway? I should look that up—

His thoughts were interrupted.

"Shit!" Joe shouted, throwing his arms into the air. He passed an old man walking his dog, which had made an unexpected turn in front of Joe.

"Watch your dog!" Joe yelled, not realizing how loud his voice was over his music.

Damn dog about made me fall... I should've asked if I needed to speak French for the job? I suck at languages. Hell, I don't even understand any Spanish, and I'm from Texas.

"That's it, *no más*," Joe said out-loud while gasping for air with his hands on his knees. He pulled out his ear buds as they spun in the air below his knees. Music blared.

"Nice ass, Man," a familiar voice said as Joe turned toward the stream. Charlie walked up out of the water beside the footpath.

"Dude, what the hell are you doing in the crick?" Joe asked standing upward with his stomach heaving in-and-out.

"Collecting water samples for the lab." Charlie held up a wire basket filled with white, four-inch-long test tubes. Water dripped from the bottom of the basket. "Crick? What the hell is a *crick*, Man? You must be from Texas or somethin'?"

"Crick... creek... whatever," Joe said, bending again to pick up a small rock to throw towards Charlie.

"Well, actually, we call it a *brook*. Hello, it's Stony Brook after all," Charlie said, lifting his nose into the air in a snobbish way.

"Dude, you're from Georgia."

"I know, but we call it a *creek* from where I'm from."

"So, how's your first week of grad school going?" Joe asked as he stopped his CD player.

Charlie approached closer. "Good, I guess. We've just been doing a lot of safety training in the lab. Hell, today's the first day I'm doing anything by collecting these damn samples."

"What are you trying to find in the samples?"

"We're looking to see what type of microbes are in the water on campus because so many people live here. I'm collecting various samples along the whole route of the *crick*." Charlie nudged Joe's left shoulder at the same time delivering his unmistakable 'Charlie laugh.'

"So, how are the interviews coming, Mr. Summa Cum Laude? I'm sure the companies are lining up to speak to you?"

They walked up from the pathway to the main street through campus. "Yeah, the interviews are going okay. I'm trying to find the right fit instead of just jumping into the first offer."

"Offer? I bet you've had some good ones? And, it has to be hard to turn down money now. Joe, guys like you and me, we didn't come from much. It must be real tempting."

"Well, I had an interview with a very interesting company this morning," Joe said. "Get this; the job's in Paris."

"Texas?" Charlie said kidding.

"*Oui, la France*," Joe said. His breath returned to him allowing Joe to speak in a normal voice.

"Ooh la la. The women there are *très bon*"

"You speak French?"

"*Merci.*"

"Dumbass, that means *thank you*. I, at least, know that," Joe said. "Yeah, this company contacted me through some headhunter agency I sent my resume. Seems like a great company, and the work is something I'm interested in. But, Paris though?"

"Yeah, I can imagine that would be a culture shock. Hell, Long Island was your first experience of a culture shock coming from Texas."

"True. But, this is another country."

"Well, you've visited New Jersey before," Charlie said laughing, almost dropping two of his test tubes. "What does Mary think about it? She will go also, I suppose?"

"Well, I haven't exactly told her about it yet. It was just a phone interview this morning."

"Man, I've only been with Becky for the last year, but I'm smart enough to know you better talk to her soon about it. Engage her. Get her opinion."

"Dude, you've been watching too much Oprah," Joe said as he lightly punched Charlie's shoulder.

"Ugh, Becky records that shit, and we watch it at night." Charlie paused for a few seconds. "She makes me watch, you know?"

"Sure. Man. Whatever."

They left campus, down the street to the Irish Pub. Charlie's lab was in the same direction as Joe's apartment. The campus was quiet, absent of students during the time between summer session and the fall semester.

"So, did the person who interviewed you at least sound interested in you on the phone?" Charlie asked, stopping to peer through the window of the bar where his girlfriend, Becky, has worked the past two years during college.

"I guess. The guy I spoke to… his name is Gabe, seemed pretty cool and all. He said they would be in touch soon about next steps." Joe stopped walking and turned back to Charlie, who had stopped.

"Gabe? What kinda name is Gabe?" Charlie asked as he put his hand over his forehead, blocking out the sun to see inside the pub.

"Is Becky working today?"

"Yeah, I see her in there." Becky waved at them from inside the bar. Charlie moved toward the door.

"Well, tell Becky I said hello. I have to run. Mary and I are having a Friday date night, and I smell terrible."

"Dude, ask that girl to marry your sorry ass already," Charlie said opening the door. "See your smelly ass later…"

Joe continued down the block and crossed the highway from campus. *That's it… it'll be perfect. Mary has always loved Paris.*

SEPTEMBER 10, 2001
PARIS, FRANCE

"WOW, IT'S SO BEAUTIFUL. But, I thought it would've been bigger?"

"There you go again, Mary, always finding a fault in something. But, I would have thought *The Mona Lisa* would've been bigger too," Joe said.

Mary grabbed Joe's hand leading him away from the da Vinci masterpiece. They shuffled through throngs of onlookers inside the Louvre Museum. "Hey, let's go over *here*." She pulled him around the corner and surprised him with a kiss. "Have I told you, thank you, yet for bringing me to Paris?"

"Uh, yeah, like a hundred times already." He enjoyed the surprise kiss.

"Well, *here's* a hundred-and-one." After kissing him, she released her grip around his waist.

They weaved through the herd of people, who were examining the exhibits. Joe and Mary were in lock-step with a local art appreciation school group, which had slowed their progress through every turn in the exhibit halls. With every magnificent work of art, a hippy-looking teacher stopped and garnished the attention of her thirty high-school students explaining the artists' interpretations.

Joe and Mary stopped in a palatial section of the museum eavesdropping on the teacher's description of the Monet paintings. Large windows lined the concave ceiling allowing natural light to fill the display hall.

Mary tugged on Joe's jacket sleeve to get his attention. "It still amazes me..." She paused a moment to take in the beauty of the Monet paintings.

"What amazes you?"

"That all these works of art are here. I've seen them in textbooks and movies. But, to see them in person is amazing." Her mouth opened wide awestruck at Monet's *Waterlilies* painting. "Oh, my God, Joe. Remember in my bedroom in high school; I used to have a poster of *this* on my wall."

"How can I not? I recall us making out many times under that picture." He playfully tickled her side through her sweater as they reminisced an innocent time.

"So, where are we going next?" Mary asked.

"You'll just have to wait and see." Joe held her hand in his excitement of his plan.

"Oh, come on, you know how I hate surprises." She enticed him with a peck on his cheek.

"You'll find out soon."

Joe and Mary exited the museum. Crowds of tourists sauntered around the gigantic glass pyramid in the main courtyard of the Louvre Museum. The ancient symbol stood as a modern beacon welcoming visitors to the museum.

They continued through the sea of people. The Paris sky was brilliant, not a cloud overhead as the sun crested through the high-noon hour.

"Here, stand up on *this*… I have an idea." Mary pointed at one of the two-foot-tall, cylindrical cement posts, which prevent entry of vehicle traffic in the pedestrian area around the museum a hundred-feet in front of the pyramid.

Always open to her requests, Joe amused her by stepping up on top of the round column. Mary backed away from him. To her face, she held her digital camera, which he had given her as a college graduation present.

"So, we talked about my interview yesterday, but you didn't say what you did while I was gone?" Joe asked.

"Okay, now turn a little to your side and hold your hand up like *this*." She demonstrated by extending her arm above her head with her wrist pointing downward. Joe followed her commands.

As he got into position, she looked into her camera and took his picture. "I told you. I walked around the *Champs-Élysées*. That's all… there… you have to come see *this*."

He stepped down and walked to her as she held out the camera. "Wow, that's so cool. I look like a giant holding down the pyramid."

They walked from the pyramid through an arched, brick doorway separating the museum area from the streets of Paris. Bicycle bells interrupted the whirring of cars passing by as they turned off the road to cross the pedestrian *Pont des Arts Bridge* over the River Seine.

Dozens of couples strolled by them as they came to a stop in the middle of the bridge. The musty, damp air engulfed them from the below river. They leaned against a railing watching the passing river cruise boats as the two-hundred-year-old bridge built by Napoleon supported them in the center of Paris.

Accordion music and scents of distant pastries lifted in the air across the river. Teenagers sat in groups dotted along both banks of the river; a popular place for the locals.

"It's so beautiful here."

"Mary, you're beautiful." Joe dug his hands into the small of her back, pulling her closer. "You make everything more beautiful."

The excitement in his voice was palpable as he kissed her grabbing her hand to lead her across the bridge. Dark-green, painted metal booths stretched down the riverbank as they stepped from the pedestrian bridge. Local merchants filled each stand with books and magazines for sale, carrying on centuries' old traditions.

"Taxi! Taxi!" Joe yelled, waving his free arm high into the air as he stepped out onto the street. A shiny, black Mercedes stopped in front of them.

"*Bonjour, monsieur?*" the taxi driver asked. He wore a light-blue, windbreaker jacket and a white, small-brim hat.

Joe leaned into the taxi window and whispered to the driver so Mary could not hear. "*Eiffel Tower s'il vous plaît.*"

Joe knew nothing of the eloquent language, but he had memorized a few selected statements such as please and thank you. He had practiced this over-and-over in their Long Island apartment before they had left.

Using the extent of his French, he whispered to the driver. "But, do not tell her where we are going." Both Joe and the taxi driver shared a smile because of the secret destination.

"No problem. Get in *s'il vous plaît*," the driver said. He motioned to Joe and Mary with his hands to get into his back-seat.

The taxis in Paris held no comparison to the ones in New York City for Joe and Mary. The rides were their first inside a Mercedes. Luxurious leather welcomed them.

"I can get used to traveling like this—" Joe said to Mary.

"American?" The taxi driver's question interrupted Joe.

"Yep, we are from Texas originally, but went to college in New York," Mary said.

"*New York, New York,*" the driver sang with a thick French accent. "I love Broadway."

The taxi darted in-and-out of the maddening traffic of central Paris. Street lanes seemed to be only suggestions to Parisian drivers. Random car horns wailed around them.

She giggled under her breath at the driver's musical abilities. "Yeah, we love the shows too. Our favorite is *Phantom of the Opera*."

The driver made eye contact with Joe in his mirror. "So, how long are you in Paris?"

"This is our second day here, but we leave tomorrow." Joe felt the challenge of conversing with the driver as the taxi entered a four-lane traffic circle.

"Oh, why such a short stay in our beautiful city?" The whirling traffic did not faze the driver as his tone remained calm in his question.

Joe found astonishment at the driver's ability to simultaneously talk to him through his rearview mirror and surmount the crazy traffic. "I came for a job interview and brought my girlfriend." Joe squeezed Mary's hand on his lap.

"First time to Paris?" The driver raised himself higher in his seat to look at Mary in his rearview mirror. His wrinkled forehead proved his decades of experience.

"First time? Huh, first time either of us has been out of the United States—" she replied. The cars traveling in the gigantic round-a-bout were too nerve-wracking for her to watch.

"*Attention!*" the driver yelled, interrupting her as he drove across the other three lanes of the circle in one move.

"Please, please tell me what's next." Mary jerked Joe's jacket sleeve with each word.

"You'll see in a few minutes." Joe made quick eye contact with the driver through his rearview mirror. The driver smiled seeing her excitement.

After their start-and-stop driving along the River Seine, the taxi turned onto the *Quai d'Orsay*. An orange-pink hue sky gave the perfect backdrop for the top of the Eiffel Tower, which had come into view. The taxi made its final turn onto *Quai Branly*. The glorious iconic structure of the entire *Eiffel Tower* appeared before them.

As the taxi stopped at the Tower, Mary yelled, "Oh, my, it's so beautiful." She kissed the side of Joe's face, while pushing his head back to peer out the rear-side window.

The driver opened the door. "Here you are, the *Eiffel Tower.*"

Mary fell out the taxi with excitement. "Wow, I can't believe I..."

The sound of her voice drifted away through the hundreds of tourists as she walked from the taxi toward the structure. Joe caught up with her after he paid and tipped the driver. Young Gypsy girls came up to Joe selling flowers, as he pushed by them to find Mary lost in the crowd. He found her looking skyward at the icon.

"It's beautiful, isn't it?" Joe asked as they stopped taking in the visual grandeur. "How does the size of this compare to what you thought it would be?"

"I don't know. I can't believe I'm seeing this in person." Tears filled her eyes.

"You want to go to the top?" Joe asked knowing the answer.

"Hells yeah!" Mary gave him the tightest hug he could ever remember. "Thank you for bringing me."

"I'm just glad we could see things this afternoon after my interview before we fly back in the morning."

Conversations and laughter filled the lower concourse under the Tower. The line for the elevator seemed never-ending. At least a hundred-people stood waiting in front of them. They moved forward a foot at a time every few minutes. With each step, Mary perched her head against the side of Joe's shoulder. She grinned with anticipation.

Joe interrupted her happy thoughts by blurting out, "This line is taking forever."

"It's okay, Joe." She laughed at his impatience. "It ain't going anywhere."

"I mean, it's just taking forever." Frustration filled his voice.

"That's okay, I mean we've got all night and nothing planned. Unless we're going somewhere else?"

"Uh..." Joe paused for a few moments. "It's just that I want us to get to the top so we can see the sunset, that's all." He kissed the top of her head.

"Oh, Mr. Romantic, aren't we?"

The line continued to move... inch-by-inch. Joe has never been one with much patience.

"Hey, look at the bright side, if you get this job and we move to Paris, then we can come here anytime." She gazed upward at the supporting steel structure of under the Tower. Her hand held the top of her red beret with I ♥ *Paris* in white letters written across the front.

"Well, let's not get ahead of ourselves, Sweetie."

Joe was always one for cautioning about things to not get their hopes too high. "I had a great conversation over Sunday dinner, and this morning I did great in the interview, but we'll see."

"What company invites someone over for dinner on a Sunday, anyway?"

"I didn't quite ask that... maybe it's a French custom or something?"

"So, you'll find out in a couple of weeks if you got it or not?" They finally stood a few feet from the steps of the elevator.

"Yeah, a couple of weeks. But, we'll see."

They took their first step up to the elevator platform. "I mean, if four years ago when we started college, you would've told me I'd be in Paris with you after graduation, I would've said you were crazy," Joe said. "Who knew that a genetic biology degree could pay off like this?"

"I am crazy. Heck, we're both crazy," Mary said, exaggerating a slow fake laugh. "No, but seriously, that company will be lucky to have you. Plus, I look fabulous in a beret, don't you think?"

Her smile reassured Joe they were making the right decision about possibly moving to Paris. "Darlin', you look fabulous in anything." Joe kissed her lips as they stood before the elevator. "Well, if this job falls through, then it's just a sign for me to pursue my Ph.D."

"Okay Doctor, it looks like we're next?" Increased excitement filled Mary's voice, as they were next in line.

After a few seconds, the elevator opened in front of them. "Are you ready?" Joe asked.

With little effort, they felt the push of the people queued behind them pushing Joe and Mary inside the elevator. They stood in the back against the glass window with at least forty people cramming inside behind them. The doors closed. Anticipation filled the tight compartment. The elevator ascended one of the angled legs of the Tower.

"Check out that sign, *Beware of Pickpockets*." Joe pointed above the closed elevator doors.

"Sure, and as you're reading *that* sign, that's when they pick your pockets." People beside them laughed at Mary's comment.

The elevator inched its way up the incline of the Tower support. Through the spider web of gray steel crossbeams with rivets the size of baseballs, Paris teased them through the iron structure as the street below came into view.

"Oh, look. That's where we came in under the Tower." The last time Joe had heard her this excited was this past Christmas morning. "Oh, it's just to die for."

The elevator continued further up, slowing down as it reached the top of the inclined support. They stopped at the mid-section platform. The doors opened. A rush of cool air filled the car.

Joe placed his mouth next to Mary's ear. "Let's keep going to the top. We can get out here on our way back down."

His words did not register with Mary, as she stood frozen peering out the elevator window. At the first stop, about half of the people got off as new people crammed inside to continue to the top. Once full, the doors closed. The elevator began the slow vertical ascent up the Tower.

Their view changed from peering through crossbeams at the street below to an unobstructed view of the city of Paris. Words came out one at a time from Mary as she said, "Oh... my... God."

Wow was the only word Joe could say as the view exceeded his expectations as they continued upward. Once they reached the top, the doors opened.

"Okay, let's go." Joe stepped ahead of Mary while holding her hand behind his back. They pushed through the standing crowd of tourists outside the elevator on the platform.

A cold wind hit their faces as they stepped out into a mass of people wandering around on the catwalk nearly one-thousand-feet above the ground. Joe led Mary into the observation deck encircling the top. Glass windows wrapped around the Tower, covered in fingerprints from the earlier visiting tourists.

"Look!" Joe pointed to city names above the glass window overlooking Paris below them. "*New York 5849 kilometers.*"

"So, that means New York City is *this* way." Mary placed her right index finger on the glass under the sign. This action explained the dozens of faded fingerprints on the glass. "Then, if I move my finger just a little bit more to the left, then *that's* the way to Texas."

"Pretty cool," Joe said affirming back to her, "yep, somewhere out there is home." He placed his arms around her waist from behind grasping his hands together in front of her.

Joe and Mary strolled around the entire observation deck, coming to the door they had entered from the elevator. They felt like salmon swimming upstream against the sea of people as they left the observation area.

Stairs led to the uppermost observation platform. A small group of Japanese tourists, wearing matching shirts with I ♥ *Paris* printed in red letters against a black backdrop, ran by them. Once the group passed, Joe and Mary stood alone beside one of the mounted telescopes along the railing.

Joe bent down and turned the gray-colored telescope straight away from them to scan out over the city. The telescope made a creaking-metal sound. It had seen better days. Joe peered into the eyepiece and said, "Cool, you can see the *Arc de Triomphe* clear from here… you have to see this."

Mary grabbed the eyepiece from him and brushed her hair away from her eyes. She looked into the telescope. "Where is… oh… there it is…" She paused taking in the full view the *Arc de Triomphe.*

"I love Paris. It's such a beautiful place." Joe placed his hand in the middle of her back between her shoulder blades as she looked through the telescope. He rubbed small circles on her back, bending to whisper in her ear. "Sweetie, I love you so much." He kissed the side of her face.

Feeling him, she released the telescope. Gravity lowered it back into its original position as the creaking sound returned. Mary turned her head toward Joe and whispered back. "I love you, too."

They stood behind the old, metal telescope pressed together in a tight embrace. A slow, soft kiss emerged alone in the moment even though dozens of people were around them in the open air.

Joe brushed Mary's hair from her eyes holding the sides of her face. "You've dreamt about coming to Paris and seeing the *Eiffel Tower*."

Mary nodded her head slowly in agreement, while he held her.

"And... I could not think of a better place to ask you to marry me." He released the sides of her face, her head feeling light from the altitude and the reality of his statement.

To her shock, Joe knelt to one knee. At the same time, he held a small, black velvet jewelry box he had hidden inside his coat pocket.

Tears were immediate accompanied by the warmth of a beaming smile forming on her face. She squealed with excitement.

Joe opened the box in his hands displaying an engagement ring glittering against the sunset sky. "Mary Warner, will you make my dreams come true and be my wife?" A single tear fell from his left cheek as he looked up to her. Tears continued pouring from her eyes; her bottom lip quivered.

"Are you... are you kidding, me?" Mary somehow asked in a high-pitched voice, cracking with pleasure.

"Is that a, yes?"

"Yes! Yes! Yes!" Mary shouted out the words as she used her free hand to wipe the tears from her face. Joe placed the ring on her left hand.

He stood grabbing Mary around her waist. A kiss exploded with the passion of the announcement. A thunderous applause and cheers rained down on them from everyone who witnessed Joe's proposal. Camera flashes bounced off their faces.

Joe and Mary pulled a few inches apart and said, "I love you," at the same time making them laugh. They kissed to the applause of their new-found fame.

"Did you plan to propose like this on top the *Eiffel Tower*?" Mary asked poking his side while kissing him.

"Well, you have always talked about how much you would love to come here someday. Once I got this job interview, I knew I just had to propose to you here." Joe kissed Mary again.

Time stood still for the next several minutes. They wandered around the Tower. People, who had witnessed the proposal, congratulated the new rock stars. Some even asked to have their pictures taken with Joe and Mary

As nighttime fell over Paris, a mass of people stood between them and the elevator. Joe and Mary entered the elevator to go back down to the street. During their descent, they stood in the corner kissing, oblivious to the passing scenery of Paris in the evening.

Arm-in-arm, they stared at each other in disbelief. From the first moment they had met sitting on the floor in front of the television at his mama's wake, their bond had long developed. Joe and Mary strolled away from the Tower oblivious to the street vendors, who came to them attempting to sell replica *Eiffel Tower* key chains.

Joe and Mary crossed the bridge over the River Seine. Ornate statues lit in a golden hue lined their path as they walked into the night. At the fountains in front of the *Trocadéro,* they stopped. Joe looked at his watch. It was *7:59 p.m.*

Joe stared into Mary's eyes. "I have one more surprise for you." Joe spun her around to see the *Eiffel Tower* again in its full view. It looked like a golden beacon shining against the black, night sky.

Within a few seconds, tens of thousands of bright, white lights twinkled and danced across the Tower. Lights reflected off the water in the fountains next to them. The twinkling white lights looked as if thousands of tiny ferries were dancing across the iconic structure.

"Joseph, it... it's so beautiful," Mary said crying from everything, which had occurred today.

"You're so beautiful, Sweetie." He placed his arms around her from behind. After several minutes, the light show ended with a roar of applause from the thousands of onlookers filling the night air.

"I love you," was said. Neither Joe nor Mary knew who said it over the crowd as they kissed and walked off together into the Paris night.

6 - 9 / 11

JOE AND MARY SCURRIED through the madhouse of the departures area in Terminal 2 at Charles de Gaulle International Airport. Their whirlwind tour of Paris had come to an end on this, the eleventh day of September 2001.

"Okay, we need to find the check-in counter." Joe reviewed his travel itinerary and surveyed the crowd. "Oh, there it is."

The passengers were a mix of business and vacation travelers. Announcements in French preceded English translations echoing through the massive building. A smiling ticket agent greeted Joe and Mary at the counter.

"*Bonjour,* where are we going this morning?"

Joe smiled back to the agent. "We're headed to JFK. Last names are Bishop and Warner."

"Soon to be Mr. and Mrs. Bishop." Mary held up her engagement ring in front of Joe's face.

The agent typed on her computer behind the counter. "Well, congratulations… okay, here we go… Mr. Joseph Bishop and Miss Mary Warner. Can I see your passports, please?" Joe and Mary were lost in each other's eyes. A few seconds had passed until they realized the agent had asked them for their passports.

"Are you checking any bags with us, today?"

"No, we have these two carry-on bags." Joe pointed at the small bags on the floor between Mary and him.

The popping of each keystroke reverberated over the counter. A printer screeched beside the agent overtaking the clicking of the keyboard.

The agent ripped two paper tickets from the printer and handed them to Joe along with their passports. "Here are your tickets. Take a left after Security, and Gate D69 is down the terminal hallway."

"*Merci*," they said together to the agent as they left for the security line.

"Here, let me get *this* for you, Sweetie." Joe placed her bag onto the conveyor belt of the x-ray machine. A security officer sat behind the machine, while an additional officer stood on the other side of the metal detector.

"Oh, put *this* back for me, please."

Joe slipped her half-full water bottle inside her bag as Mary stepped first through the metal detector to wait for their bags. As Joe walked through, a buzzer sounded accompanied by a flashing red light.

"That's, okay," the guard said motioning Joe through to the other side to join Mary.

Joe and Mary continued through the Terminal after leaving Security. "Whew, that was a close one."

"What do you mean?" Joe asked while scanning ahead for their gate.

"I'm glad they didn't frisk me, cause I'm packing a gun on me." Mary laughed, nudging Joe's shoulder as they walked.

"You're gonna get us in trouble, someday." Joe usually welcomed her sense of humor, but smiled anyway at her joke. They held hands as they walked. "Here we go, Gate D69… and, we made it with thirty minutes to spare."

Two open seats beside each other were available in the waiting area. Joe and Mary sat and performed one of their favorite activities: people watching. "Oh, look at the baby... isn't she precious," Mary said into Joe's ear.

"Whoa, I just proposed last night. I think we can wait a little for that." Mary had been talkative all morning but with Joe's comment, she sat in silence.

A voice over the speaker erupted through the crowd. "Ladies and Gentlemen, in a few minutes we will begin boarding our flight to New York's JFK Airport by row number. When your row is called, we ask that you come to the gate for boarding."

People corralled in front of the gate agents. "So much for waiting for your row to be called," Mary said.

"Thank you, Ladies and Gentlemen. We are now boarding First and Business Class, and anyone with small children or who needs extra time getting onto the plane." The voice triggered a stampede of mostly men, carrying briefcases and computer bags through the crowd of people in front of them.

"How many people do you want to invite to our wedding?" Mary asked as Joe found amusement in the herd of people gathering in front of him.

"Uh... I guess we need to figure out who all to invite—" The voice interrupted Joe, again.

"Thank you. Okay, we will start boarding from the back of the plane going forward."

The blob of people thinned out around the waiting area. Half of the passengers boarded. The chaos in front of the gate calmed. Joe and Mary inched forward each with their bag.

"Do you want to get married in New York or back home in Texas?"

"I don't know. Most of our friends from home don't even live there anymore. I think we have more friends now in Stony Brook, anyway. Grandma loved the City the last time she visited—"

A voice over the speakers interrupted Joe. "Now, we are boarding rows ten through twenty."

"Ooh, that's us," Mary said taking his hand leading him to the gate.

"*Bonjour*, tickets, please," the agent said as Joe and Mary boarded the plane. A short man attempting to lift his bag into the overhead bin above his seat held up their path to their seats.

"Here, let me help you with that, Sir," Joe said helping the man.

"Thank you." The man took his seat giving room for Joe to lift the heavy bag into the bin. Their seats were two rows behind the man.

"Here's our seat… ah, I'm ready to take off and watch some movies," Joe said as he allowed Mary to get in first since she had the window seat.

"Okay, but during our flight, I want to talk about all the plans and ideas I have for our wedding."

"All your plans and ideas… I just asked you to marry me last night?" Joe lifted their carry-on bags into the overhead bin and joined her after getting the bags situated. As they each fastened their seatbelt, the flight crew came over the speakers to review the safety features of the plane. Joe and Mary continued their conversation during the flight attendants' announcement.

"Maybe so, but I've been dreaming of this moment since I was a little girl."

Joe scanned the aisle to the front of the plane. "Hey, I think we have the row all to ourselves."

After the attendants performed the safety presentation, the plane taxied around the airport before taking off. It was a beautiful day. With the roar of the engines, they floated above the runway. Neither would have known they were flying unless they looked out the window at the ground growing distant beneath them.

Prior to takeoff, Mary had fired off one wedding question after another. Much to Joe's relief, Mary had fallen asleep as soon as the plane reached its cruising altitude.

SEPTEMBER 11, 2001, 10:07 A.M.
SOMEWHERE OVER THE NORTH ATLANTIC

FOUR HOURS into the flight, Mary awoke, her head resting on Joe's shoulder. "Was I snoring?"

"Were you snoring? Um, a lady four rows away came up and asked if you were okay with all the noise you were making." Joe laughed as Mary jabbed his side and shook her head trying to wake.

"No, you were not snoring. I was just kidding."

"Ah... uh... Ladies and Gentlemen, this is your Captain speaking. We will be taking a little detour in our flight. Air Traffic Control is asking us to land in Halifax, Nova Scotia, delaying our arrival into JFK. Just so no one is alarmed, there is nothing wrong with our plane. It is most likely due to weather conditions or technical issues at the airport. Once we have more information, we will update you. For now, I ask the flight attendants to please prepare the cabin for landing. We will be making a quick decent, so everyone please make sure your luggage and items are secure in the cabin."

"Well, okay, I have never been to Canada," Joe said turning to Mary, while holding her hand, which shook from the Captain's announcement.

"Is this normal?"

"I don't know. I'm sure it's weather-related that's all." Joe did his best to reassure Mary.

Their plane developed a noticeable downward motion. To the passengers, the feeling was that of going down a hill of a roller coaster with a sharp turn at the bottom. The Captain made an unusual approach for a commercial aircraft to the airport. A chorus of gasps came from the passengers.

The landing strip came fast at the Halifax Airport. Mary peeked out her window. A long line of jets nose-to-tail ran the full length of the opposite runway. "Wow, look at all the planes out there," Mary said to Joe. "I didn't know this part of Canada was this busy?"

"Ladies and Gentlemen, this is your Captain, again. As you can see, it looks like we are not the only ones being diverted... With this many planes, it may be some time before we can take off. Halifax Ground Control is asking us to park at Gate 1 since we are the closest plane. If you would like to get off, we ask that you stay nearby to hear updates on our flight. As soon as we know anything else, I will be back with you."

"Oh my, it seems like we may be here awhile. How much longer is our flight going to be to New York?" Mary asked Joe, who had grabbed the airline magazine in the pocket of the seat in front of him.

"Looking at this map, we are just east of Maine. If we were in a car, it's a full day's drive." He studied the map and peeked outside at the other planes on the runway.

"Hey, I've got an idea. Since the company is picking up our travel expenses and we didn't check any bags, let's get off here. We can rent a car and drive home faster than waiting here to leave. Plus, we can see some of Canada along the way."

"Are you sure? Seems like a long way to drive, doesn't it?"

"Look at *all those* planes. It doesn't sound like we're leaving soon. And, they're all behind us. I bet they will have to leave first before we can leave. So, that will take a long time."

The Halifax Airport is one of the first major airports in North America reached by aircraft flying over the North Atlantic. On a typical weekday, four international flights land in Halifax. However, today, Joe and Mary's late morning flight was the twentieth with twenty more to follow.

Mary turned her head between the window and Joe. "I don't know? Can we do that? What if it takes off sooner than you think?"

"So what? The plane takes off without us. But, by that time, we'll be near Boston in a car. What do you say? Let's be spontaneous."

Seeing the growing parking lot of planes, Mary agreed. "Okay, let's do it."

Joe stood and opened the overhead compartment. "Here are our bags. Let's get off."

"Excuse me, but where are you going with your bags?" an attendant asked, coming up to him gasping for her breath.

"The Captain said we could get off the plane if we wanted to. We've decided to go ahead and rent a car to drive the rest of the way home." Joe explained their plan only loud enough for the attendant to hear. He did not want to give away his idea to the other passengers nearby.

"I don't know if that's..." The flight attendant's attention left Joe as she glanced up the aisle to her colleague, who nodded her approval for them to leave. "Well, I guess it's okay, then," the Flight Attendant said as she passed Joe and Mary to help another passenger behind them.

"C'mon, let's hurry to the car rental place in case others have the same idea." Joe walked ahead carrying Mary's pink bag, while she carried his beaten-up blue one.

As they shuffled down the aisle, the noise of the still-seated passengers grew louder. Most of them were on their cell phones attempting to make a call. For most, they heard a message saying all circuits were busy, now. The few able to connect to someone sat in horror listening to the other end of the line.

To Joe and Mary, none of this mattered. They passed everyone wearing smiles on their faces. Joe's due to his brilliant plan. Mary's due to all the wedding ideas floating around her mind.

SEPTEMBER 11, 2001, 10:45 A.M.
NOVA SCOTIA, CANADA

HUNDREDS OF PEOPLE packed the terminal building inside the Halifax Airport. Joe waited for Mary in front of the restroom next to Gate Number 1. The airport is exponentially smaller compared to the larger JFK.

Joe turned from the restroom and stepped behind a crowd curious to what everyone was watching. Their heads fixated on a television in the waiting area of the gate.

A tall man who had blocked Joe's view turned around when Joe tapped his shoulder. "Excuse me, but what—"

"Joe?" Mary's voice calling for him interrupted his question to the man. Joe turned around and grinned. Mary seemed lost standing outside the restroom as he weaved his way through the crowd to her. "Oh, there you are. I got worried 'cause I couldn't find you," Mary said.

"I went *over there* to see what everyone was watching?"

"And?"

"I don't know, I couldn't tell, and no one said anything."

"There's a lot of people in here," Mary said as Joe contemplated going back over to everyone.

Joe looked around the terminal. Most of the gates near where they stood had passengers exiting into the terminal building. "Uh... yeah, we better go now to get a rental car. If not, we must come back here to re-board our plane." Joe took Mary's hand and led her through the terminal following the overhead signs.

"I was thinking we should have blue in our wedding. I've always loved that color," Mary said following Joe.

"The car rental place is just down the escalator." Joe could not hear Mary's questions behind him; his focus remained on the signs pointing the way.

"Whew, you were walking pretty fast." Mary gasped for her breath as they reached the escalator.

"I want to make sure we don't have to wait in a long line." Joe twisted around to Mary. "I don't know what's happening. There's a lot of planes here for a small airport... and, if we're renting a car, I am sure others are, too."

"See, that's why I love you. You're always planning ahead and trying to look out for us." Her chest pounded from keeping his pace as they had darted through the people.

The escalator ended in the baggage claim area with the car rental counters behind the luggage carousels. The few people in the area stood motionless talking on their cell phones. Joe and Mary found the first car rental counter. "Huh, I guess we tap *this*," Joe said.

He pushed down with his index finger on the silver bell on the counter. A few seconds had passed as a man, no older than Joe and Mary, came out from an open entryway behind the counter.

"Hello, my name is Anthony. How can I help you today?"

"We were traveling to JFK but landed here, and we would like to rent a car one-way to New York City, please," Joe said.

"Sure, I can imagine air traffic will be a nightmare there, so I understand... okay, let me see what we have. Is there a particular car you have in mind?"

"Not really, any will be okay, since the company I interviewed with will pay us back."

Mary stood beside Joe connected to his right arm. "We're driving home and only have *these two bags* with us... Have you heard what's happening by any chance... why all the planes are here?" Joe asked.

"I don't know. My co-worker in the back yelled earlier something about a plane crash, but I am not sure. I stepped back *there* just before you guys rang the bell..." Anthony scrolled through his computer screen. "Okay... here we go. We have a nice Ford Taurus available." Anthony passed a printout to Joe, showing the price and details of the rental.

"Cool, that'll work," Joe said as he completed the transaction.

Anthony opened a drawer behind the counter. "Here are the keys and a local map. Just walk straight out the door, and—"

"Oh, shit! Anthony, get back here and look at this... " The command from behind the wall interrupted Anthony's instruction of where Joe and Mary needed to pickup the car.

"I'm sorry about *that*. Just go straight through the door, and your car is in space number 102. Is there anything else I can help you with?"

"I think we're good."

"Have a good day," Anthony said pointing toward the o exit.

"Well, I think you're needed in the back. Thanks for your help," Joe said as Anthony left and joined his co-worker behind the wall. "Come on, Sweetie, let's get on the road."

"Holy shit," came the voices of Anthony and his co-worker at the same time as the doors closed behind Joe and Mary as they exited the building.

"Wow, *that* was very professional," Mary said with a sarcastic laugh.

The open parking lot was easy to find. Half the spaces were empty. Mary followed beside Joe as his paced slowed.

"There it is." Joe pressed the key fob as the car's running lights flashed. He placed their bags in the trunk and inspected the car before getting inside the car. As Joe started the engine, he studied the map Anthony had given him plotting out their route home to Long Island.

"We should be at the US Border in about five hours, coming into Maine." Joe showed the map to Mary to validate his plan.

As Joe placed the map in the backseat, Mary stared out the front windows. "I've always wanted to see the autumn leaves in Maine. Do you think they've changed color yet?"

"I'm not sure. It's what... uh..." Joe paused, "it's September 11th." Joe scanned the trees around the perimeter of the airport. "The leaves here are just now changing, so I don't know." They drove out of the parking lot and down the highway away from the airport.

Joe turned on the radio. Through the speakers, they heard, "The President this morning spoke from Booker Elementary School in Sarasota, Florida."

Mary reached for the radio control knob. "No radio. Let's just talk more about our wedding. I am so excited. When do you want to have it? What colors should we do? Do you want live music? Oh, the food... we need to plan a menu."

The questions came in rapid fire from Mary. "Whoa, slow down, Mary. We've got a long ride ahead of us. Let's discuss one topic at a time."

SEPTEMBER 11, 2001, 4:11 P.M.
NEAR THE CANADIAN / U.S. BORDER

MILES DROVE BY THEM. Seaside villages every so often had broken through the isolation of the Canadian countryside. The autumn leaves turned from green to golden yellow the further inland they traveled. Mary rifled off question-after-question about their wedding. Hours had passed. The only sounds came from the racing asphalt under the car, the wind crashing the windows, Mary's questions and Joe's answers.

"Okay, I think we're coming up on the Border." Joe slowed the car as they approached a short line of vehicles stopped at a guardhouse. "Can you, please, hand me my driver's license. It is in my wallet in my coat pocket in the backseat."

Mary reached behind them. "Here's your license and passport, just in case." Mary held the items as the other cars passed ahead through the Border. Joe pressed the button on his armrest as his window hummed down.

Three heavily armed guards wearing green camouflage pants and black jackets approached their car. The American Flag emblem stood against their black, flat brimmed hats. Each guard held their hands on the trigger area of their machine guns pointed to the ground. They surrounded the car. One walked to the back, another stood by Mary's side of the car, and the last bent down to Joe's opened window.

"What was your business in Canada?" the guard asked Joe. There was no small talk. The guard asked his question with an interrogating tone.

Joe extended his hand through the window holding his driver's license and passport. The guard was quick to snatch the documents from Joe. "Well, our flight from Paris got grounded in Halifax. So, we rented a car to drive home instead of waiting." Joe's eyes followed the guard behind their car inspecting underneath the trunk.

The guard grunted outside Joe's window as he held his finger on his trigger. Joe jumped when the guard standing outside his window yelled to his colleagues. "They were on a plane from Paris." The guard's interrogating gaze pierced through Joe in the front seat. Mary could not take her eyes off the guard on her side of the car, his gun a few feet from her.

After a few tense moments at the normally friendly Canadian Border, the guard handed him back his license and passport. "That was probably a good idea. I bet no planes are going anywhere for a few days. Did you notice anything strange on your flight?"

Stunned at his question, Joe said, "Not that I can think of. We were flying along and then the Captain came on the speaker saying we would land, but never said why? We landed pretty fast, and there were dozens of other planes also on the runway. That's when we decided to rent a car to drive home to New York."

The other two guards not speaking to Joe stalked the car. Their faces tensed with their right index fingers hovering near their triggers.

"Okay, you are clear to go through." The guard speaking with Joe motioned them to go ahead.

"Thanks..." Joe pressed the button on the armrest as his window rose. He pressed the button again as the window reversed down. "Is there something going on, Sir?"

"Is there... you've not heard?" The guard's eyes widened, his mouth opened in shock looking at Joe.

"No, what? As soon as we decided to rent a car, we ran to the counter. We've been making wedding plans during the entire drive."

"You need to turn on the radio, then. We are under attack. New York and Washington have been hit, and they believe other cities are next." The guard yelled over to the other two standing on Mary's side of the car. "*They* don't know what's happening."

"Hit? Hit by what?" Joe asked.

"Planes. Those damn terrorists finally did it and attacked us using planes. That's why your... hell, all planes for that matter, are grounded."

The guard standing on Mary's side tapped her window and motioned them forward as other cars queued behind them.

"What?" Joe did now understand what the guard was saying as he reached for the radio releasing his foot from the brake. Joe repeated the guard's words to himself. *We are under attack?* "What radio station?"

"Awe, hell, it doesn't matter, Son. Any of them," the guard said as Joe drove away entering Maine.

Joe pressed the scan button on the radio. Hurried reporters appeared on every station. Announcements came about plane crashes into the World Trade Center and the Pentagon.

With the reports, Joe and Mary drove in silence. The road twisted ahead of them through a thick section of forest. Hillsides grew with bright, golden leaves creating a kaleidoscope of magnificent color. It was beautiful. The sight went unnoticed by Joe and Mary.

"Joseph, I'm scared."

"I know Mary. It'll be okay. We should be near Bangor in an hour. We'll find a hotel room for the night and find out what's happening before we go any further."

A reporter's voice said on the radio. "Here's what we know… at 8:46 a.m. this morning, a plane crashed into the North Tower of the World Trade Center… at 9:03 a.m., a second plane crashed into the South Tower… at 9:37 a.m., hijackers flew another plane into the western side of the Pentagon in Washington…"

"Washington, too… what's going on?" Joe's concern heightened his sense of urgency to find any hotel along the desolate stretch of road.

"… At 9:59 a.m. the South Tower of the World Trade Center suffered a complete collapse to the ground. A horrific sight of smoke and debris filled lower Manhattan."

"Dear, God… those poor people," Mary said with a faint voice as she supported her head with her hand against the window.

"… Then reports came of another plane crash at 10:07 a.m. this morning in rural Pennsylvania. We can only speculate that this plane crash is connected to the events happening in New York and Washington…"

Joe held Mary's shaking hand as she cried beside him. "We'll find a place to stop soon, Sweetie."

With each turn, the passing golden trees disappeared behind them. Terrifying radio reports played inside the car.

"... At 10:28 a.m., the World Trade Center's North Tower collapsed. Countless numbers of fire and police rescue teams were in that area..."

"Okay, looks like Bangor is a few miles away... oh good, there's a sign for a motel ahead in two miles. Let's stop there."

Joe stole a glance over to Mary; tear-tracks etched across her cheeks. "It's okay, Sweetie."

The area outside the motel was empty of people as they pulled into the roadside motel parking lot. Joe parked the car. "Okay, I'll be back in a few minutes. I'll get us a room."

He opened the door. Mary grabbed his arm, pulling him back to her. "I love you," she said letting him go as she continued to listen to the radio.

A little bell clanged against the glass door as Joe walked inside the small motel. The entire motel staff of six people had gathered around a television in the lobby.

Joe approached the group as he caught his first images of smoke rising above New York City. A cleaning lady consoled a crying older man, who wore an apron. He must have worked in the motel kitchen.

"Uh, hello... my fiancée and I would like to get a room for the night."

A large, tall man stood from his chair. His eyes remained locked on the television screen. "Um, okay, I'll be right there." As the man turned around, it was visible to Joe the man had been crying. The tip of the man's bright red nose matched the corners of his eyes.

He led Joe back to the check-in desk. "Terrible... just terrible. What a helluva a day, isn't it?" The man pulled a key off the wall behind the desk. "Here's a key to one of our rooms."

"Don't you need my credit card or anything?"

"Hell, Man, can't you see? It's the end of the world. Just take the damn key. Consider it a gift." The man gave Joe the key and rejoined the group gathered around the glow of the television.

Joe walked back to the car to get Mary. He opened her door. She limped out of the car falling into his arms. "I am so tired. All the traveling and talking today... then, *this* news... it's killing me."

"It's okay, Sweetie. We have a room. Let me get our things out of the car. We'll rest and figure out what to do next."

As they walked inside the lobby to the elevator, Joe purposely stood between Mary and the television blocking her view. "Don't look. We'll turn on the TV in our room and see what's happening for ourselves."

They found their room and opened the door. Mary pushed ahead of him, grabbing the remote to turn on the television. As each channel passed, the same images appeared. Scenes from New York City, from Washington, from Pennsylvania reported the grim news.

Arm-in-arm, they sat on the edge of the bed. With their very own eyes, the horror unfolded before them for the first time, today.

Time had stopped.

It felt like a movie. The horrific images of the World Trade Center falling over-and-over-and-over again replayed providing a sense the day was on a constant repeat.

After an hour of the sad reports bombarding them, Joe could no longer take it. "I've seen enough." He stood from the bed and walked into the bathroom. "I will take a shower and then go find us something to eat."

A few minutes later, Joe finished and came out of the bathroom, wearing the same clothes as earlier. Mary had not moved. He kissed the top of her head. "Sweetie, I won't be gone long. I'll bring us back a burger or something."

Mary bolted from the bed and hugged his shoulders. "I love you," she whispered.

"I love you, too… while I'm gone, how about you take a shower. You'll feel so much better. I'll be back, soon." Joe walked Mary back to the bed and then left her alone in the room.

Finding a diner a few miles up the road, Joe returned twenty minutes later. He opened the door to the room holding two brown paper bags. Dark, grease spots decorated the bottom of each.

Joe was happy Mary had taken his advice and gotten a shower. She sat propped up on the bed. Her wet hair draped across her naked shoulders. The white, cotton robe from the back of the bathroom door provided warmth. She was reading a *Bible* she had found in the desk beside the bed.

"Mary, I don't think I've ever known you to read that before?" Joe sat the two grease-soaked bags on the desk.

"Come here, you've got to read *this*. It's the end of the world, I tell ya. I wanted to know what was coming next?"

She held the *Bible* between them as she read out loud. *"The Sun will be darkened, and the Moon will not give its light; the stars will fall from the sky, and the heavenly bodies will be shaken. At that time, the sign of the Son of Man will appear in the sky, and all the nations of the Earth will mourn. They will see the Son of Man coming on the clouds of the sky, with power and great glory."*

"But, you've never really gone to a church before, so you can't just read that and understand what it means? There are so many different meanings of things in the *Bible*." The smell of the greasy hamburgers floated through the air. Their stomachs rumbled from not having eaten since breakfast.

"You're right. And, I haven't. But, what the hell is going on?" Mary asked as she closed the *Bible,* placing it on the bed. She sat up and cried. Joe held her close to him.

"Look, I don't know what's going on either. I am scared too. But, right now... right here, we are together, and we're safe. And, I will never let anything bad happen to you. I will always protect you."

"I know, but all those people. New York City. I mean—"

"Shh, I know. It's so terrible," Joe said trying to console her. He said this more to convince himself everything would be okay. "Hey, let's eat, and then I'll come to bed with you. We can read more of the *Bible* together."

"Okay..." Mary paused glimpsing the television. "Joseph, I know we've never done this together, but can we say a little prayer right now?"

"Sure..." Joe grabbed her hand as they slipped down from the bed onto the floor.

Mary began, "Dear God... "

OCTOBER 3, 2001
STONY BROOK, NEW YORK

"GOOD MORNING, Professor Baptiste," Joe said in a loud voice. "Ah, seems like old times, again."

Joe loved Professor Baptiste's office. The familiar scent of thirty-year-old books with a hint of cigar smoke filled the room. Joe had spent many hours over the past two years with Baptiste with the professor serving as both his advisor and mentor.

Baptiste rose from behind his desk and took off his glasses, which fell to his chest connected to his metal-linked necklace. "Joseph, it's so good to see you, again." Baptiste greeted Joe with a handshake in the middle of his office.

"Yes, you too, Professor."

"I'm happy you've joined our graduate project team." He grabbed both of Joe's hands. Joe's wedding ring pressed against the professor's fingers. "Oh, I see you have exciting news to tell me?"

As the professor released his grip, Joe held up his left hand showing his wedding ring. "Yep... that's right. I'm married."

"So, you had an eventful summer after graduation?"

"Oh, if only you knew the half of it."

"*Here*, sit down," the professor said pointing to a brown, leather sofa against the window in his office.

Joe sat. A familiarity rushed over him. He had spent many an afternoon in this same spot. Professor Baptiste loved to discuss biology, genetics, and various scientific theories. Now, Baptiste served a new role as Joe's PhD Advisor.

"Oh, Professor. Where do I begin?

"To be sure... Mary, right?"

"Well, yes, of course."

"Just checking. I never know these days with you kids."

"Yes, Mary. I proposed to her in Paris on top of the *Eiffel Tower*."

"Well, that's—"

Joe continued, cutting off the professor. "We were there because of a job interview I had. We wanted to plan a nice, big wedding. But as soon as we got back, we knew we did not want to wait and went to the courthouse."

"That's a lot right there in your sentence, Joseph," the professor said. Baptiste crossed his legs as he sat back into the chair beside the sofa. "You went from proposing at the most romantic spot in the world to getting married at the courthouse?"

"Well… you know…" Joe said stammering sensing the professor's disapproval. "When I proposed, it was last month on September 10th. We flew back to New York City the next day. And, that's when all hell broke loose."

The professor uncrossed his legs and leaned forward to Joe.

"We wanted to get married right away because you just never know if today will be your last day or not."

The professor leaned back again into his chair signaling his approval to Joe. "I can't believe it… so, you were on a plane when it happened."

"Yes, and that's just it. We were flying to New York at the same time. Hell, we weren't even aware what had happened until that night in a motel room in Maine. We felt we were so lucky because that could have been us." Joe's voice cracked. A sense of fear from his memories four weeks earlier had returned.

"In the motel… You didn't drive home from the airport when you landed."

"No, our plane got diverted to Canada. On a whim, we decided to rent a car and drive back from Halifax." Joe reached out to unwrap a peanut butter cup from the candy tray on the table in front of him.

"Hell, Mary and I, we were so excited about planning our wedding that's all we talked about. On the plane… walking through the airport… driving the car… not until we got to the US Border did we find out."

"Wow," the only response the usual talkative Professor gasped.

"Yes, *wow*, is right. Where were *you*?" Joe asked.

"I was here in the office getting ready to go teach Biology 202. One of my students barged in here and told me I had to go watch the TV in the lobby." The professor raked his hands over his baldhead. "I got there in time to see the second plane hit the Tower, and I felt my heart drop into my stomach."

"Yeah, there were TVs in the airport and people were standing around. But, we were not even aware what was happening."

"I couldn't stop watching. To think this happened less than an hour away, and felt so helpless as the Towers fell." The professor rose from his chair. "Well, let's talk about a happier topic, your research plan."

Joe stood from the sofa and placed the empty candy wrapper into his pants pocket. "Yes, let's."

"But, first, we must go get some coffee," the professor said, opening the office door. Joe and the professor walked across the hall into the lab. "So, tell me about this job offer in Paris."

"Not much to tell, really. It was a great opportunity. The work sounded very exciting. The salary was great. Hell, any salary to a college student is great. But…" Joe hesitated to finish his sentence.

The thoughts about whether he had made the right decision rushed to him. "But, the job was in Paris. And, what we had experienced, we didn't want to live outside the country… at least for now."

"So, you came back to me." Baptiste turned back to Joe stretching out his arms with a smile on his face.

"Yes, I did. And, thank you again for allowing me to join your group to work towards my doctorate."

"Joseph, my pleasure. I've been teaching for almost thirty years now. And, you have a real talent in the lab." The professor poured himself a cup of the worst-tasting coffee in the world. "You remember your first day of class with me?"

"Yes. Like it was yesterday."

"That speech I gave. I have given it on the first day in my class many times," the professor said sipping his coffee. "What do you remember most from that speech?"

"I remember you challenging us to find our passion and to follow it." Joe poured sugar into his coffee to kill the terrible taste.

"And, during that semester and in our later work together, I saw that passion firsthand."

Joe's numbed taste of the coffee did not faze him after years of working with the professor. "You challenged me, but I had another reason pushing me into this passion."

"Your mother, right?"

"Yes, my mama. Losing her at such a young age, I... I..."

"No need to explain. I understand."

"If having a passion for genetics can help someday determine what caused her cancer, then it can help determine a cure. And, then... then, I'll understand the reason behind losing her. If nothing else, maybe I can prevent some other ten-year-old from losing their mother."

"Love... it's a strong motivator isn't it, Son?" the professor said, placing his hand on Joe's shoulder.

"It sure as hell is. Now, let's go figure out how I will save the world."

7-DISCOVERY

NOTEBOOKS with printed coordinates, mathematical simulations, scenario analyses, and pictures of decades' old research lay in front of Joe. Gabriel had excused himself from the room giving Joe time alone to review the information.

Joe's appearance had changed. He was a disheveled man. Long gone was his pressed shirt, which he had tucked neatly into his dress pants in preparation of his speech he would not deliver. Noticeable coffee stains were on both knees.

Joe reviewed the information. Unless the Eden Foundation had fabricated the data, it became clear to Joe he was validating the same results. On a notepad, he had written *2020* at the top of a page, circling the year over-and-over.

The door to the room opened. Gabriel walked inside holding Joe's favorite beer.

"*Here*, I thought you could use *this*," Gabriel said extending his hand.

Without a word, Joe chugged it as fast as he could, conjuring brief memories of his undergraduate days. When the last drop of beer emptied from the bottle, Joe slammed it down on the table as he pushed his notebook away.

Gabriel noticed the black circles drawn around the year 2020. "I see you came to the same conclusion." Gabriel placed his hand onto the written note and pushed it back to Joe. "That's only five years away."

Joe could not force himself to make eye contact with his own handwriting. The same conclusion taunted him from the paper.

"The data shows it will happen on September 11th, 2020. And, if the size, speed, and composition of that son-of-a-bitch are truly what these readings show..."

Gabriel grabbed Joe's shoulder. "Yes. It's correct. I can assure you. We have studied the calculations for the past sixty years."

Joe stood, threw Gabriel's hand off him, and pushed the notebook across the table until it hit the floor on the opposite side. "The results seem correct, but how in the hell can I believe the data is not made up?"

"I'm afraid all you have is faith in us."

"Faith? Hell, the last person I saw talking about the end of the world and using the word *faith* held a *Bible* in front of our church."

"You may not know me, but I know you, Joe... I know you very well. At this point, you must have faith in our program and me. You've got a great opportunity here to help ensure mankind continues to survive."

"But, on Mars?"

"Yes, as I explained yesterday, based on all the simulations, Earth will no longer exist. The impact will immediately explode everything."

Joe sat dumbfounded.

"Too much debris from the explosion will hit the Moon. So, we could not build Salvation there. We decided our closest, possible option is Mars."

Gabriel gave Joe a red notebook he had held under his arm upon returning to the room.

"What's this?"

"These are the plans and pictures of Salvation. We developed the plans based on our experiences on the Moon."

Joe studied the pages inside the red notebook. "The modules... how did these get transported to Mars?" Images showed white, honeycomb structures connected across the red Martian landscape.

"Each module took nine months to build. We sent them from the Moon to Mars once completed."

Joe lifted his head from the notebook delivering a piercing gaze to Gabriel. "From the Moon? *These* were built in the three years between '69 and '72?"

"No, the Public only knows about the Apollo Missions, which ended with Apollo 17 in December of '72. But, the Eden Foundation continued missions to the Moon as recent as 2005."

Gabriel dragged the remaining metal chair across the floor to the table across from Joe. The metal etched along the floor.

"The missions continued? How can that be?"

"After Apollo proved it possible for Man to land on the Moon and return, we started Project Salvation. We continued missions from top-secret locations in the southern Indian Ocean."

"But, why continue to go to the Moon?"

"We needed to establish a construction base on the Moon. The Salvation modules were constructed there and transported to Mars. It is easier and cheaper to lift off from the gravity of the Moon rather than from Earth."

"How many missions occurred to the Moon after Apollo?"

"Between 1974 to 2005..." Gabriel paused reviewing the information in the notebook. "There were three missions each month. 1,116 missions in total."

Joe stood from his chair and paced the room in disbelief. "One-thousand... holy shit. There had to have been an army of people on the Moon?"

"The missions sent the initial components of the living modules for Salvation. Also, along with the actual workers, equipment and supplies were sent. Our workers lived in modules like what you remember from the Eagle Module of Apollo."

Joe scanned the pictures from the construction teams over the decades.

"During the '80s, that's when crews of twenty workers left for a year at a time to build the modules. They took delivery of new materials three times per month."

"Once the modules were built, when were they sent to Mars... I mean, when was the first mission to Mars?" Joe could not believe he had asked that question.

"With all the Moon missions, our project engineers modified the requirements to go to Mars. Eden started the planning during the early '70s, and the first Mars landing happened on March 13th, 1978."

Joe sat back down in his chair almost missing his seat. "1978?" He ran his hands through his hair and pulled the binder closer.

"Yeah, 1978. It took time to change the systems used for the Moon flights to go to Mars. The flight takes longer to get there... there's an atmosphere on Mars to consider."

"How long does it take to travel to Mars?"

"That's where we have had fantastic technical advances through the years. Mind you, it's not like you've seen in the movies or anything. Missions which took six to nine months in the '70s and '80s... we now can get to Mars from Earth in three weeks."

"Three weeks? How in the hell is that even possible?" Joe flipped the pages in the notebook.

"In our research of lasers to try and destroy CIE.57.20, we discovered a way to use them to propel our transport rockets. It's a system we call photonic propulsion."

"What? The movies had already taken the name hyper-warp speed from you?"

Gabriel responded with a fake laugh. "Basically, our rockets launch into space, like you have seen on TV. The module with the crew and materials onboard ejects from the rocket. We can land the rocket safely back down on its original launch pad."

Joe's focus never veered from Gabriel as he spoke. If Gabriel was making this up, the description he provided Joe ignited his childhood daydreams of rocket travel based on stories he had heard his grandma tell him about his grandpa, Eli.

"Once the module is in an orbit around Earth, a receptor shield, like what you would think of as a satellite dish, extends on the back of the module. From an orbiting satellite, we fire a laser to the receptor shield. Its force pushes it forward. The satellite continues to pulse the laser. With each pulse, the forward speed of the module increases exponentially because of zero gravity."

Joe imagined the concept using rudimentary calculations in his mind. "And, Eden kept all these missions and landing on Mars a secret from the Public?"

"As you can imagine, with all the people working on Project Eden and Salvation over the years, we have had our challenges."

"Challenges?"

"We put great efforts to control our staff and the information. But, sometimes leaks occur. We have gotten good at creating diversions in the public eye away from any leak."

"Diversions? Like?"

"Joe, I don't want to get into all that… but, I'll give you one example. I want to give you a sense of the Foundation's capabilities and how powerful we are. It relates to our development of the photonic propulsion system."

The tease from Gabriel intrigued Joe.

"To place satellites into orbit with laser-firing capabilities… do you remember in the '80s all the news stories about the *Star Wars* government projects?"

"You mean where Reagan planned to put laser, missile defense systems into orbit to protect the US from Soviet nuclear missiles?"

"Yeah… those are our satellites… our missiles to fire at CIE.57.20 and our lasers to propel our flights to Mars."

Joe sat in silence.

"But, what about more recent news headlines about Mars… like the Curiosity Mission and other rover flights?"

"Yeah… this has been a tricky decision made by the Foundation. As best I can figure, sometimes the best way to stop rumors about something is to place something actually there in complete view for the Public."

"I don't follow?"

"This way, part of the truth is there for people to see. If other rumors surface about Salvation, we can use these rover missions to deflect them. Also, the Foundation does an excellent job making the Public believe anyone spreading rumors is a crazy, conspiracy theorist."

Joe's mind raced. Part of him believed every word Gabriel had said, fascinated by the science of it all. But, the critical part of him remained skeptical. It seemed too amazing to be true.

"So, to be clear… the Soviets were not the real reason for our race to the Moon in the '60s. There's a construction base on the Moon. We've been going to Mars since 1978. And, you float half-truths to divert the Public. Is there anything else you're not telling me?"

"Everything is in *this* notebook."

"Are we still going to the Moon, now?"

"In 2005, all work stopped there because of the development of 3D printing capability."

"3D printers? My friend, Charlie, used one of those to build crystalline lattice structures in his lab."

"That technology enabled Salvation to stop sending building materials to the Moon for construction. Instead, the missions now go direct to Mars. We sent several, large 3D printers able to construct the modules physically on site."

"The largest thing I've seen Charlie make was a foot-tall beer keg one day when he was playing around with it."

"Our printers are a little larger… larger than a double-decker bus. They print single module walls, seven meters tall by seven meters wide. Now, the only missions to Mars take epoxy materials for the printers, supplies, and people."

"Who in the hell agreed to live on the Moon and Mars to assemble them in the first place?"

"Joe, the exact details of the people selected are classified. That information usually is kept from me."

Joe sat quietly for several minutes. Pages rattled as he flipped through both notebooks Gabriel had given him. The pictures confirmed everything Gabriel had said. Frustrated, Joe pushed them both away at the same time.

"Many people had to have been involved with this. Not to mention the cost of it all."

"Yeah, the amount of money would amaze you. Let's just say through fear mongering and deception, the Public will fund anything. The ups-and-downs of Wall Street have been our best friends."

"How in the hell have you kept this a secret for—"

Gabriel interrupted him. "Just like you, Project Salvation has identified *those people* critical to its success and recruited them. Construction workers, scientists, engineers, even politicians."

"But, I don't understand… how do you persuade someone to go to the Moon for a year or to Mars for the rest of their life?"

"We identify people who can fulfill our requirements. We watch and evaluate them. Then, the Foundation decides to recruit them to join us, or not."

"But, what if they say *no*… what if I say *no*?"

With a cold, direct look, Gabriel said, "*No* is simply not an answer. Once we approach someone, then *yes* is the only acceptable answer."

"Again… what if I say *no*?"

"That's my job, to make you say *yes*. You will see what I'm telling you is real, and we need you for this program."

"But, surely you have approached others, and they ultimately said *no*. What about those people?"

"Let's just say we have forced no one to join us… we hold no one at gunpoint on the Moon or Mars. But, once we tell you about Project Salvation, we do everything possible to keep this classified and a secret."

Gabriel stood from his chair and walked behind Joe placing his hands on Joe's shoulders. His grip was firm and strong pressing into Joe. "And, Joe… I mean *everything possible* to keep this a secret."

As he made this statement, the television screen illuminated with an image appearing. The image was fuzzy at first but came into focus. Joe sat shocked seeing Mary at their kitchen table eating dinner by herself in New York.

"What the hell is this?"

Gabriel felt Joe's muscles tense under his grip. "Joe, we are approaching you, because we need you. Your work is the closest we have seen to actually creating cures for diseases such as cancer."

Gabriel's words fell on deaf ears. Mary's image caused Joe's heart to pound through his chest.

"Mankind will need your work and continued research. It will help develop ways to fight current and potentially new diseases Project Salvation may face."

"But, why the hell are you watching Mary right now?"

"Joe, as I said, we do not accept *no* as an answer in joining us. We will do *everything possible* to keep Project Salvation a secret."

"What do you mean *everything*... if you hurt Mary, I will kill you, you bastard." Joe attempted to stand from the chair, but Gabriel held him in place.

Gabriel released his grip on Joe as he continued to sit in front of Gabriel. "Nothing will happen to Mary or you. *No* will not be an answer, and you will join us."

Joe approached a retreating Gabriel, who came to rest against the wall beside the television, standing nose-to-nose with Gabriel. Joe pierced Gabriel's eyes with a menacing stare. "If you hurt her... I will kill you."

Gabriel smiled and lifted his hands up to Joe's shoulders. "Joe... nothing will happen. But, *you will* join us."

Joe moved his gaze from Gabriel onto Mary on the screen. This gave Gabriel an opportunity to step to the side and bend down to pick up Joe's notepad. He held it up between Joe and the screen. The black circled *2020* broke his stare.

"2020 is only five years away... this *will* happen... join us, and on 2020, you and Mary will continue to live... along with the rest of the chosen ones in Salvation."

Joe took the notepad from him throwing it across the room onto the table. The pad landed and bounced into the air. Joe walked away and paced the room, circling the table and Gabriel like a shark circling a seal in the ocean.

Minutes had passed. "So, I cannot tell anyone about this, right?"

"Absolutely, no one can know... not even Mary. In fact, don't even tell her about me or give her my name. When the time comes, you will tell her before you leave... I will help you with that."

"I'm not sure I can promise that... we don't keep secrets between us."

"Mary must not know, Joe... full stop. We are telling you now because you need time to collect your research and identify the equipment you will need at Salvation."

Joe continued circling the room. His chest heaved in-and-out. His forehead glistened from the overhead fluorescent lights.

"The Foundation will provide the needed equipment and make arrangements to send you and Mary to Salvation. From there, you will have a few years to request any additional equipment, supplies... whatever else you will need."

Joe did not pay attention to his last comment. His thoughts remained with Mary. He noticed how sad she appeared sitting in the kitchen alone.

"But, I need to tell Mary... I can't keep this to myself."

"Let me say this again, in no uncertain terms. Joe, we will do *everything* to keep Salvation a secret... *everything*."

February 20, 1960
Palomar Mountain Observatory, California

JACKSON WHEELER DROVE the ninety-minute drive from his seaside apartment in Carlsbad, California, to the Palomar Mountain Observatory. Countless switchbacks make the road treacherous through the mountain range, especially in winter.

But, Jackson did not mind. To him, the drive meant he was on his way to his favorite place in the world to look back into time, as he liked to think about it. As a child, Jackson had a fondness for astronomy. It amazed him that light from galaxies and planets within our universe takes thousands of years to reach Earth.

For the past four months, Jackson had operated the Samuel Oschin Telescope at Palomar, which uses a camera to view the night skies. He had extra motivation on tonight's trip. Jackson's dream was coming true to view the heavens with the world's largest, reflecting telescope, the Hale Telescope.

Going from a forty-eight-inch telescope to two-hundred inches is a significant difference. It is the same as driving the Palomar switchbacks in his 1957 Chevy Two-Ten Series pickup truck versus a candy-apple, red Corvette Convertible Stingray, his dream car.

Jackson pulled into the observatory's parking lot and performed his usual routine before getting out of his truck. He kissed his right index and middle fingers placing them on the pregnant belly of his girlfriend's picture tucked into the sun visor.

Jackson arrived as the sunset in the western sky over the mountaintops. Nighttime is the favorite time for any astronomer, and tonight was perfect. The weather forecast called for clear skies.

He rushed inside the observatory. On the desk beside the platform leading up to the Hale Telescope, he placed his briefcase and lunch. Butterflies swirled in the pit of his stomach reminding him of his first date with his girlfriend.

"What is our target tonight?" Jackson asked the astronomer he was replacing.

"The next area on the schedule is Columba. The constellation is coming into good view, up from the Equator."

"Columba?" Jackson asked with hesitation, "Columba is the most boring constellation to review. No bright stars. No meteor showers emanate from it."

"Jackson, we don't get to choose. Take it up with the boys up at Caltech. They send the assignments down," the astronomer said collecting his things to go home.

Jackson reviewed the coordinate sheets from the desk and climbed up the platform. In front of him was a control panel, which operates the impressive telescope. He took a deep breath recalling his countless weeks of daytime training; Jackson was ready. His excitement grew even though Columba was not his first choice of Space to scan.

On the control console, he pressed the button labeled *Shutter Doors*. The sound of a motor reverberated through the empty observatory.

Large-heavy, white shutter doors opened from the top of the dome down along the side. The doors stopped as the black sky came into view. The crisp, cool winter air rushed inside encompassing Jackson.

Under the large telescope, Jackson flipped a small, black lever activating the analog computer. The control room vibrated. The telescope's motor powered on, ready to receive its coordinates. The behemoth two-hundred-inch monster was ready to move.

He used the levers to position the telescope to the proper right ascension and declination coordinates. The building supporting the telescope moved to the right. Jackson checked the gauges reading out the hour angle of the telescope.

Once at the correct position, the rotation of the building stopped. The telescope was ready to scan the night sky through the constellation of Columba.

Jackson's years of study and internship had finally paid off at this moment. This week would change his life forever.

FEBRUARY 25, 1960, 3:17 A.M. PALOMAR MOUNTAIN OBSERVATORY, CALIFORNIA

THE WEATHER HAD been perfect for Jackson every night for his first shift on the Hale Telescope. The skies over Palomar Mountain have been crystal clear.

With the clear skies, this time of year brings cold weather in late February. Even in this part of southern California, the temperatures approach near freezing during the winter.

Jackson peered through the telescope's eyepiece and wrote notes in his journal. *Nothing new tonight. Hopefully, next week I can look at a more exciting area?*

He focused on his last section of Columba, steadying the telescope. With a press of a button on the computer console labeled *Picture,* his telescope captured an image of the stars.

Astronomers compare multiple pictures taken at the same coordinates at different times. They attempt to identify any differences between the sets of pictures. In theory, the photos should look the same. The positions of stars should not move from picture-to-picture. Any variance shows something requiring attention.

Jackson pushed up the small, black lever labeled *Computer.* The humming sounds of the telescope's motor stopped. He collected his paperwork, closed the dome's shutter doors, and climbed down the platform.

He gathered the exposed photo tablets, which popped out of the camera affixed to the bottom of the telescope. Finished for the evening, Jackson entered a glass-windowed office across the room and poured a cup of hot cocoa. Jackson sat behind a desk to enjoy his drink, but the rising steam forced him to wait.

His hot cocoa rested on the corner of the desk. After years of study and realizing his dream to operate one of the world's largest telescopes, he studied the pictures of his first week's work.

The five-inch-by-five-inch pictures on thick, plastic paper popped like thunder as he shuffled through them. The smell of drying developer ink emanated from his hands.

After a few moments of rifling through the pictures, the folder fell onto the desk. He sipped on his warm cocoa, allowing him to make it through the next few hours until daylight.

Jackson glanced down through the steam above his drink to the photos on the desk. They had fallen out of the folder spread across the desktop. He pushed the pictures back into the folder.

His eyes grew wide. Something was different about the pictures.

Jackson sat his mug down on the desk with such force, causing cocoa to slosh over the rim. He held two pictures at arm's length in front of him.

That's interesting.

He stared at the pictures while moving them side-to-side. After moving the pictures closer to his eyes, he placed them both down on the desk beside each other. Jackson turned on the overhead light in the office creating an interrogation room. The pictures sat in the middle of the bright beam of light waiting to reveal its deadly secret.

"Jesus!"

Jackson's voice echoed through the empty observatory from the office. He opened the desk drawer and pulled out a red marker.

"What is *that*?" He circled the same position on both pictures; a faint, fuzzy gray dot.

The pictures were on the opposite corner of the desk as he again flipped open the green folder. He searched in vain for other pictures taken in the same location. Those were the only two.

With his last sip of cocoa, he grabbed the black, rotary phone sitting on the desk. Protocol from his training referenced a new policy established since the new year. Any deviation in the pictures required an immediate call to Caltech, no matter the time of day or night. This would allow a record search to begin.

Jackson dialed the number taped beside the phone to the Caltech office. Even at this early hour, he could call though no one would be there. When Caltech made the policy change, they installed a new, state-of-the-art telephone-answering device.

After four rings, Jackson heard a long beep through the phone. He recalled his training instructing how to leave a message.

"Hello, this is Jackson Wheeler at the Palomar Observatory. Columba coordinates, right ascension 05 hours, 03 minutes, 53.8665 seconds. And, declination minus 27.0772038. Anomaly identified. Going back to take another picture. I will contact your office in the morning."

Jackson hung up the phone after leaving his message. He stood taking both pictures and walked toward the office door.

I'll start the telescope back up. Maybe I can see it and snap another picture.

As the office door closed behind him, the phone rang from inside the office. On the second ring, Jackson stopped.

"Dammit!"

He turned back toward the office. The ringing echoed with a violent sound in the early morning hours inside the lonely dome structure.

He picked up the phone. "Palomar, hello?"

"Jackson! Jackson…"

A woman's voice shouted through the receiver. The phone cord knocked the pictures from his hand.

"Tina, everything, okay?"

"Jackson, it's… it's time, my water just broke."

"Okay, we practiced this. Call your sister, and I'll meet you at the hospital."

"How long will you…" Tina said pausing. Jackson heard two deep, quick breaths coming through his earpiece.

"The hospital is an hour away, I'm going now. I love you."

"Love you t—" Tina said as Jackson hung up before she could finish.

"Great, where are my keys?"

Jackson grabbed his briefcase and threw the two pictures inside before taking his coat off the hanger. He rushed out of the observatory to his truck.

"Shit!"

His voice reverberated through the observatory as he ran back into the office. Jackson scribbled a note on a sheet of paper and left it on the desk:

> *Gone to hospital.*
> *We're having a baby!*
> *I found something.*
> *We need to talk!!*
> *Jackson*

8 - J . F . K .

THE DOOR OPENED to the brightness of a new morning. Gabriel escorted Joe from the main building of the Eden Foundation's compound to a central courtyard. Joe desperately needed fresh air after a tireless night.

The information Gabriel had shared with Joe upon his arrival was too much to comprehend and believe. Joe moved like a zombie unsure whether to continue walking through the courtyard or sit on any of the open benches along the pathway.

From experience, Gabriel followed Joe giving him space to collect his thoughts. His erratic path led Gabriel through the courtyard.

"So... I cannot tell anyone... not even Mary?" Joe asked loud enough for Gabriel to hear him a few yards back.

"Unfortunately, no... again, like I said, Salvation is meant for the chosen few. Telling anyone about it or what's coming will only cause mass panic. Surely, you can imagine the hell that everyone will go through on Earth until the end?"

"But, if people knew... people could prepare... do things they would never do."

"Joe, I know that sounds like an ideal scenario, but let me tell you what will happen. News will spread about the end of the world coming… people will learn that there's nothing no one can do to stop it."

Gabriel continued following Joe, who had stopped in the middle of the courtyard looking toward the sky.

"But, shouldn't people know, anyway?" Joe asked interrupting Gabriel.

"Human nature tells us there will be too much havoc if people knew the truth. Especially if people are aware there is only one safe haven built, even if that place is on Mars."

Gabriel heard faint grunts as Joe attempted to comprehend the potential scenario. "Yeah, but the end is not until five years from now… that gives people a lot of time to—"

"Rape and kill each other… what, total anarchy?"

"Joe, we've known about the end for almost sixty years now. We've performed countless simulations to determine all the possible ways to extend human life. And, this is the plan developed and put into motion."

A gentle breeze blew across the top of the building into the courtyard refreshing to them. A bench under the shade of an oak tree at the end of the courtyard welcomed them. Gabriel placed his hand on Joe's shoulder, as they sat.

"This is so much to take in right now. But, over time you will realize this is the best decision. It's a hard choice to leave those that you love behind, but your work is vital to the future of mankind."

"I still feel like I'm dreaming. That I will wake up in my hotel room and start yesterday all over again."

"Joe, many times I've told myself this was a dream."

"How long have you known?"

"I normally don't tell recruits this… but, the Foundation contacted me in the late '90s to do some HR work for them. I took the job. They gave me names of people to contact, setting up phone interviews with them for potential job openings my company had."

"Did you know what was happening then?"

"At first, no. I did the standard interview-type questions over the phone. Questions like... tell me about your background, your strengths and weaknesses, where do you see yourself in five years? We recorded the conversations, and I never knew what the next steps were for the people I spoke to. I asked a lot of questions to my supervisors. Then one day, I got an invitation to visit our company's headquarters overseas to interview for a different position—"

"So, you got a promotion?" Joe interrupted smiling.

"Yeah, that and I learned French along the way." Gabriel paused and smiled; as it was obvious to Joe he must have enjoyed the experience. "That's when someone, like me now, presented the same information to me... and well... I've been doing this ever since."

Gabriel finished giving his history and stood from the bench looking across the courtyard. Shadows from the passing clouds swept across the ground pushed by the increasing wind.

"So, if Mary and I leave in a few months to go to Salvation, when do you leave?"

Gabriel lifted his head slowly toward the sky and placed his hands in his pockets. He stepped away from Joe still sitting on the bench.

"I'm not leaving." Gabriel continued walking.

After a few seconds with Gabriel in the middle of the courtyard, Joe comprehended Gabriel's comment. Joe stood.

"What? You're not leaving?"

Gabriel stopped and turned back to Joe. "Like I said, you have a talent vital to the future of mankind. I do not."

"So. What? You're like some kind of freakin' HR guy still doing interviews with people and telling them some pretty messed up shit?"

"Yes. To be blunt about it, basically, I'm your HR guy."

For some strange reason, unbeknownst to Joe, after only less than twenty-four hours with Gabriel, Joe felt connected with this man. Usually, making friends was not Joe's forte. Maybe it was the secret, which Gabriel was sharing with him about Salvation that drew Joe's connection to Gabriel.

"What the hell?" Joe was in disbelief. "You're kidding now, right? I mean, if this is real, and what you're saying will happen… and, you don't even get to go. Then, why are you doing this?"

"Trust me. I have those conversations with myself all the time. But, it's my job. I was always a loner. No family to speak of. And, when the Eden Foundation approached me, I found my purpose… to help ensure human life continues by making sure I help those here, like yourself, prepare before leaving for Salvation."

"Gabriel, you sound exactly like my preacher growing up." Joe laughed as quick memories of Minister Greene flashed in his memory.

"I'm glad you are laughing because this is an initial sign of your acceptance." Gabriel turned and led Joe back to the main building.

"So, what happens in the end for you?"

"Well, that's it. I haven't decided if… I end it myself, or just experience it… I… I try not to worry about that for now as I have too much to do to continue the Foundation's work."

For a moment, Joe refused to move from the middle of the courtyard. Joe imagined if it were him in Gabriel's position.

Joe looked up into the sky. Clouds had floated by the surrounding mountaintops and eclipsed the sun. He slowly walked to Gabriel staring at the darkening sky.

"It just hit me. If I was told about the end of the world, and there was no hope for me. I don't know what I would do. And, you're right. Too many people would do terrible things to each other."

Joe and Gabriel made it to the closed door of the main building, where they had exited fifteen minutes earlier. "Exactly, so, you see, the end has to remain a secret. No one can know about Project Salvation."

"But… how had the Foundation kept this secret for so long?"

Joe's question went unanswered as they entered the building. The door closed behind them blocking the rolling thunder from following them as drops of rain fell.

Joe was not ready for the full truth of the Eden Foundation.

APRIL 1, 1961
WASHINGTON, D.C.

MULTIPLE DISCUSSIONS filled the Oval Office. Three groups of two men, all wearing black suits, stood in front of the President's Resolute Desk.

Everyone spoke on top of each other, while the President stood with his back to the men. His hands clenched together behind his waist as he gazed out the East Door into the Rose Garden.

Without turning around, in a raised voice to garner their attention, the President spoke. "Men, we cannot stand by and do nothing. If we have known about *this* since 1957, then we are already four years behind."

"Mr. President, our group has been underway developing plans. But... uh, what we need now is serious financial backing. We need to get our program moved from theoretical planning to reality," the elder man in the group said.

"Your *group*..." the President said as he turned toward the men all looking at him. "Who is in your group and how is this work coordinated?"

"We are officially not on the books, Sir," the group's leader said sliding a cigarette from his inside coat pocket. "Mr. President, mind if I smoke?"

The President nodded his affirmation. The elder man lit his cigarette and continued.

"President Eisenhower created the Advanced Research Projects Agency or ARPA in '58 in response to the Soviet's launch of Sputnik. I was assigned to research the Soviet's observatory capabilities. That's how I met Dr. Alexi Mikanrrovich. He's the director of the Pulkovo Observatory in Leningrad."

The President sat in the chair at the head of a small coffee table flanked on both sides by sofas. The six men followed and sat on the sofas.

"So, you met with a Soviet?" the President asked pushing himself back into his chair.

"Well, yeah. Being scientists, we try to break through political barriers. So, I reached out to him," the oldest man said.

"You had to have known any contact would alarm the KGB?"

"To be honest, Mr. President as an astronomer, I admire the Soviet's capabilities. I thought nothing of the KGB monitoring our correspondence." The man paused and pressed his cigarette butt into a blue ashtray with its presidential seal on the table.

The man had the full attention of the President and his five colleagues as they looked on. "Shortly after joining ARPA, I get this package delivered to my office. It was from Dr. Mikanrrovich. He sent me the coordinates of something he wanted me to look for in the Columba Noachi Constellation."

"Columba?" the President asked, his eyes pressed together creating several wrinkles on his forehead.

"*Noachi* means *Noah's Dove* in Latin. It is a constellation visible in the southern skies," one man said.

"And, this Doctor... he's the one that identified this?"

"Yes. His letter said he had found something curious at these coordinates. And, he asked if I could also confirm what he saw."

"So, the scientists at the Soviet observatory know?" the President asked as he leaned toward the oldest man, who lit up another cigarette.

"Well, any records kept at the observatory were destroyed in a suspicious fire last year. We've tried to contact Alexi, but cannot locate him." The oldest man puffed billowing smoke from his lips as he spoke.

"And, at no time then, no one thought to contact other officials in our government?"

"Mr. President, in '58, it was just a couple of astronomers exchanging notes. The following months, I contacted *these guys* in the Agency," the oldest man said pointing around to his colleagues. "I needed to confirm my findings."

All the men sitting around the President looked to each other.

"Because we couldn't get in touch with Alexi, we felt it better to keep this all to ourselves until we could completely confirm our results."

"And, this has been validated, now?"

The oldest man paused. "Yes, Mr. President. We have validated the information. That's when we arranged this meeting. We did it under the pretense of giving you an update on our space program."

"And, 2020, that's when *this* will happen?" the President asked.

"The date... yes. What can we do to prevent it or at least minimize the impact? We need to develop our plan of attack," the oldest man said. He pressed his expired cigarette into the ashtray beside his last butt still smoldering.

"I'm afraid any plans developed will take a tremendous financial effort. Not to mention the technological support the likes of which this country, or this world has never seen," the oldest man said.

"Who knows about this in ARPA?" the President asked.

"Mr. President, the six of us in the room, and now you, are the only Americans aware. From the Soviet side, Alexi knew but we're not sure if he contacted others or not?"

The President paused pushing himself back into his chair. "Gentlemen, with your position in ARPA, you've got this meeting with me today. I want to get all our Joint Chiefs on board and plan our actions."

"Sir, Mr. President, if I may," one man said, who looked to be the youngest of any in the room. "In your Administration, we believe the fewer people that know about this for now the better."

The pushback shocked the President. He looked at the baby-faced man, who had not spoken a word until now. "Go on. What are your reservations?"

The young man sat straight in his seat, full of astute conviction in his words he was about to speak. "Mr. President, taking the worst-case event into account, we're talking about the complete destruction of Earth. There will be mass panic and chaos until the very end. In our opinion, there needs to be an extremely tight control of this information, Sir."

"Gentlemen, if I may, if you have concerns about my staff knowing about this, then what stops other astronomers from finding out?"

"Good question, Sir," the youngest man said. "We've already taken measures to prevent this information from leaking out from other US observatories. And, we're developing methods to monitor observatories elsewhere around the world. We feel this is dangerous information if it were to be made public knowledge."

The President stood, followed by the other six men. "I appreciate your advice, and it is noted. I will take your information, and I will meet only with my Chairman. From there, we will take our action."

The President placed the sheets of paper given to him by the oldest man inside of a brown folder. Large, red letters were on the front: *TOP SECRET.*

He sat the folder on top of his desk and turned to shake each person's hand. The last man to leave the Oval Office was the young man who had the courage to interrupt his superior, earlier.

As they shook hands, the President said, "Thank you, Mr. Bishop, for your candor."

"Thank you, Mr. President. My honor and my duty, Sir, to express my thoughts." The other five men were busy speaking with the President's secretary, Jocelyn.

"*Your* thoughts? Your colleagues don't share your opinion?"

"No, in fact, I seem to be the only one taking drastic measures to do *anything* possible to keep this information secret. That's why we came to you about this first," Mr. Bishop said in a softer voice to not be overheard by his colleagues.

"Mr. Bishop, I agree with your assessment. Until we know more, there is no cause to raise the alarm."

"Thank you again, Mr. President," the oldest man said followed in unison by the other four.

As the President waved with his free hand to acknowledge their thank you's, he gripped Mr. Bishop's hand tighter. In a low voice, so only Bishop could hear, the President said, "Our Administration will get back to you soon, Eli."

NOVEMBER 20, 1963
WASHINGTON, D.C.

"JOCELYN, CAN YOU come here?" The President's voice shouted from the Oval Office with a pronounced Massachusetts accent.

His secretary entered the doorway. Thick-framed, black glasses hid heavy wrinkles around her eyes. "Yes, Mr. President?"

"Jocelyn, I need you to cancel all my meetings for the afternoon."

"Yes, Mr. President. What about the House Committee review session at three o'clock?"

"Reschedule it. Thank you, Jocelyn."

Jocelyn was used to short commands given to her. "You're welcome, Mr. President." She pulled closed the soundproof door leaving the Oval Office.

Moments after she had left, the East Door to the Rose Garden opened. One of the President's Secret Service Agents entered.

"Yes, Agent Boyd?"

"Good afternoon, Mr. President." Agent Boyd walked the perimeter of the Oval Office. A cloud of smoke from his daily pack of Winston's followed him. Agent Boyd reached under the corner of the coffee table in the center of the floor. Inside a hidden pen socket, he pressed a small button.

"Agent, why did you turn off the recording system?"

"Mr. President, I have the information you wanted me to get."

Agent Boyd paced the floor between the Resolute Desk and the East Door. His hands shook holding a folder thick with files.

"Sir, I have to ask... are you sure you want to go public?"

Sam Boyd was more than the President's personal assigned Secret Service Agent. He had become one of his most entrusted confidants, given his proximity to the President.

"Sam, without a doubt. I have struggled with the truth for over two years. I've lied to the American People about our hidden intentions to go to the Moon—"

"But, Mr. President. You've done so with great conviction because *it* has to be done."

"I believe if we tell the People the truth, then we can garner the support we need to go forward with *our true mission.*"

Agent Boyd continued pacing. Sweat rolled down his face even though an early snowfall had enveloped Washington.

"I'm convinced *the truth* will bring us together as a nation... as a planet." The President stood from behind his desk and walked to the facing sofas in the center of the room and sat beside Agent Boyd. "Surely, you are aware this is the right thing to do, or you wouldn't be helping me?"

"Mr. President, I serve at your pleasure and follow your orders."

"The same orders you promised when you took your oath to protect this Office." The President wanted to confirm what he knew to be true with Agent Boyd.

"Yes. When Project Eden contacted me to develop security protocols for them based on my familiarity with our protocols here at the White House, I knew I must inform you straight away."

The President could tell his friend was not his normal self. He placed his hand on the Agent's shoulder to regain his focus.

"Sam, thank you for coming to me when they approached you." He patted Agent Boyd's shoulder. "And, thank you for bringing me the project plan documents."

Agent Boyd poured himself a glass of water and took a sip. The water rippled from his shaking hand.

"You asked me to get any information I could on their plans."

"Sam, don't worry. I will take the complete blame for this."

"Sir, I am not worried about me. I read the plan documents before coming here... and..."

Agent Boyd scanned around the Oval Office in complete paranoia. He lowered his voice. "I'm worried about this Country and how Eden intends to fund their programs."

The President stood from the sofa with the documents from Agent Boyd in hand. He removed the stapled papers and flipped through them as he walked toward the East Door.

"Mr. President, from what I saw, they are planning diversion tactics to extend the conflict in Vietnam."

Papers ruffled in the President's hands. Murmurs under the President's breath floated to Agent Boyd on the sofa.

"They talk about getting involved down South to stir up trouble with the Negros… all to deflect attention away from Eden when they funnel money to their project."

The President listened while he read the documents. He turned to Sam.

"This is exactly why I wanted this information. I can tell the American People the truth… about 2020… about how certain elements in the government wish to create these diversions impacting so many lives. The People will support the funding necessary for this project. We mustn't do this in secret."

Agent Boyd joined the President standing by the East Door. The agent placed his hands in his pockets preventing them from shaking noticeably in front of the President.

"Mr. President, hasn't Eden made you aware of their plans? It appears they are extremely detailed. I imagine they will not stop for anything to protect their project."

"No… I met with the six men two years ago when they first learned of it. They prepared my speech I gave to Congress about our mission to the Moon."

Agent Boyd raised his eyebrows to the President in disbelief. The President's admission his speech, which has rallied the entire country behind the mission to the Moon, were not his words.

"And, I had one follow-up meeting with Eli Bishop to get his further insights into the discovery. If I recall correctly, Mr. Bishop was the only one who cautioned me about keeping this information secret from the public."

"Mr. President, if you look at the plan documents. They are all signed by *E. Bishop*."

Flipping again through the documents, the President confirmed the signatures. He slammed the folder on his desk causing the papers inside to slide across his desk.

"I gave them orders to continue with their project without keeping me updated. I needed to maintain a sense of plausible deniability." The President pushed his hand through his impeccable brown hair. "This was clearly a mistake."

Agent Boyd placed his hand between the shoulder blades of the President. He sensed the President's frustration.

"All the agony going on, all the suffering in this land. I'm confident we can truly unite the World behind this just cause. These petty issues will go away since we all will come together to ensure our survival," the President said.

"Sir, it's a beautiful dream, but what happens if you're wrong and chaos rules."

"Sam, that was what Mr. Bishop told me during our first meeting."

The President walked behind his desk and pressed the speaker button on his phone.

"Yes, Mr. President," Jocelyn said, her voice coming through the speaker on the desk.

"Jocelyn, please set-up a meeting with Eli Bishop here in the Oval Office as soon as you can."

The President turned his head to Agent Boyd and whispered, "I will talk with him first to inform him of my plan to tell the Public."

"Mr. President, your first available date is this Saturday the 23rd, when you come back from Dallas."

"Very well. This November has been busy. Please set that meeting up with him and with Agent Boyd."

"Yes, Sir. Is there anything else?"

"No. Thank you, Jocelyn."

"You're welcome, Mr. President." The speaker on the desk clicked indicating the microphone had turned off.

The President led Agent Boyd back to the East Door as both men left the Oval Office and stood outside. Crisp air smacked them as large snowflakes fell at their shoes under the awning of the Rose Garden.

The President took the agent's hand. "Sam, thank you again for bringing me the information. The Country owes you a tremendous debt for your service."

Agent Boyd did not make eye contact with the President as he thanked him. Guilt grew inside him as he dealt with an internal conflict. *Do I support my President, or follow through with the plan Mr. Bishop instructed me with?*

The snowfall stopped as the dusting covered the ground with patches of green grass across the North Lawn. Agent Boyd walked down Pennsylvania Avenue turning on 15th Avenue. Darkness had fallen over D.C., as office workers left for the evening. At the corner of K Street, Agent Boyd entered a payphone booth and dialed.

"Yes," a voice said on the other end of the line.

"He wants to meet with you." Agent Boyd hid his face under the collar of his jacket and held his head down.

"When?"

"Saturday… you promised me a place in Eden, if I helped you."

"So, he has seen our plans."

"Yes," Agent Boyd replied.

A static-filled pause came through the receiver. "Good. Where will he be before our meeting?"

"Dallas."

"Okay, we will take it from here." The line died.

Agent Boyd hung up the phone and left the phone booth continuing down Vermont Avenue. Office workers from nearby congressional buildings passed him.

God help me… what have I done?

9 - SOMEBODY'S WATCHING

FIVE DAYS HAD PASSED since the limo had picked up Joe from his house in New York. Gone was his excitement of getting paid to present his research. Instead, paranoia ate at Joe as Thomas drove Joe back to his house in Stony Brook.

How am I going to keep this a secret from Mary?

The familiar sights of his neighborhood flew outside the windows. Ivy-adorned, brick buildings of campus peeked above the treetops. Joe was home.

Okay, get yourself together. Act normal.

Somber, Joe sat in the back of the limo. His hair combed perfect, his white dress shirt tucked into his dress pants, and his clean, freshly pressed suit jacket masked Joe's anxiety caused by little sleep since meeting Gabriel. The limo stopped in the driveway of Joe and Mary's townhouse.

Here goes.

Joe took a deep breath just before Thomas opened the rear door and removed Joe's bags from the trunk handing them to him.

"I'm sure we'll be seeing each other again." One of the longer statements to Joe, which Thomas had made during the past several days.

Joe staggered to his front door relieved to be home, but worried. The engine of the car roared behind him as Thomas left. Joe fumbled in his pockets searching for his keys when the door opened. Mary stood in the doorway.

"How was your trip? Did they love your presentation?" she asked reaching through kissing him.

Joe did not respond. Instead, as she kissed him, he reached his arms around her waist pulling her close. Relieved Mary was okay, he held her tighter and longer than a normal hug should last.

"Wow, I missed you too," Mary said with a soft whisper pulling her lips from his. Joe held her, not letting go. "Everything, okay?"

Joe released his grip. Mary pulled away. "Uh, I just... I missed ya, that's all." He kissed her again and took his bags into the living room.

"Sorry, I didn't call you. Things got real busy." Joe walked to the bookcase examining the area where he had expected to find a camera.

This should be where it is because I saw Mary sitting right there.

Joe looked toward the kitchen table in eyesight from the bookcase in the living room.

"Oh, that's okay. That's what I figured. So, how was the presentation?"

Joe heard Mary's question but continued searching across the bookcase finding nothing. "Uh... the presentation? It went well." *As well as it can be considering I never gave it.*

"How many people did you speak in front of?"

"Oh... um... I'd say at least fifty or so." Joe recited the answers he had practiced with Gabriel before he had left Colorado.

"How long did you get to speak?"

"I was scheduled for two hours, but with the questions, we went all afternoon."

Mary's interrogation continued. Joe felt her excitement since she normally did not show too much interest in his daily research.

"Did you get good feedback about it?"

"Oh, yeah." His eyes examined the different ornaments and decorations in the room. "Um... uh... yeah. I had several people come up after saying they wanted to learn more."

"Anyone offer to finance any of your projects?"

"You can kinda say that."

Unsatisfied he found no cameras, Joe plopped down on the sofa releasing a large sigh. Mary sat beside him rubbing his shoulders.

"Long trip, I bet?"

"Too long. I'm just glad to be back."

Joe reached inside the front pocket of his suit jacket and pulled out two envelopes full of hundred-dollar bills. "*Here*, check *this* out." Joe's heart thumped in his chest, his eyes continuing to scan the room.

Mary opened the envelope. Joe saw the whites of her eyes expand as she ran her thumb across the stack of hundreds. "So, the organization was real then?"

"Oh, it's real all right." *Too real.*

"Did you get more information about what this organization is, and what they're about?"

Joe darted his eyes around the room. The truth he had learned the past several days wanted to creep out of his mouth.

Tell her the world is coming to an end. Tell her a planet will collide with Earth. Tell her not to worry because they will be okay... they will escape and go to Mars. His thoughts sounded insane just thinking them to himself. Joe released a quiet, sarcastic laugh.

"It's a philanthropic group that wants to fund programs which can advance cancer research. And, they want me to support their organization."

"Does that mean you will work for them? What about your lab?" Mary placed the envelopes on the coffee table in front of them as she continued massaging Joe's shoulders.

"They want me to continue at my job for the next six months. We'll discuss them funding me either at my lab or a full transition to their group."

"That means we're moving?" Mary stopped moving her hand across his back waiting for Joe's response.

Joe slowly spun around sliding off the sofa and placed his knees on the floor in front of Mary facing her. He placed his hands on the sides of her hips and looked up into her eyes.

"Mary…" he said wanting desperately to tell her the full truth. "I think we'll be moving, but I don't have all the details yet."

She placed her hands on his cheeks. The warmth of her palms was soothing. "If this organization will support you and your work, I'm okay to move *anywhere* with you."

"I'm glad you said that." He turned his head to the right and placed his head on her lap. A familiar comfort fell upon him.

"I love you," he said pressing his hands tighter on her hips.

"Maybe *you* should travel more often. I like how clingy you are right now," Mary said running her hand through his hair.

Joe lifted his head and kissed her. "I'm going to get a shower. And, I think I'll rest this afternoon."

"Good idea. Take a shower and a nap. I should go to the school anyway… I'll see you tonight." They stood together giving each other another hug and a kiss.

A few minutes later, Mary left for work as Joe carried his luggage upstairs with his backpack draped across his shoulder. The bottom of his bag clanged against each stair step. His strength had left him.

Relieved and anxious, Joe opened the door to their bedroom. His eyes scanned the room. Memories of sex with Mary flashed through his mind.

They've watched us…

Joe unpacked. The clean, folded shirts, he never had worn, returned inside the dresser beside the bed. He inspected his alarm clock yielding no apparent cameras. His image reflected in the black mirror of the television screen.

Huh, no cameras here in the TV.

He straightened as he stood seeing his image in the mirror above the dresser behind the television. Picture frames hung on the wall behind him. Joe inspected those, but they hid nothing but memories.

Where are they?

Pissed off, Joe walked into the bathroom.

They've watched us in the shower.

Joe opened the medicine cabinet, quickly closing it again. He saw no signs of any cameras or microphones. He inched his face closer inspecting the mirror above the sink staring into his own eyes. Fog from his nostrils frosted the glass.

Is this a two-way mirror?

Nothing was out of the ordinary. Joe stood before the sink cupping his hands in the running water washing his face. Refreshing, cold water dripped from his nose as he grabbed a hanging towel.

Screw it. If they're watching me… they're watching me.

Joe placed the towel back onto its holder and undressed. Delirious from his lack of sleep, he gyrated his naked body mocking the thought of anyone spying on him.

The tension in his body released as the hot water bombarded his head and shoulders from the shower. Joe stood motionless, his head pressed against the wall tiles. He replayed how he had wished his conversation with Mary had gone earlier when he came home.

Hey, Mary… oh, the trip? It went well. Yeah… um… like we're all going to die. A freakin' planet will collide with Earth.

He rinsed the shampoo from his hair, soap ran down his face. His body ached from its lack of sleep.

Are we going have to move? Hell yeah… we're moving to Mars.

Somewhat refreshed out of the shower, Joe dried himself wrapping a towel around his waist. The fogged-over mirror had a clear, large streak diagonally across it from the side of Joe's fist.

Oh… and there are cameras and microphones everywhere in the house, even at work, and we're always being followed. Hope you don't mind?

Joe brushed his teeth. His internal conversation continued with a mouthful of toothpaste and water.

Yeah… we can't tell anyone… they're all going to die.

He rinsed his mouth clean. "How long has anyone known about this?" Joe said out-loud in a higher pitched voice imitating Mary.

Uh, only since the '60s… the race to the Moon… it was a cover-up… the Cold War… another lie. Hell, who knows, maybe even the assassination of JFK was a cover-up for this shit.

Joe stared back into the mirror. The clear path his fist had made earlier fogged over again.

The person monitoring Joe, today, watched as Joe brushed his teeth in front of the mirror. A camera installed in the overhead light fixture provided a perfect, unimpeded view of his activities.

Joe walked out of the bathroom turning out the light. His Monitor watched Joe leave as the camera automatically switched over to its night-view lens.

A camera in the ceiling fan picked up Joe entering the bedroom. He sat on the edge of their bed putting on his socks. His Monitor switched to the camera in the power button of the television zooming in on Joe's face.

"Hell, if there are cameras here, then watch this." Joe stretched his arm toward the television extending his middle finger. "Screw you!" His final release of frustration into television eased his tension.

I'm going crazy. There was only one shot of Mary in the kitchen... there can't be cameras everywhere?

Joe stood and dropped the towel from his waist throwing it across the room. His Monitor observed the towel land on the chair with the camera in the handle of the bedroom door activated by the motion sensor.

"Yeah, I'm being paranoid," his Monitor heard as Joe got under the covers of the bed.

MARCH 10, 2008
STONY BROOK, NEW YORK

"JOE, WAKE UP. You're going to be late, again," Mary said as she entered the bedroom. She pushed Joe's foot, sticking out from under the cover. "I've made your breakfast and would appreciate you eating with me this morning."

He rolled over, looking at the green numbers on the alarm clock, teasing back at him *7:47 a.m.* He pulled Mary's pillow over his head to drown out the morning sun, piercing through the window.

"I don't want to get up. Can't we have breakfast in bed," Joe yelled, knowing it would not do any good.

Joe threw the pillow off his face back to her side of the bed pulling his one foot, trapped under the cover, out. When he placed both feet on the cold hardwood floor, a shiver rushed through his body.

"Damn, it's cold." He yawned and stretched.

Joe staggered from the bedroom into the kitchen. The clanging sound of dishes placed into the sink became louder.

"We only had one egg left, so I made that for you," Mary said, pouring two glasses of orange juice as she set the table.

"What are you having?"

"Just cereal," she said with a terse tone in her voice. She poured the milk too quickly spilling it onto the table. "Dammit!"

Joe raised his eyebrow toward her. "Everything all right? I'm sorry I overslept a little."

Mary wiped up the milk with a folded napkin she had laid out for breakfast. "Uh, everything's fine," she said in a short, quick fashion. She poured her milk again, slowly this time.

The spoon hitting the inside of her cereal bowl broke the awkward silence. "It's just... it's just, I checked this morning... and... we're not pregnant again this month." She continued eating, not making eye contact with Joe.

He placed his fork down with still half-uneaten scrambled eggs on its end. Joe took her free hand and said, "Oh, Sweetie. I'm sorry. We'll keep trying—"

"Trying... that's all we've been doing for three years now... is trying." Tears filled her eyes. "When will this happen for us?"

Joe rubbed the back of her hand attempting to console her, as this conversation seems to re-occur every few months. "Have you noticed any difference in things from your medication?"

Mary used her free hand and rubbed the lower part of her abdomen. "The cramps are not as bad and my period has been more regular the past few months. That's why when I was late this time, I thought this may be it."

"You know I love you, right?" Joe turned his entire body around in his chair to face her. "We'll keep trying and trying until the time is right." Joe attempted to reassure her. "Plus, you know... *trying* is my favorite part." He smiled and gave an evil, sarcastic laugh.

His joke made Mary smile. She looked up from the table and into his eyes. "Well, we are pretty good at *trying*, aren't we?" She grinned finishing her cereal.

With her smile, Joe believed he had helped the situation, making her feel better. "Hey, so it didn't work this month. But, it will happen when the time is right. Mary, I love you." He kissed her free hand.

She released her spoon as it disappeared into the milk and placed her hand on the back of his head. "I love you too, Joseph."

The morning conversation with Mary was fresh on his mind, as Joe entered his lab late this morning.

"Damn, Dude. Working banker's hours, I see," Charlie said as Joe hurried into the lab.

Stonehaven National Laboratories worked in association with the University of Stony Brook, allowing post-doc students use of their facilities. Joe's mentor, Professor Baptiste, had retired years earlier, moving to Florida. Before Baptiste had left, he persuaded Stonehaven to grant Joe his lab and office. The timing worked well as his best friend, Charlie, needed lab space, also.

"Don't start. It's been a rough morning already."

"Oh, you and the Mrs. have a fight?"

"No... no... not exactly."

Charlie sat his pen down on the table and took a sip from his coffee mug with a picture of two little girls on it. The girls both had short, blond, curly hair. "Okay, tell me. The doctor's office is now open," Charlie said.

Joe turned his stare from Charlie's coffee mug to him. "It's another month of us not getting pregnant, and Mary took it pretty hard this morning."

"Awe, Man. That's tough."

"Yeah, it is. But for me, what's tough is seeing how sad it makes her."

"Have you visited a fertility doctor or anything?"

"She's been diagnosed with Polycystic Ovarian Syndrome. We can get pregnant with medications but the chances are very low."

Joe poured a cup of coffee and returned to Charlie at the lab table.

"What kind of complications does that cause her?"

"Mainly, she has terrible cramps and her period can be a few weeks late or missed entirely."

Joe remembered the day they had visited the doctor two years earlier, and had learned about Mary's condition. The diagnosis came as a relief to them, as it had explained their struggles to conceive.

"I love my girls, but sometimes... sometimes, they can be an annoying pain in the ass," Charlie said.

"So, says the man drinking coffee from a mug with pictures of his twins on it."

Holding up his mug as if he had won a prize, Charlie said, "What can I say. They are Daddy's little girls though."

Charlie took one last sip, finishing his coffee, and sat his mug on the table. "Look, I know you guys want a baby, but maybe it's all for the best. I mean, we are lowly post-docs. And, babies ain't cheap."

"True. And, that's what gets me sometimes. Sometimes I wonder if things would have been different if I had taken that job in Paris. We would have money. Things wouldn't be so stressful, and maybe we would've already had kids by now."

"Or, maybe... Mary would have moved with you to Paris. Went into a cafe one day while you were working. Met some French dude and left your sorry ass," Charlie said standing from his desk to place his empty mug into the sink. "Man, like I always say. Don't live your life on a series of what-ifs. That will only drive you crazy."

A few seconds had passed. "Charlie, how in the hell did you go from being the party animal in college to Dr. Phil just now?"

"It's Becky. That girl done brought some sense into me that's for sure. Plus. She is so fine." The pitch of his voice rose thinking about his wife. "Joe, now in all seriousness. We've got work to do. So quit feeling sorry for yourself and let's go."

"Sir. Yes, Sir," he said mocking Charlie as he walked over to the corner to put on his white lab coat.

SEPTEMBER 29, 2008
STONY BROOK, NEW YORK

THE TRAIN TRAFFIC to Stonehaven National Laboratories was terrible this morning. Joe arrived about an hour later than his usual 9 a.m. As he hurried into his office, Joe noticed the lab he shared with Charlie was dark.

That's odd?

Charlie took pride in being early into the lab. In his words, *going into the lab was his escape from his estrogen-filled house.*

Joe unlocked the door to his office situated across the hall from their shared lab. He placed his backpack on the small sofa inside his office and sat behind his desk. His office was dark. Joe pulled the dangling-metal string of the black desk lamp. This brightened his tidy office.

Perfect stacks of paper sat in two piles on one corner of his desk. On the other was his double-flat screen computer monitor. Joe believed everything should have its proper place.

With his back turned to the open doorway, Joe's name came shouting out from the hall. Charlie rushed in his office. His presence in the open doorway brought chaos to Joe's meticulous space.

"Have you heard the news this morning?" Charlie's chest heaved noticeably as he worked to catch his breath standing with an untied shoelace and half his shirt-tale untucked from his pants.

"No. Is it about the train system and is that why you're late too this morning?"

"Hell no, Man. The news about the stock market?"

"Stock market? I didn't know you owned any?"

"I don't really. Only what's in our 401k program through the University," Charlie said as Joe logged on to CNN. Charlie stood over Joe's shoulder.

"Something must be up if you're in here talking about the stock market instead of some cartoon your kids made you watch this morning for the thousandth time," Joe said as the webpage appeared with large, bold, black letters at the top.

"See... see... big news today. Stocks are already down like six hundred points in the first hour of trading." Charlie placed his rather large index finger on his computer screen.

"I'm sure it's temporary. It'll go back up in a week or two," Joe said, pushing his finger off his screen. "Watch the fingerprints, Man."

"I don't know... it's getting bad. The stocks have been falling for months now. I don't follow them too much, but I know it'll impact our retirement package." Charlie stammered back in front of Joe's desk.

"Well, then it's a good thing I don't have that much in my 401k now, huh," Joe said as he scrolled down the webpage.

"How much is *not much*?"

"Well," pausing as Joe looked way from his computer over to Charlie, "not much... like, as in zero."

"What?"

"Bills, Man. We have too many bills to pay. I can't have any of my check going into 401k." Joe lowered his eyes, realizing his response did not meet Charlie's expectations. Joe looked again at the screen. "Well, I can look at the bright side. There're some cheap stocks to buy now?"

"Man, you've got to get your financial house in order. We're just lucky to be in academia, because if we worked for a company now, we might find ourselves out of a job soon. Have you read about the layoffs?"

"Layoffs? No, you know me. Between spending time with Mary and my nose buried in my research, I don't pay attention to the news."

"You should check it out. Tens of thousands of people are being let go," Charlie said as he walked back through the doorway. "I'll catch up with you at lunch. I have to go to the lab downstairs and cover for the teaching lab assistant there."

As Charlie left, Joe finished reading the breaking news alert. His conversation with Charlie replayed in his mind.

If we worked for a company, we might be out of a job.

Joe opened a new webpage and searched for *Sauvage Enterprises*. His eyes widened. The search results returned one story after another about *Sauvage* filing for bankruptcy. A complete liquidation of all the company's assets had occurred. The interesting item to Joe was the company had ceased to exist as of yesterday.

"Wow," Joe said under his breath as he continued reading.

Joe learned since his interview, seven years ago, none of the programs *Sauvage* had planned to launch never exited the clinical-trail phase.

He closed his web browser.

Well, the bright side is, if I would have worked at Sauvage, I'd be out of a job.

Joe pulled the metal string of his black desk lamp. The room fell dark, except for the glow from the computer monitors. He stood and walked out of his office, closing the door behind him.

I wonder where all the money goes when the stock market crashes like this?

AUGUST 6, 2015
STONY BROOK, NEW YORK

THE MIND GOES on automatic when one repeats the same mundane tasks like traveling to work. You take the same route, day-in and day-out, and arrive at your destination not remembering the journey.

This was no different for Joe on this morning's drive. It was like the countless others. Today was his day with the car, which he was proud he had kept running for so many years.

His car was the same Oldsmobile his grandma had given him as he left for college. With its faded paint, balding tires, and a small dent in the rear bumper, it contained many memories. Sometimes when driving through blinding rainstorms, memories of his graduation night with Mary would return.

"What the hell is that?"

The car lunged forward with its final breath as he pulled into his parking space at the lab building. "It's gone. Great, just what we need now." Joe snatched his backpack from the passenger's side and slammed the drivers' door in disgust as he got out headed to his lab.

"Good morning, Joe."

"Yeah, good morning, Charlie." Joe spoke with quick short breaths between his greeting as Joe placed his brown bag lunch in the refrigerator.

"Jeez, someone woke up in a pissy mood this morning?"

"Awe, Man, I'm sorry. My car finally died on me this morning."

"Well, it's about time that classic died. Hell, what... it's like as old as shit, ain't it?"

"Yeah, it's an '89."

"Damn, how many miles are on it?"

"Not as many as you'd think. My mama bought it new, but then got sick right after. My grandma had it." Joe paused as he poured a cup of coffee. "We only went to church and one time down to Brownsville for vacation. The only real miles came on our drive from Texas to here."

"Well, it's a good thing you've got some paid speaking jobs from your research, because we don't earn anything in academics." Charlie belched his booming laugh distinctive to him.

"Thanks for reminding me."

"You know what you should do? My dad just got a great deal after researching cars. Spend some time today doing that."

"Well, I'm going to surf online because I sure as hell do not feel like doing any work this morning." Joe shuffled off to his office with his head down in disappointment.

Joe turned on the lights chasing the darkness away from his office. The shimmering fluorescent light revealed research manuals stacked on the floor with scattered scribbled notes on his desk. It looked as though the janitor had overturned a recycling bin in his office.

Sitting in his chair with its gray, paisley fabric, Joe waited for his computer to boot. A blue, login screen appeared as Joe sat emotionless.

A new car? Wait until I tell Mary about this. Hopefully, I can find a good deal, or I will need to do more speaking engagements.

On automatic, Joe clicked away at miscellaneous links looking at information for different cars.

Okay, I am not getting anywhere. What I need to do is figure out what type of car, how much can I afford, and then try to…

Joe's thoughts trailed off as he noticed his email icon in the lower right of the screen flashing. With a sigh, Joe clicked opening his email. "I bet this is another bill."

The new message in his inbox had the title, 'You Are Invited to Speak at Our Next Meeting.' Curious, he pointed his mouse over the message to open it.

I hope they pay well?

The flickering, fluorescent light provided an annoying shimmer on the computer screen as he read.

Dear Dr. Bishop, we invite you to speak at our meeting in Denver, Colorado next month. You should be extremely proud of your breakthrough research in gene therapy. Our conference brings together the best minds in the world on various topics. We are excited to hear your presentation and share in an open exchange with our audience members.

"Wow, someone's kissing my ass here, aren't they?" Joe asked laughing as he continued.

Our organization will cover your travel expenses and compensate you in the sum of $50,000 for your time and presentation.

"Fifty-thousand dollars!" Joe had to re-read the email to make sure he was correct.

Compensate you in the sum of $50,000.

Joe scrolled down the message and continued reading.

Our organization is at the forefront of new technology. We only seek the best, most innovative thinkers across many industries and disciplines to attend. And, until our organization becomes well established, we are offering a competitive speaking fee.

"Well, hell, you've got me," Joe said as he pushed himself from the desk leaning in his chair which made a wicked creak with every move sounding like it was about to fall apart.

"Shh," Charlie said sticking his head in the doorway holding his finger in front of his lips. "You must have found a great deal on a car."

"Better than that, and talk about perfect timing," Joe countered back. "Charlie, have you ever heard of the Eden Foundation?"

"No… uh… um."

"Me, neither," Joe said pausing for a moment still in disbelief at the timing. "Charlie, come over here and read this email I just got."

"I will but how am I going to get through Mount Paperwork to get over to you?"

"Just get over here and read this, Smart Ass."

As Joe kicked the paper near his chair, Charlie lowered his glasses to the tip of his nose and leaned over Joe's shoulder. Charlie read the email on the dimly lit screen, mumbling to himself while reading.

"Fifty-thousand dollars," Charlie said in disbelief.

"I know, right?"

"I don't care if you've never heard of the Eden Foundation or not, fifty-thousand dollars is fifty-thousand dollars. If I were you, I'd contact them to confirm that." Charlie placed his hand on top of his head and shook it side-to-side in shared disbelief. "And, if so, wow. I never get any offers like that. The only email offers I get are for those damn penis enlargement pills."

"Yeah, Becky asked me if you would ever get those?"

"Ha, ha, Mr. Funny Guy."

"There's a link at the bottom of the email to their website. I am sure there's information about the Foundation." Joe scanned the email one more time.

"Well, congratulations. Talk about coincidences. I mean, you show up bitchin' about not having money for a new car, and then you get this offer."

"Coincidences… Yeah, I don't believe in them," Joe said.

"Okay, then Mr. Destiny, check out the small print and let me know as I'll cover your classes those days."

"Thanks, Man," Joe said yelling back as Charlie left Joe's office.

Joe clicked the link to the foundation's website. The email disappeared. A webpage opened with a spinning icon of Earth. The words, *The Eden Foundation,* were at the top of the page. After a few seconds, the spinning Earth faded away. The slogan, *The Future of Mankind Is Your Responsibility,* appeared.

Well, that's an attention-grabbing statement.

Joe clicked the 'Continue' button. An empty white screen loaded.

Fifty-thousand dollars for me? Hell… use that money to build a better website why don't ya?

A few more moments had passed. A black, Arial-font text scrolled across the screen. Joe read the scrolling message, which matched the information he received in his email.

"I knew it was too good to be true. This looks like some kind of spam. I'd be better off following up on the email from the Nigerian prince I got last week."

Joe leaned forward in his chair with a noticeable frown on his face. His hand held his forehead causing wrinkles to crease up to his scalp.

I knew it was too good…

He lifted his head off his supporting hand. A deep sigh escaped Joe as he moved his mouse to close the screen.

As soon as he clicked his mouse, the piercing ring of the black, cordless phone startled the quietness in his office.

"Stonehaven Laboratories, Dr. Bishop speaking."

"Hello Dr. Bishop, this is Gabriel D'Angelo from the Eden Foundation. I wanted to follow-up on our email invitation I sent you this morning."

Shocked in disbelief at the timing of the call, Joe said, "Yeah… um… hello. I'm sorry, what was your name, again?"

"Gabriel D'Angelo… with the Eden Foundation… I'm the one that sent you the email invitation to speak at our conference next month."

"Oh… okay. So, yeah, I went to your website, and I must say that… um, uh, what's the deal? I mean, your website looks so basic, and I have seen a lot of scams through email before."

"Dr. Bishop, my sincere apologies about our website. We are a new organization, and we really want to make a big splash on the research scene. In our excitement, to be honest, we've not spent a lot of time on our website."

No shit.

"But, I can assure you we are a legitimate organization, and we will make it worth your time. In fact, we are so confident in our mission, we believe it will completely change your life."

Joe listened to Gabriel speak as he opened the email invitation, again.

"Our organization is committed to attracting only the best minds from around the world. We truly believe the ability to share your research with our audience, and their engagement, will help further your work."

"You're a fantastic salesman, Mr. D'Angelo. I'll give you that," Joe said with a sarcastic tone. "Hell, as long as you send me a contract spelling out I'll get paid, I'll prepare a talk on my research. The worst case is I show up at some geek convention and we share information about comic books or something."

"I can assure you, Dr. Bishop, this meeting will change your life, forever."

"Send me the contract, and I'll look it over and get back to you," Joe said shaking his head, still in disbelief. "Thank you for the invitation."

"No, thank you for agreeing to consider attending. Our Foundation has been following your work for some time. We are excited to see how we can help you continue with your research."

"How long have you been following my research?" Joe asked as his eyes widened creating slight wrinkles to appear again on his forehead.

"We'll get into that when we meet. If you decide to attend, a limo will pick you up at your home and fly you to Denver in our private jet. We are backed by serious donors who are committed to our mission."

"You should have mentioned the private jet in the first place," Joe said laughing into the phone. "Okay, you have convinced me. I'll wait to review the contract and will be back in touch."

"Sure, the contract is in your inbox now. I'll be touch with you tomorrow to confirm the arrangements. Thank you again, Dr. Bishop."

"Please, call me Joseph or Joe."

"Joseph, I'll call you tomorrow." The call ended.

Crazy he called me just now as I was looking at their website. It's almost like he was watching me and knew to call.

Joe placed the phone back down on its charging base and jumped from his chair. His sudden leap created a domino effect on the stacks of paper falling in every direction from his desk.

"Charlie. Charlie, you are not going to…" Joe said, his voice trailing off as he left his office.

10-INSOMNIA

HOURS HAD PASSED since Mary had left for work at the high school on the day Joe had returned from Colorado. In that time, Joe had tossed in their bed replaying Gabriel's voice. As his eyes grew heavy, fuzzy images of CIE57.20 flashed in a bright exploding light beneath his closed eyes. Like a bad, never-ending movie, his thoughts raced from one point to another. Nothing made sense to him.

No matter how much Joe tried to calm his thoughts, he floated between consciousness and a dream world. Visions of everything he had known would come to an end.

How am I going to explain this to Mary before we leave for Salvation?

Feelings of grandeur overcame him thinking about space travel and Mars.

Is this really going to happen?

Images rushed over him in manic-depressive states. His emotions ranged from excitement about their selection to go to Mars to deep sadness for his friends left behind. As quick as those thoughts had entered, they had disappeared replaced with a sense of pride his work held in its importance to support future life. Pride fled, as fear of the unknown and of everything familiar to him destroyed had returned.

The time on the alarm clock teased him.

How will I ever sleep, again?

At 8:25 p.m., keys rattled against the front door downstairs signaling Mary's arrival home. Joe pulled the cover over his head and pretended to be asleep when she entered their bedroom.

Mary came out of the bathroom and into the bedroom where Joe lay. "Oh... sorry. I didn't mean to wake you." Her voice was soft and comforting to Joe.

He rolled toward her pushing down the covers and yawned. "Ahh... that's okay. I need to get up anyway."

"Did you get a good nap?"

"Yeah... um... it was okay." Joe rubbed his face hiding his lie. The redness and puffiness of his eyes were evidence of five nights of no sleep.

"Hope you don't mind. Tomorrow's the first day of classes, that's why I'm running late. So, I brought pizza home tonight."

"Fantastic. I'm starving." Joe kissed Mary passing her to put on a pair of sweatpants from the dresser to go downstairs.

"Let me change, and I'll be right down," Mary said.

A few minutes later she came into the kitchen joining Joe. To her surprise, he had made a place for them at the table. The smell of the hot, melty cheese smothering the thinly sliced pepperoni engulfed the tiny kitchen.

Steam rose from the box and their mouths. "You know, these last five days have been the longest we've ever been apart," Mary said.

Between bites, Joe grunted "Ahem" acknowledging his agreement. With his last slice on the plate, his focus changed from the pizza to Mary.

"What about the time I went to that conference with Charlie?"

"No, that was only three nights."

His last slice entered his mouth resting on his tongue. Joe did not bite down.

Awe shit, Charlie.

At that moment, Joe realized Charlie would die with everyone else in 2020. The past several days with Gabriel, not once did Joe think about his best and only friend.

Joe's face lost all its color. The pizza dropped from his hands slamming on the plate below him on the table. Mary's face appeared blurred. Three of her appeared. The light from the kitchen dimmed. His body slumped down from his chair to the floor.

"Joe... Joseph... Are you okay?" Mary yelled as he opened his eyes. Her worried face came into sharp focus.

"Uh... I'm fine. I'm just so tired... guess I have gotten little sleep over the last few days." Joe lay on the cold, tile kitchen floor shaking his head of whatever it was causing him to faint.

"You scared me. One minute you're talking. The next, I see your face go blank and you hit the floor." Mary helped Joe sit up where he had fallen. "You feel better, now?"

"Yeah, I guess," he said, embarrassed.

"You need anything? Water?" She rubbed his upper back reassuring him.

"Yeah... um... help me up." Joe pulled himself to the chair and rested his head in his hands with his elbows on the table. "I guess I got light-headed or something from not sleeping."

Mary came back to the table with a glass of water sitting it between his elbows on the table. "Do you want to sleep down here on the sofa, or do you want me to help you back to bed?"

"I'll stay down here tonight. That way, if I can't sleep I won't keep you awake." Joe sipped from the glass. The water refreshed him.

"Why haven't you been able to sleep?"

Joe paused. He wanted to confess everything to Mary. "Uh... um... so much happened at the conference. A lot of new information. And, it kept me up at night thinking about it."

Because everyone's going die and we're going to Mars.

"Did the nap help this afternoon? When's the last time you slept?"

Joe took another sip of water. "It helped. Probably a couple days ago?" A lie said to not worry her since it has been five nights without sleep.

"Well, maybe the pizza will put you in a food coma." She laughed. "Let me go upstairs and bring you a pillow and a blanket. I'll make you a nice, comfy spot on the sofa."

Mary kissed the top of his head as she went upstairs. After she left the room, in a low, whispery voice Joe said, "Okay, *you* saw that. I almost told her. But, I promised I wouldn't."

Joe looked straight ahead as he sat in the same spot as Mary when he had seen her in Colorado. "I know you bastards can see me."

"What did you say?" Mary asked walking down the steps, hugging pillows and a blanket.

"Oh... uh... I was talking to myself. You know, Mr. Brain Damage over here."

"Well, at least the lack of sleep hasn't taken your sense of humor away, Mr. Damage."

She unfolded the blanket and fluffed the pillows. The smell of fabric softener caressed the air.

"Come *here*, and let me get you comfortable."

Joe joined Mary on the sofa, a familiar place for him. Many a late-night home from the lab, Joe had slept there often.

"Here are your pillows." Mary gave them one last good fluff and placed them behind his head. "Now, if you need anything, just yell for me. Do you want the TV on?"

"Sure."

"I'll put it on the news channel since that usually makes you doze off." She placed the remote on the coffee table within his reach and kissed him, goodnight.

Mary went into the kitchen. Sounds rolled into the living room. The refrigerator door opened and closed. An empty pizza box crumpled into the garbage can under the sink.

She turned out the lights going back upstairs. At the top of the steps, Mary told him goodnight and that she loved him. Darkness crept through the living room.

Streetlights peeped through cracks of the curtains interrupting the downstairs shadows. The greenish glow from the LED lights on the appliances filled the kitchen behind him. Random reflections danced on the furniture and freshly painted walls from the flickering television.

In July, Joe and Mary had moved into their new rental townhouse. They had decided it was time to become adults moving from their college apartment, which they had called home for nearly fifteen years.

Their landlord had the home painted before they moved. This was a perfect opportunity for the Eden Foundation to install cameras and microphones in doorknobs, smoke detectors, mirrors, light switches, and even two televisions. Eden knew they would not get rid of the free gifts left in the home.

With no light except the television, the cameras switched to night mode. On duty tonight was Joe's usual Monitor. She observed Joe lying on the sofa, both arms under a blanket, his eyes closed.

The cameras in the upstairs bedroom captured Mary as she entered the bathroom. Her routine was the same every night: remove her make-up, wash her face, brush her teeth, and apply moisturizer before slipping into bed completely naked. The Monitors had created a checklist to quickly identify any abnormal activity from her. Joe was less predictable in his routine.

Several minutes had passed. Joe fell into a light sleep lasting an agonizing few moments. His eyes opened again to the images on the television. This pattern repeated well into the deep hours of the night.

Mary's voice came to him in a dream. *That was the longest we've ever been apart. Promise me you will never leave me that long again.*

Joe jolted awake unsure if the conversation was real. He collected his thoughts and recalled their earlier conversation when he came home.

Frustrated, he watched television. The news programs had ended hours earlier. Joe became lost in an infomercial for the latest, weight loss gimmick.

The program numbed his mind compelling him to not change the channel. Between states of reality and dreams, he awoke again. This time on the television was a man in a pale, blue suit. His white hair slicked back, and he had the most devilish wide grin on his face. The man was a televangelist barking through the screen.

"Brothers and Sisters. I'm here today to tell you the end is near. Come to know Jesus as your Lord and Savior. You will enjoy everlasting life with him in heaven."

Joe released a heavy sigh.

"Let's pray together."

The man closed his eyes in an over-exaggerated attempt to show he was praying. After a few moments, an incredible smile etched across his face contradicting the tone of his prayer. "Now, Brothers and Sisters, call our number below. Make a donation. Let God into your heart. Give what the Lord commands in you. Amen... Amen."

Joe listened to the televangelist and laughed.

God? What God will let this happen? Heaven? Well, you're all going there soon enough. That's for damn sure.

Joe's arm tangled in the cover attempted to reach for the remote. Before he could turn the television off, the televangelist disappeared. The screen turned blood red. White letters scrolled across... *Breaking News*.

A few seconds had passed. The red screen changed to a view of a newsroom from the local television station.

"Terrorists have claimed responsibility for shooting down a Russian plane en route to Moscow. All two-hundred-and-forty-three passengers and crew are feared dead."

The light from the television went dark as Joe pressed the power button on the remote. Darkness surrounded him on the sofa. Sarcastic thoughts entered his mind.

It doesn't matter... terrorists... politicians. What is real anymore? Hell, I bet somebody was on that plane and knew about Salvation.

Joe was losing faith in everything he had known to be true.

In complete silence, a slow drip from the kitchen sink grew louder. On her screen, the camera in the television captured Joe throw off his blanket. Joe stretched out his arms and yawned before standing and walking into the kitchen.

With the kitchen lights turning on, the cameras switched to daylight mode. His Monitor watched as Joe turned the faucet on-and-off. He inspected the pipe pointing down. Two large drops fell into a small puddle formed in the bottom of the sink.

Several minutes had passed. Mary entered the kitchen. She laughed seeing his backside sticking out from under the sink, his head inside the cabinet.

"Good morning, Honey... What are you doing?"

Joe crawled from under the sink and closed the cabinet doors. "I fixed a leak in the faucet."

"Oh... okay? Were you able to sleep?"

He stood from under the sink and gave her his normal morning kiss. "Good morning, Sweetie. I slept like a baby." Again, another lie.

FEBRUARY 18, 1990
PASADENA, TEXAS

THE CHURCH HAD BEEN ALWAYS a comforting place to Joseph as a child. It was the one constant he could always seem to rely on, given the sadness he so far had to endure as a child.

Joseph never knew his father, a kind and loving family man. A drunk driver had killed Jacob on the day Joseph was born. Now, it had only been less than a year since his mama, Rachel, had died. So, he looked forward to going to church on Sunday mornings with his grandma, Liz. His way to connect with his mama.

Joseph especially loved the sermons about reuniting with lost family members in Heaven someday. Even though he was only eleven-years-old, Joseph understood the meaning of Minister Greene's sermon.

"Brothers and Sisters. Please turn in your *Bible* to First Thessalonians, Chapter Four, verses fifteen through seventeen." Minister Greene held his *Bible* as he marched around his podium allowing the congregation time to follow his instructions.

Minister Greene continued, "Dear Folks, the *Bible* tells us: *the Lord himself will come down from Heaven with a word of authority, with the voice of the chief angel, with the sound of a horn. And, the dead in Christ will come to life first.*

Then, we who are still living will be taken up together with them into the clouds to see the Lord in the air."

Minister Greene finished reading the verses and looked out toward the congregation. "Folks, we have studied before in our sermons from Revelations about the end of days. I am here to tell you we are living in these times now. War, disease, natural disasters… they are all around us. But, our God said it *right here*. That all us believers will soon be called up to Heaven as the Rapture will be upon us."

The minister's voice grew louder. Veins in his forehead bulged with each passing sentence. Joseph always liked it when this happened. It entertained him when the minister solicited a chorus of "Amens" from the people who sat around him.

Minister Greene walked from the altar to the center aisle parting the two sides of the church sanctuary. He stood in the middle and continued his sermon.

"It will be a glorious day my Brothers and Sisters in Christ. For on the day of the Rapture, we will all rise up to Heaven and experience Salvation with our Father. There, we will rejoin our fellow brethren who have died before us and we will live in eternal bliss with Jesus in Heaven."

Joseph slid his body forward in his seat. The widest smile overcame him. He turned his head to his grandma. Her eyes caught his. Liz returned a matching smile. Silently, she knew why Joseph looked so happy.

"But, all will not be well here on Earth for those left behind. The nonbelievers, they will not understand what is happening. And as the antichrist appears, they will have to endure Hell on Earth during the final tribulation." Minister Greene walked back to the altar standing at the center of the stage in front of the choir.

"Then, at the end of the tribulation, Jesus will return to Earth. This second coming of Jesus and the Church will save the remaining lost souls in which there will be a thousand years of peace on Earth."

"Wow, a thousand years," Joseph said, whispering to himself. Joseph slipped back into his seat and leaned his head onto his grandma's shoulder. Liz lifted her arm and hugged him to her as he pressed against her listening to the sermon continue.

His eyes blinked slower... and slower until he drifted into a light sleep. Even though he fell asleep, in the background Minister Greene's voice continued. His words were comforting to Joseph as he fell deeper to sleep.

A few minutes had passed. Joseph jolted awake. Visions of his grandma and everyone else standing with their hymnals replaced the darkness of his closed eyes. Sounds of music from the organ played.

Joseph took a few seconds to orient himself from his nap as now the room was full of music and singing. He stood from the pew beside Liz. She lowered her hymnal down so he could follow along in the song.

Joseph found his place with Liz's help pointing to where they were in the lyrics and sang along to *How Great Thou Art.*

As the chorus ended, he looked up to his grandma. At that moment, all the color in Joseph's face disappeared as he opened his mouth in horror without a sound. Instead of looking into the eyes of his grandma, the eyes of his mama looked back to him.

It was not the same warm, loving expression Joseph remembered from his mama. Instead, it was the last expression Rachel wore before going into the hospital. How she looked when she had passed out this past Easter in the Minister's arms.

Her expression was one of someone gasping for their last breath. Rachel's eyes rolled into the back of her head. All Joseph could see now were the whites of her eyes.

Joseph released the hymnal as the book fell. It passed without hesitation through his and her hands together slamming to the floor. The sound of their book hitting the floor multiplied by a hundred. All the other hymnals everyone held hit the floor at the same time. A sickening thud rumbled throughout the church.

The cascade of books hitting the floor came to him like a tidal wave as the organ music stopped. Standing in complete shock, Joseph's mouth opened wider-and-wider. Fear in his eyes grew.

Joseph slowly said one, single word. "Mama?"

The word *Mama* escaped his lips as Rachel floated away from him toward the ceiling. Everyone else in the church joined her in the air. He was the only person left on the floor as the bodies floated through the ceiling. Joseph yelled, "Mama!"

In an instant, Joseph was in complete darkness. His clothes were soaking wet with sweat. He realized he was lying in his bed. He wanted to cry but was in a state of confusion unsure where he was or what had happened.

A few seconds had passed. His heartbeat slowed as he calmed down. After a deep breath, Joseph lay with his eyes open replaying the dream over in his mind. He realized the sermon he had heard caused his dream. Satisfied, he rose from his bed.

His footsteps seemed lighter than normal. Darkness of the room surrounded him. The room felt familiar, but different.

He looked at his watch to check the time. Pressing the left-side button, a greenish glow lit the black air as *2:30 a.m.* reflected. Joseph lowered his arm not seeing the date, which had scrolled across his watch, *September 12, 2020.*

What a dream? Joe thought as he walked into the bathroom without making a sound. The dream had haunted Joe as it had reoccurred with greater frequency the past few weeks.

OCTOBER 12, 2013
STONY BROOK, NEW YORK

DARKNESS FILLED THE HALLWAY between Joe's lab and his office. An eerie red light emanated from the emergency exit sign at the other end of the hall in the Stonehaven building.

Inside the lab, Joe sat behind his workbench. All the lights were on. His normally neat hair was disheveled. Hours had passed as he peered over mountains of new data from his latest simulation the past three days.

A plate sat beside him with clear plastic wrapped over a half-eaten piece of apple pie. On top was a yellow sticky-note in Mary's handwriting. *I know you said you would work late tonight.*

Steam rose from his mug beside the plate. The aroma of coffee filled the lab. Three, wet filters sat on top of the trash can below the coffee-maker beside the lab sink. Evidence of spilled water lay on the floor between the sink and coffee pot. Signs pointed Joe had been here for quite some time.

"Can this be?" Joe asked of no one in his lab as the early hours of Saturday morning crept upon him. Papers fell to the floor. Across the table, three thick research books with well-worn pages sat open to different places.

He reached into his white lab coat's front pocket and pulled out a small voice recorder. To remind him of his various notes during his research, he pressed record and spoke.

"The RNA codex miR-182 from Sample 10.09.2008B has proven to be an identical match to Sample 10.09.2008A. The simulated statistical probability of an exact match between the two samples is 0.000001%. So, one out of a million people could potentially share the same RNA codex. Sample 10.09.2008A was taken from the female patient with a maternal relationship to Sample 10.09.2008B taken from the male patient."

Joe stopped the recording as the hallway light turned on. To both their surprise, the cleaning lady peeked into his lab. She was pulling her mop bucket with its squeaky wheel following her. Joe pressed record again to speak.

"The miR-182 Sample 10.09.2008A was administered to mouse subject number one and mirR-182 Sample 10.09.2008B was administered to mouse subject number two at 14:20 and 14:25, respectively on October 4th, 2013. The injection points were into the cerebral cortex."

"Tests conducted on both mice after forty-eight hours show a ten percent increase in positive markers for potential GMB tumor growth. Further tests are needed to determine the genetic relationship between the identical codex development of miR-182 as well as the ability of this

RNA codex to reduce the expression of several oncogenes promoting cancer development."

"Joe, you look like shit," Charlie said shouting, as he entered wearing his University of Stony Brook sweatshirt. "Man, it's ten o'clock and kickoff starts in two hours. Have you been here all night?" Charlie asked as he picked up the plate with the half-eaten apple pie to his nose.

Joe stopped his recorder. He glanced toward the window as bright daylight shined through the horizontal metal blinds. "Charlie, I've got to show you this." Joe's voice cracked from not drinking anything for the past several hours. "I think I've found it."

"Joe, it will have to wait. Becky's waiting on me. I needed to run in here to pickup my tickets that my stupid ass left in my desk. We still have two extra tickets if you and Mary want to come?"

Charlie rummaged through his cluttered drawer, through empty candy wrappers.

"Ah, there they are." Charlie slammed the metal drawer closed and started toward the door. "Whatever it is, it has to wait until Monday. I left the tickets on my desk if you want to come." Charlie's voice trailed off as he walked away.

Joe looked at Charlie's desk at the tickets and then back to the plate with the now missing piece of pie. As he looked toward the window, a twinkling glimmer of light bounced off the side of his eyes. Leaves deflected the sunlight, which shimmered on the clear, plastic wrap on the plate.

He placed the plastic wrap back over the plate to stop the glare from bouncing off of his face. Once in place, the yellow sticky-note fell off and floated down to the floor. Joe bent to pick it up and place it back on the table.

"Dammit!" Joe shouted as he realized he had been in the lab since Thursday morning.

Mary had made her famous, homemade apple pie for Wednesday's dinner. Joe had missed this because he again worked late. Before Joe had left Thursday morning, he had seen the plate with two pieces of apple pie and with a yellow sticky-note on top.

"Mary is going to kill me," Joe said as he picked up the papers from the floor, arranging them in neat stacks on the tabletop. He emptied his full, now-cold coffee mug into the sink, turning off the coffee pot and lights. Before Joe left, he closed the blinds filling the lab with darkness as he locked the lab door behind him.

Joe walked across the hall to his office and got his backpack to go home. The light from his office reflected through the lab door. It illuminated one sheet of paper left on his tabletop beside the computer. The bold, black letters on the paper stood out against its white backdrop:

Sample 10.09.2008.A (Rachel Bishop)

11-PARANOIA

DAY FIVE WITHOUT meaningful rest, Joe forced himself to get out of bed this morning to return to his lab. He figured maybe a normal routine would trigger his body's response allowing him to fall asleep this evening.

Once he stepped out of the shower, the strong scent of bacon wafted up from downstairs. Joe followed the trail of maple and pork as the sizzling grew louder as he entered the kitchen.

Mary wore her orange sports bra and black spandex shorts as she cooked. She has always been an early riser enjoying a morning jog. With her teaching classes starting today, Mary got an even earlier start than usual.

"Good morning, looks like you're refreshed this morning," Mary said feeling his warms lips against the back of her neck as his hands rubbed across her bare, flat stomach.

"Smelling bacon always puts me in a good mood." Joe backed away from her playfully tapping the backside of her shorts as he sat at the table.

"Busy day, today?" Mary joined Joe at the table and sipped her orange juice between bites of crispy toast.

"Uh... just need to catch-up on some work. I owe the Eden Foundation information. So, I'm working on that the next few days."

Steam rose from Joe's plate of buttery, scrambled eggs. "How's your day looking?" Joe savored his bites of crispy bacon. Grease glistened on his lips in the morning sunlight peeking through the window.

"Well, today is the first full day of classes."

"Oh, yeah, I totally forgot. You excited?"

"First day of class is always the best. I'm happy I get to teach the sixth-grade honors math class this year because I'll have a lot of the same kids from last year."

Mary rushed through her breakfast placing her dirty dishes in the sink and ran upstairs to change. A few minutes later, she came back into the kitchen fully dressed for class.

Mary was a low-maintenance person with a natural beauty. Joe loved this about her. She loved the fact she could easily get dressed and leave quickly not having to apply makeup in the mornings.

Joe sat at the kitchen table pretending to read the morning paper at the table. He admired Mary watching her collect her things to take to class. Her lips were moving, but Joe heard no sound. Mary kissed him before leaving, which brought him out of his momentary trance he had fallen.

Joe and Mary's new rental townhouse was in a perfect location. They lived on the opposite side of the Stony Brook campus; a perfect location close to the middle school for Mary and near the train station for Joe.

Before going upstairs, Joe washed the dirty dishes cleaning the kitchen. He went upstairs for a quick shower, got dressed, and left for Stonehaven.

First time I've gone to the lab in over a week.

Joe enjoyed his walk to the train station. The gorgeous weather on this clear, warm morning refreshed Joe. If only the clouds could exit his mind caused by his insomnia.

Ten minutes had passed waiting at the station. A dozen or so people stood around him, most looking down to their smartphones. Various flavors of coffee breezed by Joe as he held his hand across the top of his forehead to block the blinding sun.

Squealing from the approaching train lurched around the bend in the tracks from the West. The Pavlov noise created a stir from the crowd waiting on the platform as they jostled their positions.

The Number 7 had arrived for Joe's fifteen-minute ride to Stonehaven. Each train car has seats arranged on both sides of an aisle allowing two passengers to sit side-by-side facing another two. The layout maximizes the number of people, which can sit in one car, but creates an awkward intimacy of strangers whose kneecaps are less than a foot apart from touching.

Joe found an empty seat by a window as an older, white-haired woman sat beside him. A boot appeared on the floor between the closing doors causing them to re-open.

The boot belonged to a young African-American girl, who was pushing a baby stroller. They sat across from Joe and the older woman.

The doors closed causing the baby in the stroller to cry. It was a cry so violent, it could pierce the eardrums of a heavy-metal, rock God.

Great… I'll have to listen to this screaming the whole way.

Joe's new neighbor reached out her pale, wrinkled arm and pointed at the baby. "Is she your daughter?" Her voice came feeble muffled by the moving train.

"Yes, Ma'am. Her name is Janice."

"Oh, such a beautiful name. How old is she?" the woman asked. The baby's screams became even louder.

Beautiful, hell. Listen to her.

"She's… uh… like six months. Shh. Shh." The girl rocked the stroller in a failed attempt to hush her daughter.

The train car vibrated passing over the tracks. A gentle, bouncing motion rocked everyone from side-to-side. Bright sunlight shined through the windows. A strobe effect occurred as the sunlight flashed fast through the passing trees.

With Joe's lack of sleep, people inside the train car moved in slow motion. A perfect opportunity for a short nap killed by the non-stop crying.

Joe closed his eyes for a moment hoping this would drown-out the infernal cries of Satan's spawn… but, this did not work.

"Does she sleep during the night?" the woman asked.

The mother said something back, but Joe could not understand her. To pass the time, he had his own responses in his mind to the woman's questions.

Of course, she doesn't sleep for God's sake. Can't you hear?

The baby hijacked Joe's bright and cheerful morning. His eyes attempted to zone-out the merciless noise by staring out the window.

Joe listened to the woman and the young mother talk. Joe knew she was attempting to make the young mother feel better.

"Can she eat any solid foods, yet?"

Are you listening? It sounds like they are feeding her broken glass.

"We just started with some baby food," the mother said.

"Do you have any other kids?"

"Uh… a son. He's ten."

Why can't he be here instead of her?

"Have you heard about Mars?" the woman asked.

Yeah, like you mean, we've been going there since the '80s.

"No, what's going on with Mars?" the young mother replied.

"That's where we will escape when a planet destroys Earth," the woman said.

"What planet? Destroy Earth?" the young mother asked.

Shut that freakin' baby up.

"When is this going to happen?"

Five years from now, in 2020.

"2020, in five years," the woman replied.

"Yes, you're all going to die!" Joe shouted opening his eyes after falling asleep.

Joe scanned around at everyone. Silence filled the train car. The vibrating wheels screeched beneath them. Joe's announcement scared the baby into stopping her crying. All eyes stared back at Joe.

"Oh… sorry… bad dream." Joe shrugged his shoulders and lowered his head failing to make eye contact with anyone. The train slowed.

Thank God. It's my stop.

"Excuse me," Joe said as he stood and stepped out of the stopped train into the bright, early September air. Joe made his way to his lab walking through the Stonehaven campus. Flower gardens with pink and purple New England asters reflected the bright rising sunshine.

Except for the time back in 2012 when Joe and Mary contracted a terrible case of the swine flu forcing them to miss two weeks of work, this past week was the longest time Joe had been away from his laboratory. Today, Joe knew he had the place all to himself, since Charlie was still away with Becky and the kids for an extended Labor Day vacation. This was a relief for Joe, as he was unsure if could handle any more conversations about Colorado.

Joe entered his office and closed the door behind him without turning on the lights. He sat behind his desk. Stacks of paper and countless numbers of research books were around the room. Musty, the unopened room smelled.

I should take all this, but how?

Going on his sixth night with little sleep, thoughts raced through him.

What do I need to take? I'll tell them I need all these books… Oh, I can just scan the papers. Why does it smell like ass in here?

The silence in the room was deafening until the phone on his desk rang startling Joe wide-awake. On the second ring, he picked up the phone. "Stonehaven, this is Dr. Bishop."

"Good morning, Joe. This is Gabriel. Hope I'm catching you at a good time."

"Uh… hi… um… yeah, I'm good." The wrinkles on Joe's forehead suggested his curiosity of the call given he was just with Gabriel two days earlier.

"Thought I'd check-in to see how you're doing since our meeting? We thought your presentation was perfect, and our donors can't wait to hear more from you."

Huh… what presentation? I never gave my… oh, yeah…

"Oh, yeah, the presentation. It's my first day back, and uh, I need to gather my thoughts about what's needed."

Joe remembered what Gabriel had told him in Colorado. If he called Joe, Gabriel would do so under the pretense of calling about the presentation. This is just in case someone was with Joe or if the call was on speaker.

Joe looked around his office. "No one's here, Gabriel."

"Well, I was calling to see how you were doing, and if you needed anything. Remember, if you need to contact me, call me on the number I gave you. It's a private line."

"No, everything's good. I'll be back in touch in a couple of days. Let me pull myself together, and I'll call you, then."

"That's fine. Oh, and one more thing. No more outbursts like that on the train, okay?"

"I was having this crazy dream, and I…" Joe stopped talking. He realized someone must have been following him from Eden for Gabriel to know so soon.

"Good. As long as we are clear about that," Gabriel said in a stern voice.

"I'll be careful, I promise. So, I have to go. I'll call you soon." Joe faked his sense of urgency to get off the call.

"Well, good talking to you, Joe. Take care, and we'll be watching."

Huh, you'll be watching.

After Gabriel hung-up, Joe placed the cordless phone down on its charger in slow motion. His eyes darted around the room. Already on edge from no sleep, Gabriel's last comment amplified Joe's paranoia.

They're watching me everywhere. Someone was following me on the train? I bet it was that lady beside me. She was way too nosey about that damn baby.

Joe leaned back in his chair and placed his hands behind his head for support. His books and papers spread around the room appeared and disappeared repeating in slowing intervals. His eyelids opened-and-closed, slower-and-slower.

Several hours later, a car horn woke him wailing away outside his office window. The daylight had disappeared into complete darkness. Joe looked down at his watch. The time was 11:20 p.m.

I must have passed out here.

He reached for the phone to call Mary to apologize for being late. But as he placed it to his ear, he slammed it back down.

I can't call her. She might be asleep.

He got his backpack from the corner chair and left his office locking the door behind him. Darkness filled the hallway except for the eerie glow of the red light from the exit sign.

No wonder I slept all day. It's so quiet. Everyone's still on vacation.

Gone was the warm morning. Cold, misty air filled the darkness of night as he ran to the station to catch the last train for the evening. As he stepped up the platform at the tracks, he looked behind him.

Is someone following me? They must be. Doubt they'd only follow me in the morning and not at night?

His platform was up a flight of stairs from the parking lot of the train station. Each footstep up the metal stairway reverberated down the platform into the quiet night.

Ten minutes to wait.

He sat on a cold, metal bench under the arrival time board. Joe could not sit still. His eyes turned faster than his head. Paranoia had joined him in his wait.

It has to be a person, right? I mean, there's no way cameras are watching me from inside the train?

Light footsteps floated from the opposite side of the train tracks. He peered through the misty fog between him and the opposite platform. A petite shadow walked up the steps. As Joe squinted his eyes, the veil lifted as the shadowy image became clear. A young girl under a hooded parka waited for her train.

Joe stared as she sat down on a metal bench across the track from him at least thirty yards away. She waited for her train going in the opposite direction into New York City. His eyes slowed their wandering and focused on the girl.

The glow from her smartphone illuminated her face. She was a black woman, but he was too far away to identify the details of her face.

She glanced up at him and looked away once she caught Joe staring at her. Joe saw her mouth moving.

She must be talking to someone on her cell phone.

Joe kept studying the image.

She looks like that girl with the baby this morning.

He flashed back through his fuzzy memory of the young mother and her devil baby.

That can't be her, right? Why would she be out so late by herself? Maybe, she's the one following me?

Joe stood and walked to the edge of the platform trying to get a better view. She looked at him as a train approached on her side of the tracks. Within a minute, a train had arrived stopping on her side of the track blocking his view.

Seconds later, the train inched away. Electricity bounced off the overhead cables with the movement. He looked on the platform. The young girl was gone.

I'm going crazy. She obviously got on the train.

After a few minutes of peering through the fog, a distant light appeared accompanied by the familiar squeal. Joe's train had arrived. An empty car, typical for this time of night, comforted Joe.

Good. No one's on following me.

Joe sat by the window and looked through it to the opposite platform. As his train lunged forward, he saw the same young girl. She was leaning against one of the support columns of the platform's metal roof.

What the hell?

"Okay, he's on the train now," the young girl said. She spoke into a Bluetooth microphone connected to her ear.

After her confirmation, the Monitor watching Joe tonight switched to a video feed from the train's security camera. Joe's train rumbled down the tracks on its way toward Stony Brook.

I'm just being paranoid. There's no way that could have been the same girl from this morning?

12 - THE WILL

"MARY, HERE are our bags." Joe pushed through the crowd in the baggage claim area at the Houston International Airport. Two black suitcases with red ribbons tied to the top handle spun off the carousel.

"Good idea with the ribbons, Honey," Mary said pulling her bag behind her, "it made them so easy to find."

Joe and Mary walked to the rental car counter. "Joe, it's been a long time since we've been home?"

"I know, what? It's been at least two years." He collected the paperwork from his backpack. "Okay, Mary, wait here and I'll get the car."

Mary remained behind as she watched him zigzag through the roped-off maze at the counter to speak with an agent. A few minutes later, Joe returned to her holding a set of keys and paperwork.

"Okay, we're all set," Joe said, dangling the keys in front of her to get her attention, as she was busy people-watching.

"Oh, Joe, look *at that*. See how happy everyone is."

"Yeah, well," he said picking up a bag he had knocked over, "their happiness can balance out our sadness." He clutched the handle on his bag. "Are you ready?"

Mary turned away from the happy reunions and pulled her bag following Joe to the rental car parking area. "So, what kind of car did we get?"

"It's a black Jeep, perfect color for a funeral."

"Joe, you didn't?"

"No, just kidding… that just happened to be the color of the car… *there* it is… space number eight." Joe pointed in the general direction and clicked the key fob to unlock the doors.

The lights flickered on-and-off, creating a yellow strobe light as they approached. Joe opened the back and placed both bags inside, pulling out a folded piece of paper from his backpack.

Mary got into the car as Joe walked around, completing his inspection to make sure everything was okay. Satisfied, he opened the driver's side door and adjusted his seat.

"Here are the directions I printed off from the Internet."

"Aye, aye, Captain." Mary lifted her right hand to mock a salute to Joe. "Just trying to lighten the mood, Babe."

"Thanks," he said while adjusting his mirrors. The windshield wipers moved. He played it off like he meant for that to happen. "Well, at least I know what that button does." Joe started the car and followed the exit signs out of the parking deck.

"Have you ever met, Robert Spivey before?" Mary asked as she studied the directions.

"No, the only time I've spoken to him was when he called Wednesday morning."

"Okay, turn left at the next light."

"He told me he first met Grandma many years ago, when she had that property line dispute with the neighbor."

"Okay, at the stop sign, you will keep going, straight."

"I still can't believe it. I never want to hear a phone ring at 3 a.m. ever again."

"It says to go for one mile and then merge onto Highway 3-South."

"Damn… a heart attack… I still can't believe it?"

Mary peeked over to him and said, "Heart attacks? Do they run in your family?"

"Mama died from a brain tumor, and she was adopted. So, I know nothing about her birth family. Dad died in the accident with a drunk driver. Grandpa Eli was killed in a robbery. Hell, I can only hope for a heart attack."

Joe sensed the dirty look Mary had given him. She did not appreciate his joke in the moment. "I think because of so much sadness when I was a kid that subject just never came up?"

"Okay, take the next exit and it looks like you will stay in the right, left lane because our next turn is a left."

"I am happy though Grandma had a lot of friends through the church. I've always felt a little guilty leaving her down here when we left for New York."

"The office should be at the next light."

"Now, I hate it we didn't come home for Christmas," Joe said, turning into the parking lot of a small, brick building. A lone, candy-apple, red Corvette Convertible Stingray sat near the building. A tinted-glass wall stretched along the entire front. Two doors were in the center of the building.

Joe parked the car. Mary placed her hand on top of his hand as he held the keys turning off the car. "Honey, you can't beat yourself up over that. Remember, she had a great time taking the Christmas singles' cruise down in the Bahamas."

"I know, but…" Mary rubbed his hand. A tear formed in his eye. Joe took a deep breath. "Okay, let's get *this* over with," he said before opening his door.

Joe pressed the button on the key fob. Two quick chirps came from the horn. They hurried across the parking lot to the building. A sign written in gold letters was above a door: *Law Offices of Robert S. Spivey.*

Joe opened the door. Mary entered first. He followed as the door shut behind them. The office was a throwback to the '80s with wood paneling along the walls. In front of a closed, white door, sat a receptionist. A small woman, she had muscular arms coming from her flowery blouse.

She made eye contact with Joe and Mary as they entered the lobby. "Well, hey, y'all must be the Bishops. My name is Alice. Come on in. Can I get you folks some water? Coffee?" Alice reached out to shake their hands, welcoming them.

"Thanks. No, I'm good," Joe said.

"I'll take a coffee," Mary said, smiling at Alice.

Alice turned back toward the desk and pressed a button on the phone. "Bobby, the Bishops are here."

"Okay, I'll be right out." The familiar voice Joe had heard through his phone earlier in the week echoed back.

"Dear, how do you take your coffee?"

"Two sugars and a little cream, please." Mary followed Alice to the coffee pot in the opposite corner of the lobby.

Joe turned his head following the ladies, only to turn back to his right as the office door opened. Through the doorway walked Mr. Spivey.

Brown wing-tips were the first noticeable things about Mr. Spivey in his dark navy suit. What grabbed Joe's attention most was Mr. Spivey's white tie with bright red hearts dotted across it.

"Good evening, Folks. Happy to meet, Y'all. Just wish it was under better circumstances," Mr. Spivey said. He had a crushing handshake.

"Nice to meet you, Mr. Spivey." Joe attempted to loosen his grip.

"Oh, please call me Bobby. And, you must be Mary?" Mary walked over joining Joe.

"Nice to meet you too, Bobby," Mary said sipping her caffeine-laden coffee.

"First, let me wish you both a belated Happy New Year. I just wish this was a happier meeting."

"Thank you," Mary said with a smile as she pressed her head into Joe's arm, lifting it off again to sip her coffee.

"Here, let's go into my office and we can get started."

Bobby extended his arm into the doorway. "Alice, that's all for now. Go home and enjoy your evening with your husband."

"Okay, Bobby, I'll take care of our earlier situation, and I'll see you later," Alice said as Bobby closed his office door behind them.

Joe and Mary sat before his desk in matching black leather chairs beside each other. Bobby walked up behind them and placed a hand on each of their shoulders.

"It has pained me to no end losing Elizabeth. Your grandma was something very special. And, I'm truly sorry for your loss."

Bobby released his grip and sat in his desk chair across from them. A brown folder sat on top of his desk. He grabbed a small string hanging from the folder and spun it around its clasp, which had kept the folder closed.

Once opened, Bobby pulled out a small stack of documents. "So, if it's okay with y'all, let's get on with the reading of the Will as we discussed earlier on the phone."

Mary grabbed Joe's hand as she turned to Joe, who had fixed his gaze on the documents in Bobby's hands. To Joe, it was as if Bobby was holding his grandma at that moment.

"Now, before Liz left for her cruise, she met with me to update her Will. I told her there was absolutely nothing to worry about… to enjoy her cruise. But, you know, she wanted to be careful is all."

Joe sat uncomfortable in his chair. Memories of other family members he had lost at such an early age flashed in his memory. The difference between then and now, Joe had no responsibility as a child.

Liz was his second mother, who had taken care of him as her own after Rachel's untimely death. The lady who had sacrificed so much, so he could go off to college, graduate with honors, and get his PhD. Liz was his grandma, and Joseph missed her.

"So, I will read this out loud to y'all. Please stop me at any point if you have questions." Bobby pulled a pair of wire-rimmed reading glasses from the front pocket of his shirt underneath his jacket breast. He took a sip of water from the glass on his desk, clearing his throat.

"I, Elizabeth Esther Bishop, an adult living at 207 Chatham Lane, Pasadena, Texas, being of sound mind, declare this to be my Last Will and Testament. I revoke all wills previously made by me with this Will being effective as of December 1st, 2003."

Bobby spoke the words on the paper. The words were from Liz. Beads of sweat formed on Bobby's forehead, his voice sounded like cotton balls crammed his mouth.

It's not that hot in here. Bobby must have really liked Grandma.

"I appoint Robert Stephenson Spivey, Esquire, as my Personal Representative to administer this Will, and ask that he be permitted to serve without Court supervision and without posting bond."

Uneasiness consumed Joe as his thoughts raced.

Who is this man Grandma trusted with this? Why didn't I come to see her before? Where did he get that ugly tie?

Bobby continued his reading. "I direct Mr. Spivey to pay from my residuary estate all the expenses of my last illness, administration expenses, all legally enforceable creditor claims... "

Bobby spoke the words, but Joe lost focus on what he said. Memories of his grandma rushed to him, which he had repressed over the years.

A sense of guilt crept back again as small tears fell down the side of his cheek closest to Mary. She glanced over to Joe and extended the back of her index and middle fingers together wiping his tears. Mary placed her hand on the back of his neck as Bobby continued.

"I devise, bequeath, and give my house and all its possession to Middle Creek Baptist Church of Pasadena in full care and responsibility to Minister Samuel Greene. If Minister Greene is no longer the pastor of Middle Creek Baptist Church, then I ask the current minister to assume full responsibility."

Mary squeezed Joe's hand.

"The Church and the members there became my family, seeing me through the darkest of days. And, in their honor and in the presence of our Lord Jesus Christ, I pledge my eternal love. Please do what you see fit to do with my house."

"So... uh... um... everything in the house, including the house, goes to the Church?" Joe asked. He turned to Mary, but she did not look back. Joe saw her eyes were pink as her ability to keep from crying had been a challenge.

"Joseph, Liz spoke very candidly during the afternoon when we prepared this document. She confided in me that if it had not been for the church that there is no way she could have made it. Could have provided for you. Could have helped get you to college. Your success made her so proud of you."

Bobby took another sip of water. "Shall I continue or give you folks a moment?"

Mary saw Joe nod his head and said, "Let's continue."

"To my loving grandson, Joseph Jacob Bishop… "

Joe closed his eyes hearing these words from Bobby. He imagined hearing his grandma's voice, as Bobby spoke the words she had written in the Will.

"I love you more than words can even imagine. That night of Rachel's funeral, when I told you that your mama and daddy would always be with you, you became my hero."

A lump formed in Joe's throat.

"You were so strong as a little boy, who had been through already too much. That little boy grew into a handsome young man, who married the love of his life in Mary. The both of you have made me so very proud and happy to be your grandmother. And, I promise you. I will always be with you. Always."

The crack in Bobby's voice in reading the last sentence made Joe open his eyes. His grandma's voice had disappeared as Bobby's voice became clear again.

"So, I Elizabeth Esther Bishop, devise, bequeath, and give the following items from within my household possessions to my grandson, Joseph: all my photo albums, home movies, and scrapbooks. These are the collections of our family and our wonderful memories. I want you to have these. To share with your family, and to continue our memories as you proceed in your life."

Mary's hand became cold and wet in Joe's.

"Also, I give to you the antique writing desk that belonged to your grandfather, Eli. My fondest memories involve watching you study long hours into the night while at that desk. Remember, Joseph as I always would say to you that the truth is in this desk."

Bobby took another sip of water.

"Under penalties of perjury, we, the undersign Testator and witnesses declare Elizabeth Esther Bishop to be of sound mind and in good health. All of which is attested to this first day of December 2003."

As Bobby concluded the reading of the Will, silence filled the room for an uneasy few seconds. Joe glanced up from his lap to Bobby. "So, what's next?"

"Next? It's a lot to take in I'm aware. Our office will contact Minister Greene to start our proceedings accordingly. This includes filing all the necessary paperwork with the cities of Pasadena and Houston. And, the State of Texas for that matter."

"What about the items mentioned, should we… uh… go collect those?" Mary asked, trying to ask the questions she imagined were in Joe's mind.

Joe sat emotionless.

"We've already made arrangements to have them delivered to your apartment in New York. Unfortunately, because the house and said property will turn over to the Minister, we cannot allow you to go inside."

"Uh, I understand," Joe said, turning to Mary. "There's too many memories in that house, and… and, I am okay with that."

"It's tough… a tough situation… such a good, church-loving woman. And, again, I am truly, deeply sorry for your loss."

Joe stood from his chair, signaling Mary to stand also. He reached out his hand across Bobby's desk. "Thank you, Bobby. I can tell you thought very highly of my grandma."

"Joseph and Mary, everyone, who met Liz, loved her." Bobby reached over to shake Mary's hand next.

"I'm happy because the church can always use the donations, or even use the house in other ways. So, I am at peace with this," Joe said.

Bobby walked around his desk and opened the door to an empty lobby.

"So, will we be seeing you tomorrow at Liz's funeral service?" Mary asked as she stepped out of Bobby's office.

"No, unfortunately, I'm leaving on vacation tomorrow." Bobby's eyes darted around the lobby as he walked Joe and Mary to the front door.

"Well, Bobby, thank you again. And, thank you for the kind words about my grandma. It really means a lot to know she had such wonderful friends near her."

Joe placed his hand on the small of Mary's back nudging her toward the front door. He wanted to run away from his building sadness inside the lobby.

"Again, you're welcome. It was my pleasure knowing Liz. Now, if there's anything you need over the coming days, please don't hesitate to call the office. Alice, she will help y'all in any way."

"Thank you," Mary said as she leaned over to kiss Bobby's cheek. "Have a good time on your vacation."

Joe opened the door of the office and stepped out into the muggy, Gulf Coast night air. "You have a good night," Joe said, shaking Bobby's hand one last time.

"And, it's bad timing and all, but, again, Happy New Year to y'all. Have a good night ya hear," Bobby said as he waived good-bye.

Joe and Mary walked across the parking lot to their car. "So, that must have been Alice's Corvette parked out here earlier," Joe said attempting to divert their attention from what had just happened. Joe pressed the key fob. The rental cars lights flickered with a quick horn chirp. Joe walked hand-in-hand with Mary, leading her to the passenger side of the car. Mary placed her hand on the door to prevent Joe from closing.

"I love you," Mary said.

"I love you, too." Joe kissed her before closing the door. As he walked to the driver's side, one statement in the Will bothered Joe.

Remember, Joseph, as I always would say to you that the truth is in this desk.

Joe opened his door, sat down, and placed the key into the ignition. He paused for a moment before backing the car out of its space.

I don't remember Grandma ever saying that?

Bobby locked the front door of the office from the inside. As he was about to turn out the lights, the connecting door to the empty, adjoining office opened.

Only two offices were in the small, brick building. The building sat alone in a business park in southeast Houston.

A smile appeared on Bobby's face as a man appeared in the doorway. "Were you listening?" Bobby asked.

"Yes. *They* seemed to take everything well. And, *you* did an excellent job," the man said.

"Do you think they suspect anything?" Bobby asked.

"Hell, you sounded like a real lawyer there for a moment, I didn't even recognize who you were," the man said. "If *they* were monitoring Joe, then *they* will think he visited with Mr. Spivey."

As Bobby and the man continued their conversation, Alice appeared through the darkness of the empty, adjoining office. She stepped into the lobby standing between Bobby and the man still in the doorway.

Alice turned to Bobby and said, "Luther, you need to help me with these bodies. Spivey's a fat son-of-a-bitch, and I can't lift him into the barrel. But, I was able to take care of that bitch with no problem."

"Okay, Alice, I'll help," Luther said.

"What a stupid name. Don't call me that shit, again. It was hard enough playing your secretary."

"Ruth, Luther... " the man in the doorway said getting their attention with a firm voice showing he was in charge, "you both played your parts well. We've put in motion, tonight, hopefully the steps to help us find *him*. Then, we will have all the proof we need to tell the World everything."

"Do you think this Joseph knows where *he* is?" Ruth asked.

"Time will tell. But, for now, Luther, you've got to continue your part as Mr. Spivey and take care of the house with the church. Ruth, you move ahead with getting *those items* delivered to New York."

"Sure thing, Boss," they both said together. Ruth again passed the man through the doorway, disappearing into the empty, adjoining office.

Luther walked over behind the man still in the doorway and placed his hands on the back of the man's wheelchair. Luther spun the man in the wheelchair around, pushing him into the darkness next door. They followed Ruth to help dispose of the bodies of Robert Spivey and his secretary, Alice.

JANUARY 15, 2004
STONY BROOK, NEW YORK

LONG ISLAND IN JANUARY can be a brutal time of year. But, tonight felt different. It was like an early spring in comparison with the temperature near freezing and no breeze.

The weather made for a rather pleasant time to walk home from dinner, as the Irish Pub was next door to Joe and Mary's apartment in Stony Brook.

Large, fat snowflakes floated across the air. Their college town appeared like the inside of a snow globe.

"Joe, it is so beautiful tonight." Mary stuck out her tongue to catch one of the many snowflakes falling around them.

"Yeah, it's crazy, because a few days ago, we were in eighty-degree weather back home in Texas."

She caught two flakes with her tongue and pulled herself closer into his arms. They meandered their way back to their apartment.

"We better not get sick because of it…" Mary paused as she hugged his arm tighter. "That's the first time you've said the word *home* when talking about Texas in a long time."

Joe stared into the distance of the white veil ahead. "It's just we've been *here* almost five years now and Long Island feels more like home to me than Texas."

"Yeah, but you still say *y'all* instead of *yous guys*," she said, laughing at him while tugging his arm. "So, there goes to prove you're still at least a Southern boy at heart."

"Yee-haw," Joe replied in an exaggerated voice.

"Do you miss home?" Mary asked staring up at him. Snow collected in small patches in his hair.

"I miss Grandma, but as far as missing home. Not really. I have you, here... Charlie... my work." Joe gave her a quick kiss, while the snow fell faster.

"Yeah, I don't miss home either. The weather I miss *sometimes*, but barbecue, now that's another story."

They did not mind shivering outside, as snow still was new to them, even after five years of living on Long Island.

"Mary," Joe held her hand stopping them from continuing, "this whole funeral thing got me thinking. We should try to have a baby."

Her eyes widened leaning back her head as she smiled. "That would be wonderful. But, last time we talked about this, we weren't sure about money, bills... you know, whatever."

"But, we shouldn't wait any longer? Life's too short."

Mary stood on her tiptoes. The streetlight shined through the thickening snowfall. She placed her hands behind his neck and kissed him. Snowflakes tickled their faces. Moments had passed. She pulled away. Snow crunched under her as her feet landed back to the ground.

"Yes," she said.

Joe placed his long arms around her, hugging her tight against his body. "Okay, let's go, I'm freezing."

"Well, when we get inside, I'll warm you up," she said, taking her hand and swatting his butt.

The motion of her hand propelled them forward kicking through the snow-covered sidewalk home. Four feet pounding collected snow from their shoes disrupted the silence inside the building's foyer.

As Joe turned on the stairway light, he glanced up the flight of steps to their apartment. "Mary? Did you lock the door when you left?"

Earlier in the afternoon, Joe had called her to meet him at the Pub on his way home from the lab for dinner. Mary saw their door, opened about an inch.

"Yeah... well... I'm sure, at least, I thought I did. I was home at two o'clock when the delivery guys showed up to drop off the desk and box of pictures from your grandma. Then, you called, and I left to go to the pub to meet you."

Joe searched the open space of the stairwell. "I'll go—"

She interrupted him, "I must have forgotten to pull it shut or something?"

"Mary, stay, here. I'll go in and check."

"Check for what?" she asked puzzled as Joe walked upstairs. Mary grabbed his arm stopping him and said in an exaggerated whisper, "Stop. You think someone's in there?"

"I don't hear anything, but just stay here." Joe removed her hand from his arm.

He went upstairs. Taking each, slow step seemed to make the situation for Mary even more alarming. Loud, creaking sounds came from the fifty-year-old wooden steps.

Reaching the top, Joe slowly pushed open the door. He stretched his hand inside the room. Light escaped through the opened doorway, down the stairwell refracting off the melting snow on his jacket.

Joe disappeared into the apartment. Mary followed up the steps. Air escaped fast from her as Joe appeared in the doorway.

"All's clear," Joe shouted, not seeing Mary standing there because he thought she was still downstairs. "Oh, sorry about that." Joe grabbed her hands. "I didn't mean to scare ya."

"Give me a heart attack why don't ya." Mary rolled her eyes at her own comment. "Oh, sorry. Bad choice of words."

"I checked the rooms. No one's here. You probably just didn't pull it closed tight when you left like you said."

"I guess?" Joe's paranoia had developed since moving to New York serving as a constant reminder to Mary to lock the doors and windows of their apartment.

"Well, if someone was here, we'd see their footprints. Look at *these* I made walking in here without taking off my shoes."

"Good point, Sherlock," Mary said almost tipping over taking off her first boot. She did not want to track any more snow and water than necessary into the living room.

"You know that part about not missing home we were talking earlier? It's coming back inside from the snow I will never miss when the time comes to leave here," Joe said.

He untied his shoes and placed them in the tray next to the door and hung his coat on the nearby hook. "So, show me what came today."

Mary finished taking off her boots, placing them and her coat beside his. She led him into the guest bedroom. A red futon sat in the far corner of the room with his grandpa's antique writing desk on the opposite side near the door.

"It fits perfect in here," she said, walking to the desk with Joe still standing in the doorway. "I remember in high school coming over to your house and seeing you do your homework at this." She rubbed one hand across the top of the writing surface.

"Yeah, I always liked doing my homework *here*. Just something about it, I guess. I always thought it was pretty cool."

Mary sat in a black metal chair behind the desk, opening-and-closing the many drawers.

Joe walked behind her and grabbed a small wooden tab at the top of the desk. In one quick motion, he pulled it down as a flexible wooden screen rolled over the writing surface.

"Grandma used to get on me about playing with this. It made this awful noise throughout our house."

"So, Grandpa Eli bought this desk?"

"Evidently... to be honest, I know little about the history of it."

"Oh, but Liz must have loved it or something for *this* to be the thing she left you."

"Yeah, no kidding. Honestly, I remember doing all my homework and playing with this roll-top thing, but I thought nothing more of it."

"Well, Liz must have thought you loved it. What about her comment in the Will about always telling you something about the desk?"

"Really, I don't know what she meant. Maybe she used to tell me something nice when I was doing my work and it meant something to her." He lifted the roll-top back up into place. "And, I don't understand what she meant by *the truth being in the desk*."

"Maybe there's a million dollars hidden here somewhere." Mary gave a fake, evil laugh while opening one of the side drawers.

"Wouldn't that be awesome?"

"So, you want to see the box that came too?" Mary asked as she stood, passing by Joe to walk out of the room. After a few seconds, she returned carrying a box she had placed in their bedroom earlier.

"Hope you don't mind, but I peeked inside the box right before you called." She sat the box down on the edge of the red futon. Inside the opened box were two picture albums and one scrapbook.

"Oh, great… pictures of me and my goofy haircuts in middle school," Joe said with a sarcastic laugh. He reached for one of the picture albums.

"Remember, I loved your goofy haircuts." Mary ran her hand through Joe's hair as he sat beside her.

Joe took the largest of the albums and placed it between them. The turning pages crinkled, caused by the plastic protective covers, which had become a dull, yellow color along the edges.

"Awe, how cute?" Mary placed her finger on a baby picture of Joe. She pointed to a picture on the opposite page. "Wow, you look like your dad *in this picture?*"

"Yeah, this was taken about the time Mama and Daddy met when she came back home her freshman year of college."

"So, he's like, what… eighteen in this picture?"

"Yeah, something like that." Joe stood. "Let me get our high school yearbook." He bent down to the bottom shelf, pulling out a dust-covered, blue book and returned to her.

"You're right. Looks just like me." Joe pointed to his senior picture. "I never noticed that? Grandma would say it every now and again, but no one ever wanted to say too much around me about him."

"How long were your parents together, before—"

"Well, they met when Mama came home from school, so that would have been at least in May of '78. They got pregnant with me that summer…" His last few words came slow remembering the events.

"That's why Rachel didn't go back to college?"

"It probably gave her a good reason. Grandma told me once that Mama told her she got really homesick her freshman year, and that was why. But, being pregnant with me does sound like the real reason, doesn't it?"

"Why did she come all the way here to Stony Brook for college?"

"To be closer to New York City, I think... as Grandma said, *to get the Hell outta Texas.* The bad thing is Mama gave up a full academic scholarship, here, majoring in biology."

Mary turned the next page in the album. A picture trapped behind the plastic covering was of Rachel as a teenager. Joe placed his hand over the bottom of his mama's high school picture.

"I wish I could have met your mama. She was so pretty."

"Yeah," Joe said as he removed his hand away from Rachel's picture at a slow pace. Painful memories of her last few days hit him.

"So, let's see. I was born on April 1st in 1979, which is also when Daddy died..." Joe paused as Mary turned the page. "It's crazy. I'm older now than both my parents were in *any of these* pictures."

Upon hearing his comment, Mary slammed the picture album closed. She reached inside the box and placed the bulging scrapbook on her lap.

"Okay, enough of the sad talk. Show me your macaroni necklace or your drawing of a turkey you made by tracing your hand. C'mon, you know all scrapbooks have these things in them?"

"Well, I've never seen *this* scrapbook, so I couldn't even begin to tell you what Grandma kept?"

Mary opened the book. The smell of twenty-year-old glue and dust-covered papers rose to them. "See, I told you. *Here* is your hand turkey." She laughed at his crooked turkey with its weird, bumpy curved feathers.

"I don't even remember making that?"

"Here are your report cards. And, your certificate for good behavior in kindergarten... Oh, look, a first-place ribbon in the science fair."

"Yep, nerd-of-the-year," Joe said, mocking his achievements as he took the book from her lap. Joe turned the pages. "And, here's my swimming certificate from the Y... so much random stuff in here."

Mary searched inside the box and left the room for few moments before returning beside him. "I could've sworn there were two scrapbooks I took out of that box before I left?"

She checked again inside the empty box as Joe continued turning the pages. "Strange? There were four books in there, I'm sure of it?"

Joe closed the scrapbook on his lap and placed it back into the box. He stood, turned to Mary taking her hands into his.

"That's okay. You were sure you locked the door too before you left." Joe had a devilish grin on his face. "Now, where were we? We were talking about starting a family, huh?" His voice was soft and deep as he bent down kissing the side of her neck.

"Mmm, that feels good," she whispered. Her lips followed along the side of his face, reaching his to kiss him back.

Joe pulled away and turned toward the box sitting beside them and kicked it to the floor. He turned back toward Mary.

Joe said, "There... now, where were we?"

NOVEMBER 18, 2014
STONY BROOK, NEW YORK

HUNCHED OVER his laptop, the light in the laboratory flickered above Joe as he reviewed the results of his latest experiments. With a sudden jolt, the lab door swung open slamming against the inside wall. The horizontal, metal blinds over the door's window rocked side-to-side ushering Charlie into the lab holding Joe's wireless office phone.

"Joe, call for you." Charlie held his hands over the bottom microphone.

"Who is it?"

"What do I look like, your secretary?"

Joe took the phone from Charlie's out-stretched arms and landed back on his stool. "Hello, this is Dr. Bishop."

"Hello, Dr. Bishop. I hope I am catching you at a good time?"

"Well, actually, I was just in the middle of—" The caller interrupted Joe.

"Yes, well, I am with the Delhomme Agency. I'm calling about an outstanding amount due to one of our clients, First Bank of Long Island. Your outstanding balance due on your credit card has been transferred to our agency for collection."

Joe rolled his eyes as he listened. *Jeez, another one.*

"Your outstanding balance is \$1,750.23, and it's one-hundred and twenty-two days past due. Does this information sound correct to you, Dr. Bishop?"

Running his free hand through his hair and looking up toward the ceiling, Joe responded with a heavy sigh into the phone. "Yeah, that's sounds about right. But as I explained to the bank, we'd like to lower our minimum payments."

Fingers banged away on a keyboard through the phone. "Okay, our records show your last conversation with the bank two weeks ago. The original minimum payment was five percent of the outstanding balance."

Joe stood from his stool pacing around the lab. His nostrils flared with every keystroke in his ear without anyone speaking.

Dammit, it's just a two percent difference. It's not like we can even pay that anyway.

"Okay, here's what we can do. We will send a new bill to you in the mail, today. Your new monthly bill will indicate a minimum payment calculated at three percent of the outstanding balance due. Our mailing address will be included on the bill, and if you have any questions please contact us."

Sure, whatever. "Okay, will do."

"Well, thank you, Dr. Bishop. On behalf of the Delhomme Agency, you have a nice day." The caller's faked pleasantry was apparent given how fast the call ended.

"You have a nice day, Dr. Bishop," Joe said in a high, mocking voice. "Dammit, another collection agency!" He screamed in frustration slamming the phone down onto the tabletop.

"Yeah, the wife and I get those too," Charlie said as stood at the lab sink washing his beakers.

"I mean, we're trying the best we can. We're even selling some of our shit."

"How's Mary doing at finding a second job?"

"She teaches all day at the middle school and picks up some nights at the Pub. She's trying to see if the Community College has any teaching assignments, but nothing yet."

Joe looked toward the ceiling with heavy sighs escaping from his body. The call had violated his research sanctuary.

"And, it ain't like we're getting rich here with our research," Charlie said as he walked over and sat across from Joe. "I tell you who's getting rich. It's these pharmaceutical companies that take our research and use it in their drugs. You ever thought about leaving this post-doc work?"

"Sometimes. But, Man, I feel like I'm just so close, you know? I identified the RNA codex for the markers of different cancers. But, I... I still can't quite get to the next step in finding a cure and shit."

"Hell, Joe, you've been hanging around me too much, cussin' like that." An approving smile stared back at Joe.

"Mary, says that too." Joe returned a smile and head nod to Charlie. "It's just all this frustrating shit with our bills, Man."

"Hang in there. It's not like you own a house, and your car is paid for. So, what's the worst that can happen?"

"We get evicted from our apartment and have to come live with your sorry ass."

"Hell, it ain't like you and me are home much anyway. Becky would love the company because our twins can get on her nerves."

Joe stood from the table and rinsed his coffee mug in the sink. "We'll figure it out. At least we think we're getting it under control, now."

"Why don't you call it a day? Go home to your beautiful wife, and make sweet love to her." Charlie's voice became deeper doing his best Marvin Gaye impersonation.

"Like, uh, that's another thing. If we do ever have kids, how will our finances be then?"

"Dude, look at me and Becky. I'm in the same boat as you doing this research. Becky hasn't been back to work since the kids. So, when the time comes, y'all will make it happen."

Joe replayed Charlie's words as Joe left the lab building heading to the train station. His reassurance comforted Joe.

Even though it is a short fifteen-minute train trip, the time usually allowed Joe to decompress and unwind before coming home. Joe's work consumed him. His thoughts raced all day and night mentally reviewing his numbers and comparative research. Joe believed he was close to answers in his research.

Laughter and conversations against the backdrop of howling train wheels typically were enough to snap his thoughts away from his work and back to the normalcy of his family life. Today's train ride did not calm him.

His thoughts raced between the phone call, his talk with Charlie, his past conversations with Mary about starting a family, to turning down a lucrative job offer after college. His manic mind twisted and turned his thoughts into a jumbled mess.

The train stopped in Stony Brook. Joe collected his backpack and left down the platform to the sidewalk outside the station. During his four-block walk home, his thoughts pressed him.

All we have really left we can sell is the china we got from Grandma after our wedding… The only other thing is our car.

Joe fumbled in his backpack for the keys unlocking the door to his apartment.

But, we need to have a car. Charlie's right. It's not like we can get anything for that piece of shit, anyway.

He entered the apartment and placed his jacket on the back of the door. Mary was not home yet from teaching. Their place felt empty. The stereo was gone. The television was sold. Echoes bounced through the living room with his recliner absent.

Joe placed his hands to his lips and blew into them. *It's cold in here?* He checked the thermostat on the wall. *Sixty-two degrees?* Joe tapped his fist on the thermostat.

"That's just great. Our heat's turned off."

His hands were no longer cold. Blood boiled throughout his body pulsating a rage he had kept suppressed.

Joe walked into the office, threw his backpack on the red futon, and sat in the chair behind his grandfather's antique desk.

Why, why, why, Grandma did you not give us the house or at least something else we could sell?

The chair moaned as Joe leaned back placing his hands behind his neck. "Well, this desk is probably worth a couple thousand." Joe's words were biting and sarcastic, as the desk had sat useless in their apartment for ten years since arriving from Texas.

But, why this, Grandma? I know you were proud of me, but a desk?

His mind flashed back to his childhood. He remembered doing his math homework, while his grandma knelt beside him attempting to help. This memory made him smile. Joe realized she did not understand anything about statistics or calculus, but Liz tried to help, anyway.

Joe searched his memory for any semblance of meaning as to why his grandma had left the desk to him. A smile appeared to Joe as a memory flashed from the time he had sat at this desk talking to Mary on the phone after an eighth-grade dance.

As fast as his memory appeared, is as fast as his thoughts shifted to Mr. Spivey's reading of the Will. After ten years, Spivey's voice repeated clearly in his memory.

Remember, Joseph, as I always would say to you that the truth is in this desk... the truth is in this desk... the truth is in this desk.

Spivey's mental voice grew louder as Joe balled up both fists and banged them on the desktop. With each pounding sound, Joe shouted sarcastically, "The truth is in this desk!"

The fist banging and his yelling filled their apartment like the chanting of an ancient witch doctor. "The truth is in this desk!" Bang!

With a heavy sigh, as if to signal his last assault, he yelled, "The truth is in this desk!" This time, he slammed both hand down together. He felt blood pumping with each heartbeat on the bottom of both fists against the wooden desktop.

An eerie silence filled the apartment except for a small click from the bottom of the desk where Joe's feet were.

Great, now I've broken the damn thing?

Joe slid off the edge of his seat as his chair rolled away behind him. He got on his knees to determine what he had broken after his violent tantrum.

The shadow from above made it impossible to see. He opened a desk drawer and pulled out a black flashlight with a white Stonehaven Labs logo.

His back muscles tinged as he positioned himself on his knees and elbows under the desk holding his head turned sideways against the floor. Joe moved the flashlight to the floor.

To his surprise, he reached under where a small, wooden drawer had popped down about two inches. The angle made it impossible to see. Joe slipped his hand inside the small, hidden drawer.

His fingers slipped across something square. It felt like a piece of thick paper with a smooth, plastic covering on it. Joe was unsuccessful in his first attempt in grabbing it with his fingertips. On his third attempt, he got a fingernail under the thick paper.

Joe pulled his hand out of the drawer holding a square piece of black plastic. He flipped it over. A Polaroid picture stared back to Joe.

What the hell?

The picture was in his right hand and the flashlight in the other. His elbows supported him while he stared at the picture with his knees still on the floor and his butt stuck up in the air.

The faded picture appeared to be several years old. The shadows from the desk and the flashlight glare made it impossible for him to make out who was in the picture.

Joe turned off the flashlight, crawled out and pulled himself up. He knelt with his wrists on the edge of the desk's writing surface. Gone were the shadows and glare from his earlier vantage point. Joe could make out whom he saw.

"That's, me? That's at my high school graduation?" The tone of his voice questioned what he saw.

Why was this picture hidden in here?

The sound of keys and the front door knob turning broke his stare on the picture. Mary came into the living room carrying two plastic grocery bags.

"Hey, Sweetie. You're home early," Mary said.

"Um… huh." Joe grunted as he stumbled into the living room. Mary went into the kitchen to put the groceries away. The smell of freshly baked bread rolls followed her.

Mary's voice was faint blocked by the rustling of plastic bags from the other room. "So, I got a call today from someone asking about our credit card bill. I pretended I was Mary's sister. Ha, I don't even have a sister—" Mary stopped talking when she entered the room with Joe standing there.

She knew something was wrong. No matter how terrible Joe's day was, he always would kiss her when either of them came home.

"Everything all right?"

"Uh… oh… hey." Joe broke his concentration as he gave her a quick kiss. "So, what'd you get at the store?"

"I thought I'd make hot dogs, tonight."

"Remember what Mr. Spivey said?" Joe asked.

"Mister, who?"

"Spivey, at the Will reading."

"Oh, yeah, you mean, Bobby?"

"Remember when he was reading the part from Grandma about why she left me the desk?"

"Yeah, I guess, so? That was so long ago."

"The part about the truth is in this desk?" Joe held his discovery to her face.

"What? You finally found the million dollars." Mary laughed as she held the picture Joe had given her. "What's this?"

"Found it in the desk." Joe stood behind her peering over her shoulder.

"That's you… at our high school graduation." She pulled the picture closer making sure. "You've not seen this in there before, now?"

Joe took the picture from Mary stepping in front of her in the middle of the living room. "I've never seen this picture. I accidentally hit the desk and heard something pop-open on the bottom… um… I looked, and found *this*." Joe did not want to confess to her about his tantrum.

"Crazy, because we were joking about money being inside," Mary said as she walked into the office. "Where was it hidden?"

"It was under *there*." Joe grabbed the flashlight and shined it in the area of the hidden drawer.

Mary took the light from him and got down on her hands and knees. The desk muffled her voice. "This is pretty cool. You think there are other drawers under here?"

"I'm not sure," Joe said as he tapped her waist with his hand. "I'll lift it. Shine the light and look for anything else in there."

The antique desk was solid oak with three drawers on the bottom right side and a roll-top section with numerous small drawers and shelves. Joe grunted as he lifted the corner. "Okay... uh... anything?" His fingers turned white as the weight of the desk prevented his circulation.

Mary pressed her body against the floor as she crawled under the desk. "Don't set this down on me."

"See anything?" Joe tightened his lips. The weight grew in his hands.

The familiar pop sound to Joe occurred again as Mary pushed the drawer up into place. "You really can't even tell there's a drawer here when it's closed. I don't think there's anything else." She tapped various spots around the bottom.

"Okay, I need to set it down, now."

Mary grabbed the chair and pulled herself up to sit. Joe sat in the red futon staring at the picture.

"So, why was *that* picture hidden away in a secret drawer?" Mary asked as her gaze lingered on the desk.

"Uh... I don't know." He paused and placed the picture down on his lap. He made eye contact with her. "Do you think this is what Grandma meant by the truth being in the desk?"

Mary stood, walked over to him, and plopped down beside him. "Sweetie, who knows? But, the truth is, you were so damn cute then." She took the picture off his lap.

"What I don't understand is why hide this picture?"

"Did y'all even have a Polaroid camera?"

"No, not that I remember. Grandma took her purple, thirty-five-millimeter camera everywhere because it was always in her bag."

He paused taking the picture from Mary and studied it a hand's distance from his eyes. "But, all the pictures I ever saw of me from graduation were taken from her seat in the stands. This is a Polaroid, I mean, it's like it's zoomed in on me. Either that, or whoever took it was right in front of me?"

Joe moved the picture in-and-out as if he were looking under his laboratory microscope to find any hidden details. "Well, from what I remember, Polaroid cameras didn't have a zoom. So, *this* had to have been taken as I left the stage because I'm holding my diploma *here*."

Mary sat with a smile as she asked, "Do you remember anybody taking pictures down there? All I remember was shaking the principal's hand, getting my diploma and looking over to you as I walked off the stage."

Joe held the picture down in his lap as he looked toward the ceiling trying to access his memory of that night seventeen years earlier. "Don't know, it was all a blur."

Mary stood and positioned herself between Joe's legs sticking out over the red futon to the floor. "I'll tell you what I remember about that night."

She took the picture from his hands and placed it on the floor beside them. She bent over and placed her hands on his sides pressing into him causing him to lean back.

"I remember us driving your car around to the back of the school later that night," Mary said pressing her lips against his forehead.

"Mmm," was the only sound Joe made as he tried to lift his head to kiss her.

She pushed his head back down and climbed on top of him, her legs spread over his hips as she kissed him. A few seconds had passed. Mary pushed herself up sitting on his lap as he supported her. His chest heaved up-and-down.

"Let's see if I can help you with your memory," Mary said.

13-POLAROID

PRESENT - STONY BROOK 12:22 A.M.
SEPTEMBER 9, 2015
1,829 DAYS PRIOR TO IMPACT

JOE'S BREATH HUNG in clouds of condensation from his mouth as he walked up the steps of their townhouse. The cold, night air lingered making his walk from the train station that much faster.

As he unlocked the door to enter, Joe attempted to be as quiet as possible not to wake Mary. With his phone's flashlight app, he managed the obstacle course of furniture from the front door to the kitchen and then to the home office.

Joe shut the door and turned on a desk lamp. Before lying on the red futon to rest, he sat behind the antique desk. He flipped through pictures of Mary and him saved on his phone in search of anything to make him sleepy.

Awe, the Shore. We had fun down there this summer.

A warm, yellow light emanated from the lamp lighting the dark home office. One-by-one, he scrolled through the images remembering a simpler time. A time before he had learned about the end of the world and their pending escape to Salvation.

And, to think, my only concerns were bills and getting ready to deliver a presentation.

Time faded fast away as it became 3:45 a.m. The pictures brought memories of innocence allowing him to take his mind off Colorado. Once he got to the beginning of the pictures from Christmas of 2013, he plugged the charger into his phone.

As his hand moved across the desk, Joe knocked over a small picture frame sitting on the corner. He sat it back into place as he smiled.

High school graduation. Now, that was a simpler time.

Joe squinted his eyes together through the half-dark room focusing on the picture.

Hmm...

He leaned across the desk inspecting it closer. A familiar question returned.

Who took this?

Joe turned over the frame, pushed up the velvet backing, and pulled out the Polaroid picture.

Mary said she didn't. And, Grandma was up in the stands. This had to have been someone standing right in front of me?

This revelation along with the young girl earlier on the train platform further increased his paranoia. Joe turned the picture on its side, upside down, and back. He hoped to discover anything, something new. A clue of whom the photographer may have been and why his grandma had hidden the picture in the desk, many years before.

I'm going crazy now.

Frustrated, he threw the picture on the desk.

Light from the lamp reflected off the glossy front of the Polaroid picture lying face-up as it landed. As Joe moved his head, the light flickered across his eyes. A hidden memory resurfaced.

Hmm...

Joe picked up the picture again. The front of it stared at him in his hand taunting him.

I think I remember someone stepping in front of me when I came down those steps. Oh hell... that's right... I remember a flash and then looking away.

Joe turned on the overhead light chasing away the shadows in the room. "Where did we put those…"

A box filled with pictures and old, home movies he had received after his grandma's death sat under the red futon. Ripped packaging tape shattered the quietness in the room. Plastic videocassette tapes banged around inside as he dug through the box and its contained memories.

Minister Greene had sent the box to him after finding it when his church took over his home. The note the minister sent along with the box showed he thought Liz had made a mistake by not giving these to him.

Success. A white VCR tape labeled *Joseph's High School Graduation - 1997* sat under an assortment of pictures.

Joe and Mary's home office served a dual-purpose as a guest bedroom. The only guest who had slept here was Charlie for the few nights he found himself in the doghouse with Becky. A small television with a built-in VCR player sat on a small dresser facing the futon.

Joe powered on the television and placed the tape inside pressing *rewind*. A whirring noise grew louder and faster as the tape got closer to its beginning. The increasing speed matched Joe's racing heartbeat pounding through his sweatshirt.

A clunking thump preceded the video automatically playing. Joe's anticipation grew waiting through the few seconds of static followed by a blue screen. His grandma's voice shouted from the side speakers of the television.

Eleven years had passed since her funeral. His thoughts of his grandma had become more infrequent. Hearing her voice brought an unexpected emotional response from Joe. He gasped. Amusement followed when Joe saw his eighteen-year-old self bouncing down the stairs of his Texas home.

"What are you looking for? I have your graduation cap right here."

"Mom's college school pin. I wanted to wear it today to honor her."

"She would be so proud of this moment. Her baby graduating high school and going off to the same college she attended."

Oh, my God, this seems like yesterday.

Static again filled the screen, fast replaced by his graduating class marching into his football stadium. *Pomp and Circumstance* played through the speakers. The image zoomed to Mary and panned across until Joe saw himself as he took his seat among all the graduating students.

Joe pressed *fast-forward*. The tape made a whizzing noise as it advanced. Amusing images of students walking across the stage one-by-one in double-time appeared.

When Joe saw his friend Bobby Avery walk across, he knew his name was soon. "Joseph Jacob Bishop," the principal said.

Through the television, his grandma screamed at the same time causing the video to shake. The tremor on the screen settled down a little as Joe saw himself come down the steps.

The video revealed a forgotten memory. A man wearing a dark-gray jacket with a black hat stepped in front of Joe as he watched himself step down from the stage.

The man stopped, a small flash occurred, and the man disappeared from the camera. Joe saw on the television the man had stood close to him in that moment. But, Joe could not recall his face, only the recent memory of seeing a flash brought on by the reflected light from the Polaroid on his desk.

Joe pressed *rewind* as the images reversed on the screen. The people walked backward across the stage. He pressed *play*. "Joseph Jacob Bishop."

Joe anticipated the moment. His finger held above the *pause* button. The video played as he watched himself shake the principal's hand, walk down the steps, and the mystery man appeared. Joe pressed *pause*.

The image froze. The eighteen-year-old video, coupled with his grandma's shaking, created a blurry image. Joe could not make out the man's face.

He pressed *rewind* and then *play*. "Joseph Jacob Bishop."

This time, Joe turned the volume up as loud as possible on the television. When the man appeared, Joe heard his grandma.

"Whoa… what?" Her words escaped from her between short breaths.

The screen panned following the man stumble out of sight. He never fell but rushed away as fast as he had appeared before Joe. The camera never caught his face, as only his back was visible.

As soon as the man disappeared on the screen, static appeared. Joe pressed *fast-forward* to check if anything else was on the tape. After thirty-seconds of nothing but static, he rewound the tape stopping it before the principal called his name, and pressed *play*.

"Joseph Jacob Bishop," the principal said.

Joe watched himself walk across the stage. He paused the video at the moment a flash from the man's camera occurred. The picture froze. Joe held the Polaroid picture beside the frozen image on the television screen.

Shit! This is the picture this man took?

The Monitor observing Joe saw his face from the camera installed in the television. It was a perfect placement for capturing all the movements made in the office.

But, the camera failed in one respect. The Monitor could not determine what Joe viewed on the television screen. Only that the name *Joseph Jacob Bishop* was said four times about a minute apart.

Upon the last time hearing Joe's name come from the television, the Monitor typed into her computer:

09/09/15 @ 04:20 a.m. - unsure what Subject is watching.

6:34 A.M.

THE IMAGE FROM Joe's graduation night remained frozen on the television screen as an unknown man stood in front of him. The Polaroid picture taken that night eighteen-years ago leaned against the television as Joe sat slumped in the desk chair.

Night Seven had passed with little sleep. Both frozen images stole Joe's blank stare. His half-opened eyelids no longer blinked.

Joe could not get beyond his discovery, he sat unsure if he was awake or seeing things. For two hours, he and the television remained in this frozen state until the living room lights came on. Mary was in the kitchen preparing her morning breakfast.

The lights snapped Joe from his trance causing him to straighten himself in his chair. He pressed the power button on the television and took the Polaroid picture to the kitchen.

"Hey, good morning. What time did you drag yourself home?"

"Uh... I... it was pretty late." Joe gave her his typical morning kiss.

"What did you have for dinner last night?"

Joe sat at the table with the picture in his hands lost in his trance. Her question went unanswered.

Mary repeated her question. "What did you have... oh, what are you looking at?" Without a reply, he flipped the picture around to show what had stolen his concentration the past several hours.

"Oh, your graduation picture. Did the frame break?"

They are watching us.

"Hey, Mary, can we go outside? The light may be better out there. I want to show you something."

"You're lucky. The trash stinks anyway, so you need to take it out. But, I'll go out there with ya."

Joe opened the cabinet under the sink. The stench of eggshells and an empty milk carton invaded the kitchen. Joe pulled out the trash can and tied the bag.

"See, I told you, that stinks," Mary said holding open the backdoor.

Mary followed Joe to the trash can in the backyard, while he placed the bag inside. He held the picture on top the closed lid.

"Are you sure you don't remember Grandma ever talking about this picture or our graduation?"

Mary grabbed the picture from him to inspect it. "No, all I remember about this picture is you found in the desk a few years ago." She gave the picture back to him. "The only thing I remember Liz saying about our graduation was how proud she was of you."

"Do you remember her taking this picture, though?"

"The only picture I remember from then is my favorite picture ever. You know, the one where I jumped up on you and kissed ya."

"Yeah, that's my favorite, too. What about a cameraman, do you remember someone taking pictures as we walked off the stage?"

"Camera man? I'm sure there was, but I can't remember anyone particular from way back then."

What the hell? Tell her.

Joe's confession about what he had seen in the video almost slipped from his lips until a strong, smoke smell followed them from the door.

"Shit! I left the eggs on the…" Mary ran by him back into the kitchen.

Joe followed and replaced the trash can under the sink. "They're okay, I must've dropped some eggs on the stove," Mary said.

He sat again and continued staring at the picture.

"Did you get *any* sleep last night?"

Joe looked at Mary and stuttered a response. "Uh, um."

"Can you stay home today and promise me you'll sleep?"

He placed the picture down on the table. "That's a good idea. I'm so tired."

"How 'bout this, after breakfast, go upstairs and sleep. We've got that party to go to at Becky's on Saturday, and it's going to be a late night."

"Party?"

"Don't *party* me, Joseph. She invited us a month ago, because it's the twins' birthday, and they asked us to stay for drinks at their house."

"I forgot."

"That's okay," she said.

"No, it's not. That's right, Charlie wanted me to come over Friday night to help put together the swing set they're giving the girls."

"So, see. You need to stay home, today."

Joe looked at the picture sitting on the table. "Yeah, you're right."

"I'm glad I don't have to convince you." Mary finished her breakfast and kissed the top of his head. After placing her dishes in the sink and putting on her jacket, she prepared to leave for work. "I love you. Now, go back to bed." She blew him a kiss as she closed the door.

Joe sat alone in the kitchen. His mind was in a haze. Remnants of smoke curled through the air.

She's right. I need some sleep.

With a heavy sigh, Joe stood to go upstairs seeing across the living room he had left on the desk lamp. The closer he got to the office, his desk chair looked inviting. He sat turning off the lamp. Darkness filled the room. After a few moments, light reappeared as Joe put the picture back into its frame. He leaned back in the chair.

Memories of finding the picture several years earlier came to him. The angst Joe had felt from his grandma's cryptic note in her will, haunted him. Liz's voice grew louder in Joe's head repeating the words Mr. Spivey had said at the reading: *the truth is in the desk... the truth is in the desk.*

Joe leaned forward. The spotlight of the lamp reflected off the picture, its origins continuing to taunt him.

What the hell? What did she mean by the truth is in the desk? All I ever found was this damn picture?

Minutes had passed. The Monitor observed Joe, who only stared straight ahead at the desk. Notes about Joe's morning activities scrolled on the screen.

One note stood out: *Subject appears to have fallen asleep at the desk for the past four hours.*

The Monitor recorded Joe waking as he stood from his chair and left the office turning off the desk lamp. No sooner than the room went dark, bright lights filled the room, again. Joe rushed back turning on the overhead lights and got down on his knees in front of the desk.

Joe pulled his cell phone off its charger and activated its flashlight app. The phone's white light lit the underside of the desk as he lay flat on the floor.

With his hand, he pressed upward on the hidden drawer causing it to pop open. He placed the phone into the dark void to determine if he had missed something from his earlier search.

His frustration grew as he found nothing. A deep, breathy sigh left his body as he placed his head sideways, flat against the floor. His phone's flashlight created a reflection inside the small drawer.

What the hell?

He moved the phone from side-to-side. A faint reflection occurred each time the light moved. Not able to tell what he saw, he reached inside the drawer. He felt a small piece of paper pressed against the top of the desk.

Is that tape? It must help hold up the drawer?

He used his thumbnail to pick at and pull off the tape.

What the hell is this?

Something was under the tape. Careful not to pull too hard, Joe picked until it fell into his hand.

His eyes widened pulling his hand out. In his palm, he held a small piece of thin, white paper. Frayed edges framed the paper. The side touching the tape had a brown, grease stain.

Joe turned it over. His wide eyes added more light than what came from his phone.

What the... Are these numbers?

Written in pencil he found a pattern of numbers and letters in a five-by-five matrix. Joe held his discovery inches from his face, studying each number and letter.

This looks like a code or something? It was purposely taped inside there with my picture.

He inspected the paper in his hand.

Is this the truth, Grandma?

JUNE 11, 1997 - PASADENA, TEXAS *GRADUATION DAY*

THE EXCITEMENT OF Joseph's graduation had been building for months. In January, Joseph received the thick, acceptance package to the University of Stony Brook. But, before his next chapter in his life could start, he had to get through this big day, and he was running late.

Liz paced through the living room waiting for Joseph. She wanted this day for her grandson to be perfect, to capture every moment on film and video.

Joseph had saved his money during the summer while working at the A&P. He knew his grandma had wanted a JVC VHS-C camcorder for her birthday for moments like this.

Liz pressed *record* on the camera with one hand, as she held her car keys in the other. "Hurry up, you are going to be late," Liz said as she pointed the camera upstairs toward his room.

"I will be down in a minute, Grandma. I can't find my..." his response grew faint as Liz picked up Joseph's graduation cap off the downstairs bookshelf.

She pointed the camera back upstairs as Joseph came bouncing down. "Okay, I'm ready."

"What are you looking for? I have your graduation cap *right here*."

"Mom's college school pin. I wanted to wear it today to honor her."

"She'd be so proud of this moment. Her baby graduating high school and going off to the same college she attended." Liz beamed with pride as she lifted her head upward, as if Rachel was looking down on them in this moment.

"All right, well, we need to go. You need to be at the school in fifteen minutes." Liz turned off the video camera closing the door behind them as they walked out of the house.

The faded-green Oldsmobile rumbled through the neighborhood to the football stadium. Inside the car was quiet. A stark contrast to the chaos earlier before they had left. Both sat reflecting about the past years' events, and the longing for his mom Rachel to see this moment.

Oh, wow, Joseph is so quiet. He has to be excited about today. He must miss Rachel.

"I bet you wish she could be here with you now?"

"Uh... yeah? Oh, you mean Mama?"

"Of course, who else?"

"For a moment, I thought you were talking about Mary."

"Do you know who is coming to see her graduate?"

"Yeah, her dad's coming. He told me I'll be able to hear him when they call my name." Joseph sat daydreaming out the window. "Can I have the car tonight?"

I can't believe that son-of-a-bitch is actually going to see his daughter graduate.

"Sure. I'll ask Bob if he wouldn't mind bringing me back home afterward... Big plans after graduation?"

"A few parties with friends. We aren't sure which ones we're going to yet."

Oh, please don't get into any trouble.

Hundreds of teenagers ran through the parking lot in excitement. Heat from the sweltering Texas sun stirred a light breeze through the stadium. Their blue, polyester graduation gowns ruffled in the wind.

I remember when I was this young... I knew we should have left sooner... It's going to be hard to find good parking, here.

"Hey, let me out here, please. There's Tommy." Joseph jumped out of the car door before waiting for it to stop.

"Good, *there's* a spot." Liz parked and got out of the car grabbing her bag out of the back-seat. The sweltering sun had baked the makeup on her face. She was on a mission, to find her grandson in the maddening crowd.

Where the heck is he? They all look the same... Oh, there he is. Liz swam through the sea of excited students over to Joseph. Seeing how happy Joseph looked made her smile.

"Take our picture, Grandma," Joseph said seeing his grandma and placing his arm around his friend.

Liz looked in her bag draped across her shoulder. *I really need to clean my purse out. I can't find anything. Oh, there it is.*

Liz pulled out her 35mm camera. "Okay, say graduation."

"Graduation!" Joseph and his friend screamed in unison.

I better go or I won't find a good seat.

"Okay, I'll come find you after the ceremony. Have a good time," Liz said giving Joseph a quick wave as she walked passed on her way into the stadium.

As Liz turned around to go inside, she felt a hand grab her shoulder spinning her around. Joseph gave her a huge bear hug and whispered in her ear. "Grandma, I love you. Thank you for everything."

She pulled back and kissed his cheek. "It was all I could do. I did it all for Rachel, and I am so very proud of you".

As Joseph smiled, he let go of her hands and said, "Okay, I will see you in a few hours".

Liz wiped away a single tear rolling down to her chin as she walked into the stadium. "Rachel, he did it. And, he will make you very proud," she said softly.

A waiting crowd filed into the stadium as the herd of people entered through the gate. *Darn, there's already so many people here.*

Members of the junior class honor society passed out graduation programs at the top of the stands. "Can I have two, please?" Liz asked reaching out her hand.

She searched the stands. On the fifty-yard line, the best seats, she saw a familiar face. *Oh good, there's Bob.* Mary's dad, Bob, sat on the end of the bleachers beside the steps four rows down. *I'm sure I can sit beside him.* She walked down the gray cement steps to the row where he sat and tapped him on his shoulder.

"Well, hey, Bob. I bet Mary is so excited," Liz said, her voice going in a higher tone as she faked her excitement seeing him. Bob was not her favorite person as he partook in his fair share of public drunkenness.

Bob stood and gave Liz a tremendous hug. *Awe, poor thing looks like he's been crying.*

"I can't believe my little girl is finally graduating," Bob said.

"Isn't it something? Joseph's been so excited the past couple of days."

"I mean… she's ah, she's…" Bob said stuttering.

"Yeah, I bet she's excited too." Liz attempted to confirm what Bob was trying to tell her.

"No, she's leaving me." Bob slid over on the bench giving Liz enough room at the end of the metal bleacher. "We had a big ol' fight this morning, and uh, she says she's moving to New York with Joseph."

The surprising news caused Liz to do a double-take. Bob's stare never left the football field.

"Really? That's news to me," Liz said unsure if she believed him or not.

Mary probably just told him that in the heat of the moment in their fight.

Joseph had confided in Liz many times before about Mary's relationship with her father and their fights, which centered on his drinking. Liz had asked Joseph if Mary ever felt endangered by Bob's drinking, but Mary said her dad was a sad drunk and not violent.

He really does care for Mary.

"I'm sure she didn't mean she would go live with Joseph, just to visit." Liz attempted to console Bob feeling sorry for him.

"Mary and me, we don't always get along. But, I love that girl."

"And, she loves you, too." Liz placed her arm around his shoulders. She felt the wetness across his back from the blazing sun. "Plus, as long as I'm alive, those two ain't living together unless they're married." Her warm smile made Bob feel better.

"Liz, what say you and me... we go have dinner one night?"

Oh, God...

She took her arm off his shoulder and gave him a playful nudge on the top of his head. "Maybe, but I do need a ride home, tonight, after."

"Sure," Bob said in agreement as *Pomp and Circumstance* blared over the stadium's speakers.

The stadium lights illuminated the dark corners of the track where the students marched into the stadium. Mosquitoes and moths the size of baseballs danced around the lights.

The air was thick and humid. A typical summer night in Houston. Liz reached for her video camera. The humidity created a thin film of moisture on the camera's viewfinder. She pressed *record* and peered into the fogged-up camera.

There's Mary... so, if she's Warner, then Bishop is way in front of her.

Liz panned the camera forward through the marching file of students. At first, she passed Joseph, but realized her mistake and panned back until she saw him.

Oh, he looks so handsome.

"Way to go Mary!" Bob shouted making Liz giggle.

"Way to go, Joseph!" Liz yelled back copying Bob's excitement. Joseph was visible through her viewfinder waving his hands at her as his name came rolling down from the stands.

The graduates marched into the stadium. Rows of black, metal seats waited for them on the grassy area between the stands and the running track before the field. Liz had a great seat, thanks to Bob.

She spent the next thirty minutes filming different speakers as they came to the stage. The common theme directed to the graduates challenged them to pursue their passion and to shoot for the Moon.

After agonizing speaker-after-speaker in the inferno heat of the evening, the moment finally had arrived. The graduates stood one row at a time to go to the stage and get their diplomas.

Good, Joseph's in the first row. I can't miss him.

Liz increased her focus concentrating on Joseph's every step. The fog on the viewfinder faded. Joseph's whole body fit into the camera frame. She was certain not to miss anything.

"Joseph Jacob Bishop," the principal said as Liz shouted out in excitement causing the camera to shake. She tracked his movements with her video camera. Joseph walked across to the middle of the stage and shook the principal's hand as he received his diploma. Liz continued following as Joseph came down the steps on the other side.

This is great. I've got a great shot of him.

Liz stood in the stands beside Bob. Her left eye closed and with her right eye, she peered through the viewfinder. The camera stopped shaking as Joseph came down the four steps from the stage.

When Joseph got to the bottom step, an older man appeared wearing a dark-gray jacket and a black hat as he stepped in front of Joseph.

Move… You're in my way.

Liz watched as the man pulled up a camera to his face and pointed it at Joseph. A quick, white flash appeared, causing a memory to pop into Liz's mind. Air escaped from her lungs as she said, "Whoa… what?"

The man's image in her camera startled her enough to make her open her left eye and move the camera losing her focus. Both the man and Joseph were now out of frame. A few seconds had passed as her vision had to re-adjust through the camera.

It can't be… I've been standing in this heat too long.

Liz searched for the man as Joseph had already gone back to his seat. The next row of students stood and went to the stage.

Liz tapped Bob on his left shoulder as they stood. "Bob, excuse me. Can I meet you outside the gym afterward, so you can take me home?

I'm going to go down to get a better shot." Liz held the video camera toward Bob, so he understood what she meant.

"Sure, see you, there… try to get a good shot of Mary for me."

Liz picked up her bag and walked down to the grassy area behind the seated students. More graduates walked across the stage. Friends and family members also were sneaking down to the field to get closer pictures and videos.

Where did he go? Liz stood to the left of the seated graduates. A perfect angle to capture the graduate's steps down from the stage. But, she was not here for pictures.

"Mary Alisha Warner," the principal said catching Liz's attention. Liz witnessed Mary walk across the stage and shake the principal's hand, not missing the moment.

Liz scanned the crowd. *Where is he? I can't miss him. He has to be the only one wearing a jacket.*

"Okay, will the graduating class of 1997 please stand," the principal said. Her voice boomed over the stadium speakers eclipsed by the screaming students.

Almost on cue, a blizzard of blue graduation caps with yellow tassels flew through the air. Liz had a terrific view since she stood where she had filmed the mystery man earlier.

With her proximity to the students, Liz experienced the hazard of an avalanche of square caps falling around her. One hit her across the top of her head. By reflex, her eyes followed the cap as it hit, bounced, and rolled across the ground at her feet.

What the hell is this?

The hit-and-run graduation cap rested a foot away. She looked down and found a Polaroid picture of Joseph coming down the steps. It lay face-up on the ground. The fallen cap had blocked the bottom of the picture as she bent over to pick it up.

Liz held the picture into the stadium lights. She confirmed it was the image of her grandson.

It's him. I know it… Where did he go?

The surreal scene now turned to chaos; graduates hugged and reached for high-fives. The clapping and cheering continued raining down from the stands. People moved about along the sides of the standing graduates, jostling for a better view.

Liz looked around and walked to the side of the bleachers, scanning the crowd for the mystery man. Lightning flashed overhead without thunder.

He's gone. I can't find him?

Liz slipped the Polaroid picture of Joseph into her bag. She went to the top of the bleachers. Her eyes explored through the crowd as the mass of people left the football stadium through the entry gate and into the parking lot. The sea of graduates congregated at the nearby gymnasium beside the football stadium.

I have to go find, Joseph.

Liz stopped her search, satisfied her mind was playing tricks on her on this humid June evening. Another flash of lightning in the distance distracted her as she attempted to press *record* on the video camera. Her battery was dead.

Disappointed she would not get a final video of Joseph and Mary together this evening, Liz remembered her 35mm camera. She rummaged through her bag while walking closer to the graduates. She heard Mary's voice yell out, "There you are."

Liz found her camera and pointed it at Joseph, who now held Mary. Mary's legs wrapped around his waist as he stood kissing her. Liz pressed the camera button causing a flash as Joe's graduation cap fell to the ground.

I bet that's going to be a great picture.

Liz joined Joseph and Mary. "So, where are you two headed off to, tonight?"

Please be safe.

"Don't worry, we'll be home sometime, tonight," Joseph said with a laugh with Mary's arm behind him.

"Okay, well, if you need anything call me. You both have fun." Liz hugged them together at one time.

Oh, Lord, watch over them.

Joseph and Mary passed in front of her as Liz watched them walk across the parking lot to her parked car. An immediate crash of thunder followed a brilliant flash of white light.

A smile appeared on Liz's face. Her happiness was not so much for Joe's graduation as it was for a thought, which had entered her mind.

I know it was him. I'd recognize that camera anywhere. I've always known he was still—

Bob interrupted her thoughts. "Hey, Liz, we have to go. There's a storm coming."

CHRISTMAS MORNING, 1972
PASADENA, TEXAS

THE SUN ROSE over the horizon in the Pasadena, Texas neighborhood. Frost on the ground and trees created a shimmering effect. An unusual cold morning as a chorus of chirping birds greeted the rising sun.

Normally, at this time of morning, the suburbs outside Houston come alive with the rattling of cars. Most of them headed toward the Houston Space Center.

But, this was a special day. No cars were on the roads. School buses were not beginning the usual decent into neighbors. No, on this day, all was quiet, as children woke their parents to open presents on Christmas morning.

For eleven-year-old, Jacob Bishop, Christmas was his favorite time of year. He loved the presents, the candy, and the Christmas carols he would sing with his mother, Liz. The anticipation of waking to open his presents always drove him crazy.

Liz made Jacob promise not to get up before 7 a.m. Jacob had to wait to allow his dad, Eli, extra time to sleep. Eli had planned to be home late on Christmas Eve from work at the Space Center.

Keeping his promise to his mom was harder than Jacob had hoped. Jacob could not take it any longer as he wiggled with excitement in his bed. Jacob tip-toed from his bedroom, down the hallway by his parents' bedroom and into the living room.

As Jacob rounded the corner, a smile grew on his sleepy, little face from ear-to-ear. Colors from the Christmas tree lights twinkled in his eyes, which grew bigger taking in the full sight of the gifts Santa had brought overnight.

"Oh, boy!" Jacob shouted.

Jacob ran to the tree and slid into the presents as if Reggie Jackson was stealing second base for the A's. Presents scattered from their original resting place as Jacob searched the stacks of gifts.

Jacob found one with his name and picked it up to his ear, shaking it, trying to guess what was inside.

I hope this is it...

Crinkling paper and rattling boxes continued until a light came on in the living room.

"Jacob Levi Bishop, I thought I told you to wait?"

"I did Mama. I didn't wake you up. I came in here."

Liz staggered over to Jacob and bent down kissing the top of his head as she shuffled into the kitchen. "Don't open any. Your dad's in the bathroom and we'll open them in a little bit." The coffee maker filled the room with the aroma of instant coffee.

"Merry Christmas, Jacob."

The loud, deep voice coming from the hallway startled Jacob. "Daddy!" Jacob yelled as he stood and ran to Eli hugging him around his waist.

Eli had worked many long days and nights at the Space Center. Several days had passed since Jacob last saw Eli. Jacob's surprise to see his dad was even greater because of his excitement for Christmas morning.

Jacob looked up to Eli. "Did you see Santa last night when you got home, Daddy?"

"I just missed him, Son. But, I heard the reindeer on the roof just as I came inside." Eli brushed the top of Jacob's hair side-to-side.

"Awe, Man. I tried to stay up, but I fell asleep."

"Here's your coffee, Honey," Liz said as she came from the kitchen. Steam rose from both mugs in her hands. The smell of instant coffee filled the tiny house on 207 Chatham Lane early this morning.

"Thanks, Baby," Eli said taking his coffee and kissing Liz's cheek.

"Can we open the presents now?" Jacob asked as he jumped up-and-down between his parents.

"Okay, okay, Jacob. But, you have to hand them out first," Eli said.

Eli and Liz sat in matching-yellow, velvet-covered chairs. A small table sat between them. Their coffee gave its jolt of caffeine they desperately needed this early in the morning.

Jacob handed out the gifts. He crawled between stacks of gifts and under the tree. His small arms were full of presents as he passed them out between his parents.

"Mama... Daddy... Daddy... Two for me... Mama..."

They smiled watching Jacob go back-and-forth from the tree to them with gifts in hand. The only time either of them looked away from Jacob was when Eli and Liz smiled at each other. They held hands between their son's deliveries.

"Okay. That's all. Now, can I?"

"Go on," Eli said nodding his approval to Jacob.

"Yippee!"

A Tasmanian devil appeared before them in the living room. The sight of colorful green and red paper with various pictures of snowflakes and Santa Claus flew around Jacob. The ripping of paper became deafening.

"Far out!" Jacob yelled as he disappeared from his parent's sight lifting his hands above the mountain of torn paper. Jacob held the toy he so had hoped he would get placing it on top of his Christmas list for Santa.

"What did Santa bring?" Eli asked with a grin knowing this was the one gift Jacob had wanted most.

"Evel Knievel," Jacob said as he appeared from the cloud of papers on the floor holding the box. "You set his bike on *this* red thing and wind it up, and Evel rides his bike across the floor... Hot dog!"

Liz smiled watching Jacob run into the hallway taking his toy from its box. "Look how happy he is, Eli." Liz turned to her husband. "He'll play with that thing for days."

"Go, Evel. Woo-who," came shouts from the hallway.

"Here, I got *this* for you," Liz said lifting a wrapped box from behind her waist.

Eli unwrapped his present. His eyes grew wide with anticipation. He opened the box and smiled, as he held a black baseball hat of his favorite team, the New York Yankees. Eli put on his new hat, smiled, and said, "I love it."

"But, did you see what else was inside the box?"

"I didn't see…" Eli replied peering again finding white tissue paper.

Buried at the bottom was a smaller, gift-wrapped box. He unwrapped the hidden gift. A red, velvet jewelry box sat in his hand as he lifted it to the Christmas tree lights to inspect it closer.

"Awe, Babe, it's perfect."

"I figured as much time as you're putting into work that *this* would be helpful."

"The watch is beautiful, Liz."

"Turn it over and read the inscription."

Eli + Liz = Forever.

Upon reading the words, Eli stood and placed half his weight on her armchair and the other on her lap kissing her. Her lips tasted of coffee and cigarettes.

"This is the perfect gift," Eli said.

Evel Knievel whipped through the living room. Eli and Liz jumped in the chair as Evel raced into the mound of ripped paper, finally crashing into the tree. The sight of the toy resting in the water at the base of the tree amused Eli and Liz. The spinning back wheel of the toy buzzed until it stopped.

Jacob followed behind Evel seeing the aftermath of his stunt. "Cool, Man. Far out!"

"Jacob, come, here. I've got a present for the family. I want *you* to open it," Eli said as he stood and snuck behind the tree pulling out a gift he had hidden.

Jacob sat on the floor in front of his parents holding the box with various pictures of Santa Claus and snowmen on it. The blue gift-wrapping never stood a chance against the might of an eleven-year-old.

Paper flew away behind Jacob. He pulled a box out of the paper and tried to pronounce what he was reading. "Pola... Po... it's a camera." Jacob held the box up to his parents.

"Let me see that," Liz said reaching her hands to Jacob. She lifted it closer and read what was inside the box. Christmas lights twinkled off the box's metallic lettering. "Eli, this must have cost a fortune?"

"What kinda camera is it, Daddy?"

"It's a Polaroid camera. And what makes *this* camera special is you snap the picture and you get it instantly."

"But, I've seen these advertised... it costs too much," Liz said.

"We use them at work, and they're amazing." Eli took the box from Liz and opened it.

He lifted the camera out its plastic-wrapped Styrofoam protective covering. "See, it lies flat. Then, you pull *this thing* up. The camera pops open, and you take a picture." Eli pulled the brown, square knob on the collapsed camera showing how to use the family's new present.

Eli held the camera toward Liz. "You just point the camera, click *this* button, and *voilà*."

Mechanical, humming came from inside the camera breaking the silence of anticipation. A zipping noise followed, reminding Jacob of the bug zapper they had used in the summer for cookouts.

A thin, black square piece of white-framed plastic ejected from the front of the camera. Eli grabbed the plastic and held it in front of Jacob and Liz. The blackness inside the white frame faded to a lighter gray color. Like magic, the green color of Liz's pajamas appeared.

"And, after you take *this* out of the camera, in about thirty-seconds... *there*... you have your picture." Eli extended his arm in front of them.

"Wow... that's cool... take my picture, Daddy." Jacob sat straight holding Evel Knievel in his lap.

Eli handed the picture to Liz as he lifted the camera to Jacob. "Say cheese."

"Cheeeeese."

"This SX-70 is the most current camera out there," Eli said as he took the picture from the front of the camera and gave it to Jacob, who watched his picture appear.

"But, but…"

"No, buts about it, Liz. Jacob's getting older, and it'll be good to have these memories for a long time."

Looking again at her photo, Liz said, "Okay, but as long as you don't take any more pictures of me looking like this?"

"Like what? My beautiful wife."

"No, you know what I mean… with my hair like it is." Liz pushed her hair up into her normal bun style. "Here, let me see that camera." Liz took the camera from Eli and put it up to her face to take a picture.

"Babe, you got it backwards."

"Oh, yeah… that's better." Liz pointed the camera at Eli and snapped his picture. As Eli's picture appeared through its black covering, Liz smiled. "Maybe this camera is a great gift after all?"

"Woo-who, way to go Evel. Now let's jump the tree!" Jacob yelled as he ran by his parents.

14 - THERE'S ONLY YES

AFTER A LONG NIGHT, a repeated night of many without sleep, Joe had every intention of staying home to rest. His plan failed as thoughts raced all day about his discovery last night inside the hidden desk drawer. Since he could not slow his mind, Joe surprised Mary with a dinner outside in their backyard when she came home from teaching.

Joe heard Mary opening the front door and rushed to greet her. "Honey, dinner smells wonderful, but you didn't have to do anything special." Joe used his grandma's recipe for lemon chicken, which filled the kitchen with flavors of citrus and rosemary.

Joe led Mary to the backyard where she saw a small outside table where Joe had placed the food and drinks. They sat in their backyard enjoying the beautiful early evening. Birds chirped in the overhead oak limbs. Joe's mind was at peace.

"So, how was your day?" Mary asked as she spread butter on her bread roll.

I don't need her to worry about me. Lie.

"Oh, my day? Well, I tried to stay here and rest but went to the lab to catch up on some reports."

"Was Charlie there?"

"No, they come back today from Myrtle Beach."

"Ah, the ocean. We should plan a trip someday," she said.

Joe sat in a daze looking down at his plate while Mary ate. "You're not hungry?"

"Um, not really. I nibbled a little as I cooked, and I—"

"*Excusez-moi,*" a man said as he stood between them outside asking if they wanted water to drink. The man wore a black shirt and pants with a white apron holding a glass pitcher full of water.

Huh, who are you? Where did you—

Joe looked surprised seeing the man, but Mary seemed to expect the man's question.

"*Oui, s'il vous plaît,*" Mary said as she nodded to the waiter in approval.

As the water poured, Joe heard several people walking by them. Joe spun his head around. They were alone. With disbelief, Joe turned back to Mary. "Where's the waiter?"

"The who?"

"The waiter… he was just here."

"No one's here," she said as laughter grew louder behind him. Positive he was not hearing things, Joe stood from his seat. The only thing near them was their trash can next to the door to their kitchen. No one else was in their backyard.

"Joseph, are you okay?"

Joe realized his lack of sleep must have caught up to him seeing and hearing people. He turned to Mary and sat again at their table. Seconds had passed. Accordion music played.

The sound of people walking returned, as did their laughter. Mary sat in front of the kitchen window. Joe saw the back of Mary's head reflected in the window as the afternoon sun slid lower in the horizon. He squinted causing her reflection to come more into focus, so too did the image of a black, slender, tall triangle in the background. Joe strained his eyes toward the window to better study the reflection. The image of the *Eiffel Tower* emerged.

"Where the hell are we? How did we get to Paris?"

"It's okay, Sweetie. It's okay. Everything will all be over soon," Mary said.

Mary reached across the table and clinched Joe's wrist. Her grip grew tighter. The bright sunshine dimmed like a passing rain cloud overhead.

"It's okay, Joseph. Everything will all be over soon," she said.

Mary's stare pierced his soul. The whites of her eyes turned blood-red.

"What the hell?" Joe yelled.

The more Joe struggled to loosen Mary's grip, the tighter it became. With his free hand, Joe leveraged her hand off his wrist. Joe stood and backed away from the table.

Mary rose from the table floating off her chair. Blood ran from her green eyes. She yelled over-and-over, "It's okay! It's okay!"

The sight of seeing Mary float into the air with the blood dripping down her cheeks increased his terror. As Joe backed away from her, he knocked over the table. People, who had passed by earlier, now became visible, as everyone stopped and stared at Joe. Their screams replaced their earlier laughter. Blood fell from everyone's eyes as their faces looked upward toward a darkening sky.

"It's okay! It's okay!"

The sun disappeared behind a total-black sky. The only light visible was the reflection in the kitchen window with the *Eiffel Tower* engulfed in bright, orange flames shooting upward to the heavens. Joe turned around in horror and saw the *Eiffel Tower* burning. The heat warmed Joe's face.

Mary screamed getting his attention. As Joe turned, her blood-filled eyes frightened him. Her nose was now only an inch away from his. Her sudden closeness weakened his knees as if they were about to buckle.

She floated upward six feet above the ground with her mouth opened larger than normal, while looking down to Joe. Complete darkness absent any teeth filled her mouth as a death-awakening scream shrilled from her. Joe's heart stopped.

"It's okay!"

Joe closed his eyes to hide the terrible sight filling his brain and ears. The screaming stopped. The crackling of the burning steel of the *Eiffel Tower* disappeared. Silence and calm returned.

A warm light washed over Joe's closed eyelids as they opened. Mary's face filled his complete field of vision. She bent over him as he lay on the red futon in their home office.

Mary was shaking Joe's shoulders and wrist. "Joe, it's okay. It's okay… it's just a bad dream."

Joe blinked his eyes fast to help re-gain his sight. "What the… Mary?"

"Joe, it's okay. You were having a terrible dream."

He propped himself up on the futon. She sat beside him.

"It felt so real. We were eating dinner outside. But, then, all of a sudden, we were in Paris… and… and… but, I thought we were here, though."

"You thought we were here?"

"Yeah, we were in our backyard, but it was in Paris. And, this waiter asked nicely if we wanted water…"

"A polite French waiter? What a nightmare, in deed," Mary said attempting a joke.

"Then, the sky turned black, and the *Eiffel Tower* was on fire… and… your eyes…"

"Ssh. There, there. It's okay. It was just a bad dream. You've not been getting any sleep, and—"

"Sleep? Shit, who can sleep with dreams like that?"

Mary rubbed his back as he placed his head down into his hands, his elbows propped up on his knees. "Yeah, I came home from teaching, and peeked in here. You were snoring so I thought you were sound asleep. I didn't want to wake you. So, I went to the kitchen and re-heated chicken for dinner and went outside because it's such a beautiful evening."

"Yeah, in the dream we were outside and we were eating chicken."

"But, the next thing I knew. You were yelling, and I thought you hurt yourself or something getting up. So, I ran in here and you were screaming, *this is it, it's the end.* You kept on screaming that… and, I tried waking you."

This is it, it's the end?

Joe lifted his head from his hands and looked at the desk. He saw his Polaroid picture and the small sheet of paper with the scribbled numbers and letters.

Oh, shit, that's right?

"Mary, I hate these dreams when you wake up and can't tell if it's real or not?"

"Oh, Honey, It was just a bad dream. It wasn't real."

If only the last week wasn't real.

"Whatever your dream was about, it's not the end…" She reached over him and opened the curtains. Bright, warm orange sunlight filled the room. "It can't be the end with a sunset like this?"

Joe rubbed his eyes blinded by the sun.

Huh, the sun must have been shining on my face through the curtains.

"Did we talk outside this morning?" Joe asked.

With a worried look, Mary replied, "Sweetie, when I left this morning, you were asleep and in the same position I found you in tonight when I came home. The last time we spoke was yesterday."

"Oh… that must have been another dream too? We were outside talking about—"

Mary interrupted him. "Joe, I'm worried about you."

He stood from the futon and peeked out the window. "It's okay. I'm just having crazy dreams because I'm not sleeping well."

"You were sound asleep this morning when I went into the kitchen. I thought for sure when I burned the eggs you'd come running in to see what had happened."

"You burned eggs?"

"Yeah, some dropped on the stove when I was cooking."

"That explains it… the smoke in my dream." Joe kissed and hugged Mary. "What about the party at Charlie and Becky's this weekend?"

"That's next month, Dear. They don't come back from their vacation until this weekend."

"Oh, uh, yeah… that's right."

Am I going crazy?

PRESENT - STONY BROOK, MORNING
SEPTEMBER 10, 2015
1,828 DAYS PRIOR TO IMPACT

FOR NINE YEARS, Dr. Joseph Bishop's office had been his sanctuary. A place where he could collect his thoughts and write his findings from his research in the adjoining lab.

His office was his refuge from the chaos of the world around him. Too many times, it also had served as a hotel room. Joe found it too easy to lose track of time due to his countless hours of peering through volumes of trade journals, thesis works, and lab results.

It was the place where Joe wrote his definitive research published in *The New England Journal of Medicine*. Since publication, various conferences had contacted Joe to present his discovery of the genetic marker miR-182 and its RNA codex, which potentially can reduce the growth of cancerous tumors. Joe felt with his discovery the purpose of his life finally was coming to fruition. He just did not realize how, until last week.

Still, it was another night without sleep. Joe had left early this morning to go to his sanctuary. On his way, he decided, today, would be the day he began the process to determine what stays and what goes to Salvation.

Joe stood at his desk shuffling through his papers. Years of memories and hard work trapped in binders and folders on his desk and bookshelves. It was a painstaking task reviewing everything without stopping to reminisce about his work. His thoughts about Salvation replaced his memories.

Mary and me... on a rocket? Living on Mars? We'll be Martians.

Sarcasm was his usual defense against stressful situations. As Joe sat behind his desk, he pulled closer a stack of papers, followed by pushing another pile off his desk into the trash beside him.

So, now I'm Mr. Important. I will be the one who develops cures for cancer and illnesses... on Mars... I can't even get funding to do that here.

He made two sections placing items he wanted to send to Salvation: a *keep* and a *maybe* pile. The trash can was home to his third choice, the obvious things not going on this fantastic journey.

Joe pulled out books and notebooks jammed with loose-leaf paper from his bookshelf. Dust rose into the air from the books, which had not moved in months.

Conference notes from April... keep.

Fantasy football stats from 2011... trash. Dammit, I should have drafted Brady first that year.

Climate studies and their impact on human genome development... keep. Anything in there about the climate on Mars, Dr. Jennings? Nope. That's why I'm going and you're not, Sucker.

Oh, shit... a Playboy.

Joe pulled the magazine from the shelf. It sat stuffed between two volumes of research material. He flipped through the pages. Naked women in various positions unfolded in front of him.

I told Charlie not to keep these around the lab. Maybe I should put this in the keep pile.

Joe stood with his back to the opened doorway. He turned to the centerfold admiring the picture, while facing the bookshelf.

"If I'm interrupting anything, I can come back later." A familiar voice came from behind him.

Joe rushed to close the magazine embarrassed like a twelve-year-old, who his dad had caught with his hidden porn stash.

"Uh, oh, it's not mine..." Joe's words escaped him. His face turned bright red. As Joe turned, Gabriel stood in the doorway wearing an expensive gray, Italian-made suit with thin navy blue pin-stripes. "Gabriel? What are you doing here?"

Joe dropped the magazine into the trash and went over to shake Gabriel's hand. "I know it's only been a few days since we last saw each other. But, I said I would check-in with you from time-to-time."

"Yeah, I know. But, I didn't think it would be so soon?"

The two men walked through Joe's cluttered office. Joe extended his hand out to the chair in front of his desk as Gabriel sat.

"I'll be honest. The reports I've been receiving... well, I wanted to come and see how you're doing?"

"Reports? What reports?"

The question came fast at Gabriel as Joe sat at his desk behind the stacks of papers he had created.

"I won't go into the details. But, like I said in Colorado, let me assure we are monitoring you. Mainly, we are confirming you are okay, and to know if you're keeping up on your end of the bargain."

"My end of the freakin' bargain. What bargain is that? The part where you tell me we're all dying except the chosen few who get to escape and live on Mars. Some bargain."

"This is my point. Our experience tells us we need to watch after those we recruit to Salvation. We've told others in the past... and, well, let's just say, for some... it's too much to process."

"Too much to process... you think?"

"I want to be completely honest with you because I can sense your hostility here. We've told others before, people respected in their fields. And, after about a week, we would learn they had killed themselves, or they would try to tell others."

Joe pushed back from his desk. The wheels on his chair squealed against the floor. "How many people have you told?"

"Like I said, I've been doing this for years, now. There are others like me who recruit people to join Salvation, also. Me, I've personally recruited a couple of hundred people, before you."

"Any other scientists like me? Will I have a team of people to work with there?"

"Already at Salvation, there are two staffers who will be your *go to* people."

"What the hell are staffers? What credentials do you need to be a staffer?"

"You can call them whatever you want. Basically, two people will be assigned to help you in your ongoing research, in your discoveries, in your whatever."

"My whatever? You mean a possible cure for cancer?" Joe held up a binder full of paper from the *keep* section of his desk.

"Yes, your potential cures. If humanity is to survive long term, they will always face a threat. Your work might lead to a solution someday... if not by you, by someone generations from now."

"Oh yeah, on the Venus colony, maybe they can help with the cure," Joe said as he slammed the binder down on his desk.

"Don't be foolish. It's too hot to survive on Venus," Gabriel said as he laughed. "So, are you doing okay? You look like you haven't slept?"

"Haven't slept is an understatement. Between my thoughts about the end of the world... living on Mars... everyone on Earth dying... sure, I sleep. And, then when I do, I have these terrible nightmares. So, yeah, I'm doing pretty freakin' great."

"That's why I'm here. We've not given you any options to talk to anyone about this. You have all these emotions and feelings trapped inside your head. So, I'm here to listen and answer questions to help. Eden really needs you. We don't want you to do anything foolish."

"Like kill myself or go running through the streets screaming *it's the end of the world?*"

"Yes," Gabriel said. His voice was cold and frank. "Exactly, that."

Joe stood from his chair and placed each hand on the highest stack of paper on his desk. "Can't you see I'm going through my stuff and getting ready for the trip?"

"Yes, and it's a great start. But, we'll need more than the documents you wish to take. We need to know the equipment and the lab requirements you will need to be successful."

"Successful? Hell, I don't even know what to expect by living on Mars. How does the body react in a different world, in a different gravity..."

"It's overwhelming, I know. It's like a crazy science-fiction movie you've found yourself in. But, trust me, there is no Bruce Willis... there isn't any last-minute heroics which will save the billions of people, here."

Joe grunted in frustration. He ran his hands through his hair, which remained out of place.

"Your task at Salvation is to continue your research hoping one day to develop cures from your work either by you or by others. This will help ensure the survival of our species beyond Earth."

Gabriel's statement hung in silence as Joe loosened his grip of the papers. Joe stared out his window. Gabriel watched Joe.

"Okay, the requirements I'll need. What limits are there?"

Gabriel stood and joined Joe at the window. "Basically, tell me what you need. Trust me, there is no budget limitation on this."

"There's always a budget limit on something, somewhere."

"Not when it concerns Project Salvation... if you only knew the real costs associated. But, seriously, contact me in a few days with your list of requirements. We'll accommodate you as best as possible."

"And, my documents?"

"Once you have everything you need to take, let me know and we'll take it from there. We'll scan everything instead of sending the actual books and papers."

"I figured as much because we're not talking about your typical office move here," Joe said. An unfamiliar smile appeared on Joe's face, something missing the last several days.

"I'm happy to see you smile." Gabriel placed his hand on Joe's shoulder. "So, how's Mary doing?"

Joe's shoulder lowered as a new thought of Mary entered his mind. "She's worried about me not sleeping. I did freak her out last night."

"Yeah, what's this about talking about *the end* with her?"

Joe turned to Gabriel. "How did you know... You son-of-a-bitch." Joe knew the answer before Gabriel could respond but wanted to restate his displeasure of being watched.

"I showed you in Colorado we are watching you."

"In my whole house... how long have you been *watching*?"

"Like I said before, you and your work have been on the Eden Foundation's radar for quite some time. I cannot get into the specifics about how long and our exact methods. But, what matters most now is going forward... how I can help you... and make sure you do your part."

"You mean, you're spying on me to make sure I don't tell anyone else?"

Gabriel placed a firm grip on Joe's shoulder and looked direct into his eyes. Gabriel's smile disappeared. "Don't kill yourself or tell anyone else. You understand me, Joseph."

Joe's eyes grew wider at Gabriel's harsh and honest response. "Well, I'll do my best at the not killing myself part." Joe laughed trying to diffuse Gabriel's terse tone.

"Am I making myself clear here?"

"But, Mary... when can I tell her?"

"I'll come back to you on that. You've known now, for what... almost a week, and look how you're dealing with the news. From our past observations, we determined you can keep this information safe... but, Mary would not."

Joe thought about what Gabriel had said. *You think I can keep this secret?*

"Hell, you're right. Mary loves to gossip too much."

"It's not that. Again, from our past experiences, we found it's best *for some* that we tell them just before they leave... and for others, like you, we can tell you months before, so you can prepare."

"This makes me think of another question... what about those you've told but refused to take part or later told someone?"

"As I mentioned last week, there is *no alternative* but to join Salvation. It is the only way."

"Yeah, but, surely there's been someone who told you, *no?*"

"That's where our observations play a huge role. We fully determine those who will fit our program and assess their willingness to join before we even approach them."

"Gabriel, look, I'm a scientist. I've performed many experiments that were supposed to be true. But, I was later disappointed in the outcome because the results did not yield what I understood to be true. So, surely, you've had one person who either refused to join or told others?"

"Please hear me, Joe, with all seriousness. There is no alternative but to join us. If anyone in the past refused or told others, let's just say Salvation does anything possible to keep its activities safe... I mean *anything.*"

Joe sensed the somberness of Gabriel's statement, which sunk into Joe's head as he realized its meaning. "What did you *do* to those who refused or told?"

"Let me repeat my words, there is no alternative but to join Salvation and we will take *all measures* to protect it."

The unspoken words became clear to Joe. He understood the seriousness of the situation. Project Salvation will do anything and everything to protect itself from the billions of people who know their fate to die in a few years. Salvation must prevent mass chaos to ensure human survival, even if this survival is on Mars.

This revelation became clear to Joe. Peace filled his mind with the fate of Earth, of Mary and himself, and why Eden had chosen him to join… as crazy as it sounds.

A few minutes of uneasy silence had filled the office. Joe stepped over to the half-emptied bookshelf and looked at Gabriel. "Okay, it's sinking in. I can read between the lines here. I understand."

Gabriel smiled.

"I'm not going to tell anyone. You can count on me for that. I'll get those requirements about the lab to you soon and contact you when I'm ready to send these documents."

Gabriel stood by the closed door. "I'm happy to see you coming around. If you need me, call me."

"Hell, I'll just talk out-loud to myself because you're spying on me anyway, right?"

Gabriel nodded and winked acknowledging *yes* to his question. "By the way, what were you watching on TV the other night in your home office?"

Even though they just spoke about the Eden Foundation watching him, Gabriel's question startled Joe. "Oh, it was nothing. I can't sleep, so I thought watching old, home movies might help."

"They must mean something to you because the report I have states you kept watching the same one? We can save those for you also and send to Salvation," Gabriel said as he exited through the doorway and down the hall.

Joe turned toward the bookshelf to finish his sorting routine. He smiled as he opened the next binder from the shelf holding it above the trash.

"Well, Miss July, at least some things at home *are* still private." The binder smacking the magazine echoed across the empty office.

15-ELI

HIGH SCHOOL GRADUATION is a special time anticipated each year. Tonight's ceremony at Bethlehem Senior High School is like the hundreds taking place across south Texas on this hot, muggy evening.

Cars stretched for miles in both directions on the small, two-lane highway in front of the school. Everyone in the community seemed to arrive for the evening's festivities. Volunteers in orange, reflective vests guided cars into the football stadium's parking lot beside the high school.

An attractive, older woman drove a faded-green Oldsmobile through the pedestrians and traffic of the two-thirds-full parking lot. Her long, brown hair flowed in the air rushing through the opened windows. In the passenger seat sat a senior wearing his dark-blue graduation gown accompanied by his smile from ear-to-ear.

An older man stood among the tall, slender east-Texas pine trees lining the perimeter of the parking lot. His gaze fixed onto the green Oldsmobile as it pulled into a parking space among the hundreds of other cars. The man stepped his way around the trees; dry pine needles crunched with each move.

At the edge of the tree line, the man lurched onto the black top of the parking lot. Heat sizzled from his feet in the late afternoon, summer sun.

The old man lumbered through the parking lot; his eyes never veered from the green car. He froze as the woman stepped out of the car.

People walked by the old man, as he stood motionless in the middle of the parking lot. They gave him a double-take as they passed. After all, the man wore a gray jacket on a ninety-five-degree day with sixty-percent-humidity.

"They *are* calling for storms tonight," a woman said to her husband as they passed the old man, who stalked the attractive older woman like a lion on the plains of the Serengeti.

His attention never left her. He was careful not to get any closer than a few cars away. His eyes peeked over the top of the parked cars as the older woman approached the young graduate who earlier had jumped out of the car.

The old man heard the senior and his friend yell "Graduation!" as the woman he had followed snapped a picture and kissed the senior on his cheek. The woman left toward the stadium; the old man followed.

The old man saw the senior run after the woman grabbing her shoulder and spinning her around to give her a huge bear hug. The senior whispered something in her ear as she pulled back and kissed him, again.

This happy scene repeated many times across the parking lot. But, it was this family, which had gained the old man's full attention. The old man stood close behind them and heard the woman's response to the senior. "It was all I could do. I did it all for Rachel, and I am so very proud of you."

This response brought a soft smile to the old man's wrinkled face. A jagged scar ran across his left cheek across to his right eye stopping at his right temple. A stoic face soon returned as the old man looked behind him. Paranoia consumed the old man as if someone was watching him… was watching this same family.

The old man regained his composure realizing he was safe. Turning back to his prey, the old man lost sight of the family.

The sun showed mercy by setting behind the tall, pine trees along the horizon. Beads of sweat ran down his scar as an escape route from the heat building underneath his black New York Yankees hat.

"Would you like a program?" a young girl said wearing a white dress standing at the stadium entrance.

The old man pushed her hand away and released a faint grunt under his breath as he passed her. Once inside, to his relief, the old man found the familiar sight of the attractive older woman's flowing, brown hair.

He followed as she entered the stands at the fifty-yard line. She stopped beside a seated, balding man. His potbelly resting on his lap flattened when he stood to greet her.

The old man remained stationary, a safe distance away. Rage brewed within him as the balding man hugged the woman. The repeated grunt came from under the old man's breath, again.

Throngs of people filed into the stadium to find a seat. The old man remained motionless on the pathway from the concession area to the stadium seats. He looked like a small tree standing in a stream as water rushed around him.

Time had passed. Stadium lights replaced the blaring sun. Moths, the size of grapefruit, darted around the lights dancing to the music of the marching band.

The breeze, which had blown earlier, stopped. Oppressive humidity swamped the stadium. Flashes from cameras throughout the stands matched the flashes of lightning along the horizon.

More time had passed. Everyone had taken their seats. People jockeyed to take the perfect pictures of the ceremony. The old man stood in the same position. His gaze froze on the brown-haired woman sitting beside a balding, heavy-set man.

At an instant, the mood of the sweltering crowd changed. An excitement arose throughout the stadium as the graduation march played from the band. Everyone cheered snapping the old man out of his trance. He turned and saw the hundred graduating seniors march onto the track around the football field.

A soft smile returned to the old man. This time, the smile never left as the graduates took their seats before the stands.

The music stopped. The crowd released one last roar, which came rolling down to the stage where the principal welcomed everyone. After the speeches and a song sung by one of the female graduates, the principal retook the podium.

"It is now time to present the graduating class of 1997 with their diplomas."

This statement signaled the old man as he unzipped and reached inside his jacket. The old man pulled out a rectangular piece of metal with light-brown, faux-wood on its top.

He zipped up his jacket and pulled up on a small, square knob on the wood grain surface. The rectangular metal propped-open revealing an old Polaroid camera. The old man stepped down the side of the stands in the shadows and onto the field.

The crowd was behind the old man, and the seated graduates were to his right. The old man stood near the steps where the graduates were coming down from the stage to go back to their seats.

Camera flashes flickered all around the old man creating a strobe-light effect. His head turned side-to-side attempting to shake his triggered paranoia caused by the lights.

The principal said, "Joseph Jacob Bishop." The old man lifted his head. He felt his shoulders swell and his chest expand as his attention went to the same senior he had followed since arriving in the parking lot. A large smile replaced the soft one from earlier. Gone were all the old man's teeth.

The old man watched as the graduate walked across to the principal and shook her hand taking his diploma. The Polaroid camera blocked the old man's eyes with his toothless smile visible underneath the camera.

Flashes from other cameras bounced off the old man as he stepped in front of the graduate walking down the steps from the stage. With the graduate about five feet from him, the old man pressed the red button on the Polaroid camera. The picture slid out the front.

"Hey, Jacob!" one of the other seated graduates yelled to the graduate coming down the steps making fun of his middle name. To the older man, hearing this name sent a cold chill over his body. A frightened expression overcame him as the old man turned his head side-to-side as fast as he could. The old man was visibly upset.

A fellow cameraman bumped the old man causing him to turn and run from the field into the shadows cast by the stage. The old man ran away so fast he did not notice the Polaroid picture had fallen from his hand.

Brown, parched grass supported the small, square piece of plastic. The white side of the picture faced up to the sky. Camera flashes and an ever-growing flickering of lightning filled the sky.

People kicked the small picture a few times, but it never turned over. The white side grew dim fading away releasing like magic a familiar sight. A happy graduate with his diploma in-hand appeared as the image stared toward the sky.

More minutes had passed. The picture witnessed a rainstorm of falling blue, graduation caps. In one sudden motion, someone rescued the picture from being trampled or ruined by the brewing storm.

Now safe, the image looked at the face of the attractive, older woman with brown hair, whom the old man earlier had followed. Her face frozen as she searched for picture's lost owner. The old man was nowhere in sight. Darkness engulfed the picture as it disappeared into the safety of her purse.

Eighteen years later, the picture sat safe on the corner of a desk staring at an older version of the graduate. His jaw opened as he searched the picture for answers.

THANKSGIVING DAY, 1997
PASADENA, TEXAS

THE BISHOP FAMILY had experienced too much suffering by unfortunate deaths throughout the years. Liz always had attempted to make the year-end holidays as festive as possible. But, this year was a first for her. Joseph would not be home for Thanksgiving, as he was seventeen-hundred-miles away.

Three months had passed since Joseph and Mary had left their home in the Houston suburbs. The University of Stony Brook on Long Island may as well had been in a foreign country. Given the distance, Joseph and Mary had planned to come home once his freshman year at Christmas.

This decision was difficult for them, especially for Liz. Thanksgiving held a terrible anniversary for the family, one, which changed their lives forever.

Twenty-two years earlier, in 1975, Liz had prepared her first, large Thanksgiving dinner, since Eli had taken the week off from his work at NASA. The turkey had cooked overnight filling the house with a savory smell. Steam rose from the buttery mashed potatoes.

As Liz placed the bread rolls in the oven, she set out the drinks and glasses, realizing they were out of ice. With the convenience store only a block away, Eli offered to walk there hoping they were not sold-out. Their son Jacob would have gone, but he was recovering from the flu.

Three hours had passed. A thunderous knock came from the front of the house. Liz's heart raced to the pit of her stomach as she opened the door with two policemen on her front stoop.

They delivered grim news about Eli. As he was paying for the ice, two masked robbers entered the Quick Stop holding him and the store clerk at gunpoint. The police said an altercation had occurred with one robber shooting both the clerk and Eli in the head.

The hardest part for Liz was not being able to say goodbye to Eli. Damage to his face was too brutal; they held a closed-casket service the following Wednesday.

Jacob, then fifteen, would beat himself up for not feeling well that day or he would have gone to the store. Jacob had believed the outcome on that fateful afternoon would have been much different, and his dad would still be alive. Jacob had carried his guilt until his untimely death by a drunk-driver ten years later before Joseph's birth in 1979.

Thanksgivings were therefore a difficult time for the family. Through determination, Joseph's grandma had reinforced the true meaning of the holiday, to be thankful for what you have. This year, rather than celebrate alone, Liz volunteered with her church to help at the local homeless shelter.

If I can't have family here this year, then I can at least help others.

"Good morning. Happy Thanksgiving, Liz," Bob Warner said. He rushed to Liz taking her tray of cookies she held.

"Thanks, Bob," Liz said delighted to see familiar faces. "Happy Thanksgiving to you, too. Have you spoken to Mary this morning?"

"Oh… uh, yeah, sure. I called her this morning to wish her a happy Thanksgiving." Bob walked away from her carrying the cookies into the kitchen through swinging double-doors.

"Why, there's a gorgeous sight, happy Thanksgiving, Liz," James Unger said pushing by Bob. James hugged and kissed Liz on her cheek, which lingered a little too long for her comfort.

"Now, now, Jim, you let Liz go now you hear. I swear one of these days, she's going to slap you," her best friend Martha said. Martha grabbed her husband by his shoulder in a playful manner. "Hey, Sugar, happy Thanksgiving. Come *here* and hug my neck."

The two ladies had been friends through church as long as either could remember. They hugged in the entrance as a steady stream of haggard-looking men walked inside passing them.

"How are you holding up, Sugar?" Martha asked knowing how hard today must be for her.

"Oh, I am great. The Lord has blessed us with a beautiful day, and we're here to do his work."

"Amen, Sister… Okay, we're set-up in the back to prepare the food," Martha said. She took Liz by the hand through the double-doors into the kitchen.

"Yum, look at *that sight*. Now, that's what I'm thankful for, today," James said as the two women walked away from him in the shelter's entryway.

"Jim, hush now, I heard that," Martha said turning and giving him a stern stare.

Martha leaned and whispered into Liz's ear. "Shh, let's not let Bob use the stove. I think he's already been drinking this morning."

Yeah, you called Mary this morning, you bastard.

"Okay, what do you want me to do?"

"Sure. It's simple. We mainly heat the food and place it in *these* aluminum pans. When it's time to serve, we set everything out and give the guys what they want."

"When do we start serving?"

"We always start at noon. This gives everyone time to eat, and us time to clean up. After that, everyone is welcome to watch the Oilers game in the Rec Room."

"Don't you mean the Cowboys? I'm not a big football fan, but I at least know that much."

"I'll tell you what, them Cowboys better kick their ass," James said as he entered the kitchen.

"Jim! Language!" Martha said.

"Sorry, Honey. But, that son-of-a-bitch, Adams, took our Oilers up to Tennessee… first time ever I'm pulling for Dallas," James said. He lifted the plastic wrap off of the plate of cookies. "*These* are delicious, Liz."

"Jim, you couldn't handle *my cookies*," Liz said as she and Martha laughed together at him.

The next hour had passed. Clanging pans echoed through the kitchen. Wonderful aromas of turkey and ham with all kinds of sides hovered into the dining area.

The men who had come today took seats at the folding tables set-up outside the kitchen. The number of homeless men who had frequented each year seemed to increase closer to the holidays.

Nearby manufacturing companies tend to cut positions this time of year to make their annual numbers. This creates a negative effect on the local community. Several people who were already living paycheck-to-paycheck had found themselves with little-to-no money for Thanksgiving.

New faces appeared this year in the crowd. The most unsettling sight for Liz was seeing a woman with a baby, who had entered the shelter. This problem in southeast Houston no longer had seemed to impact just men.

"Doesn't that break your heart, Sugar?" Martha asked.

"Have you seen her before?" Liz asked.

"This is the first time I've seen anyone but men here in all my years. She was here yesterday. I tried speaking with her, but she doesn't speak any English."

"Oh, bless her heart. I'll be right back," Liz said as she walked to the woman with her small baby.

Liz welcomed her and told her 'Happy Thanksgiving' in Spanish. The woman continued with her frown until Liz asked her in Spanish if she needed anything.

A smile chased away the frown on the woman. "Oh, *gracias*. Thank you." The woman continued speaking to Liz in Spanish, as Liz placed her hand on top of the baby's head before walking back to the kitchen.

"She doing okay, Sugar?" Martha asked Liz when she returned.

Liz opened the refrigerator pulling out a jug of milk and poured it inside a bottle the woman had handed her. "She's okay. She just needs milk for the baby."

"When did you learn to speak Spanish?"

"I've been taking lessons over at the community college. We're getting more students in our classes from Mexico. And, I find it easier when I'm teaching to help them in their language."

Liz warmed the milk by running warm water over the bottle in the sink. After a few minutes, she tested the warmth of the milk by squirting a few drops on her wrist.

Liz gave the full bottle back to the woman. The baby drank, and the woman looked up to Liz from her seat. Small tears formed in the corners of the woman's eyes. Liz melted with emotion as she bent down to hug and comfort the woman.

The team of volunteers assembled the food onto the outstretched tables forming a buffet line. At noon, Minister Greene had arrived in time to lead everyone in prayer before dinner.

A record number, one hundred thirty-two people, formed a line to wait their turn. The volunteers served everyone. Liz's duty was to serve turkey stuffing to each outstretched, white paper plate presented.

Joy and happiness filled the shelter for the afternoon. This masked the pain and sorrow many had felt. Everyone ate and enjoyed the fellowship.

As the last pieces of pumpkin pie vanished, everyone stumbled into the adjoining recreation room fighting off their pending food comas. The big football game between the Oilers and the Cowboys was about to start. The room was split with their emotions around their once beloved Oilers.

The game had started. Cheers and jeers roared into the kitchen as the volunteers began the daunting task of cleaning. Bob, now feeling hung over from his morning bender, washed dishes with James. Martha and Liz were on trash duty.

"Liz, I've been volunteering here for many years, and this is the worst part of it," Martha said as she stacked empty food trays to take to the kitchen.

"Well, at least all the food is eaten and nothing's gone to waste."

"At my house, we're eating leftovers for days, and still throw out so much food," Martha said, as she left for the kitchen. "Would you go around the tables and get any trash that may be there?"

"No problem," Liz said as she pulled a large black trash bag across the sticky floor. She shook the bag. Air rushed inside creating a loud plastic-popping noise as it opened.

Looks like my house after one of Joseph's parties.

Liz walked between the tables placing used napkins, paper cups, and dishes inside the bag. More cheers came from the Rec Room, as the Cowboys scored a touchdown.

On the last table in the back of the room, farthest away from the buffet table, Liz found one last empty plate. She picked it up and placed it inside the bag. As the plate fell into smelly darkness, Liz saw handwritten numbers and letters on its underside. Curious, she reached in and pulled the plate back out of the bag.

Bits of turkey stuffing and mashed potatoes fell from the plate to the floor. Liz smeared a brown grease stain on the back of the plate to get a clear view.

What's this? It looks familiar?

As fast as the questions entered her mind is as fast as Liz dropped the plate back into the bag. She used a dishtowel clipped to her waist to bend down and clean the food particles, which had fallen on the floor.

No? It can't be?

While crouched on the floor, she pulled the paper plate again back out of the bag. Liz pulled herself up to the chair next to her at the table.

This looks like the game that Eli and I used to play. It can't be, because I remember we made it up as we went along.

"Hey, Sugar, no sitting on the job," Martha said walking over to Liz. "Oh, just kidding. I need a break, too."

Martha sat across from her. Liz slid the plate to Martha with the letters and numbers showing. "Do you notice anything about this?"

"Yeah, they're super thin. We had hoped to get those thicker ones, but we didn't want to turn down the donation."

"No, I mean *look*—"

Before Liz had finished, a roar rushed out of the Rec Room toward them as the Oilers scored a matching touchdown. The screams caused Martha to stand and run away to see the replay.

Liz carried the paper plate by her waist as she followed Martha. The room seemed split down the middle. The remaining loyalist Oilers' fans sat on one side, and Cowboys' fans on the other.

Who could have written this? I can't remember who sat at that table.

Liz scanned across the room for any familiar face. Martha motioned for Liz to join her in an empty seat in the back. Liz joined watching the rest of the game with about sixty, remaining people.

As the Cowboys scored the next touchdown to go up by seven, Liz's attention was on the letter and number scramble written on the thin, white paper plate with a small grease stain.

How did we used to solve this?

"Touchdown!" came the shouts from the Oilers' side of the room to tie the game.

I... I can't think with all this noise.

"Excuse me, Martha, I'll be back in a few minutes."

"Okay, but hurry up, the Oilers are getting ready to score, again."

As Liz stood and walked out of the room, a ruckus erupted as Martha's prediction came true. Liz slipped out a pencil from her hanging coat pocket and sat at a nearby table.

The back of the plate stumped her. It appeared to be a random pattern of letters and numbers, which read:

K	N	Q	T	W	
Z	3	6	9	12	J
15	18	21	24	A	3
D	G	J	M	P	
S	V	Y	2	5	

2.4, 3.5 4.4, 3.5 2.5 2.4 5.2 5.5

She racked her brain studying the pattern. Her left elbow rested on the table and her left pinky was stuck inside the corner of her mouth. In her right hand, she held the pencil tapping the eraser-end on the table.

"Touchdown!"

Liz recognized Martha's high-pitched scream from the crowd. The Oilers had scored again.

I'm going crazy. I remember Eli would give me these puzzles to solve and I would send the answer back to him. Heck, but that was so long, ago.

As the distance of the years came to her mind, Liz looked from the table toward the ceiling in disgust.

Dammit, it's this stupid anniversary. It's making me see things that can't be.

Her curiosity disappeared as fast as the Cowboys' lead based on the group's reaction in the other room. The Oilers had kicked a field goal to go up 27 to 14.

Okay, if this is even real, let's see... The letter 'J' on the side starts the matrix. So, the first letter would be the next letter in the alphabet, K.

Liz studied the matrix. Her memories with Eli helped her.

Then, this number 3, below the J, is what I count to get the next letter. It would be L, M, and then N.

The rules of their puzzle game flew back to Liz. So far, it worked correctly by explaining the letters K and N she saw on the first row. This realization snapped her out of her pity state, which had developed earlier.

So, I repeat this logic and fill in the first row by counting 3 letters away from N. This is the letter Q, next would T, and then W.

Liz sat in amazement. Her logic matched the first row of the handwritten matrix.

How can this be? I thought Eli and me were the only ones that played this code game. I used to think this was a stupid game he made me play.

Memories of her husband, Eli, flooded her.

This stupid game paid off, though. I remember we used to send these messages back-and-forth as we watched TV with Jacob in the room. He didn't even know we were talking about getting him his Evel Knievel bike for Christmas.

Liz smiled with the memory. In an instant, her pencil's eraser tapping fell quiet. Liz shot up in her chair studying the rest of the matrix.

She wanted to believe this had to be the same type of coded message. But, who could have known how they played this game? Who wrote this message? And, most important to Liz, what did this message say?

Okay, so if this is real, then I start with the next row and a Z. Check. Next, I use numbers counting by 3 like with the letters until I get to 26, and then start over with letters.

So, the rest of the row is 3 6 9 12. The third row... 15 18 21 24 A...

Liz saw how her logic matched the letters and numbers written on the back of the paper plate.

There's no way this can be a coincidence.

She was ready to take the next step in deciphering the matrix. However, with the game being over, the group of people filed out of the Rec Room passing her seated at the table outside the doorway.

"Sugar, you missed the game. Our Oilers, uh, I mean Tennessee won," Martha said as she sat down beside Liz. "What are you doing?"

"Uh, um. Just thinking about Eli, a little. He loved the Oilers." Liz did not want to share with her this strange set of letters and numbers she had found. Liz looked up at the faces of the people filing out.

Maybe someone will see me with this and give me a reaction?

Disappointed no one looked at her, Liz noticed how each face changed from smiling to a blank stare as each person headed to the front door. "Oh, this is so sad, Martha."

"I know, Sugar. But, at least we brought some happiness for them today." Martha stood from the table and grabbed the paper plate in front of Liz. "Here let me get *that* for you."

Liz slammed her hand down on top of the plate. "Uh, that's okay. I got it."

"Just trying to help… Okay, I'll be in the kitchen once your pity party is over, Sugar." Martha always knew Liz sometimes needed tough love to push her along.

Liz stood holding the paper plate by her side. "Uh, I'm not feeling well." Liz faked rubbing her forehead. "I'm going home if that's okay?"

"Sure. I didn't mean to—"

"Oh, not that. I'm fine. All this food and noise is giving me a migraine," Liz said as she took her jacket off the hanger.

"Do you need Jim to take you home?"

"No, I'm good. I can make it okay. I'll call you, tomorrow," Liz said as she hurried toward the door to leave.

"Well, call me tonight if you need anything," Martha said in a loud voice as Liz opened the door and walked out.

Liz followed the last in the group to leave closing the door behind her. Her face beamed as a smile appeared.

Only Eli knew about this puzzle.

Thoughts of a happier time consumed her as she walked home.

16-THE CODE

FOR THE PAST WEEK, Joe had walked through life in a haze. The information he had learned was too surreal. His lack of sleep had taken its toll.

But, Joe felt something new this evening. Real clarity existed. Gabriel's talk today had helped motivate Joe, which had been absent. Joe turned on the lights inside his home office and repeated his earlier method of sorting documents. The journals on this bookshelf had even a thicker layer of dust than those in his lab.

The reports Gabriel received said I ain't been doing well... no shit, how does one take the news that a planet will destroy every—

A large, yellow book fell from the bookshelf interrupting his thoughts. *Son-of-a-bitch.*

He bent down to pick up the fallen book, flipped through its pages, and threw it into the nearby trash can.

Gabriel's worried I will kill myself or tell someone... please... no one would believe me anyway... hell, I barely believe it myself.

Minutes had passed. After clearing the bookshelf, he looked under their red futon. This area was their hiding place to keep things out of sight keeping the room tidy.

The box of memories from Texas sat unopened since their move earlier this year. He wanted to review everything, so he ripped open the packing tape and pulled out one of the photo albums.

I'm not sentimental or anything, but I don't want to throw these away. Surely, they can scan these, too.

The photo album pages crinkled as he flipped through one memory after another, a simpler time. Joe reached back into the box and pulled out his grandmother's scrapbook. Old report cards, his achievement certificates, his many science project first-place ribbons, and various childhood crafts poured from the dusty book.

She really kept all this stuff? Can they even scan this stuff?

His macaroni necklace taped to a page amused him. Joe remembered Mary making fun of it when the box first arrived years ago from Texas. *Damn, has it really been eleven years since Grandma died?*

Joe had opened it only the one time when he received the box. He had failed to notice the date of *March 1986* scribbled on the upper-right corner of the page. He rubbed his fingers across the handwritten date.

1986? This isn't Grandma's, this is Mama's scrapbook... this must be her handwriting.

A smile erupted on his face below his bloodshot eyes. With each turn, he rubbed his fingers across his Mama's dated pages: *June 1986, November 1987, and July 4, 1989.*

On the next page, the handwriting changed for *December 1989*. Gone were the elegant curves of the letters. In their place were handwritten, straight lines.

Oh, wow... Grandma kept up with this book after Mama died?

His eyes darted away from the pages. Painful memories flooded him.

It must have been so hard for Grandma. But, she was always there for me, that's for sure.

Joe turned the brown, construction-paper pages. Happy memories chased his sadness away. Joe remembered his grandma's facial expressions when he would bring her things from school. Never asking what she did with them, Joe now realized where she hid her treasures.

In the next pages, Joe found his high school graduation program, his college orientation notice, and a letter he had written to her his first week at Stony Brook.

Oh, I remember this... I felt so guilty leaving her and wanted to tell her how much I missed her.

On the last page, his grandma had written, *Thanksgiving Day 1997*. The only item there was a small picture of Grandpa Eli.

She must have been missing him on this anniversary?

Joe turned the page and reached the end of the scrapbook. Written by his grandma on the bottom of the book's cardboard backing was, *Our Story Continues in the Next Book.*

Joe immediately threw open the flaps of the box. A noticeable sigh escaped him.

Empty... She must have started another one? Maybe, Mary's seen it?

He stood and placed the photo album in the keep pile on his desk. *What do I do with this?* He held the scrapbook over the trash can. *Hell, I can't throw this away. I'll ask them to scan it or take pictures of everything.*

Joe sat the scrapbook down in the *keep* area; its bulging pages prevented it from closing properly. The weight of the book caused an avalanche of papers to slide across the desk. His graduation picture was no match for the onslaught as it fell.

Last night's discovery of the mysterious paper fell to the floor from under the fallen picture frame. As Joe picked up the frame, the paper recaptured his imagination.

What the hell? This has to mean something for Grandma to tape it under the desk, out of sight. Shit, not to mention her cryptic note in the Will?

No matter how much Joe persuaded his mind with the numbers and letters, they kept their secret safe. Before Joe could finish with the files in his desk, he heard keys rattling outside the front door.

"Honey, I'm home... where are you?"

"In the office."

Mary stood in the doorway of their home office. "Have I got news for you."

She entered the room and kissed him on the top of his head. Mary seemed to bounce as she walked by him to sit on the red futon. "So, at the planning meeting tonight... guess who will be the new chairperson for our branch of the teacher's union?"

As Joe opened his mouth to answer, Mary interrupted him. "Me, that's who. What this means is now, I can go to Albany and talk to the administration about improving the funding for our school."

"That's... that's great, Mary. Where is the other scrapbook from my Grandma?"

In disbelief, Mary stood. Her face turned red as she released a noticeable huff. Heavy pounding footsteps replaced her once light entry into the room. A few seconds later Joe heard the refrigerator door slam shut. Mary came back to the office doorway. She held one earring as she worked to remove the other.

"Joseph, can you not at least be happy for me? I come home with what I think is great news, and you just sit there, and—"

"I'm sorry, Sweetie," Joe said trying to diffuse the situation. Anytime she called him *Joseph* he was in trouble.

"Sorry. You're always sorry, Joseph. How about ask me questions about the news I just told you?"

"Okay... so how often do you get to go to Albany?"

"Dammit, Joseph that's not even the point. The point is now I can voice the changes I see that need to happen at our school."

"Oh, uh, I just mentioned Alb—"

"Well, you did at least listen enough to hear *that part* I guess," she said sarcastically. "There are two meetings a year there..."

Mary stopped to concentrate to finish removing her last earring. "If you don't mind, I may need your help to listen to me as I practice any speech I may need to give."

"Sure, I'll be happy to."

She stepped back over to him and kissed him again. "Joe, sorry I snapped. I've had a long day... I don't know how you put in those long hours every day at the lab."

Joe sensed Mary was no longer upset. "Because it's me and my work. I don't have students coming to me throughout the day, like you do, draining all my energy."

She disappeared from his view for a few moments as she walked back into the kitchen. Water ran for a few seconds and stopped. She returned in the doorway holding a glass of water.

"Okay, love you. I'm going upstairs to bed, now."

"Love you, too."

The wooden steps released a moan with each of her steps. The creaking stopped too soon.

From halfway up the stairs, Mary shouted, "Joe, there is no other scrapbook. Remember... that was the night we came home and thought someone had broken into our apartment."

That was so long, ago.

"That's the day that box came from your grandma. And, remember I had thought there were two scrapbooks, but there was only one."

Joe looked at the scrapbook sitting in the *keep* area. He heard Mary laugh.

"Maybe that's what was stolen?"

The creaking returned with her sarcastic laugh as she continued upstairs to their bedroom.

"Okay, thanks," Joe shouted back to Mary.

Well, one book it is. She must have not started another one, I guess?

Joe heard the bedroom door close. He sat alone in the office with his thoughts staring at the book and holding his discovery from last night. Joe unfolded the paper. His gaze captured again by the numbers and letters with its tantalizing mystery.

There are twenty-five letters and numbers on this paper. There are twenty-six letters in the alphabet... It couldn't be as simple as replacing the number with it matching letter, can it?

Joe pulled out a blank sheet of white paper, which sat under the scrapbook. With a nearby pen, he recreated the same pattern of numbers and letters on the paper.

The first row is all letters K N Q T W, but the second row is both Z 3 6 9 12... out of curiosity... if I change the 3 to the letter C... the 6 to F... 9 to I... and 12 to L.

He had reproduced two rows of letters: $K N Q T W$ and $Z C F I L$.

Great, so that doesn't help? Screw it. I will finish the rest of this matrix the same way.

He replaced the remaining numbers with their corresponding letters of the alphabet. His new third row was $O R U X A$. The fourth row was $D G J M P$. And, the fifth row was $S V Y B E$.

Well, that solves it, Sherlock. Now, there are no numbers, only letters... the only letter missing is an H.

A heavy sigh of frustration left him. Joe slammed his pencil on the paper and went into the kitchen for coffee.

Why can't I break this code?

The aroma of fresh coffee filled the kitchen. Hot water percolated from the single-serve coffee pot. Joe sipped on the hot coffee, but before he could finish his caffeine fix, he sat the cup in the sink. Hot coffee shot over the cup's edge onto his hand.

That's it... It's a code.

Joe ran back into the office. His stare took turns between the original grease-stained paper and his reproduction.

The letters are arranged in a pattern. If I wanted to spell out words, I could reference the column and the row number... it can't be that simple, can it?

The chair groaned as he leaned in the seat, his hands pushing his hair off his forehead.

Let's assume this is true... this means this is a code key.

Joe paused his thoughts and stared at the ceiling.

The truth is in the desk? That's what Grandma told me and I've been racking my brain for years over that.

He looked again at his new listing of letters:

K	N	Q	T	W
Z	C	F	I	L
O	R	U	X	A
D	G	J	M	P
S	V	Y	B	E

If this is a code key, then what's the message... the truth, about what?

PRESENT - STONY BROOK, 7:11 P.M.
SEPTEMBER 11, 2015
1,827 DAYS PRIOR TO IMPACT

DAYS OF NOT SLEEPING finally took their toll on Joe. Friday night after dinner, Mary had found Joe passed out, face-down on his unmade side of their queen-sized bed.

Mary woke the next morning. Joe lay motionless in the same position as the night before. Worried, she held her hand near his nose. Not satisfied, she bent over and placed her ear over his nose. A gentle breath released through his nostrils. Relief overcame her.

Poor baby.

She tried to be silent during the day, checking in on him every now-and-again. Each time she peaked inside the bedroom, he was sleeping in a different position. It became a game to her. Once he slept on his back, the next curled up in a fetal position.

Saturday turned into Saturday night. Joe still did not wake. As Sunday morning arose, Mary rolled over facing Joe. His chest moved up-and-down with each breath.

Maybe I should wake him... He's so tired. I should let him sleep... Maybe something is wrong with him... No, he's fine.

PRESENT - STONY BROOK, 12:15 A.M.
SEPTEMBER 14, 2015
1,824 DAYS PRIOR TO IMPACT

AS DIFFICULT AS IT WAS, Mary let Joe sleep. And, a restful sleep he had. By the time Joe awoke, it was after midnight. He was aware it was late because Mary was fast asleep beside him. The only light shining into the room came from the streetlights.

Wow, I finally slept… I wonder what time it is? I'm going to guess it's three?

Joe lifted his head above the pillow stuffed beside him blocking his view of the nightstand. His alarm clock with its bright-green numbers stared back to reveal it was only a little after midnight.

I only slept a few hours… but, I feel so… so rested.

Joe lay flat on his back staring up at the ceiling, his mind empty of thought. Gone were the horror stories of his imagination, of the events in-store for everyone left on Earth. His stress had left since he had completed going through all his documents and files at work. Gone, it seemed, were all his cares in the world as a sense of peace and acceptance of their fate overcame him.

Joe opened and closed his eyes slower each time. One last time his eyes opened before coming to a final close. His breathing slowed.

With a sudden motion, Joe jolted his eyes open as if someone had pressed a stickpin into the bottom of his bare feet. He turned his head again. His alarm clock teased him with the date in smaller letters below the time.

What the hell… it's Monday?

Joe sat spinning himself around on the bed. His feet landed on the cold, hardwood floor.

I've slept the whole weekend?

Not wanting to wake Mary, he tip-toed out of the bedroom. He made sure not to land his entire weight with each step to leave as quiet as possible.

"I cannot believe I've slept this long?" Joe said as he walked into the kitchen, again checking his cell phone for the correct time and date.

Well, hell, I've not slept in over a week… Man, I'm hungry.

The smell of leftover pepperoni and mushroom pizza rushed over him as he opened the refrigerator. He popped two cold slices into the microwave.

No wonder I'm hungry, I've slept for what… two-and-a-half days.

Joe waited in front of the microwave for his dinner, lunch, breakfast... food. The time counted down increasing his anticipation of enjoying the melting mozzarella.

In a dark room in a half-empty office building on the upper-east side of Manhattan, the Monitor assigned, tonight, recorded her observations of Joe. All notes are time-stamped. A long, blank space in the log appeared before the new entry about Joe waking at midnight and eating pizza.

On the Monitor's screen, Joe went into his home office and sat down at the desk to eat his pizza. In one hand, Joe held a slice of New York's Best Pizza, and in the other his computer mouse.

I've probably got a ton of emails to go through. Charlie may have sent me pictures of their trip to Myrtle Beach.

He took another bite of his pizza as the computer screen illuminated in front of him. The desktop picture of Mary walking along the beach appeared.

Subject is accessing his email account, the Monitor typed.

The Monitor looked at her split screen. On the left side was the video feed from inside his home office. And, on the right was the email Joe was accessing in real-time on his computer.

Damn, I must be like Rip Van Winkle as long as I slept... Jeez, one-hundred-plus emails.

The Monitor reviewed Joe's emails as they opened on the right side of her screen. Most Joe opened were from financial companies and school.

Here's one from the credit card company... guess, I don't have to worry 'bout paying that son-of-a-bitch, ever again?

Joe read his emails deleting those obvious as spam. *Make your penis two inches larger? Delete. For God's sake, we better not have spam where I'm going? Ah, here's one... find singles in your area. Delete... Looks like no emails from Charlie, yet.*

The Monitor recorded her log entry. *Subject reading emails and finished eating.*

Joe scrolled to the bottom of his inbox. *I get all this spam email and I never look at it?*

He paused at the last email in his inbox. His cursor moved over the 'X' to delete it, but a mouse click never occurred.

Another spam… let's see what it says.

Joe clicked on the email with its listed subject: *IMPORTANT INFO.*

Ooh, it must be real important… it's in all caps. Joe's well-rested thoughts remained sarcastic.

The email opened. Pictures appeared on the screen. Joe scrolled down. Several pictures were in the email: President John F. Kennedy, Princess Diana, and the Murrah Building after it was bombed in Oklahoma City.

What the heck?

Joe was about to close the email, but the urge to continue scrolling tempted him. The images continued. Scenes came of riots in Los Angeles, groups of starving children in Africa, a screenshot of the Dow Jones ticker from the 2007 market collapse, and the Waco, Texas complex fire.

This is a strange grouping of pictures?

Pictures continued of a hypodermic needle with the letters *AIDS* across the top of it followed by another needle with *H1N1*.

The last image was one of a shadowy plane crashing into the World Trade Center. Joe stopped scrolling. The hair on his neck stood straight up as he and Mary always believed it could have been them on that plane.

Joe continued scrolling. No new pictures were present. As he was about to close the email, the top of a row of numbers appeared. He scrolled down further. A string of numbers came into view: *5.1 3.5 2.5 5.2 3.5 1.4 2.4 3.1 1.2.*

Huh? Um… okay?

His right index finger spasmed as he scrolled the cursor back to the top.

Who sent this email? Who is friend@xmail.com? … Delete.

The split screen on the Monitor's computer still showed Joe sitting at the desk. On the right side was Joe's email program closing in real-time. Joe's desktop image appeared on her screen as his computer shutdown.

The Monitor typed her last entry into her log: *@12:56 a.m. — email received with pictures and a row of numbers from friend@xmail.com.*

As Joe's computer closed, the Monitor's split screen resumed to a full screen. The video feed showed Joe walk out of his home office turning out the lights.

She watched him enter the living-room and sit on the sofa. *Subject is watching television. Nothing new to report. Send alert about receiving email from friend@xmail to Command.*

9:35 A.M.

INSIDE HIS OFFICE at Stonehaven, Joe sat in darkness with his blinds drawn shut. Peeks of morning sunlight poked through the metal, horizontal blades of the blinds.

Stacked boxes full of years' worth of work sat high on his desk, on the floor, and on the small black sofa in his office. His desk chair creaked as he reclined back and placed his feet on top of his desk. A cascade of papers fell to the floor when his black sneakers hit the side of a box.

"Shit!"

He placed his feet on the floor. His desk chair released a loud creak as it straightened itself when he bent forward to pick up the fallen papers.

"Jeez, a brother leaves for a week and you're leaving? That must have been one hell of a conference you went to?"

Charlie's familiar voice came booming into his office. Joe lifted his head from the side of the desk. The sight of his best friend brought Joe relief.

"Charlie, how the hell was your trip to Myrtle Beach?"

"Man, it was great. Becky and the twins had a wonderful time." Charlie stepped through the obstacle course to sit on Joe's sofa. "Uh, seriously, Man. You going somewhere?"

"Uh… um… uh, no. I just got tired of looking at all this stuff in here, you know?"

"Dude, it looks like you're getting rid of everything?"

Joe looked around his office in agreement. "I am sending *all these* to my house. That way my office will be empty and I can have it cleaned."

"Yeah, I've been meaning to tell you it smells like shit in here." Charlie released a laugh, which bellowed down the hallway matching his deep voice. "Why not just move this stuff into the empty office next door and then clean your office?"

"Ah, see, Charlie. That's why I missed ya, Pal. Nah, I thought about that, but this will let me spend a little more time at home working instead of all my time, here."

"Don't say no more. Mary's giving you a hard time about working too much, again."

"Uh, no... uh," he paused realizing this sounded like a better reason, "yeah, she's been bustin' my balls lately."

Charlie stood and walked into their shared lab across the hall. "What you guys need is to go on a vacation." He returned into Joe's doorway, again. "You two need to get away and spend *quality time* together... our vacation was just what we needed."

Dude, you don't even know what kind of trip we are getting ready to go on.

"Um... yeah, a trip... we'll look into that."

Charlie smiled as he turned to go back to the lab. He yelled from across the hall. "Hey, I can't wait to hear about your trip to Colorado and your presentation. Maybe you can catch me up over lunch, today?"

"Sure thing," Joe yelled back.

Joe's words held hostage his recent sense of happiness seeing his friend again. An overpowering feeling of guilt had returned.

For a moment, Joe had forgotten everything about Colorado. Charlie's reminder caused all his thoughts to flood back at once. Guilt balanced sadness as Joe bent down again to finish picking up the papers.

"Hey, some guys may come here in a few days to pick up my stuff."

Joe looked up expecting to hear a response from Charlie from the lab. Instead, Charlie stood in the doorway looking back at Joe with a phone stuck between his shoulder and his ear.

Charlie mouthed the word, *Okay.*

Joe felt bad for disturbing him and mouthed back, *I'm sorry*, as Charlie closed Joe's office door. The light from the hallway disappeared. The boxes on the floor looked like stalactites in the caves of the east-Texas hills Joe remembered from a school field trip.

To awaken the darkness, Joe pulled down on a faded-yellow string hanging from the top of the window. A tidal wave of light rushed into his office as the blinds raced upward.

Damn, that's bright.

Joe shielded his eyes from the flowing sunshine filling his office. Dust particles from the paper-filled boxes danced in the air. The sunrays made it appear as though he stood inside a mad hatter's dusty snow globe.

His eyes followed in amusement one rather large dust particle seeming to hang in the air. As his eyes focused beyond the dust particle, it became blurry.

A sheet of paper hanging onto the edge of a box sitting on the floor next to him caught his attention. He bent over to push it back into the box, but he stopped. The contents of the paper captured his gaze like the beautiful artwork in the Louvre Museum.

VLOOKUP formulas in Excel? Hmm...

Joe snatched the paper before it fell and walked back to his desk chair. The piercing creak occurred as he sat studying the various Excel formulas he had used in his research.

This formula returns a value of the cell in a column of data.

He ran his right hand through his hair.

Okay, say Grandma's letter matrix is the data set. If someone wanted to communicate something, they could send something like a VLOOKUP formula.

An audible laugh echoed through his office.

Yeah, like Grandma knows anything about Excel?

His head was full of mixed emotions. Frustration overcame him. He was reaching for any answer.

Why did Grandma tape the matrix inside a hidden drawer with my graduation picture?

The determination to solve this mystery stole Joe's thoughts away from the mind-numbing information he had learned in Colorado.

To release his frustration, Joe balled up the paper with its equations and shot it toward a lone empty box in the corner of the room. The paper ball floated through the air slashing through the glowing dust particles. He missed the top of stacked boxes in the middle of the floor as the ball arched its way down into the box.

"Yes, swish… two points."

Silence returned once the paper ball stopped rattling inside the box.

Two points? If someone wanted to use that letter matrix as a code key, then you could send two points to tell the coordinates on the matrix to select a letter.

Dust no longer floated in the air as enough time had passed to allow them to settle. "That's it," Joe yelled. The particles of dust jumped into the air as if he had frightened them. He ran to his door with his keys in hand.

When the office door closed behind him, a small stack of boxes tipped over beside the doorway. He stuck his head into the lab across the hall.

"Charlie, I'm going home now… rain check on lunch 'till tomorrow?"

"Sure thing, Boss… Go enjoy your afternoon delight," Charlie said with a grin.

Joe rolled his eyes as he left the lab. He ran down the hallway slamming the door against the wall.

I only need to find two points…

11:15 A.M.

JOE STOOD WINDED in the front doorway of their home after running from the train station. His heavy breathing drowned out the jumbling keys left swinging in the door.

He made a beeline for his antique desk. A heavy, loud sigh rushed from his lungs as Joe waited for his computer to start.

Joe grabbed his mouse and double-clicked the Internet browser to open his email program. His eyes darted around the screen.

That's right… I deleted that email.

He clicked on the trash folder scrolling through its emails.

I deleted it. It was just after the penis enlargement emails.

He kept scrolling.

Not here?

He clicked on his inbox again and scrolled.

Not here, either?

He clicked in his draft folder and scrolled.

Maybe it got saved, here?

After ten minutes of searching, he pushed himself away from the computer with a blank stare.

I know for sure I saw an email last night with all those random pictures in it.

He raked his hands through his hair.

At the bottom was a row of numbers... that's it... I'm losing my mind. Hell, I am making things up, now?

Joe stood to walk out of the office. He froze in the doorway.

Wait, I remember some of them...

He sat and pulled out a sheet of paper from the trash can beside his desk. With a pencil, he wrote out the numbers he tried to remember.

I'm sure the first number was 5.1... then 3.5... and I think 2.5 was next.

He placed dashes for the remaining ones he could not recall.

I can't remember how many numbers there were?

Joe reached into his pocket pulling out his black wallet to retrieve the small paper with his earlier solution.

Okay, the first number... 5.1... If I look at the fifth column and then the first row, the matching letter is W.

He wrote the letter *W* on his paper.

So, 3.5 is the third column, fifth row... that would be the letter Y. And, 2.5 is the second column, fifth row... V.

Wrinkles creased along his forehead. The letters made no sense.

W Y V... uh... what the hell is that... maybe it's the row first, then the column?

He put his pencil to the paper again.

Okay, so 5.1 is the fifth row, then the first column... the letter S. And, 3.5 is the third row, fifth column... the letter A. Then, 2.5 is the second row, fifth column... the letter L.

His eyes grew closer together. The letters *S A L - - - -* taunted him.

Who the hell is SAL - - - -?

He replayed the pictures from the missing email in his memory.

One of those must be related somehow to a name starting with SAL.

Joe has a talent for recalling images and lists. If he would have studied the pictures last night or had a normal sleeping pattern, he could have recalled everything. Unfortunately, this email was fading from his memory.

I can remember the Oklahoma City Building and the Twin Towers. I'm pretty sure there were even pictures of JFK and Princess Diana.

He stared at his graduation picture on the desk leaning in his chair.

I remember something about AIDS and the stock crash…. and the Waco fire.

His lack of sleep and with all his stress from the past week, his frustration grew too much to take. Joe folded the small, thin paper and placed it back into his wallet.

Maybe, I'm just making everything up? I mean, where the hell is the email? It could not have just disappeared.

Air escaped his pursed lips. His mind froze. The lower part of his mouth opened. This same expression came to him one other time in recent memory, several days earlier in Colorado.

Maybe it's not a name… maybe it's… Salvation?

Joe sat in front of his computer screen. His emails taunted him. He laughed as he slipped his wallet back into his pants.

A new Monitor had taken his shift watching Joe, today. On his observation screen were the split images of Joe on the left and his opened email program on the right.

The Monitor typed in the ongoing log:

Subject came home in a hurry and looked through his email. He appeared to be looking for something. No voices were heard. He took something from his wallet, but I am unable to see what it is. After a few minutes, Subject is staring at his computer.

The Monitor pressed *enter* to record the log. In Colorado, the Eden Foundation received the entry recorded into a database. The entry was for *Subject 147889.*

Deep in the recesses of the Command Center was the mainframe room. Since the 1970s, Eden had recorded countless records for other Subjects, here.

The room's dimensions are large, some six hundred-feet-square. With today's modern advances in computer systems, gone are the large mainframes. Much smaller equipment servers store records for all the Subjects watched by Eden.

A computer terminal connected to the server enables a technician to perform diagnostics. The screen illuminates with sets of numbers scrolling upward. Each number belongs to a watched Subject.

Subject 147889 appeared at the bottom of the screen immediately upon entry by the Monitor in New York City. Within a few seconds, it scrolled upward as a new record for *Subject 189125* appeared. A new record for *Subject 101112* followed. After twenty seconds and one hundred entries, the record for Joe had disappeared off the top of the terminal.

Gabriel sat at his office desk on the ground floor. He had established an alert on his smartphone when a new record was submitted for Joe, or *Subject 147889.* An alert appeared on his phone.

"Joe... Joe... Joe... Forget about it and stay with our mission at hand," Gabriel said as he glanced over at his laptop. On his screen, he read the deleted email Joe had attempted to locate.

Gabriel clicked his videoconference icon on his screen. After a few moments, a live image of an older woman appeared. She wore black-rimmed glasses and a black microphone from her left ear to her mouth.

"Have we made any progress in finding the source of the email to *Subject 147889?*" Gabriel asked.

The woman responded through the video screen, "Unfortunately, not. Whoever sent it, sent it through an encrypted email server with a temporary IP address. I cannot identify the location of the address."

"Does it match the IP address of the other emails?"

"They all have different addresses. The last one was registered in the Philippines and bounces around the world on hundreds of servers before ending up on the inbox of *Subject 147889.*"

"That's disappointing... keep working on it and let me know immediately if you identify the exact location from where it was sent."

"Yes, Sir," the woman said before ending the video call.

Gabriel scrolled to the top of the email and looked at the sender's information.

"Okay, 'Friend' who and where are you?"

17-Singles Cruise

Thanksgiving Day, 2003
Pasadena, Texas

THE SIXTH THANKSGIVING alone for Liz meant volunteering again to serve dinner at the homeless shelter. Liz loved her new annual tradition. It kept her mind off the anniversary of Eli's death, and it became such a rewarding experience for her.

As Liz closed the front door of her home to leave, the phone rang in the kitchen. She opened the door and ran inside. Her decoration style was trapped in the '70s. Dark, shag carpeting in the living room lead to bright, yellow-painted kitchen cabinets in the kitchen. Another remnant from the past was the lime-green phone hanging in the kitchen. Its extension cord was long enough to reach all the way into the living room.

"Hello," Liz said in a rushed breath as she darted into the kitchen grabbing the phone on its fifth ring.

"Hey, Grandma, it's Joseph. Everything, okay? You sound outta breath?"

"Oh, hey Joseph... Oh, you know me, I'm runnin' 'round here like a chicken with my head cut off fixin' to get ready to go somewhere." Liz giggled as she calmed down.

"That's right... the homeless shelter is today. I wanted to call and wish you a happy Thanksgiving."

"Happy Thanksgiving to you and Mary, too. I saw where they're calling for snow, there."

"Yeah, only a few inches. We've lived here long enough now where that seems normal."

"You know everything here would be closed for days with only an inch." Liz walked into the living room and sat in a corduroy-covered chair. The lime-green phone cord spun in the air behind her.

"So, Grandma, Mary and I were talking the other day about how we're looking forward to come see you at Christmas."

"Well, uh... um, Joseph." Liz stammered her response. "I've been trying to find the right time to tell y'all."

"Grandma, you're finally coming to see us at Christmas? Oh, that's great. Mary will be so—"

"Oh, no... no, not that. Well, I'll just come out and say it. I'm going on a trip over Christmas."

"A trip... at Christmas... to where?"

"Month or so ago, Martha and I were talking about dating. You know, she and Jim got divorced."

"No, I didn't know that?"

"Yeah, it was all the news here. Martha found out he'd been cheating on her for years... anyway... we were talking and she asked me why I never dated anyone after Eli."

"Yeah."

"I didn't have a good reason for her. I guess the whole situation just broke my heart too bad that I never really wanted to. Plus, I had you to look after, and the church."

"Yeah, but Grandma, I've been gone now for, what... about six years, and Grandpa, well that happened, what... like a million years ago."

"That's exactly what Martha told me."

Liz stood from her chair and walked into the kitchen to her shiny, stainless steel refrigerator — the only new appliance she had bought in the last ten years. Under two fruit-shaped magnets, she stared at a cruise brochure of her future trip.

"Well… about this trip. Martha mentioned a singles' cruise we could take to the Bahamas… so, that's what we decided to do."

"Grandma, a cruise… a singles' one at that? Totally doesn't sound like something you'd do?"

"After Martha gave me the information, I looked at it forever. I got furious at myself because that's exactly right. It doesn't sound like something I'd do. That's why I'm doing it… even after Martha said she couldn't go."

"What? Is Martha not going with you? You're going by yourself?"

"Yeah, she gave me some excuse about the grandkids and Christmas. But, I think she's still dealing with handling the divorce. And, I didn't want to press her about it."

A few moments of silence fell on the line. They both had to process the news.

"Joseph, I hope that's okay. I was going to tell y'all sooner. I had to convince myself to go… I hope y'all didn't buy plane tickets already to come see me?" Liz asked.

"Oh, that's, okay. No, we've not flown since 9/11. It still freaks Mary out. We were planning to go by bus." A pause occurred. "I can't wait to tell Mary about this. We'll miss you and hope you'll have a good time."

"Oh, Sweetie, I will miss y'all, too." After a few seconds of silence, laughter came through the other end of the call. "What's so funny, Joseph?"

"Awe, nothing. I was thinking about what I said about having a good time… but, don't have too good of a time… Grandma, do we need to have *the talk*?"

Liz could not help but laugh as she responded, "Now, now Joseph. I may be trying something new, but I ain't that crazy."

"I'm happy you're doing this Grandma. I can't wait to hear all about it."

"Me, too. I'll call y'all though before I leave, so don't worry… Well, tell, Mary I said happy Thanksgiving and that I love her and you, too. I have to go now before Martha goes nuts at the shelter."

"Okay, I love you, too, Grandma. Happy Thanksgiving. I'll call soon. Bye, Grandma."

CHRISTMAS DAY, 2003, 8:08 A.M.
PASADENA, TEXAS

A BROWN SUITCASE SAT by the front door full of beach clothes, dresses, and shoes. All, items one would take on a seven-day cruise to the Bahamas. Its owner paced the living room floor. Thoughts raced through her mind, unsure if this was the right thing to do?

Liz had always been conservative by nature. She would never leave the house without putting on her makeup and fixing her hair. Floral prints were her favorite. They flattered her new curves she discovered after changing her diet and walking two miles each day. The night of her daughter-in-law's funeral made it clear to her she needed to get healthy. She had the responsibility of raising her grandson, Joseph.

Today, the trip Liz was taking may be the most adventurous thing she has ever done. Between her pacing bouts throughout the front rooms of her house, she sat on the corduroy-covered chair in the living room. Liz lifted the family scrapbook from the table beside her turning its pages of happy memories calming her nerves.

She had memorized every item on every page. The familiar order slowed her racing thoughts. On the last page, she saw her handwritten date on the top, right corner: *Thanksgiving Day 1997.*

Wow, this seems like a lifetime ago since I put Eli's picture here.

Liz flipped over the last of the brown, construction paper pages. A smile appeared on her hurried face as she read her note: *Our Story Continues in the Next Book.*

Boy, did it ever.

She paced the floor again creating ruts in the thick carpeting. Her impatience to start her adventure became too much to take.

A car horn blared outside her house. She peeked through the curtain attached to the small window of the front door. No one was in her driveway.

Coffee percolated on the counter by the sink; its aroma called her. The scent grew stronger as Liz followed its trail to the kitchen. The hot coffee refreshed her caffeine addiction as she returned to the living room chair.

The coffee had no taste as the anticipation of her trip created numbness throughout her body. Liz reached under the table and lifted a second scrapbook onto her lap. At the same time, the coffee cup clanged against its matching saucer as she sat it down too hard on the table. Her attention was elsewhere.

She took a deep breath and opened the cover of the second book. The same brown, construction paper sheets filled this new scrapbook.

Taped to the scrapbook's first page was a thin, white paper plate affixed upside down. The paper plate had a torn, missing section in its center. A smile grew through her made-up face.

Huh, to think... it all started with this.

She placed her index finger on the plate and rubbed toward the missing center. Jagged edges from the torn section felt like feathers to her fingertips.

I'm glad I hid this just in case.

The missing section had contained handwritten rows of letters and numbers forming a matrix. The plate's mystery owner from that Thanksgiving in 1997 never identified. Visible to Liz below the missing section written on the plate was a string of numbers.

Funny, when I saw this, I couldn't even remember how I used to solve these codes with Eli.

Her index finger made its way down to the original string of numbers: *2.4, 3.5 4.4, 3.5 2.5 2.4 5.2 5.5.* An audible giggle came as she rubbed her hand across the numbers.

Liz remembered how she had rushed home on that Thanksgiving night over six years ago. Her mind racing almost as fast as she walked home. She ran through the front door, threw off her coat, and sat in this same corduroy-covered chair.

Her memory flashed to taking a blue ink pen from the table. Liz's body shook as she placed the tip of the pen on the thin, white paper plate below the handwritten numbers.

The numbers give the instruction to the column and row of the selected letter in the matrix.

Now, six years later, she sat in the same chair where she made her discovery. Her finger rubbing over the faded-blue ink of the words she translated that night.

A screeching ring from the lime-green phone hanging on the wall from the kitchen interrupted her. *Give me a heart attack why don't ya.*

Liz sat the second scrapbook on the table beside her. The page with the paper plate still open. She raced to the kitchen and picked up the phone handle dancing in its cradle.

"Hello?"

"Merry Christmas, Grandma," Joseph and Mary said at the same time through the phone.

"Oh, Merry Christmas, y'all."

"We were hoping to catch you before you left for your cruise."

Liz turned and saw the clock hanging on the opposite side of the room. It was 8:45 a.m.

"I'm running late. I'm going to miss my flight."

"Well, we wanted to call to wish you a Merry Christmas and hope you'll have a great time in the Bahamas."

"Awe thanks you two. I'll miss y'all, and hope you're having a good Christmas there in New York?"

"It's snowing, so it's a white Christmas for us."

"Okay, well, I really need to go. I love you both so very much," Liz said; her tone became serious.

"Hey, Grandma, we know. We love you, too. I can tell you're worried about the trip, but it'll be great."

"Uh, yeah. You're right… I'll call you when I get back at New Year's."

"Okay, well, Merry Christmas, and we love you."

"Love you, both. Merry Christmas."

Liz sat the phone handle back onto its cradle. The matching lime-green cord twisted and swayed back-and-forth as she rushed from the kitchen.

I hope I'm not too late.

She hurried to the small table beside the corduroy chair and turned out the lamp. Light escaped from the room. The last image she saw was her handwritten note in faded-blue ink below the numbers: *I am alive.*

The words she had written six years earlier brought a smile to her, which hid in the now darkness. Liz lifted the handle on her bag. With a deep breath, she opened the door and pulled the suitcase behind her, closing the door as she walked out.

The sound of keys clanging against each other echoed across the front yard. The opening and closing of her car door broke the silence in the neighborhood. Early on this Christmas morning, her car's engine roared to life in the driveway.

Liz was on her way to the airport unaware of the adventure she was about to endure. Unaware, she would never return home.

CHRISTMAS DAY, 2003, 11:15 A.M.
HOUSTON INTERNATIONAL AIRPORT

HOLIDAYS LIKE CHRISTMAS increase the organized chaos of an airport. This morning at the George Bush Intercontinental Airport was the textbook definition of chaos.

The normal busiest time for air travel is the days before Christmas. A blizzard in the Northeast had canceled countless numbers of flights. So, today was the catch-up day for the airlines.

People hurried in different directions with mixed emotions, many traveling to be with friends and families. For Liz, there was no sense of frustration, only apprehension as she was about to embark on her own adventure.

The wheels of her brown suitcase squealed as they rolled across the tiled floor in the ticketing area. One wheel performed a whirly dance as it spun at different speeds based on how fast Liz walked.

She found the check-in counter for her flight and waited in line to get her boarding pass. The sigh of relief did not come from her, but from the suitcase as it struggled to keep up with her hurried pace through the manic maze of people.

"Good morning, where is your destination?" the young girl behind the ticket counter asked.

She's not much older than Mary.

"Merry Christmas, uh… um… yeah, I'm going to Ft. Lauderdale, Florida."

A myriad frenzy of typing came from the young girl's fingers. "Merry Christmas to you, too. Name and ID, please?"

Liz presented her passport to the young girl. "Here you go. My name is Elizabeth Bishop."

The ticket agent took her passport; the frenzied typing grew even more frantic. "So, has it been busy, today?" Liz asked trying to make small talk calming her nerves.

"Oh yeah, earlier it was crazy, but it's like slowing down now a little. Most of the flights are arrivals today being Christmas and all."

The young girl handed Liz back her passport and continued typing. "Ah, Florida. I bet the weather is super awesome there since it's snowing everywhere else."

"Uh… yeah. I'm going on a cruise and it should be great."

"How many bags are you checking in?" the young girl asked as the sound of a printer rang out from behind the counter.

"None, *this* is a carry-on, is that okay?"

The young girl leaned forward across the counter to get a better view. "Sure, it's just the right size."

More printing came from behind the counter. Liz stood there turning her head as if she was looking for someone.

"A cruise, huh? From Florida, is it to like the Bahamas or the Virgin Islands?"

The girl's question snapped Liz out of her spastic trance causing her to focus her attention again. "Oh, uh… yeah, the Bahamas. I can't wait."

"Okay, here is your boarding pass. Your gate is B2," the young girl said as she used her ink pen to circle the gate number. "Just go to your left through Security, and your gate is not that far from there."

Liz took the boarding pass from the young girl and looked down in the direction the she had mentioned. "I go *that way*?"

"Yes, like just down on your left."

"Okay, great. Thank you, and merry Christmas."

"Merry Christmas to you, too. Enjoy your cruise."

Liz grabbed her suitcase with its squealing wheels. The same one as before pin-wheeled around as she walked. In her right hand, she made sure she had her passport and boarding pass as she had rehearsed.

She saw a line of passengers waiting to go through Security. Along the side of the waiting passengers stood friends and family. It was obvious to Liz the sadness some had while waiting. Liz watched as some kissed and hugged their loved ones as they walked away.

Their sadness became her sadness. Guilt crept into her mind not being with Joseph and Mary this year for Christmas. But, her own new adventure was about to begin.

I can't believe I'm doing this.

18-Liz

THIS TIME OF YEAR, the Long Island weather can change from the heat of summer to the chill of winter, all in the same day. But, today... today, was absolutely gorgeous.

Birds chirping in the trees added a relaxing soundtrack to this cloudless day. A light, gentle breeze blew. Leaves swayed, not yet wanting to release their summer color to the ravages of autumn.

The beautiful weather was not the reason for Joe's walk. No, his racing thoughts pushed him outside to rid his mental anguish.

Children's laughter playing in the nearby schoolyard was enough to break his dark thoughts. He stopped to absorb their happiness. This faint release did not last long for his morbid thoughts crept back.

Well, kids enjoy it now. In five years, you're all dead.

The schoolyard laughter drifted into quietness behind him. Joe continued down the sidewalk to where it emptied into the local park frequented by dog walkers. A lone park bench gave him relief as he sat and watched two young lovers walking their black lab around the park.

Every so often, the two stopped and kissed as their dog longed to visit the nearby trees.

I didn't even think about what will happen to all the animals? I need to ask Gabriel if there's an ark planned for Project Salvation?

Two pigeons chased each other through the air between him and the couple. The distraction did not faze Joe.

Did that email even exist? I wish I could remember the numbers. Hell, I'm not even sure if it is real. Dammit, I'm going crazy.

A rustling sound grew louder as a jogger entered the park. The pounding footsteps startled the couple's dog across the field from Joe.

I mean, all this shit Gabriel told me about Project Salvation, maybe I was dreaming about the email?

The jogger ran a path along the edge of the woods encircling the park. He waved to Joe as he passed his bench.

That's it. You, continue to run, for what reason? Ugh, I really need to stop this...

Joe stood from the bench. His lower back and neck ached from the deepening stress of his thoughts. As he walked across the grass field reaching the middle, he stopped. The clear, blue sky was in a complete, unobstructed view. He tilted his head back rubbing his neck for relief, as he looked straight up. An epiphany overcame him.

Okay... I just need to accept this. Mary and I have been chosen. All our family is gone. My mind needs to calm the hell down and prepare for this.

His reassurance helped, but it was short-lived. A new thought pounded through his tense muscles across his forehead.

Charlie, Becky, and the twins... what about them?

The fate of his best, his only, friend haunted him. Joe thought of Mary's friends and co-workers at the school.

What about them?

No matter how much he tried to keep everyone out of his mind, their fate weighed too heavy on his shoulders. The crushing stress rounded his upper back down as he walked to the opposite side of the park. The jogger stopped nearby to stretch.

There's no way that email had anything to do with Project Salvation? I mean... Grandma taped that damn paper inside the desk drawer as a game or something... It means nothing.

As Joe left, the jogger pulled his cell phone from his shorts. "Subject has left the park. I will continue to follow."

CHRISTMAS DAY, 2003, 11:45 A.M.
HOUSTON, TEXAS

THE GATE B2 waiting area bustled with groups of people who sat on blue chairs in front of the ticket agent's desk. The red LED letters above the agent indicating *Ft. Lauderdale - Boarding 12:15 p.m.* teased the anxious crowd.

Around Liz, parents attempted to corral their children. An old man read his newspaper. A teenager talked on her cell phone, possibly to her parents from the tone in her voice. A man tried in vain to wrap a last-minute gift from the airport newsstand.

Liz sat with her brown suitcase at her feet watching everyone. In one hand, she held her passport and boarding pass while in the other was a folded note. She took amusement watching the people while looking around the terminal.

The agent approached his microphone as Liz peeked at the note she held. "Good morning and merry Christmas. We will be boarding Continental Flight 1541 to Ft. Lauderdale in a few moments. Please check that you have your boarding pass and identification ready. I will make an announcement when we are ready to board."

His voice created a stir among the waiting passengers, like poking a beehive. The parents collected their children's toys. The old man put away his newspaper. The teenager continued talking. And, the poor man, well, he was still having troubles wrapping his gift.

For Liz, the announcement elevated her breathing. Her heart pounded. It had been years since she had last flown.

Okay, here goes nothing... the note says that I should go to the restroom before boarding begins.

Liz stood and straightened her yellow skirt down to her knees. Her white, flowery blouse waved as she pulled her suitcase to the nearby women's restroom.

Her makeup and hair were perfect in the mirror as she admired herself. A deep breath came from her as she peeked inside her note and took her suitcase with her into the handicap stall.

She propped her suitcase next to the door and slipped her hand inside the unzipped top part. After fumbling for a few moments, she pulled out a pair of gray sweatpants and a black, hooded sweatshirt.

Another peek at her note and she fished out a pair of white sneakers from the bottom of the suitcase. Her shoes were on the floor and her sweat clothes were on the top of the suitcase, which wobbled with its top-heavy adornment.

Her heart pounded as she removed her blouse and exchanged it for the black, hooded sweatshirt. Liz reached behind her waist to unzip and step out of her skirt slipping into the gray sweatpants.

I cannot believe I'm doing this.

The toilet lid slammed down shocking her. Liz sat and changed from her black flats into the sneakers. The crackling of a white, plastic masked her heavy breathing as she shoved her flats, skirt, blouse, and pocketbook inside a shopping bag from her favorite boutique store.

Her heart jumped into her throat as the restroom door banged open against the wall causing her to freeze. Not wanting to move to make a sound, Liz peered through the crack of the toilet stall. A young woman with her child stood at the sink.

"Hurry up, we're boarding soon."

"Okay, Mommy."

Liz sat in the stall, frozen. She watched as the woman looked at her reflection in the mirror and adjusted her makeup. The child entered the toilet stall two doors down from Liz, who let out a sigh of relief under her breath.

An announcement came over the speakers in the bathroom ceiling. "Continental Flight 1541 to Ft. Lauderdale is now ready to board. We ask those requiring assistance or those with small children to proceed to the gate."

"That's us... we need to go."

Her mom's voice was a cue. The toilet flushed followed by a small voice. "Okay, Mommy."

As the stall door closed, water flowed in the sink. "Quick, wash your hands, and let's go."

A few seconds had passed when the vibration of the slamming door ricocheted throughout the women's room. All was quiet. Liz released a deep breath and unlocked her stall.

Liz opened her door and stepped to the sink. As she stared in the mirror, she turned on the water and grabbed paper towels in the nearby dispenser to wipe the makeup from her face.

Her hand shook as she applied a new shade of lipstick from bright red to a darker magenta. She threw two pins holding up her hair into the trash. A mix of brown and gray hair flowed down into her face and over her shoulders as she brushed it with her fingers.

She was barely recognizable from before.

I look terrible.

With her skirt, blouse, and flats in the shopping bag, she left the empty, brown suitcase pushed under the sink. Her note instructed her to keep it open to prevent any alarms of a potential bomb threat of an unattended bag in a bathroom.

Liz walked to the door and pulled her black hood over her head. One last deep sigh came from her as she looked down to the floor and walked out of the restroom.

The crowd of people had grown since Liz went inside the restroom. The passengers hoarded like cattle to the boarding gate area. A small passageway between the restroom and the growing crowd gave her the perfect opportunity.

Liz walked away from the boarding area unnoticed, going by the neighboring Gate B1 and out through Security back to the ticketing area of the airport. People still flocked into and out of the terminal building on this extra busy Christmas Day. She blended in with everyone as she exited through the sliding glass doors to the outside world.

CHRISTMAS DAY, 2003, 1:20 P.M.

THE MANIC EXCITEMENT around the airport was palpable with familiar Christmas carols playing from the speakers under the bright lights inside the terminal building. Hundreds of eager passengers waited in queues in front of the different airline kiosks. Travelers, weary from weather delays, exited the airport. Excited travelers entered ready to get to their final destinations. Outside, honking horns, squealing timing belts, and spinning tires provided the musical chorus.

This chaos allowed Liz to walk easily unnoticed from Security to exit the airline terminal. In her inconspicuous sweat clothes and sneakers; Liz drew no attention to herself. This is how she wanted it to be.

She hurried across the street dodging an arriving taxi and a departing shuttle bus.

Good. There's the sign for the Ramada Inn bus.

A heavy sigh released her stress as she waited. A young couple, each pulling their luggage, approached.

Ah, there it is.

A red-and-blue-painted bus stopped at the waiting area. Liz stepped up into the bus and took a seat in the back as the young couple sat in front. The driver attempted to make small talk.

Oh, thank, God, they will talk with him.

Liz drew no attention. The couple replied to his banter.

She overheard the driver explain the three stops needed before they arrive at the hotel. Her chest heaved as these stops gave her time to catch her breath from her excitement of sneaking away. Her shopping bag crinkled with each jolt over the speed bumps. No one else got on the bus... to her relief.

As the bus left the airport, Liz slipped her hand inside her bag. She carefully held a folded note cupped in her palm. The paper contained sets of numbers. Her handwritten letters formed the secret words instructing her actions.

Liz held her head down avoiding eye contact under her black hood. Strands of gray hair slipped from their cover across her shoulders. A sudden shift left in her seat snapped her attention from her note. They had arrived at the hotel.

The couple exited first followed by Liz passing the driver without a word. She stopped short of entering through the hotel glass doors. A roar from the bus engine caused Liz to look back. Her head turned side-to-side.

I don't think anyone is following?

She inhaled filling her chest full of the cool Christmas air. The hotel glass doors opened. Air escaped from her lungs. The glass doors closed behind her. Her gray hair flowed as she pulled her hood off her head and approached the front desk.

Be confident. Like I've been here before.

"Good afternoon. How can I help you?"

Liz had practiced her response for days. "My son, Joseph, is flying into Houston tonight and checking-in here later. Because of the snowstorm, he wasn't sure if he'd make home in time for Christmas."

She remembered to look sad as she spoke. "We've never missed a Christmas together." Liz forced a tear that fell down her face. "But, just in case, he mailed me a package, here."

"Oh, uh, okay…" The hotel clerk paused. His upper lip pressed down as Liz spoke. "Let me check. What's your name?"

"Yes, my name is Martha Flemington."

"Flemington… Flemington, ah…" The clerk typed into his computer. "Yes, I have a reservation for him tonight. Excuse me one-second."

The clerk stepped around the corner of the wall behind the front desk. A few seconds had passed until he returned holding a large manila envelope. "Here's your package. Can I see some identification please?"

"Oh, uh… sure." Liz hesitated shifting her eyes from his. "*Here*," she said giving the clerk her driver's license.

An earlier note had instructed Liz on how to obtain a fake license. Living in Houston with the influx of illegals, finding a place was easy to locate for the right price.

"Okay, great Ms. Flemington. Here's your package, and we hope your son enjoys his stay with us."

"Okay, thank you… merry Christmas." Liz grasped the package tight against her chest and turned away from the clerk.

A red, over-sized sofa welcomed her across the lobby. In her lap, she held the padded envelope addressed to her, or at least to a Ms. Flemington. Liz inspected the package holding it inches from her eyes.

I don't recognize the handwriting?

She pulled the tab on the corner of the envelope. The darkness inside the opening kept its contents secret. Her fingers reached inside to the bottom.

Feels like a credit card.

Liz slipped the item between her fingertips and freed her hand from the envelope. She held a hotel key. Written in black ink was the number *201*.

Is this where I'm supposed to go, next?

Fear froze Liz. Uncertainty caused her heavy, quick breathing to return. Her confidence was gone.

I should have told Joseph what I'm doing… I should have made Martha come…

The hotel glass doors opened, startling her. She threw the key back into the envelope. Liz turned her head toward the opening doors; a man in a wheelchair rolled into the lobby to the front desk.

Okay, Girl. Calm down. You've been looking forward to seeing him for six years, now. And, today… it will finally happen. All the questions I have… like why did he leave us?

Her internal pep talk worked. Confidence returned catapulting her to the elevator. Liz pressed *up*. The arrow above the elevator illuminated red. A simultaneous chime signaled the opening doors. Air gulped down her throat as she pressed the second-floor button.

As the elevator doors closed, a hand entered appearing in the gap two feet from the floor. The low placement of the hand frightened her.

The doors reversed open. "Room for one more?" the man in the wheelchair asked smiling.

"Oh, sure," Liz said as she stepped back giving him room to enter. "What floor?"

"Three, please."

The elevator doors closed. Relief overcame her since he was not getting off on her floor. A secret part of her wished he was in case she needed to scream for help.

The elevator stopped on the second floor. The doors opened.

"Merry Christmas," the man said. She jumped with his silence-piercing comment.

"Oh, you too, merry Christmas," Liz said not able to turn around in time to see the man's face as the doors closed.

A narrow, red-carpeted hallway with matching red walls stretched from the elevator. Her breathing matched her slow, short steps. The blue doors counted down from Room 210 as she dragged her feet down the hall. She stopped at the last door. Room 201. Her breathing was shallow.

Liz clenched the key tight in her sweaty right hand. The white shopping bag dangled by her left side. She paused the key an inch from sliding into the key slot.

Maybe I should knock, first?

With a needed deep breath, she spun her right hand around and gave three light taps on the door.

Run, get out of here. Her thoughts rushed to her. *No, I have too many questions.*

She tapped three more times. Louder. Each knock echoed through the empty hallway. No answer.

"Okay, here goes nothing," she said in a quiet voice.

Sweat rolled down her palm as she slid the key into the slot. Two small red lights flashed; the door did not unlock. Liz tried again, slipping the card slower. One small green light appeared with a faint click; the door unlocked.

She grabbed the handle and opened the door ajar. "Hello? Anybody here?" Her voice cracked into the darkness of the room.

No reply. She pushed the door open. Her reservation about going into a stranger's hotel room was clear with the door's slow pace.

"Hello? This is Liz... Eli, is that you?"

CHRISTMAS DAY, 2003, 3:45 P.M.

LIZ SAT IN THE CORNER of the empty hotel room in a brown, leather recliner. Her white shopping bag rested on the made, queen-sized bed. The rhythm of dripping water from the bathroom alternated with the ticking clock on the nightstand beside her.

The wooden door muffled conversations of people as they passed the room. Faint beats of music from a radio or television in the adjoining room pounded in sync with her anxious heart. No clothes were in the closets or inside any drawer. Nothing was under the bed. The room was empty.

Liz was alone with her thoughts. *These instructions must be a joke. I've been fooling myself. There's no way Eli's alive... We had his funeral... But, I never saw his body... The messages I've received... No one knew our secret coded language.*

Her internal conversations of doubt drowned the silence in the room. That was until a quick knock occurred on the other side of the door. The tapping caused Liz to jump from the chair and stand in a defensive position unsure what to do.

"Housekeeping," a female's voice said from outside in the hallway.

Oh, it's just the cleaning lady.

Liz peeked through the door's eyepiece. A Hispanic woman in a gray uniform stood outside beside a cart full of towels and toiletries.

It really is housekeeping. Liz sighed as she opened the door.

"Housekeeping, can I come in?"

Liz's relief to see, to speak to anyone pressed her quick response. "Oh yeah, sure." Liz stepped back to allow the lady to come into the room with her bucket of cleaning supplies in hand. "The room is not that dirty or anything?"

"*Sí,* dat's okay," the lady said as she walked in and out of the bathroom dusting the furniture.

Liz sat again in the chair and asked, "Have you seen anyone else in here?"

"*Señora,* it's a hotel," the cleaning lady said sitting her bucket on the floor by the door.

"No, I mean, have you seen anyone else in *this* room, today?"

The lady continued cleaning. "No, *Señora.*"

Liz kept staring at the lady as she cleaned.

Huh, she looks familiar... "Have we met before? My name is Liz... uh... Elizabeth."

The lady stopped her dusting motion. Her cloth swung back-and-forth in the air. She stood straight, turned and faced Liz. "Did anyone follow you?"

Gone was her Hispanic accent replaced by a noticeable Texan drawl. The question pushed Liz down on the chair. Her eyes widened. Wrinkles deepened on her forehead.

"This is important, were you followed?" the woman asked.

Liz scanned around the room. "Uh, um... no... I... I don't think so. I followed all the instructions from the messages."

"And, you went through Airport Security to your gate and changed clothes?"

In a state of shock, Liz replied, "Uh, yes."

"And, you took the shuttle bus here and left your car in the parking lot?"

"Yes."

"Good, then they'll think you're on that flight to Florida?"

"They?"

"Yes, *they,* the people responsible for the events in all the pictures I sent?"

"Wait, it... it was you that sent me the coded messages?"

The lady went to the window and pulled the curtains closed. The room fell into complete darkness until she turned on the floor lamp beside the air conditioning unit where Liz sat. "Yes, I sent all those to you."

"But… but, the codes… how—"

"Sorry about that. It was a dirty way to contact you, but I didn't think you'd believe me if I hadn't." The lady walked over and sat on the edge of the bed facing Liz. "I'm sure you have a lot of questions, but we have to be very careful."

Liz stood from the chair to leave the room. The lady grabbed Liz's wrist as she passed her on the bed. Her grasp on Liz was as tight as someone trying to climb a rope.

"Liz, I knew Eli." She released her wrist.

"What do you mean, you knew Eli? You can't be but what at most thirty years old… he's been dead since—"

"Thanksgiving 1975, right?"

Confirmation of the date stopped Liz from leaving. Liz faced the woman. "Who are you?"

"My name is Ruth… and, I knew your husband, Eli."

CHRISTMAS DAY, 2003, 4:11 P.M.

AN UNCOMFORTABLE SILENCE settled in the hotel room. Several moments had passed. Liz remained motionless in the middle of the floor. She glared at Ruth, and Ruth stared at Liz.

Liz sat back in the chair facing Ruth, who sat on the edge of the bed. "So, other than knowing our code and my husband's name, how can I believe you?"

"Liz, you have to have faith in me. I… I met Eli in the hospital."

"When?"

"In 1996, I had attempted suicide, and my aunt had me committed."

"Committed?"

"Yeah, I was a danger to myself. For days, I sat and stared out the window of the common area on our floor. That's when I met him."

"Eli? My Eli… my Eli, who was shot and murdered in 1975… that Eli?"

SECRET SALVATION ♦ 253

Ruth paused. "Yes, that Eli. Someone had committed him several years before I got there. One day, he pulled up a chair beside me, and we talked. He kept calling me *his Elizabeth*. To be honest, that place scared me, so I just played along."

"Okay, help me here? You're saying that my dead husband was in a psychiatric hospital with you?"

"Yes."

"That's it; you're a crazy person. What you're saying explains everything," Liz said with an uneasy laugh leaning forward.

"If he died in 1975, how do I know his name... your name... the stupid code y'all used to do?"

Liz did not answer her questions.

"He kept calling me *his Elizabeth* and passed me these notes... but, they were just a bunch of numbers. One day, I asked him to explain, and that's when he showed me how to understand his code."

Liz sat quiet, still in a state of disbelief to what Ruth had explained.

"He talked for hours about the codes and the messages in them. I thought he was crazy at first. But, I realized he was a genuinely nice man. So, I listened... eventually, he told me about you and your son, Jacob."

"Look, so you know about our code and my son's name... that doesn't prove you met him, especially since he's been dead since 1975, Honey."

"Explain *this* then," Ruth said as she reached into the front pocket of her gray uniform. "Here, take *this*."

Ruth stretched her fist to Liz, who instinctively met her hand as Ruth dropped something into Liz's palm. "What, an old watch—" Liz stopped. Her complexion became as pale as the white towels Ruth had carried into the room earlier. Liz turned it over and read the words of a faint inscription: *Eli + Liz = Forever.*

"Eli gave me *this* watch to give to you when I left the hospital."

A large, single tear fell from Liz's left eye. "Eli... How? ... I remember filling out a form at his funeral listing everything in his casket. *This* watch was supposed to be inside... How?"

"It's okay, Liz. I'm sure it has to be a lot to take in right now?"

254 ◆ CHAD JOSEY

More tears formed on the top of her cheeks below her eyes. Liz held her breath. "But... but, he was... the robbery?"

"Eli told me the same people responsible for the things in those pictures were behind faking his death."

"Faking his death? Huh... uh, why?"

"He never explained it. I just listened. I'm sure he thought I was you he was talking to."

"But, let's see... if you met him in what... 1996 and were released the next year... then... he's still there?"

"I'm afraid he's not anymore. I left the hospital because the doctors thought I was no longer a threat. A couple of months later, I went back to visit him, and he was not there."

"But, why didn't *someone* at the hospital inform me he was alive?"

"I don't know if the people at the hospital believed him? He kept saying his name was Eli. But, the name tag on his wrist said his name was Robert."

"But, you... why didn't you come tell me when you got out?"

"I wanted to so badly... But, the things he said... the people responsible for faking his death... what they did... I was afraid they would come after me."

Ruth darted her eyes around the room.

"I did finally get up my courage. That's when I came to the homeless shelter on Thanksgiving."

Liz stood from the chair. "I... I remember you, now. You were the woman who didn't speak English. But, you had a baby with you?"

"My cousin... I had to babysit her for Thanksgiving while my aunt worked."

The air came out from under Liz's feet as she plopped down back into the chair. "But, why didn't you say anything?"

"Would you've believed me? Do you even believe me now?"

"Huh, good point. I don't know what to believe."

"That's when I went back to visit him at the hospital. I wanted to tell him how nice you were to me and that you were doing okay. But, no one there knew who I was talking about. They claimed to have never had or released anyone by the name of Robert or Eli. I even described his old gray jacket and black Yankees baseball cap he loved."

Liz smiled at the memories of the Christmas when she gave Eli the hat from his favorite team.

"That's when I got scared and ran away from the hospital... as far away as I could. I have family down in Mexico, so I went to stay there for a while."

"So, that's when you sent me the coded messages?"

"Yes."

"But, if we met on Thanksgiving in 1997, why did it take you so long to send me the next message?"

"I don't know. I believed what he had said and was afraid the same people after him would come after me. I tried to forget everything. Then 9/11 happened."

"9/11, you mean Osama Bin Laden, that 9/11?"

Ruth laughed. "Yes, that 9/11. Several of his coded messages in the hospital warned that in the future the same people responsible for faking his death, and the countless despicable other things he told me about, would do something very terrible someday."

Liz listened rocking slowly side-to-side in her chair.

"And, the way 9/11 happened... Eli didn't talk about planes into a building or anything like that; just that something tragic would occur that would stop the whole world. As soon as I saw the second plane hit the tower, I knew what he was talking about was true, and needed to reach out to you."

"But, why me... why tell me all those terrible things you sent in the notes?"

"Uh... um, I needed to prove to myself that I wasn't crazy. So, I sent them in a code to the only other person I knew who could read them."

"But, you sent me encoded messages with no way to contact you back. You spoke of things about my family and me that only Eli would have ever had known."

"I'm sorry if I've upset you... I... I needed to reach out to you."

"Gray jacket and Yankees hat... I knew... dammit, *that* was him."

"What? You saw him?"

"It was my grandson's high school graduation. I was filming the ceremony and saw this man take my grandson's picture. I didn't want to trust what I thought I had seen, but that didn't stop me from trying to find him."

Tears filled her eyes again as the memories of Joseph's graduation night came back to her. "I felt like it was him, but I convinced myself it couldn't have been... that is until I found your note at the shelter. No one could have known about our code?"

"So, you never got close enough to him to confirm that it was Eli?"

"No, he was down on the field, and I was up in the stands. At the end of the ceremony, it got crazy, and I lost him in the crowd."

"What was he wearing... uh... I mean, did he look normal?"

"Other than wearing a jacket and a hat in the middle of June, he seemed normal... Ha! I... I still can't believe I am talking about him like he's alive... or was alive."

"But, if you had doubts about thinking it was him sending you the messages, why did you go along with my plan to bring you here?"

"Uh... good question... I... I wanted to believe it was him and that it would be him in this room."

"I'm sorry to trick you like that. I knew if I didn't make you think I was him you would never have agreed to meet me."

"I still can't believe I went through with these instructions. Chalk it up to an old woman's fantasy for her dead husband."

"Do you believe the things in my messages I sent?"

"You mean like saying some organization is behind assassinating JFK or that the same people also killed Princess Diana?"

"Yeah."

"To be honest... not really. It's too much to accept conspiracies like that. But, in the same notes, you would mention trips we had taken in the past or other personal details... and—"

"Liz, Eli loved you so much. He spoke of you all the time. And, I got to know you well through his stories. I added those comments because I thought you would keep the messages and not throw them away."

"You didn't even know if I knew what these codes were about, but you kept sending them anyway. For all you knew, I could have been throwing them all away each time they arrived."

"True," Ruth said, "I wanted to think you would keep them. In my way, I was having a conversation with you." Ruth walked over to the closed curtains, peeking through to scan across the parking lot. "Did you tell anyone else about the messages or anything?"

"No. No one would have believed me if I said I was getting encoded messages from my dead husband."

"What did you do with the messages, if you didn't throw them out?"

"Funny. I didn't know what to do with the codes, so I kept them in a scrapbook."

Ruth closed the curtains and spoke in a softer voice than before. "Okay, I need to go, now. I don't like to stay in any one place too long."

"Go, but, I've got a million questions about Eli."

"All in due time, Liz. But, here's what I need you to do." Ruth motioned her over to the window and opened the curtains a single inch, wide enough to peek through. "You see that blue Toyota *there*?"

"Uh, yeah."

"*Here* are the keys. I'm leaving, but you stay in the room until nighttime. Take the car and drive to *this* address." Ruth handed her a slip of paper along with the keys to the car.

"Why don't I come with you?"

"Liz, we can't be too careful. One, or both of us, may be followed. That address is a safe place. I can tell you more about Eli, there," Ruth said as she walked toward the door. "And, remember to be careful and make sure no one is following you," Ruth said as she left.

The room fell silent, again. The dripping of the water and the ticking of the clock returned.

Did that conversation just really happen?

Liz looked down at the keys and address in her hand.

Is Eli really alive?

A smile appeared on her face followed by a worried feeling.

But, what was he involved in that would make him fake his death?

CHRISTMAS DAY, 2003, 4:44 P.M.

THE FLOOR of the hallway cracked under Ruth's feet. She left Liz alone in Room 201 and proceeded to the stairs, walking up one flight.

Ruth opened the door to the third floor and walked down the matching hallway to Room 301. She knocked on the door.

"It's me," she said.

The door opened. A man in a wheelchair greeted Ruth as she entered the room. He closed the door behind her.

"So, has she been in contact with Eli?" the man asked.

"No. We thought sending Liz those messages would trigger an attempt by her to reach out to Eli. If she knew he was still alive, surely she would have tried to make contact. She really believes he died in '75."

"Well, that's disappointing to hear," the man said as he wheeled over to the window.

"But, I do have some good news. Liz saw Eli at Joseph's high school graduation. So, we at least know he was still alive in 1997."

"*That* is good news because we lost his location after '96 at the hospital."

Ruth joined the man at the window. They saw Liz walking fast across the parking lot to the parked car Ruth had pointed out earlier.

"So, what do we do with her now?" Ruth asked.

The man spun his wheelchair away from her rolling to the desk. He grabbed and pressed a button on his cellphone to make a call.

"We'll try *our way* to get more information from her when she comes to the address you gave her. We'll make sure she's telling the truth about him, whether she knows where he is or not."

"And, if she doesn't have any more information?" Ruth asked.

"Even if she does or doesn't, she's as good as dead now anyway, isn't she?" the man said as turned his attention to the cellphone. "Luther, she will be there soon. Make sure she doesn't leave until we get there."

19-Secret Told

L AUGHTER FILLED the tiny house on Harbinger Street tonight after the twin's birthday party. Mary helped Becky with dinner while Charlie and Joe were in the garage. The twin girls were in the living room watching television. A typical house, on a typical street, all seemed normal to Joe for a change.

"You see *this* driver right *here*? I can knock the shit out of a ball on the course with this thing." Charlie took two slow, practice swings with his new club he had bought in Myrtle Beach. Each swing almost knocking over his bicycle.

Joe reached out and said, "Let me see it before you break something." He took the club from Charlie. "Wow, this club is so light."

"Yeah it's light, but it'll drive a mutha fuc— "

"Dinner's ready, Guys," Becky said poking her head into the garage from the door leading into the kitchen. The smell of stewed tomatoes and gooey cheese followed her.

"I need to get you out on the course someday," Charlie said.

"Yeah… maybe… one day," Joe replied.

As the guys came into the kitchen, the aroma of homemade lasagna and garlic bread smacked them in the face. "Smells great, Honey," Charlie said standing behind Becky. He placed his large hands on the sides of her hips kissing the back of her head.

"Thanks. Now, go take Joe and Mary to the table, Mr. Host," Becky said with a sarcastic giggle. Becky pulled the aluminum foil off the oven dish. The lasagna bubbled with mozzarella cheese. A spray of steam rose across the countertop.

"Girls, dinner's ready," Charlie yelled as he walked into the dining room.

"Honestly, Mary, I love that Man, but why does he have to yell through the house," Becky said as she cut the lasagna into squares.

"Oh, you know you love his deep voice," Mary said smiling.

"Did I ever tell you the first thing he said to me when we met?"

"No?"

The twins turned off the television and came to the table. With no sound coming from the living room, Charlie and Joe heard Becky's question to Mary.

"What I told her was how beautiful she was." Charlie's deep voice came thundering at Becky and Mary as they entered the dining room from the kitchen carrying the food.

Becky gave Charlie a dirty, playful glance as she sat across the table from him. "Yeah, not exactly. He came up to me in the Quad at Stony Brook. It was the first day of our Junior Year… Joe, you were there."

Joe laughed remembering what had happened.

"So, here comes this big—" Becky said until Charlie interrupted her.

"Go on… say it, Honey… this big black man."

"Uh… no, I was going to say, here comes this big guy coming up to me with a handsome smile."

"That's better."

"And, I thought he was going to ask me something bright and intelligent. Or ask me for directions. But, no. Mr. Big Smile *over here* comes over to me and tells me, *hey you know you've got a nice…*" Becky mouthed in silence the word *ass* because her ten-year-old girls were at the table.

Everyone erupted in laughter knowing this sounded like something Charlie would do.

Joe interrupted and said, "Yeah, and that's when I saw Becky *here* slap Charlie's face."

As the laughter subsided, one of Becky's daughters said, "Mommy, you do have a nice ass."

Horror came over Becky's face at her daughter's comment. At the same time, what his daughter had said caused Charlie to erupt into a frenzied laughter joined by Joe and Mary.

"Honey, thank you, but we don't say *that word*," Becky said. Her girls sat on opposite sides of the table from each other.

As soon as Becky was confident her daughters understood what she meant, she turned to Charlie. "What have you been saying around them?"

"Me? It's you, Miss Potty Mouth."

"Huh, well, I don't know what you're talking about?"

"What did you call the Giants today?"

Not answering his question, Becky said with a smile, "So, everyone, please dig-in. The food's getting cold." She lowered a piece of lasagna onto her plate. "Well, *they* are."

"What did you call them, Mommy?"

"Oh, your Mommy just called them a bunch of pleasant guys," Charlie said. His response made Becky giggle sending wine up her nose as she sipped from her glass.

"See, You Guys, that's why I love *this* man. He makes me laugh. I don't know how you put up with him in the lab, Joe."

"Becky, this lasagna is delicious," Mary said with steam escaping from her mouth.

The next few moments no one spoke. Scraping silverware against plates chimed across the table. "Thanks, it's a family recipe from my grams. She was originally from Sicily, so I'm like half Italian."

"So, where did your blonde hair come from?" Mary asked.

"Grams was a waitress, and I remember her telling me about my gramps who one day came into her restaurant. Once she saw this tall, blonde German come in, she said it was love at first sight."

"Awe, that's so sweet," Mary said looking over and smiling at Joe.

More silence fell across the table as the lasagna disappeared.

"So, Joe, Charlie tells me you're getting new funding for your research."

Joe looked over at Charlie before responding to Becky. "Uh... yeah, it's not a big deal."

"Not a big deal? Did Joe tell You Guys about this organization that's funding him? They picked him up in a limo and flew him out to Denver in a private jet," Mary said.

"No. Joe... never... mentioned... that," Charlie said. "In fact, he's not told me much about the trip. He has been acting a little crazy since though."

"Charlie... uh... I, it wasn't a big deal." His words stuttered as Joe attempted to find the right thing to say, next. "They're just excited about funding my research. They see the potential it could lead in helping find a cure for cancer or other diseases."

"Yes, Charlie, you've noticed it too. Joe's not been acting the same since he got back," Mary said.

Everyone looked at Joe. Even the four, ten-year-old eyes peered at him. "Uh, yeah... sorry about that. I think I'm just feeling the pressure since I've never had my research funded like this before."

"Awe, Man, it's all good. We're just bustin' your b—"

"Charlie!" Becky interrupted him by slamming her fork on her plate.

The banter at the table continued. Joe was relieved the focus of the conversation changed from no longer talking about him or his research.

I wonder if Salvation has this house bugged since Charlie's my best friend?

The conversation shifted from politics to vacation to the twins' outfits for Halloween. Joe injected comments where he could, but his thoughts drifted to Colorado.

"Mommy, we're done now, can we go watch TV?"

"Yes, but first take your plates to the kitchen," Charlie said in his fatherly tone to the girls.

"Okay, Daddy," the twins responded in unison.

"Oh, that's so cute. Do they do that a lot... speak at the same time?" Mary asked.

"Yeah. To be honest, I find it creepy sometimes." Becky tapped Charlie on the wrist.

He understood Becky's unspoken request as Charlie left the table and followed behind the twins. "Here let me help you with those," Charlie said with sounds of running water coming from the kitchen.

Everyone's heads turned to the kitchen and smiled. Charlie appeared in the doorway. Both of his daughters hung on the opposite sides of his hips, their legs wrapped around his pudgy belly. "Okay, girls, what do we give Daddy for dessert?" he asked.

On cue, each of his daughters leaned over to his cheek and yelled, "A raspberry," as they blew air out their puckered lips against his face.

Charlie lowered them to the floor to the roaring laughter of everyone seated at the table. "Yum, delicious. Okay, go watch TV now, but not too loud." Small running legs rushed by the table as the twins went into the living room.

"*That* kind of thing in unison though is too precious." Becky reached for Charlie's hand as she spoke looking at him.

It was *the* look. The look two people give each other that are madly in love. The same look Joe and Mary still have for each other. But, Joe was now seeing the look from someone else. From his best friend.

The look bothered Joe. *I… I've got to tell Charlie.*

The conversations continued. Laughter from the girls floated into the dining room. The food on the table disappeared. The hands on the clock turned into late evening.

"Wow, I should go put the girls to bed. It's eleven-thirty." Becky jumped from the table oblivious to where the time had gone. "Mary, can you help me, please?"

"Sure."

"Charlie, can you and Joe clean the table?" Becky asked.

"Sure, but let me go give them a goodnight kiss first," Charlie said running passed Becky and Mary into the living room.

"He loves those kids so much," Becky said smiling at Joe and Mary.

As everyone left Joe alone in the dining room, Joe picked up the plates and silverware.

"Here let me help," Charlie said when he returned.

On their second trip into the kitchen carrying the dirty dishes, Joe stopped Charlie at the sink. "Hey, Man. What are you doing tomorrow afternoon?"

"I've got to rake the leaves in the morning, and then I'm watching football. Want to come over?"

"I was wondering if we could meet at *our* spot. I need to talk about some things."

When Becky had gotten pregnant, Charlie was under a lot of stress, especially when he had learned they were having twins. He had asked Joe if they could take a walk and talk. They had found themselves along the creek that flowed through campus at Stony Brook.

During that walk, Charlie broke down to Joe in tears as the stress had been building too long. At the end of their talk, to lighten the mood, Charlie said, "Man, we'll consider this *our* spot from now on, when we need to have another deep talk, again."

Charlie sensed the seriousness of Joe's request to go to *their* spot. "Uh, sure. What time?"

"Does two o'clock work okay?"

"Sure. I'll bring us a couple of beers."

"What's this, you're now going to start drinking at this time of night?" Becky said returning to the kitchen.

"Uh, no. But, that sounds like a good idea," Charlie said laughing going over to Becky to kiss her.

"Well, thank you guys for inviting us over tonight." Mary walked over to Joe placing her arm around his waist. "We really enjoyed it."

"Anytime, Dear. Love having you guys over, and we'll do it again, soon," Becky said patting Charlie on his butt out of view from their guests.

Joe and Mary left out the kitchen back door. Joe said, "Thanks again. And, Charlie, see you, tomorrow."

PRESENT - STONY BROOK, NY, 2:15 P.M.
OCTOBER 4, 2015
1,804 DAYS PRIOR TO IMPACT

JOE PACED along the dirt path covered in golden leaves from the trees. The path led along the length of the creek flowing through campus and was a popular jogging route for the students.

Where is he? Okay, I made sure if anyone was following me I ditched them. Joe continued pacing back-and-forth.

I did as they do in the movies. I went inside the mall and the movie theater. I snuck out the back entrance. Hell, I even ran through the woods to get here. I'm positive no one followed.

"Boo!"

Joe's heart stopped beating for a moment as he jumped spinning around in the air. "Dammit, Charlie! Scared the shit out of me."

"Sorry, Man. Couldn't resist. You've been fun to watch walking and talking to yourself."

"Oh... um... yeah."

"That's okay. I do it now all the time... here's your beer." Charlie reached into his backpack. "Sorry, I'm a little late, but the leaves took longer than I had expected."

Joe popped the top of his beer can; a little foam slipped down its side. "That's okay. Thanks for coming. No one followed you, did they?"

"Followed... followed *me*? Aren't we too old to play cops and robbers?"

Joe ignored Charlie's joke. "I mean, uh... no one that you know of was following you, were they?"

"No, Man, I guess not. You okay? You're acting kind of strange?"

"I don't know? I'm not even sure where to begin?"

"How 'bout starting with what's got you all messed up lately."

Joe motioned to Charlie to follow him to a quieter place along the path away from the passing joggers. "My funding... the organization that wanted me to come out to Colorado to present to them?"

"I knew it... they're the Mafia, and they want you to deal drugs on campus?"

"Dammit, Charlie. No. I'm serious here."

"Sorry, Dude. Just trying to lighten the mood. What gives? What do you need to talk about?"

The golden leaves floating to the surrounding ground gave the appearance of Charlie and Joe trapped inside a bright, yellow snow globe. A colorful scene of contradiction to the darkness of Joe's confessions to Charlie about Colorado... of meeting Gabriel... of the information Joe had learned.

Minutes had passed, as did many joggers. Joe told Charlie everything about Salvation. Charlie listened not saying a word.

Each, on their third and last of the six-pack, Charlie said, "Joe, you're my best friend, right? But, have you lost your mind? You sound like a crazy person."

"Exactly. I'm going crazy here. I reviewed all the data myself. I saw the pictures and videos."

"And, you don't think they made this shit up as part of an elaborate scheme?"

"But, why include me in this?"

"Why does *any* cult include any of its members?"

"That was my first belief. They were a cult or something," Joe responded finishing his beer.

"And, it sounds like that to me, too."

"But, Gabriel knew things... things about me, like he's been watching me for a long time."

"So, he's a stalker?"

"It seems like he's telling me the truth about everything."

"So, let me get this straight, a planet-like thing will destroy Earth. It's orbiting the Sun in a different plane than all the other planets?"

"Yes, and its path will intersect Earth's in five years."

"You know how crazy you sound?" Charlie asked. "My brain is melting. I just can't process it all."

"No, not that... you're crazy, Man. No way in hell is that going to happen. I mean we both are scientists, right?"

"Uh-huh," Joe grunted shaking his head in agreement.

"We've taken tons of science courses and attended many lectures. And, even though neither of us studied astronomy, a discovery like this would make its ways through the scientific community."

"Man, I know. I know," Joe said shaking his head side-to-side. "That's why I'm struggling with this. And, Gabriel told me his organization had done many things to keep this a secret."

"Like what kind of things?"

"I don't know for sure. But, when he talked about the things the organization had done, Gabriel seemed like a totally different person. I got a terrible vibe about it, and that makes me imagine the worst things as far as how they've gone about keeping Salvation a secret."

"Sounds like all this conspiracy theory shit about 9/11 being perpetrated by the government or some evil corporation or something."

Should I even tell him about my weird email and my Grandma's encoded matrix?

"I mean, there's no way something like this could be kept secret for what... how long did you say, since the '60s? Next, you're going to tell me you know who the second shooter was who killed JFK?"

"Dammit, Charlie. I'm telling you about what happened in Colorado, and why I've been acting the way I have."

Charlie crushed his beer can and threw it into his backpack. "Sorry, Man. I'm giving you a hard time about this because it sounds too unbelievable. So, if this Gabriel guy told you not to tell anyone, why in the hell did they tell you now instead of waiting until February when you're leaving?"

"He said they wanted to give me time to assemble my work and identify equipment needed for the lab."

"Your lab on Mars?" Charlie laughed as he sat on the side of large rock outcropping along the creek side.

"Man... *that* does sound crazy when it's spoken out loud doesn't it? But... um... yeah, on Mars," Joe said.

"So, that's why you've been cleaning out your office? Are you going to put all that shit in a suitcase?"

Joe sensed Charlie did not believe him from his sarcastic responses. "Those men who came by our lab last week… they're taking everything I boxed-up to digitize everything. Now, I've been working on what equipment I will need on Mars."

"Okay, okay… but, what about Mary?"

"What about her?"

"What did she say when you told her?"

"Charlie, you're the only person other than Gabriel who I've even spoken to about this."

Charlie sat silent staring at his friend. Joe knew Charlie was attempting to process the information.

"Assuming this is real, and you're leaving in a few months… and by leaving, I mean you freakin' going to Mars… You're just going to surprise Mary?"

Joe crushed his last beer can and handed it to Charlie to place in his backpack. "Gabriel gave me explicit instructions not to tell her or anyone."

"But, you're telling me?"

"I had to… to tell someone. After last night… after I saw you with the twins and Becky… I just… just had to tell you."

"What? So, I can throw an 'Earth is going to end' party before 2020?"

"No, Jackass… I told you so you could live the next few years together, you know what I mean?"

"Oh, like running away together and spending every moment with them?"

"Uh… I… thought that—"

"Wait, a minute. If this shit really is true. They've been building equipment on the Moon and assembling it on Mars. How much would that cost? Who the hell has funded something like that?"

"I asked, and Gabriel gave me some cryptic response about various world governments funding programs for their military efforts. In reality, the money is diverted to Project Salvation."

"Yeah, but we are talking about trillions and trillions of dollars."

"Charlie, *this is* where my mind has been going. What if Project Salvation has caused things like… uh, hell… I don't know… like AIDS or the stock market crash? How much funding goes into programs to fight diseases and there's still no cure. Or, the amount of money flowing in-and-out of the markets… uh… I don't know; maybe that's how?"

"Jeez, that's a leap there don't you think? Hell, if that's true, are you sure you want to be part of an organization like that?"

"No. I… don't know. I've gone back-and-forth a million times. Do I run through the streets yelling the end of the world is coming or call up CNN? No one would believe me anyway."

"Yeah," Charlie replied. The tone of his one-word response made Joe realize Charlie, his best friend of fifteen years, did not believe him.

"See, you think I'm crazy… everyone will. That's why I am going along with it… if it's not real, then I'll have a good laugh about it in a straight jacket. But, if it's real, then… then…"

"Then, we're all going to die, and you and your research will help humanity continue to live… on Mars."

"Yeah, something like that," Joe said.

"Now, not to piss you off or anything, but you're not the only one researching for a cancer cure… so, why you?"

"What Gabriel said was my research is very specific to the human genome and predicting various cancers from our genes. And, the Eden Foundation feels my research seemed to be the most promising to find a cure someday."

"Plus, you never know what kinda cancer-causing stuff you will find up there on Mars?"

"True." Joe laughed unsure if Charlie was serious or not.

"Any idea on the number of people on Mars or planned to be there before the end of Earth?"

"From my research, the least amount of people is five thousand to ensure genetic diversity and a healthy population. But, I've read other research, which indicates ten thousand. Numbers fewer than this requires genetic screening to make sure reproduction can occur with no problems."

"Joe... that's not my question. 7.4 billion people are on Earth... how many of this number will be saved by this Project Salvation?"

Silence fell between them as they sat on the large rock looking at the creek and back at each other. "I'm not sure?"

"You're not sure? You're being asked to help save the human race and you don't even know how many will be there?"

Joe shook his head and said, "Damn. I was so in a fog when Gabriel told me everything... I... I... never asked?"

"Well, Dr. Savior, you've got some homework still to do here before you leave? And, while you're at it, is Noah taking with him any animals?"

"Awe, shit... the animals... I was thinking about those the other day."

Charlie held his hand firm on Joe's shoulders, who sensed his attempt to comfort him.

"Man, has our conversation helped any?" Charlie asked.

"Uh... yeah... it has..." A sense of relief overcame Joe, who now had even more questions for Gabriel.

"Well, I'm happy I helped. But, I have to go. Since the world is ending in five years, I better get back to my family," Charlie said with a hearty laugh as he stood from the rock.

"Hey, Man. I know you don't believe me, and I'm still working on believing it myself... but, thanks for listening."

"No problem. That's what brothers are for," Charlie said.

"Just promise me you won't tell Becky what we talked about here."

"Um, yeah. She'll think I'm totally nuts anyway, so I'm not saying anything."

"Charlie, I'm not joking here. I wasn't supposed to tell anyone, and I don't want you to share what I've told you with anyone else either."

As Charlie swung his backpack over his shoulders, he said, "I promise. Your secret is safe with me, Brother... I'll see you tomorrow in the lab, right?"

"Sure, I'll see you, then. Thanks again for meeting and for the beer."

"Later, Man," Charlie said. He left Joe standing beside the rock outcropping. Charlie disappeared up the dirt path back to the Student Quad area on campus.

As Charlie walked out of the woods and into the Quad, he looked up toward the sky.

He's really lost it. So, a planet will destroy Earth in five years? And, there's a colony on Mars that Joe and Mary will be joining?

As this thought entered Charlie's mind, an audible laugh escaped his body. A group of nearby students, who had been talking to each other, stopped to look at Charlie. To them, Charlie was a crazy man laughing alone as he walked.

"Oh, don't mind me? I just learned the end of the world is coming," Charlie said as he passed the students.

5:55 P.M.

EARLY OCTOBER is an inviting time on Long Island. Visions of golden, autumn leaves fill one's view. The air has turned crisp but not yet cold enough to lift the smell of chimney smoke.

An hour outside New York City, the University of Stony Brook sits on a small campus nestled among the suburbs. Today, the campus bustled with laughter and yelling. Coeds in different groups spoke of their conquests of last night. Cheers rang out at the flag football and soccer games played in the Quad.

But, for Charlie, his mind was elsewhere. He passed everyone enjoying the relaxing afternoon on the Sunday before mid-terms. Across the Quad was his chained bicycle among the dozens of others in front of Harris Hall.

When Charlie had agreed to meet Joe at their spot, he thought his friend needed to talk about Mary or financial troubles. Instead, Charlie left concerned for his friend's mental health in hearing his wild tales.

Charlie walked across the Quad to his bike. He stared at his shadow stretched out in front of him on this late afternoon. Given his familiarity with the campus, he could have walked to the bicycle rack blindfolded.

Joe's crazy... What he told me can't be real?

After unlocking his bicycle, he retrieved his helmet from inside his backpack. The cold, wet spots caused by the empty beer cans comforted his sweaty brow.

2020… that's in only five years…

The sun fell below the golden treetops. Charlie peddled through campus. Sunlight passed in-and-out between the trees creating a strobe-light effect.

Should I believe him? Has no one heard about this before?

The only traffic on campus was from pedestrians, bicycles whirling by, or the occasional rollerblader. Campus police restrict vehicles over the weekends only allowing maintenance crews to position equipment in various locations for building repairs or landscaping.

Charlie's thoughts and concerns about his best friend accompanied him as his bike meandered its way through campus.

Hell, I'm not sure I want to believe him. Mars? Really?

His bicycle bounced from the sidewalk onto the blacktop road jolting him back to reality. He did not notice the crosswalk he had ridden through without slowing.

I need to pay attention. I didn't even look when I crossed there.

Charlie continued through campus. Sun rays flashed from light-to-dark as the sun slipped lower behind the golden trees.

And, they picked Joe and his research? Why not mine? Treating water-borne bacteria in drinking water is just as important.

The red, crossing light flashed as Charlie approached a four-lane intersection of the highway encircling campus. He braked placing his left foot on the ground and staring at the light until it turned green. As he lifted his foot onto the pedal, his front wheel entered the intersection.

Car headlights raced toward the intersection. In an instant, the rear wheel of his bicycle locked lurching upward behind him. His heavy body pushed forward in his seat.

"Stop! You son-of-a-bitch!"

Charlie raised his hand extending his middle finger into the air toward the rear of the car racing passed him. Satisfied he got the driver's attention; he pedaled across the remaining lanes of traffic.

Charlie and Becky live on the opposite side of the small park across the highway. He took a shortcut through on his way home.

My God, I need to tell Becky just in case... my girls... they will be fifteen when—

Charlie emerged from the park, his bicycle on the sidewalk in front of their house. A pickup truck rode fast behind him speeding up as it closed quick on Charlie. The violent impact interrupted his thoughts.

Charlie lifted off his seat. Twisted metal and the exploding fiberglass frame pushed ahead faster than his body through the cool, crisp autumn air.

The remaining pieces of his bicycle flew beyond him in slow motion. By instinct, Charlie's arms reached out to brace his fall onto the sidewalk.

His body tensed bracing for impact with the ground, which did not occur. The front bumper contacted Charlie in the instant before landing. A sickening thump of his body rolling under the truck ended as the rear, passenger tire pushed through his mid-section.

The driver had not tried to brake evidenced by the lack of tire marks across the pavement. A fifty-foot-long trail of blood, broken glass, and large chunks from both the twisted wreckage of the bicycle and Charlie were the only markings visible. The truck left the scene as fast as it had hit Charlie.

Golden leaves falling from the heavens mesmerized Charlie as he looked upward. The crisp air grew colder against the sensations of hot blood rushing across his face from his helmet.

His legs bent twisted in several directions. Charlie looked as if someone had thrown a six-foot-tall rag doll out the window of a moving car.

What remained of him below his shoulders was numb. A blessing for Charlie as he lay in a pool of blood and internal organs spilling from his stomach onto the sidewalk.

Through the blood spitting from his mouth, he managed a smile. A growing white light replaced his view of the falling golden leaves around him. His beloved Becky's face appeared inside the light. Her smile gave him peace as his eyes opened-and-closed at a slowing pace.

The image of his twin girls on either side of Becky joined their mother looking over him. Charlie saw all three of them smiling, not saying a word.

His eyelids opened one last time. Fifteen years of memories flashed by in an instant. With a final sigh, Charlie's head and neck went limp in Becky's hands.

Becky had been sitting on the porch watching the girls play in the front yard. She saw Charlie leave the park and turn onto the sidewalk riding his bicycle.

"Look, Girls, Daddy's home."

As the words escaped her, she saw Charlie's body tumbling under the pickup truck along the sidewalk. She sprinted to him screaming. Charlie died as soon as Becky had lifted his bloody head from the pavement.

The only sound worse than the truck trampling his body was the shrill of terror coming from the twins. They ran to their mother.

Minutes had passed. In the Eden Foundation's Colorado office, a cell phone rang sitting on top of the desk belonging to Gabriel.

"Yes?" Gabriel said

"It's done," a voice on the other end said.

6:01 P.M.

THE DIRT PATH along the creek meandered its way through campus. After Charlie had left, Joe took his time and the long way home.

Water rippled over rocks and tree branches strewed across the creek bed. Joe enjoyed this relaxing atmosphere on his stroll home.

Golden leaves fell around him. Infrequent joggers and occasional bicyclists were his only interruptions to his enjoyment.

Man, what a relief to talk to someone about this. His secrets shared with Charlie made Joe four times lighter. He was relaxed, and dare we say... happy. Paranoia though stuck around in his mind.

I'm sure no one followed us there. I took so many precautions... unless they followed him... no, they can't possibly follow everyone I know... can they?

The pathway ended. Joe had a choice of directions: continue the longer way home under the bridge or leave the trail taking a direct route.

I should get home. Mary will have dinner ready soon.

Joe left the pathway and came to a pedestrian crossing at the four-lane highway encircling campus. He waited until the light changed to green so he could continue.

Halfway across, four police cars and an ambulance rushed around the corner coming toward him. A chorus of flashing lights and sirens intensified the closer they came. Joe ran to the other side. As they raced passed, the sirens faded in the distance.

For the next twenty minutes, Joe resumed his stroll home. His house was on the opposite side of campus from Charlie's.

I should've told Charlie sooner because I feel so much better, now.

The golden leaves became visible to Joe. On his way to meet Charlie, he did not take the time to notice their deep, vibrant color.

Hell, if I feel this good after talking with him, maybe it's okay to tell Mary?

Joe turned the corner on his road and walked along the sidewalk to his house. As he stepped on his front porch, the door flew open.

Mary ran to him, falling into his arms crying. Her body fell limp as she hugged Joe. An uncontrollable cry erupted from her.

"Mary! Mary, what... what is it... are you okay?"

Her crying did not allow her to respond. Mary's body heaved between short, shallow breaths.

Joe pried his upper body away. Her face was full of terror. "What happened? What's wrong?"

Concern consumed Joe. He has known her since they were ten-years-old, and he had never seen her balling uncontrollably. Not even in high school when she told him the stories of her dad's drunken episodes.

"Charlie's... Charlie's," Mary said between crying breaths.

"Charlie? What about Charlie? I saw him less than an hour ago?"

"He's... dead."

Joe nudged her shoulders away. "What?"

"Beck... Becky called... I could... could hardly under... stand her."

"What?" Joe went numb.

"She… she said… she… she saw him get hit… by a truck outside their house…"

Joe pushed her arms off him and rushed inside their house. "Are they at the hospital?"

"Uh… um… she called me from their house."

Joe paced the living room looking for something. But what, he did not know. The car keys hanging beside the door caught his attention.

"Mary, let's go!"

She followed him as they left their house. Tires screeched and pierced through the quiet neighborhood. Mary was inconsolable in the passenger seat.

"I can't believe it? I was just with him."

The stoplight was red. Joe blasted through the intersection having peeked both ways to make sure no cars were approaching. He turned onto the road fronting the park between campus and Charlie's neighborhood. Flashing lights of four police cars and an ambulance appeared ahead.

"Oh shit," Joe said as he realized those were the same vehicles, which had passed him earlier.

Police blocked traffic a hundred feet from the scene of the accident. Joe pulled into a neighbor's driveway and parked. Both of them bolted from the car to Charlie's house.

Before they made it there, two police officers grabbed their arms preventing them from going any further. Becky saw Joe and Mary as she attempted to speak with two other officers closer to the house. Becky let out a horrific scream and pushed by the officers running toward her friends.

As she reached them, Becky fell into Joe's arms passing out. In the distance, the crying of the twins grew louder from their front porch seeing their mother collapse. The officers holding Joe and Mary back let them go as Mary ran to the front porch and the twins.

One officer saw Becky collapse and motioned to a paramedic. Joe sat with her on the ground. The paramedic snapped a small, white packet below her nose awakening her. Becky looked up to Joe.

"The truck… it… it didn't stop… it… it… kept going."

The officer, who earlier had spoken to Becky, walked to them sitting on the ground. "Ma'am, can you describe the truck?"

"I… it happened so fast… Charlie! Charlie!" She cried out for him.

The screaming from the twins stopped as Mary got them inside their house.

"Officer, what happened?" Joe asked as he supported Becky in his arms. They sat several feet away from the ambulance, which blocked their view of a white tarp draped over Charlie's body.

"It was an apparent hit-and-run, while he was riding his bicycle. Ma'am, anything… anything at all you can tell me about the truck or a license plate number?"

"It… it was a white pickup… with wide tires… it came out of nowhere and hit my husband… Charlie! Charlie… No." Her cries were painful.

"Officer, I was with him about two hours ago. We met on campus. I left him and walked home, and he was going back to his bike."

"Miles," another officer said, "*here*, look in this." The officer held a blood-soaked backpack.

Officer Miles took the backpack. With his white-gloved hand, he reached inside and pulled out two of the six crushed beer cans.

"Sir, do you know anything about *this*?" Officer Miles asked Joe.

"Oh, that? We had a few beers down at the creek when we met. Since I was walking back home, he took them to throw away for me."

Officer Miles dropped the cans back into the backpack and gave it back to the other officer. "Take *this* and tag it." After the officer had taken the backpack away, Officer Miles wrote in his notepad. "Sir, and your name is?"

"My name? Uh, yeah, Joe…um, Dr. Joseph Bishop."

"And, how many beers would you say the deceased had before he left?"

The word *deceased* sent Becky into another crying rage in Joe's arms. "We split a six pack… I don't see what that has to do with this?"

"So, how many would you say he had?"

What part of split do you not understand? "We each had three… over two hours ago."

"So, you're saying he left you to ride his bicycle soon after drinking three beers?"

"Uh, I guess... but... I don't—"

"Okay, that's all I need, now. Ma'am, we can take you to the hospital if you'd like, while we stay here to investigate the scene more. We need to get a full statement from you when you're able."

Mary staggered out of Becky's house. Becky pressed herself up from Joe's arms and ran to her. "How are the girls?"

"Oh, Sweetie, they're okay. How are you?" Mary said as she took Becky into her arms and walked back to the house.

"And, Sir, we'll need you to come to the station to make a full statement, also," Officer Miles said as he turned away from Joe.

Joe stood assessing the scene in front of him. The red and blue lights from the ambulance and police cars flickered in the evening darkness. Police officers were taking pictures of the blood and bicycle debris lying across the sidewalk.

What has just happened?

20 - Aftermath

FOR YEARS, JOE had found solace in his laboratory. His lab was a place where he could escape the stresses of his everyday life.

When credit card companies hounded him attempting to get payment, work was his refuge. When the struggles occurred of not being able to have a baby, he left his sadness at the lab's door.

What made his research a sanctuary was his best friend, Charlie. Gone was the laughter, which normally had filled the lab. Gone was his confidant. The person Joe could go to when he needed a voice of reason, other than his wife.

Joe told Mary he would meet her at the church later in the afternoon for the funeral. Mary had stayed with Becky the past week to help with the twins as Becky made the arrangements.

Joe has been like everyone else, in a state of disbelief at what had happened. To prepare himself for the funeral, he needed his alone time in the lab this morning. Without plans to work, Joe knew in his way; he was going there to say goodbye.

I still can't believe you're gone... We were just talking earlier... Man, I can't believe the cops say alcohol contributed to your accident...

A knock interrupted his internal conversation with Charlie. Joe turned to the door. Gabriel stood in his lab to Joe's surprise.

"Hi, Joe. I'm truly sorry about your friend."

Joe shook his head in disbelief not expecting Gabriel to be in his lab this morning. "Thanks. How did you hear? Oh... wait... never mind."

Gabriel walked into the lab. "Like I said, we are watching you. But, I'll be honest. Our folks lost you though for a few hours on Sunday until you came home and got the news from Mary."

That's a relief. I lost you, son-of-bitches.

"Yeah, I went for a walk on Sunday, and came home to Mary. She was hysterical... and... the scene at Charlie's house was terrible. I can't even explain it."

"I would have reached out to you sooner this week, but I wanted to do it in person and not over the phone or email."

"Thanks, Gabriel. It means a lot you came."

"Well, I'm only here to see you. I'm not going to the funeral because I can't make myself too public."

Joe walked by Gabriel entering his office across the hall and motioned for Gabriel to come in and take a seat. "To help take my mind off the funeral this afternoon, I have a few questions for you."

"Sure," Gabriel said as he followed into the office closing the door and sat beside him on the sofa.

"To help me prepare for the equipment needed, how many people will be at Salvation?"

"I'm sure I've mentioned it before. The plans are to staff Salvation with a minimum, viable population to sustain humanity."

"Minimum, viable population? Out of seven-and-a-half billion people is how many?"

"The numbers change. We choose everyone because of the purpose they fulfill for example technicians and construction workers. There are scientists like you, doctors, teachers, engineers—"

"That's not my question. How many people? I need to know a number because this determines the amount and equipment I'll need."

"Eden is building Salvation so after 2020; it will be possible to expand the facility as the population increases."

"Gabriel, you are avoiding my question. Of the people currently on Earth, how many will be at Salvation, let's say by the time 2020 happens?"

Gabriel stood and walked to the window. As he peeked through the metal blinds, he said, "You want a number? The plan calls for having ten-thousand people there."

Joe knew this number from his calculations but wanted confirmation from Gabriel.

"They come from different places across the world to ensure enough gene pool diversity. Part of your responsibility will be to use your research to help plan conceptions based on gene pairing."

A roar came from behind Gabriel. "What the hell? You said Eden chose me because my research will continue cancer research to help mankind."

"Well, yes, Joe. That's still true. But, also your research will make sure we select the correct pairs of people for conceiving children to sustain human life. Your ability to identify genetic markers for the predisposition of certain diseases is crucial."

"So, I'll be playing God?"

"No, not exactly. Your input will help us decide, you won't be the one *making* the final choice."

"Why, not tell me this up front?"

"Let me be honest. If I told you *this*, would you have joined us in the first place?"

Joe backed down his stance. "Um, I thought you were about being honest with me from the beginning, Gabriel? And, I thought *no* was not an answer."

"I've been nothing but honest with you."

"Okay, let me test you on that. Where did the funding come from for Salvation?"

Joe knew his question surprised Gabriel from the reaction on his face. Gabriel sat at Joe's desk.

"I told you in Colorado. Salvation gets its funding through various government programs."

"But, Salvation is supposedly a huge secret. How can the government fund something that's this big without it getting out to the Public?"

"Governments around the world fund programs established for many things. Part of the money never goes there. It goes to Salvation."

"Governments? What countries are involved?"

"All the major, industrial governments contribute. The funding involved with military programs creates tons of money for us."

"But, how does Salvation receive the funding?"

"I am being honest with you here. I hope my honesty helps answer your questions, so you will accept your destiny at Salvation."

Joe's eyes pierced Gabriel from across the room in anticipation.

"Eden has positioned elements within the various militaries around the world. As funding comes, they funnel part of the money through different contractors and intermediaries. You would be surprised what governments are willing to spend when war and chaos rules."

"What? I get a sense you are saying Salvation has started wars to get funding?"

"Um, yes. That's one method we have used... this so-called *war on terror* has been a fantastic funding vehicle for us."

Joe could not believe Gabriel had confirmed his conspiracy suspicions about Salvation.

"So, yes, to answer your earlier question, we are selecting you to join us. We need your help to maintain humanity with ten-thousand people. How we funded Salvation is not important."

Joe sank slowly into the sofa. He sat speechless.

"I know... it's a lot to take in. But, it's the only way."

"But, I'm still having trouble accepting how people like you and the others watching me don't get to go. I mean, what's in it for you?"

"Eden studied and recruited me, and others like me, to join Salvation. We all perform our role. For us who don't go, we enjoy a certain power here on Earth in our time remaining. This power is very intoxicating for us, and that's how we manage."

Joe stood from the sofa as Gabriel continued talking.

"You think Salvation is powerful in keeping its secrets. Imagine the things we can enjoy *here* in our remaining time in agreeing to support Salvation."

Joe stood in silence. Gabriel's words sank into Joe's overflowing, melting brain. A few moments had passed.

"You mentioned you selected everyone based on a purpose they are to fulfill, there."

"Yes."

"What about Mary? Why did Eden select her? I mean, you could have just kidnapped me or something?"

"You know the answer to this, Joe, don't you? Come on, really. Do you think you could have brought any value to Salvation knowing Mary was still on Earth, or if we forced you to go?"

The question lingered unanswered for a moment. "So, Mary has been chosen because of me, because you need me?"

"You're finally getting it. Your research is so critical in helping select who gets pregnant and who doesn't. And, if you create a cure for cancer along the way or your research contributes to this in the future, then all the better."

"But, what is she expected to do there?"

"She's an excellent teacher and an administrator, now. As more children are born, they will need caretakers and teachers. You can say Mary has a critical role in helping the future children learn and grow."

Joe relaxed somewhat as he paced in front of him. Gabriel's response relieved his building anxiety about her. His questions about Mary had been bothering him.

More silence lingered in the office. "Another question… what about other life on Earth like the animals and plants, how are they being accounted for at Salvation?"

"Well, we have limited room there. So, no animals will be part of the program. And as far as plants, we have been shipping tons of seeds to Salvation. Some have survived, others have not. But, there is an effort to send the seeds—"

The alarm from Joe's smartphone blared through the office interrupting Gabriel.

"Gabriel, I have to go. I told Mary I was coming here this morning. She said it was fine as along as I made sure I left on time."

Gabriel stood and headed to the door. "Joe, we'll continue our Q-and-A later. But, now you need to mourn your friend. Again, I'm so sorry about the accident."

"I still have lots of questions... but, thanks again for stopping by. I'm not surprised you knew where I was since you're watching me."

"And, let me remind you again, Joe, tell no one about this. I will give you instructions about what and how to tell Mary."

Joe again sensed the seriousness in Gabriel's statement. *Hell, I tried telling Charlie. He thought I was insane, so I'm not telling anyone else.*

"I'll wait until you tell me it's okay to tell her... I'm still not sure how she will take it."

"I'll help you. But, for now, be with Mary and Becky. And, again, I'm so sorry for your loss, Joe."

Gabriel opened the door and left. Joe gathered his coat and a few mementos for Becky he had taken earlier from Charlie's desk.

Only ten thousand people? ... I help to choose who gets pregnant? ... Everyone else really will die? ... Hell, on that happy note, let's go to a funeral.

1:00 P.M.

BECKY HAD JOINED the church as soon as she had enrolled at the University of Stony Brook. Charlie had joined to impress her in college, never belonging to a church of his own. Her happiest moment there came seven years later when she had married Charlie at the altar. The same place now where his body lay inside a casket in front a hundred people who turned out for his funeral.

Amazing Grace echoed through the sanctuary. Not a dry eye was present. Tears fell silent down Becky's face in the front pew. She did not waver in her appearance; she was through crying.

Her new mission was to be a rock for her twin daughters, each sitting on either side of her as they both cried. Their faces buried into her black dress.

Becky's parents from Indiana sat on her left. To her right sat Charlie's parents, who had flown up from Georgia. His parents cried the loudest doing their best to console each other.

Joe and Mary sat behind Becky. The reality of the service was surreal. Joe's thoughts consumed him as he relived the memories of the times he had with his best friend.

Heck, I've spent as much time alone with Charlie as I have with Mary.

As the music stopped, the minister stepped to the podium to deliver her sermon.

"As Jesus said, *Blessed are those who mourn, for they shall be comforted.* Charlie was a loving man, a loving husband, a loving father, and a loving friend."

The words floated over the casket and remained lifted in the air by the sounds of crying and sniffling noses.

"Also, as Jesus said in John, Chapter Fourteen, Verses One through Four, *Let not your hearts be troubled. Believe in God. In my Father's house are many rooms. If it were not so, would I have told you I go to prepare a place for you? I will come again and will take you to myself that where I am you may be also.*"

The words the minister said entered the recesses of Joe's memory. He had attended unfortunately too many funerals in his life: his parents, Mary's dad, and his grandma.

I can't believe he's not here... I was with him just before the accident.

"In times like these, we always seem to question God. Why Charlie? Why now? But as Ecclesiastes Chapter Three, Verses One and Two tells us, *For everything, there is a reason, and a time for every matter under heaven: a time to be born, and a time to die...* "

"How are you doing?" Joe said in a whisper in Mary's ear.

Mary said nothing in return. When she made eye contact, Joe saw two, large tears roll down her face. She worked to give a small grin to show she was okay. The grin was a lie hiding her deep sadness.

Joe held her hand tighter leaning over to kiss her forehead. *I want to cry, but I can't.*

The music of a hymn played. The choir sang. Childhood memories overcame Joe as he whispered in Mary's ear, "This was one of my favorites to sing in church with Grandma." With a gulp of breath, he sang along with the choir.

Once the hymn ended, the minister retook her podium. "What a beautiful song… how great Thou art, indeed. Charlie lived a wonderful life. Now, in this time of sorrow, we should give our shared strength to Becky and the children," the Minister said.

Becky continued to look at Charlie's casket. She knew if she made eye contact with anyone during the service she would start crying.

"We can also look to Psalms Chapter Forty-Six, Verses One through Eleven to see how God will provide his strength to us."

The minister flipped the pages of her *Bible* and read out-loud. *"God is our refuge and strength, an ever-present help in trouble. We will not fear. Though the Earth give way and the mountains fall into the heart of the sea, though its waters roar and foam and the mountains quake with their surging."*

Joe followed along from a *Bible* he found in front of him. The words had an eerie familiarity.

"The holy place where the Most High dwells. God is within her, she will not fall; God will help her at the break of day. Nations are in uproar, kingdoms fall; He lifts his voice, the Earth melts."

Mary stroked the back of Joe's hand, which held the *Bible*. Joe did not feel Mary as the minister had his complete attention.

"The Lord Almighty is with us; the God of Jacob is our fortress. Come and see what the Lord has done, the desolations he has brought on the Earth. He makes wars cease to the ends of the Earth."

As the minister concluded her words, six large men stood. They walked and surrounded Charlie's casket. With ease, they lifted and carried it to the back of the church. Everyone stood turning to follow the men as they passed.

The words the minister had spoken still rang in Joe's ear. *Psalms Forty-Six… I need to remember this passage.*

The men carried the casket down the front steps of the church and into the graveyard. Along the tree line, a pile of fresh, brown dirt lay beside a six-foot deep, rectangular grave. Mountains of different colored flowers provided a bright setting for the somber moment.

Charlie's casket came to rest on a platform over his grave. The congregation followed. Once everyone was in position, the minister stood in front of a seated Becky and the twins. The cries within the audience contrasted to the love songs sung by birds in the trees overhead.

"And, we commit his body to the ground. Earth-to-Earth. Ashes-to-ashes. Dust-to-dust. The Lord bless him and keep him. Amen."

"Amen," the congregation said in unison.

As the casket lowered, Joe looked across the graveyard. He saw a figure in the distance.

Is that Gabriel? Looks like the suit he was wearing?

The service ended with the congregation dispersing from the graveyard. Joe and Mary watched Becky and the twins in a tight embrace with Charlie's parents.

As the people cleared out in front of him, Joe noticed the figure in the distance was no longer there watching.

I still can't believe Charlie's gone… What a terrible accident… It was an accident, wasn't it?

A black limo left the church parking lot. A faint purr of a motor lowered the tinted window dividing the driver from the passenger.

"Thomas, make sure your team watches *him* even more closely. If even any hint exists he may talk about Salvation, call me immediately like you did last week. Do I make myself clear?"

"Yes, Gabriel, I understand," Thomas said as he drove the limo away from the church.

"Oh, and great job in cleaning up *this* situation last week."

21-ACCEPTANCE

PRESENT - STONY BROOK, NEW YORK
DECEMBER 24, 2015
1,723 DAYS PRIOR TO IMPACT

THE PAST WEEKS in the lab have been a constant reminder of Joe's heartbreak since Charlie's funeral. Uneasiness fills his sanctuary.

For years, Joe would complain to Charlie. His work area was untidy with books and papers everywhere. His music would echo through the undecorated hall bouncing against the stairwell door. But, now, what Joe would not give for Marvin Gaye or Otis Redding to come blaring into his office.

Cataloging his equipment needs for Salvation has been a Godsend. This monotonous task cleared Joe's mind. His newfound solitude allowed no fear of Charlie asking too many questions. Joe had the entire floor of the research building to himself. Joe was alone.

Since the funeral, Joe and Mary have gone through the motions of their days. Joe spends his time in the lab, and Mary puts in extra time at the school.

Becky took the twins to go live with her parents in Indiana. She sold their house in Stony Brook with its horrific reminder along the front sidewalk. The twins had constant nightmares of their Dad rolling under a pickup truck.

With her, Becky took Charlie's possessions from his lab and office. This unintended consequence made Charlie's presence disappear. Joe's confidant, his best friend, was gone.

On the selfish side, Charlie's death brought a sense of comfort to Joe. He can focus on Project Salvation without the worry of Charlie being left behind.

The holiday season has arrived which was never the happiest time for Joe. Too much family tragedy brought a foreboding sense to him. Joe always wondered what sad event was next.

On this Christmas Eve morning, Joe sat on a stool in Charlie's work area. The stairwell door opened at the end of the hallway. Footsteps grew louder. For an instant, Joe imagined seeing his friend come bouncing through the entry.

With anxious anticipation, his wish did not come true. The footsteps belonged to Gabriel, who was visiting for the first time since the funeral.

"Merry Christmas, Joe."

"Hi, Gabriel. Merry Christmas... what do I owe the visit?" Joe stood from the stool and shook Gabriel's hand.

"I wanted to personally give you the good news."

"Good news, that's long over-due."

"First, we've completed the electronic transition of the items you sent. The second thing is we have obtained the equipment you have requested. We are making arrangements to send this to Salvation."

"I may have a few more items to include."

"Not a problem, let me know. But, the biggest news is I can finally give you the instructions for leaving."

Joe's heart pounded at the news. The reality of the pending journey was becoming surreal.

"I've been waiting... keeping this from Mary has been the hardest thing I've ever had to do. This includes burying my family and friends."

"Damn, Joe, so morbid."

"What? I'm supposed to be happy over seven billion people will die in a few years, and they don't even know it?"

"Like I've said many times, you can't focus on those left behind. Focus on sustaining the future."

"But—"

"Focus on the fact you and your wife will get to live," Gabriel said cutting Joe off from his argument.

Joe did not respond. He walked by Gabriel across the hall to his office and sat behind his desk. Gabriel followed shutting the office door and sat in the chair across from him.

"So, tell me, how are we doing this?" Joe asked.

"*Here* is the information and instructions you will need," Gabriel said as he gave him an iPad.

Joe read the instructions on the screen as Gabriel explained the events. "On Friday, January 29th, a limo will pick you and Mary up at your house taking you to JFK. There, you will board our private jet, which will fly you to Mauritius."

"Mauritius? Where the hell is that?"

"It's a beautiful island in the southern Indian Ocean, east of Madagascar."

"Africa?"

"Yes."

"You will give Mary *this* trip to our resort for Christmas. Tell her the Eden Foundation is giving you this as a gift for our partnership."

"What do I tell her about Salvation?"

"Nothing at the moment. We will handle this in Mauritius. But, you both can tell your friends and co-workers about taking this trip."

"Look around... " Joe waved his hands in the air, "what friends and co-workers?"

"Between you, I am sure you need to notify people of your two-week vacation? Pack the normal things to take for a two-week beach trip."

"So, we'll leave for Mars from there..." Joe stopped himself as he laughed. "Sorry, that still sounds crazy when I say it."

"We will give you the specific instructions at our resort."

"And, we will blast off, I imagine it's a blast off, from Mauritius?"

"Again, we will tell you there." Gabriel raised his eyebrows. "What's wrong Joe? Aren't you happy to be finally getting closer to going?"

"I've accepted this is real. But, I still need to tell Mary everything. These past weeks since the funeral have been so hard on us."

"Joe, this is why we do not want you to tell her, yet. Go to Mauritius. Enjoy our resort. The water, the beaches are so beautiful. Have that to enjoy."

Joe listened but imagined how Mary would react when he explains everything.

"Trust me. I've been doing this a long time. We have learned from past recruits how to handle these types of situations."

Joe leaned back in his chair trying to comprehend Gabriel's comments. "Hell, we've not taken a vacation since a job interview in Paris many years ago."

"Yeah, on 9/11, I remember," Gabriel said.

"You remember?" Joe asked as he did not recall having this conversation with Gabriel about Paris.

"Oh, no. I meant I remember from reviewing your files." Gabriel stood from the sofa distracting Joe.

"What about things associated with our house? Bills and shit?" Joe asked.

"Do you care about *that* where you're going?"

"I guess not. Hell, I should have stopped paying my rent months ago," Joe said as he laughed.

"I'm glad to hear you make jokes… No need to worry about paying rent where you're going that's for sure."

"Well, this brings up more questions about Salvation."

"Like?"

"Like, how do we pay for things? If Earth is destroyed, how does Salvation get new equipment?"

Gabriel laughed surprising Joe. He could not remember hearing Gabriel laugh before. Gabriel had a short-winded, high-pitched laugh, the complete opposite of Charlie's.

"Getting paid? Money? That's funny. No one is paid. Everyone works to support each other. People will consume everything equally. Of course, who is to say future generations may develop a new economy."

"Huh, a socialist utopia, then?"

"I don't know about that… but after 2020, everyone at Salvation will be on your own. That's why you're going now. You will establish your lab and have time to inform us if you need other equipment so we can get this to you before…"

"Before?"

"The end. Sorry. Sometimes, even when I say *that,* I catch myself."

"But, we talked about that before, that you've accepted your fate of being left behind."

"Well, yes, but Joe, we all have a role to play here. My role is to recruit and make sure the recruits go. In return, I can get anything I want here until the end. That doesn't mean that I haven't lost sight of my fate either."

"You've not spoken to anyone about trying to join Salvation?"

"It's pointless. If Salvation makes an exception for me, then next they make exceptions for all the others."

"You've never told me how many people are like you?"

"I am not sure of the number, but many people have performed my role across the world for decades."

"Decades… huh, I still can't get over we've been on the Moon and Mars all this time."

"And, I hope you're seeing why I've been so strict telling you not to speak to anyone? First, they would think you are crazy and would not believe you."

Joe listened nodding his head.

"Or, maybe they would believe you and ask too many questions. The next thing we know, Salvation is compromised, and everything will be lost."

"Trust me. I've been struggling with wanting to tell. At first, I realized you're right; people would think I am crazy. But, then it hit me. Mass chaos would happen."

A crooked smile appeared across Gabriel as he nodded his head as Joe spoke.

"I mean look at the chaos caused by the scare of Ebola or the presidential election cycle. Could you imagine what would happen if people knew they only had less than five years to live?"

"Exactly, Joe. By the way, now can you see how easy it is to manipulate people through fear?"

"Yeah, I guess. But, what do you mean by that?"

"Uh, never mind. I think your question about being paid, made me get all philosophical for a moment."

Joe scrolled down the iPad reviewing the instructions. "So, do I need to bring any paperwork, passport or anything?"

Gabriel belted out another high-pitched laugh as he peeked through the metal window blinds. "Sure, bring your passport. That has to be one hell of a passport stamp on Mars, huh?"

Joe laughed in return. "Yeah, it could be little *Marvin the Martian* stamps."

"Yes, bring them. You will need these to get into Mauritius. We will want to keep up the appearance you and Mary are there on vacation." Gabriel left the window for the door. "Okay, I'm going. We will talk again before then. Go home. Give Mary this gift and enjoy your Christmas together."

Joe reached to shake his outstretched hand. The eventual banging of the door down the hall followed after Gabriel left Joe's office.

Christmas? Will this still be celebrated at Salvation? Mauritius?...

Joe returned behind his computer and opened Google.

Where is Mauritius?

PRESENT - STONY BROOK, 1:17 P.M.
DECEMBER 24, 2015
1,723 DAYS PRIOR TO IMPACT

DECORATIONS, MUSIC, AND LAUGHTER filled Main Street in downtown Stony Brook. Last-minute Christmas shoppers lurched around the pedestrian lanes. Stereotypical men wandered shop-to-shop staggering through the crowds like the set of a zombie movie.

Joe walked a straight line through the chaotic array of shoppers. They flowed around him like a salmon swimming upstream in the swirling rivers in the Northwest. He was on a mission to find Mary the absolute best gift.

Before leaving the lab, Joe had printed pictures of Mauritius from the Internet. His plan was to place them inside a card as her present. Guilt pushed him further into the maddening gathering of shoppers.

Fresh thoughts flooded his brain. Tonight, Joe was finally confessing part of the plan to Mary. Guilt, however, ate at him for not telling her of Salvation. He was concerned about her reaction; this haunted him.

Joe pushed his way through the rugby scrum at the front door of Stony Brook Floral & Gifts. Early shoppers thoroughly had picked-clean both card aisles. Gone were the sparkling Christmas cards. A hodgepodge of random ones, most unrecognizable as belonging to Christmas, remained.

Well, this won't work.

He grunted under his breath. The rush of snowy, cold air hit Joe as he pushed his way out onto the sidewalk. Cars zoomed by on the two-lane street. Pastry smells from the next-door bakery made Joe hungry. The temptation disappeared when he spotted a jewelry shop across the street.

What the hell? Let's see what they have left.

Joe jaywalked to the store dodging a bicyclist and a speeding white pickup truck. Traffic was not his concern. Inside, the shop was peaceful being only half-full with shoppers. Joe collected his thoughts.

I've not given Mary any jewelry since our wedding. Maybe I'll get her a ring… what the hell size does she wear? Joe scanned the illuminated glass display of sparkling jewelry.

"Hello, Merry Christmas. My name is Cathy, may I help you find something for your wife?" the female clerk behind the display case said.

"Hi, Cathy, Merry Christmas… is it that obvious I'm looking for a ring for my wife?" Joe smiled at her.

"Well, I've been here for years. Nine-out-of-ten times, if a man is in here on Christmas Eve, it is for something for his wife," Cathy said smiling back at Joe. "Do you know what type of ring she likes?"

The display case was overwhelming with its choices. "Mary only has the diamond wedding ring I gave her… I imagine she would *like* anything."

"Oh, Dear. As much as I would love to sell you a ring, if you don't know what she likes, you'll be guessing and throwing away your money. What about a necklace? That's a little easier because she can match it with different outfits."

Joe appreciated her honesty. "Okay. You're the expert here."

"What kind of style does she wear? What about her job, is it corporate? Does she like to dress up?"

"Well, she works at the high school. She is on the teachers' union committee. They travel to Albany a couple of times a year," Joe said as he scanned the necklaces next to the rings. "And, we go out to dinners from time-to-time, but she never dresses too fancy."

And, oh yeah, we're getting ready to board a rocket to blast off to Mars… you got anything for that?

"Okay, that helps. Something practical but not too upscale… *here* are some nice pearl necklaces she may like." Cathy walked Joe over to the display case at the end of the showroom.

As Joe followed, a twinkling light reflected off a heart-shaped, diamond-encrusted pendant inside a glass case on the wall behind her.

"What is *that?*" Joe asked.

Cathy turned to where Joe pointed. "Oh, it's beautiful, isn't it? Would you like to see it?"

Before allowing Joe a chance to respond, Cathy took the keys attached to her hip and unlocked the glass case. She pulled out the piece of jewelry and placed it onto a black velvet cloth on top of the glass display case above the rings. The heart-shaped pendant was about the size of a quarter; its twinkling was mesmerizing.

"This is a one-of-a-kind piece in our collection. It's beautiful with twenty blue diamonds. White diamonds create the heart outline. This entire piece is thirty-two karats."

Cathy may as well have been speaking Greek to Joe. He did not care. The pendant was hypnotic.

"The chain is pure platinum, and if you push *here*… it opens. On the inside, there is space for two pictures… one of you and one of her, or one of you both and the other of your children."

"Oh, we don't have kids."

"Well, a picture of each of you works. It's a beautiful piece. *Here*, let me show you something similar." She pointed at the pearl necklaces.

"How much is *this*?" Joe asked as he held the sparkling diamonds.

A shocked expression overcame here. "This is a very exquisite piece. We've had it here a few years because it's so expensive."

Look, Lady, I'm leaving Earth in a few weeks. You can have my house for God's sake. I don't care.

"Seriously, though… how much?" Joe asked in a calm manner.

Cathy punched the keypad of a small, solar-powered gray calculator near her. After a few moments, she spun it around as she smiled. Joe recognized the smile, knowing she knew there was no way he could afford the price shown.

One-hundred-and-twelve-thousand dollars did not deter him. "I'll take it," Joe said slamming the glass case with the black credit card Gabriel had given him for expenditures Joe needed to prepare for Salvation.

"Really! Wow." Cathy flashed a huge, shocked smile. The commission on this one sale alone made for a fantastic year-end bonus. "Oh, *it* is so beautiful, and your wife will love it."

Joe could not tell if her excitement was genuine for Mary or the sale as he watched Cathy place the necklace into a black velvet box, which went inside a light-blue jewelry box. She wrapped the box with a bow of small, dark-blue ribbon.

After signing the credit card slip, Cathy gave him the small bag with the store's jewelry logo on the front. "Again, Merry Christmas. I'd love to show you more pieces after New Years."

"Thanks, we'll see. Merry Christmas," Joe said as he took the bag and left.

Did I buy that out of guilt for not telling Mary about what's happening? She'll love it, I'm sure.

Joe continued down the sidewalk. The holiday decorations seemed brighter. The Christmas music seemed more cheerful. His fog of not knowing what to get Mary had lifted. He enjoyed the atmosphere.

The brightness of the festive ambiance dimmed as his momentary pleasure disappeared. At the end of the sidewalk was the Catholic

Cathedral of Stony Brook. A sign with the letters *Open* on its doors compelled Joe closer.

Joe reflected on his purchase, on the news he needed to tell Mary, on the death of his friend. A rush of emotion overcame him physically forcing him up the stone steps and through the front door of the church.

By now, Joe had lived in Stony Brook for as long as he did in Texas growing up. In this time, he had never been inside this cathedral.

Every Sunday morning as a child, Joe had attended church with his mom and grandma. After moving to Stony Brook, he had only visited three church services: his grandma's funeral, Charlie's wedding and funeral.

Even though he grew up as a Southern Baptist, standing inside the Catholic cathedral felt familiar to him. He walked down the aisle separating two the sides of church pews and sat on the front row.

Joe gazed upward and stared upon the crucifix with a statue of Jesus. An eerie silence filled the empty sanctuary. A row of small, votive candles flickered beside the altar. The eyes of Jesus hanging on the cross looked down upon him.

So, Jesus, what's your opinion of life on Mars? I don't recall that exactly mentioned in the Bible? Not expecting any obvious response, Joe looked up and presented a smirk on his face to the statue.

All this time, people have been praying to you. And, for what? It's all going to end here anyway and continue on Mars.

Joe watched as a frail, old woman shuffled to the table with the prayer candles. She had a noticeable hunch in her back as her shaking hands lit a candle. Her wrinkled fingers with brown age spots clutched onto a walker for support.

When she finished with her prayer, she made the sign of the cross with her right hand across her chest. She turned facing Joe to pass him.

"Merry Christmas," the old woman said. Her voice cracked. Joe smiled and wished her a *Merry Christmas.*

Joe turned his attention back to the statue of Jesus.

Will there even be religion on Mars?

Joe had a bad habit of cursing after his years with Charlie. But, he knew two things: never to swear in church or in front of his grandma when she was alive.

Memories of Liz made Joe smile as a voice startled him from behind. "Good afternoon, my Son. Merry Christmas."

A man wearing a black shirt with a white square on its collar stood in the sanctuary. Over the black shirt, he wore a white robe and held a *Bible* to his chest.

"Oh, I'm sorry. I didn't mean to scare you," the man said as he gave a quick laugh. "My name is Father Alvaro... Merry Christmas."

"Oh... Merry Christmas to you, too, Father."

Father Alvaro smiled and stepped up to the altar. After making the sign of the cross with his right hand, he floated over to the table and lit a candle as he prayed.

Joe sat in amazement. He admired the way in which Father Alvaro carried himself, especially against the ornate backdrop of the altar with its woodcarvings and golden trim.

"Excuse me... Father. Do you have a moment?"

"My Son, I'm about to step into the confessional, if you'd like to join me?"

"Uh... um... I'm not Catholic, so I— "

"Oh, that's okay. We're all on the same team here," Father Alvaro said attempting to welcome Joe.

Joe followed Father Alvaro. Each walked into the separate doors of the confessional. After closing the door behind him, Joe sat in uneasy darkness.

A moment later, a small door slid open between them. A crisscrossed, wooden screen revealed a light shining through from the other side where Father Alvaro sat.

"So, how can I help you, my Son?"

"Aren't you supposed to say, *How long has it been since your last confessional?* Like they do in the movies?"

Soft laughter came from Father Alvaro. "Yes, you're right, but you've already told me you weren't Catholic... something's on your mind isn't it, my Son?"

Joe paused. "Well… I've been keeping a secret from my wife, but I am telling her about it soon. And, Father, it's been killing me not telling her."

"Are you keeping something from her that will upset her or hurt her once she finds out?"

"I don't think she will believe me, but after that, I think she will be angry at me for not telling her sooner."

"Do you think the reason you have not told her before is you're trying to protect her from something?"

"Yes, and I was told not to say anything to her about it."

"Sometimes, we protect those we love by doing things that most times we would never do. In God's eyes, if you have committed a sin, and this is what you are not telling her, then you are sinning against God based on the marriage vows you took."

Joe squirmed. "Oh, no, I've never lied to her about any of the questions she has ever asked me. I just never explained or told her any additional information about what I'm keeping from her. And, I feel so guilty not telling her."

"If she loves you, once she gets beyond the shock of what you're planning to tell her, she will understand your reasons."

Silence filled both sides of the confessional.

"Thank you, Father. That helps me a lot."

"You're welcome, my Son. Is there anything else?"

"Well… um… yes. I grew up down South and attended a Southern Baptist church. It's been so long now… " A question bubbled from the recesses of Joe's consciousness. "How does the Catholic Church view the end-of-the-world?"

"Oh, my… that's deep question for this time of year. I can tell something is troubling you if you're asking me this."

Father Alvaro cleared his throat. Joe leaned forward with anticipation hoping to receive any wisdom to help him with the burden of the secret he has carried for months.

"In the Book of Matthew, God warns us to *beware of false prophets, who come to you in sheep's clothing but inwardly are ravening wolves.* This time of year is when you hear proclamations from so many claiming the end-of-the-world is coming."

"Yes, but Father, if we knew for certain when the world would come to an end, shouldn't everyone on Earth know about this?"

"Only Jesus Christ knows when he will return to Earth. First Thessalonians tells us that *for the Lord himself will descend from heaven with a cry of command, with the archangel's call, and with the sound of the trumpet of God. And the dead in Christ will rise first; then we who are alive, who are left, shall be caught up together with them in the clouds to meet the Lord in the air; and so we shall always be with the Lord.*"

Joe's face was mere inches away from the screen. "But, what about the survival of mankind, how can we trust they will be saved?"

"My Son, the only way to *Salvation* is through God in heaven."

"Salvation?"

Joe fell back against the confessional. "Yes, by accepting Jesus Christ as your Savior can you then be assured of everlasting *Salvation* with him in heaven."

Father Alvaro's voice replayed over-and-over inside Joe's mind. *Salvation. Salvation. Salvation.*

After several seconds, Father Alvaro said, "My Son, I can tell you still have a lot of questions. I would love to see you come back and attend a service, and we can talk more."

The father's voice snapped back Joe's attention. "Oh, okay, Father… thanks for listening."

"My pleasure. Merry Christmas and peace be unto you, my Son." Father Alvaro closed the small door between them blocking the light.

Joe exited the confessional. Several people stood close by waiting their turn to enter after Joe.

Clever way of telling me my time was over, Padre.

Joe returned to the front pew. The eyes of Jesus pierced through Joe's mind with its anguish.

The only way to Salvation is through Christ, our God in heaven, huh? Okay, that's it. I've come this far not to believe anymore. From now on, who cares about anyone else… it's just Mary and me… huh… my real Salvation is on Mars… hope to see you there, Jesus.

9:11 P.M.

SCENTS OF WARM CHRISTMAS sugar cookies wafted through the air complemented by the aroma of baking honey-ham and potatoes. As a child, Joe remembered how his grandma made sugar cookies shaped as stockings after the family Christmas Eve dinner while everyone in their pajamas waited to exchange gifts. Joe had equated eating warm, Christmas cookies with opening gifts. Mary had continued this annual tradition for Joe.

His gifts to Mary enticed Joe. Impatience grew. After tonight, they are one step closer to Salvation.

Given his fresh outlook on what was to come after his talk with Father Alvaro, a sense of peace had come upon Joe. Something missing since Colorado.

As in years' past, each had only one gift to give to the other. This tradition started out of necessity with their lack of finances.

Crackling pops accompanied by a faint, smoky scent drifted from the living room fireplace. The twinkling lights from the Christmas tree danced around Joe as he sat beside the fire. Mary sat in a matching chair beside him. Between them, a small, round wooden table supported two small gift-wrapped boxes. Both gifts were the same size.

"Okay, who goes first?" Mary said; her eyes reflecting the twinkling red and green lights from the tree.

"Uh—"

Mary interrupted Joe as she grabbed his present from her holding it to his face. "*Here*, you first."

Joe ripped the paper like a small child full of excitement. Blue paper with small, white snowflakes ripped apart revealing a black, velvet box.

"Oh, wow."

With the paper crumpled in his lap, the box rested in his left palm as he opened the top. The contents inside hidden from Mary's view.

Joe reached into the opened box and pulled out a glimmering, stainless-steel watch. Without hesitation, he placed it onto his right wrist.

"Awe, thank you, Sweetie. I love it."

"You like it? Great. It's one of those that never needs a battery."

Joe admired his new watch. "Oh, cool."

"Did you read the inscription on the back?"

He slipped the watch off his wrist exposing the underside. "I will love you to the end of time." A deep breath exhaled from his lungs making his smile grow even wider. "That's so sweet, Mary."

Joe stood bending over to kiss her. His kiss lasted longer than his usual quick peck on the lips.

"I would've gotten you a watch sooner if I'd known I'd get a kiss like that," she said. Blood rushed to her cheeks.

"Okay, my turn. I know we only give each other one gift on Christmas, but *here*." Joe paused before reaching under his seat cushion.

Earlier, he had hidden this present to surprise her. "And, before you open *it*, just to let you know, we still are giving each other only one gift. Technically, *this one* is from the Eden Foundation to us, both."

She took the red envelope from his hand. "The Eden Foundation... the company funding your research?"

"They gave us this gift to prepare me for my work with them."

"Well, that's nice... what is it?"

"Open it."

She placed her index finger under the inside flap of the envelope. In one quick motion, she ripped open the back.

Pictures of sand against the backdrop of crystal-clear, turquoise water showed themselves to Mary. A bewildered look came upon her face. On the next picture, water was in the foreground. Tropical palm trees framed the outstretched golden sandy beach. A single, tall lush mountain stood in the background.

"Uh... what the heck..." Mary deflected her attention to Joe then back to the pictures.

Anticipation consumed Joe as she flipped through the two pictures. He restrained himself from bursting out everything to her. Gabriel's voice reminded him to tell her only about the vacation. *The rest will come in Mauritius.*

She flipped over the second picture, which hid a folded note. After she had sat the pictures on the table, she unfolded the mysterious paper. A shrill of excitement came from her.

"We're going on a vacation!"

"Yes!" Joe matched her excitement.

"Where? Mauritius… it looks so beautiful… where's Mauritius?"

"I knew you would ask… I asked the same thing," he said as he pointed out the location on a map with his phone.

"Wow, that's far."

"Exactly, they want us to go far away."

"It says we leave January 29th… that's not that long."

"The best part it's summer there since it's winter here."

"And, we don't have to pay for this?"

"No, in fact, remember the limo that picked me up?"

"Yeah."

"And, the private jet that flew me to Denver?"

"Yeah," which was the most excited *yeah* anyone had ever said.

"Well, that's how we're traveling. It's a private resort owned by Eden on the island."

"Oh, my God. This sounds too good to be true."

If you only knew.

"And, we're there… two weeks?"

"Yep. Two weeks of relaxing under the sun."

The building excitement was too much. Mary jumped from her chair falling into his lap kissing him in repeated fashion across his lips.

"We've never gone on any real vacations, and when we do, we're going to a place like this."

Mary's smile brightened the room over the twinkling lights. "I'm so glad you like it."

"Why would you think I'd not be happy about something like this?"

"I don't know. This is the most spontaneous thing we've ever done."

"Well, Mr.... you should have gotten your research funded like this sooner." Mary followed with a deep kiss, which outmatched Joe's from earlier.

Joe caught his breath from her kiss. "I should guess so. Wow."

With Mary sitting on his lap, she realized Joe enjoyed her kiss. He reached across her grabbing the other gift-wrapped box on the table.

"Now, *this* gift is from me."

Mary took the wrapped box from his hand, shifting her weight on his lap. She felt him underneath her as she moved.

"How the hell are *you* going to top that one?" she asked in a playful manner, sneaking a quick kiss on his lips.

Mary ravaged the gift apart. A black, velvet box emerged from the torn wrapping paper, which fell on the floor between the chairs.

She squirmed on his lap with excitement, making the pressure under her thighs grow even more. Mary opened the box.

Joe stopped her. "Now, before you see what's inside, it's something I've wanted to get you for a long time. You've put up with my late-nights. I wanted you to know how thankful I am for you."

His anticipation for her reaction ached him. Joe released her hand; Mary opened the box.

His free hand stopped her again before she saw inside. "I know, it's too much, but you deserve it."

He removed his hand allowing her to open it. Her bottom jaw dropped open, her eyes widened. Silence. The Christmas lights twinkled against the blue and white diamonds of the pendant Mary held inside the box.

Words escaped her slowly. "It... is... so beautiful."

A single tear fell across her face down the tip of her nose. Joe lifted the pendant admiring it in the shimmering lights. Her hand reached for the back of the necklace preventing it from spinning.

"*This* small notch on the side... press it," Joe said.

Mary followed his instruction. Inside, Joe had placed their picture; hers on the left and his on the right. "It's... it's... I love it."

"Here, let's put it on you."

She lifted her auburn hair. Her exposed, naked skin enticed Joe as he kissed the nape of her neck before clasping the chain.

"There," he said kissing her again.

Mary released her hair as it flirted against her shoulders. The pendant rested on the bottom of her neck. She looked down, then back to Joe. More tears plummeted from her eyes.

Joe closed the pendant on her chest forming the diamond-shaped heart. Mary attempted to say something, to say anything. Her emotions masked her voice. Instead, Joe saw Mary mouth the words *I love you* before she leaned over to kiss him.

The passionate kiss was one they had not experienced in many months, if not years. The pressure from their lips erupted. Her hands caressed the back of his head as their kiss grew more intimate.

The kissing continued. The sensation beneath her thighs raged. The only breaks from the kissing came as they took turns catching their breath, fast escaping their mouths.

A thud came as the empty, black velvet box fell from her lap to the floor. Joe grabbed her back holding her tight against his body. He lifted her off the chair lowering her to the floor before the fireplace.

The kissing continued. Each caressed the other; his hand slipping inside her pajama pants. After a few passionate moments, Joe lifted himself as if he was performing a push-up from the floor.

Her necklace shimmered in the lights from the flickering fireplace. She released a loud moan as he pressed himself into her.

Several moments had passed. Lights danced on the ceiling above them. Mary curled up beside him, her head on his naked chest. His heart pounded against her ear, his glistening skin heaved as his lungs gasped for air.

Mary kissed the side of Joe's face, then whispered into his ear, "I will love you to the end of time."

22-Holiday

"HONEY, HAVE YOU SEEN my passport?" Mary said as she hurried around the bedroom opening and closing various dresser drawers with a manic rhythm.

Joe stood in the bedroom doorway. "I've got *it* right here."

"Ugh, I swear. I'm losing my mind."

"That's okay. It's such an exciting day. You must have forgotten you had asked me to hold on to it a few weeks ago."

"Honestly, between figuring out what clothes to take and not feeling too well the past couple of days… I'll be happy to be on the plane."

"Everything, okay?"

"Aunt Flo and cramps, if you must know… what time will the limo be here?"

"Uh… 9:30 is what the information says."

"Okay, I'll be down in a few minutes."

Joe kissed her before going downstairs to wait. Usually, he was the one running late. But, with his building excitement, he was extra-early today.

Two pieces of luggage sat by the front door. Packing for a summer trip versus one in winter requires no big, bulky sweaters or jackets. The iPad Gabriel had given him with his instructions accompanied their travel documents inside his backpack on the floor next to the luggage.

Joe started his usual ritual he does every time he leaves for a trip checking his wallet. *I've got a thousand in cash and the two credit cards... ha... I guess I won't need these insurance cards anymore?*

Before closing his wallet, he flipped over a small photograph. It was of Mary, his grandma, and himself from their last visit home to Houston before she had died.

Joe sat at his desk of the home office. After he had turned on the lamp, he slipped the cardboard backing out of the small picture frame before him. He held his graduation picture and the folded, thin paper with its mysterious letters and numbers.

I should take these.

"The limo is here," Mary said as she shouted from the upstairs bedroom. "I'm coming down in a minute."

Joe folded the picture with the paper together before turning off the desk lamp. As he opened the front door, he slipped the folded items into the top, zipper pocket of his backpack.

The doorbell rang throughout the house as Joe opened the door. He saw a familiar face.

"Hello... hey, Thomas I didn't know you were picking us up."

"Good morning, Dr. Bishop. Yes, that's correct, Sir. I will drive you and your wife to the airport."

"Here I am." Mary came downstairs. Her face red from running around putting the last items together in her bags.

"Good morning, Mrs. Bishop. My name is Thomas."

"Good morning, Thomas. Wow, I've never been in a limo," Mary said stepping out on the front porch.

"Are *these* your bags, Dr. Bishop?"

"Yes, *these two here.* I'll carry *this one*," Joe said as he lifted his backpack on his shoulders. They followed Thomas to the waiting limo.

"Uh... Honey?"

"Yes?" Joe said.

"Did you go around the house to make sure everything is unplugged or locked? I know how paranoid you are when we go somewhere."

"Oh... yeah, thanks. I'll be right back."

The picture had distracted Joe from finishing his routine. To keep up his normal appearance, he investigated each room of the house making sure the windows were locked. Mary waited on the front porch watching Thomas place the luggage in the trunk.

This is weird.... I couldn't care less if anyone comes into our place... it's not like we're ever coming back.

Joe stopped in the living room for a moment to admire a picture hanging on the wall. Since they had married in a courthouse, they did not have a formal wedding. As a surprise for Valentine's Day in 2004, Joe had arranged a session with a photographer. He in a rented tux; Mary in a shimmering white dress. This picture had become their wedding portrait.

I forgot this one.

He snapped a picture of the portrait with his phone.

I have to remember to tell Gabriel I want this digital picture sent with us.

His natural instincts took over. Joe checked the back door in the kitchen. The door handle was secure. To his satisfaction, it was closed and locked.

Joe turned to walk out but stopped short of leaving the kitchen. With a wicked grin, he returned to the door.

Screw it. He unlocked the door. *Who cares anymore?*

"Okay, Mary. Everything's good," Joe said as he walked out the front door pretending to lock it behind him.

"Mrs. Bishop, this way, please," Thomas said as he held open the driver's side, rear door.

They entered the back-seat as Thomas closed the door behind them. Mary distracted her nerves with small talk with Thomas as they left their driveway. Joe gazed out the tinted windows at the familiar, passing scenery of his neighborhood.

We'll never see this place, again.

A quick sense of *déjà vu* overcame Joe flashing back to the summer after high school graduation. He remembered his grandma growing smaller in his rearview mirror as she stood in their driveway waving, as Mary leaned against him on their way to New York. But, this time was different... very different.

Thomas continued on the Long Island Parkway toward JFK. The reality of what was about to happen was becoming too surreal for Joe.

It's finally happening...

"Mary, how are you doing?" Joe asked as he attempted to distract his thoughts.

"Better now, thanks. I am still nervous because I've not flown since our Paris trip."

You have butterflies now... just wait. "Oh, it'll be okay. I still get a little nervous when I fly, but if it's the same private jet I took last time... you will love it."

Over the next thirty minutes, Joe sat in silence. The neighborhoods, which had become familiar to him passed by out of sight. Even though he grew up in southeast Houston, Long Island had become home.

I should have spent this week doing a final tour of my favorite places to eat.

Joe sat alone with his thoughts. Mary released her nervous energy by talking with Thomas. Her latest question was if he had ever driven any famous people.

Joe overheard the conversation. *Huh, all that fame... fortune... in a few years, they'll all wish they were at Salvation.*

As they arrived at the airport, traffic grew chaotic. Thomas drove them by the departures terminal to the section reserved for private flights. The snow banks on either side of the entrance ushered the limo into the parking lot of a dark-gray building.

Two heartbeats raced in the silent backseat from excitement. Thomas opened the rear door.

"Mrs. Bishop, we are here. I will get your bags and meet you inside the doors, *there.*" Thomas pointed to the front of the building.

Joe was impatient getting out on his side joining Mary in front of the car. They walked up the steps to the building. Two, large glass doors automatically slid open as they approached. Once through, the glass doors slid closed, only to open again with Thomas walking through with their luggage rolling behind him.

"Dr. and Mrs. Bishop, please this way," Thomas said.

Thomas led them to the counter. A security guard dressed in black with a red, lapel pin sat behind a computer terminal greeting them.

"I have Dr. and Mrs. Bishop for their flight."

The guard confirmed their faces matched against pictures appearing on his computer screen. "Okay, your plane is waiting. Go through *this area here* and out the doors in the back," the guard said.

Without acknowledging the guard, Thomas followed the instructions with Joe and Mary behind him.

"Thank you," Mary said to the guard as they passed. "Wow, no one needs to see any identification?" she asked Joe.

"Yeah, I wondered that too my first time through last year. We now see how the other half lives with their private jets," Joe said.

As the glass doors in the back of the building slid open, they walked onto the tarmac to the waiting, private jet. The door already open welcomed the passengers. A small stairway led up from the tarmac.

"Please follow me," Thomas said as he started up the stairway carrying both pieces of luggage.

They entered as the captain and co-pilot greeted them. Thomas placed their luggage into a cabinet in the rear of the plane.

"Hi, folks. We'll get you in the air in a few minutes and on our way to Mauritius," the captain said. "Take a seat. We'll be back with you in a moment."

"Wow," Mary said as she looked through the cabin.

She strolled down the aisle, her hand reaching out to touch the softness of the white leather seats. Golden accents complemented the wood-grain walls.

"Yeah, it's something all right," Joe said.

"Is anyone else coming with us?" Mary asked.

"Mrs. Bishop, the jet is yours for the entire flight," Thomas said as he returned from putting away their luggage. "Dr. and Mrs. Bishop, if there's not anything else I can help you with, I want to wish you safe travels on your trip."

"Oh, thank you, Thomas. I loved our chat. I can't wait to tell you about our trip when we return. Oh, I'm assuming you'll be the one picking us up when we return?" Mary asked.

"Uh... yes," Thomas replied as she selected her seat from the many options to choose.

As Thomas passed Joe who still stood in the front of the cabin, Thomas spoke in a softer voice, which only Joe could hear. "Dr. Bishop, it's been my pleasure knowing you."

Thomas shook Joe's hand, a crushing handshake before leaving down the stairs onto the tarmac.

That sounded so final... I wonder what parts of this Thomas knows... I guess it pays to be the driver who hears all the conversations?

Joe sat beside Mary as he placed his backpack on an empty seat in front of him. The captain re-appeared from the cockpit.

"Dr. and Mrs. Bishop, we'll be taking off in about fifteen minutes. During our flight, if you need anything from us, pick up this phone, *here*. It connects to us in the cockpit." The captain pointed around the cabin.

"Drinks and food, help yourself, *here*. The entertainment system is *here*. And, once in the air, we'll come back to you every so often to make sure everything is okay. Any questions?"

"Yeah, how long is the flight?" Mary asked.

"Our flight time will be eighteen hours. It's eleven hours over to Dubai, and then another seven down to Mauritius."

"Oh, my... where's the bathroom?" she asked.

"It's back *there*, and everything operates like you're used to on a normal passenger plane. Okay, well... again, if you have questions call us once we're in the air."

The captain returned to the cockpit closing the door behind them. Joe and Mary held hands across the open aisle between their seats. Joe sensed her nervousness.

"It's okay, Honey. This looks exactly like the same jet I took before, and everything will be all right."

"I know, but just in case, I'm ready," Mary said as she pulled a plastic bag from her purse she carried.

"What the hell is that for?"

"Just in case I have to throw-up and can't make it to the bathroom," she said as she laughed rubbing her stomach.

Joe always enjoyed how Mary amused him in unexpected moments. "Ha. Funny. Just be sure if you do, to not get any on me," he said laughing.

"I'm kidding. I'm sure these butterflies will go away once we take off?"

Almost as if on cue, the jet moved forward. They pressed their hands harder together across the empty aisle. The plane made a quick, right turn.

Over the speaker, the captain's voice said, "Okay, folks we're ready to go."

As soon as the captain's voice fell silent, the engines roared faster. The jet shook like an angry tiger. With a sudden jolt, their bodies pressed into the back of their soft, white leather seats. The jet raced down the runway; the bouncing tires reverberated throughout the cabin.

After few seconds of jostling in their seats, the jet tilted up in front of them, lifting off the runway.

"Okay, Honey, here we go," Joe said. The ground grew further and further away. They were leaving home.

PRESENT - OVER THE INDIAN OCEAN
JANUARY 30, 2016
1,686 DAYS PRIOR TO IMPACT

FLYING LOSES ITS EXCITEMENT after the fourth hour. The first flight segment from JFK to Dubai flashed by in an instant. Champagne flowed as they watched movies from the comfort of their reclined leather seats inside the Gulfstream 650.

After a two-hour layover in Dubai for refueling, the second flight overnight passed in slow motion. The alcohol had worn off its effects as daylight broke over the Indian Ocean.

"Good morning. We hope you've had a good flight," the Captain said over the cabin speakers. "We're on our final approach into Mauritius. Please prepare for landing."

The voice pierced through their hung-over heads. Mary pressed the button at the window beside her seat. Light shimmered through the cabin reflecting off the ocean as the blackout panel lifted.

"Oh, wow, Joe... it's so amazing."

Hours of darkness flying overnight had hidden the turquoise water of the Indian Ocean. Daytime exposed the various hues of blue water surrounding a lush, green island below their plane.

"How did you sleep?" Joe asked.

"I passed out once we left Dubai... I had too much to—"

The long flight with their many drinks forced Mary to the bathroom. Faint sounds resulting from the alcohol overindulgence leaked through the closed door. A queasiness hit Joe as well as he too had consumed too much of the champagne during their flight.

"Ugh, I am much better now," Mary said leaving the bathroom returning. As she fastened her seatbelt, she said, "Yeah, way too much to drink last night."

The jet lunged forward as it made its final descent to the runway. Joe and Mary peeked out their windows. The turquoise water had disappeared. Lush greenery expanded as the island grew close.

Their seats jolted as the wheels contacted the ground. Their bodies pushed forward with the braking and taxiing to the terminal building.

"Welcome to Mauritius, Dr. and Mrs. Bishop," came the Captain's voice over the speakers.

Joe and Mary unbuckled their seatbelts as the cockpit door opened. The co-pilot emerged opening the side, entry door. Voices from the ground crew rippled into the cabin as they positioned the gangway.

"Good morning, Gabriel," the co-pilot said to the man entering the cabin from the stairs. The co-pilot disappeared behind Gabriel out of the plane.

"Gabriel... I didn't know ... " Joe said as he stood to greet him.

"Hope you had a good flight?"

"Yes, it was wonderful," Joe said. "This is my wife."

"Hello, Mary. Joseph has said so many wonderful things," Gabriel said as he offered his hand to her as she stood.

"Mary, *this,* is Gabriel. He's the one I've been working with from the Eden Foundation."

She reached her arms around Gabriel's shoulders giving him a familiar hug. "So, you're the one I need to thank for this vacation and for funding my husband's research?"

Gabriel returned her affection. "Yes… we at Eden think highly of your husband and his work." As Mary released her hold on Gabriel, he continued, "Come, let's go. We've got an hour ride to the resort where you'll be staying."

Joe stood in silence smiling.

I'm glad they seem to get along well. I will need all his help to tell her what's coming next.

"So, if *you* are here too, y'all won't be talking about any research will you since we're on vacation?" Mary asked as she flashed a grin to Joe. He recognized Mary's signal. This trip is about relaxing, not work.

"Oh no, not at all. Our Foundation has invited several people to our resort this week to thank them for their efforts. Part of my job is to make sure we take care of everyone while they are here."

Mary clasped Joe's arm drawing him closer. "Honey, you never mentioned his name, but you always said he was a good guy."

"Yeah, Gabriel has been helpful through everything," Joe said.

"Come, let's go." Gabriel ushered them to a waiting limo.

Gabriel led Joe and Mary to the backseat. A ground crew member placed their luggage inside the trunk.

"Please, help yourself. There's a nice fully stocked bar back here." Gabriel pushed open the wood-paneled door behind the front seat hiding the drinks.

"Oh, no more for me. My stomach can't take any more alcohol… I'll take a water if that's okay?"

"Absolutely, Mrs. Bishop, here you go." Gabriel gave her a half-liter bottle of water. Beads of condensation dripped from the bottom given the humid, tropical island air.

"Oh, please, please call me Mary. Mrs. Bishop sounds too formal for me."

"I'll take one, too." The limo drove from the airport through the outskirts of a small village. "How long have you been here?" Joe asked.

"Our first guests arrived a few days ago... so, it's been about two weeks." As he spoke, Gabriel texted on his phone. "So, either of you ever been to this part of the world?"

"Are you kidding? We've been to Paris. That's about it, other than our home in Texas. Heck, we've never even been in the southern hemisphere before." Mary's voice cracked in amazement as she stared out the window at the passing landscape.

"You will find Mauritius to be an exquisite place."

"Does the Foundation own the resort?" Mary asked.

"Yes. Our resort is on the Le Morne peninsula on the south-end of the island. It's very secluded there as our guests enjoy the privacy we offer."

The two-lane road twisted through plantations of sugarcane fields stretching for miles around the limo. Gentle, rolling hills broke the monotony of the flat trail they had traversed. Small villages appeared at the end of each plantation where the locals lived who worked the fields. As the last village drifted away hidden by the fertile fields, the first glimpses of turquoise water emerged as they reached the island coastline.

"It's so beautiful," Mary said as the sunlight reflected into the backseat off the water.

"Speaking of beautiful, Mary, the stones in your necklace match the colors of the ocean," Gabriel said.

Mary placed her hand onto the diamond-encrusted pendant, "Thanks. This was my Christmas gift this year from Joe." She leaned over on Joe's arm smiling at Gabriel.

"Looks expensive," Gabriel said, his eyes piercing at Joe.

"Well, you know, she's special and deserves the best. I thought I'd get her something *out of this world*," Joe said as he smiled with his inside joke. Gabriel returned a smile to Joe.

Expensive? Hell... your Foundation has financed Salvation for who knows how many trillions of dollars. I don't think you'll miss what I spent on her necklace.

The limo continued along the coastline. Crystal-clear water bordered golden, sandy beaches. After forty-five minutes, the water disappeared.

A lush jungle of thick, green trees emerged. Branches stretched over the road creating a canopy blocking most of the sunlight.

"Wow." Mary's mouth dropped open as she saw a single mountain appear as the canopy of trees cleared.

Green foliage covered the two-thousand-foot mountain. A steep, brown cliff faced its southern side. Between the lush vegetation and metallic-gray rocks, a waterfall crashed to the jungle floor.

"I know. It's amazing, isn't it?" Gabriel said. "We should be there in a few minutes."

The tree canopy appeared again blocking the sight of the mountain. A never-ending, ten-foot-tall, black-iron fence followed alongside the road.

"As I mentioned, our resort is very secluded," Gabriel said.

The limo slowed turning into a gated driveway. Two large metal doors with the resort's red-triangle logo opened allowing the limo to pass. Iron crashed together following the car as the gate closed behind them.

They stopped in front of a thatched-roof building. Two small, dark-skinned men in white suits waived. Each man approached either side of the limo opening both back doors in unison. The passengers left the limo as one man retrieved the luggage.

They walked through a courtyard overflowing with yellow and orange orchids. The sweet-scented pollen was a delight to the purple dragonflies dancing across the flower tops.

"*They* will take your luggage to your room. Before you go to your room, I will show you around our resort," Gabriel said.

Gabriel led Joe and Mary through a covered walkway absent any walls allowing the sea breeze to pass through from the Indian Ocean. Lily pads with lavender stems floated on the ponds under the elevated walkway. Bumblebees chased their competition for their turn of the flowers' nectar.

Swaying palm trees lined the deep-blue water of an infinity swimming pool stretching ahead to the ocean. The blue sky kissed the horizon in the distance. Fountains on either side of the pool sprayed water high into the air splashing over fish statues as if they had jumped in from the sea.

"It's just so... " Mary said pausing to take in all the sights as Gabriel explained the different restaurant options.

"So, *this* is the swimming pool area. There's a pool bar, *there*. The restaurant is down *this way* beyond the spa. And, on the other side is the beach." Gabriel pointed the directions to the jet-lagged couple. "All the people you see in the pool, they're our guests. You'll get to meet them in due time."

Are they coming with us too? How many of us are going together? Do they all know about Salvation?

"So, they're researchers, too?" Joe asked.

"Some are. Our Foundation represents many interests... but, we'll talk more about it later."

Gabriel completed the tour around the grounds of the resort returning to the open-air entrance. A different small, dark-skinned man greeted them.

"*This* is Sami. He will be your butler for your stay. If you need anything, anything at all, Sami is your man," Gabriel said. After handing Joe and Mary over to Sami, Gabriel said, "Okay, you two get settled in. I will stop by to see how you are doing, soon."

"Welcome to paradise, Dr. and Mrs. Bishop. Please, follow me. I will take you to your bungalow." Sami motioned them to follow him down a path between the main thatched-roof building and the spa.

Similar to the other two men, who had greeted them upon their arrival, Sami was of Indian descent. His uniform was immaculate. A pressed, dark-blue cotton shirt complimented his bright, white pants and matching white gloves. Sami, as a butler, stood-out among the others working at the resort.

"*Here's* our spa. We have a wonderful menu of options there to relieve any stress. Here, please." Sami led them to a parked, white golf cart with three rows of leather-covered seats.

Sami drove. A small, black paved road, only wide enough to allow a single cart to pass, meandered through the resort. Small bridges crossed streams connecting different ponds and flower gardens between the bungalows.

"*Here* we are," Sami said. The cart stopped at a bungalow near the edge of the beach.

Sami guided them up the few steps to their bungalow and pushed open the door. Joe and Mary followed. A rush of cold air hit them as the muggy, tropical air stayed outside.

"*Here* is your bedroom… over *here*…. is your bar… and, *here* is the bathroom…"

"Oh my, look at *that tub*," Mary said. A deep, large stone tub enticed her in the center of the floor.

"Out *this door*, is your shower."

"Wow, it's outside," Mary said, her eyebrows lifted to Joe.

"And, *here* is the best part of our whole place." Sami walked through the bedroom to two large curtains drawn together pushing them apart in one quick motion. Like a magician, he revealed a glorious view. "*Here* is your beach."

French doors opened outward to the sandy beach. Two bamboo chairs sat around a small table. A hammock stretched between two, fat palm trees provided the perfect shade from the summer sun. The golden sandy beach tempted them a few feet from their door.

"Oh, my God," Joe and Mary said together as they stepped barefoot on the warm sand.

"I can't wait to get in *that* water, Joe."

"Again, if you need anything… anything at all, please call me at *this number*." Sami presented Joe his small business card. "*This* number will ring *my phone*. I always have *this* with me."

The three of them went back inside the bungalow. Sami started toward the front door. "Is there anything you need, now?"

"I'm a little hungry," Mary said looking at Joe.

"Okay, I'll have fruit brought to your room. Here's the room-service menu. You can order anything you'd like, or you can visit any of the restaurants. As we say here, *whatever you want*, we will make it happen."

"Thanks, Sami," Joe said.

The door closed behind Sami as he left them alone. Mary placed her arms on Joe's shoulders pulling her closer. She looked up into his eyes. "Thank you for bringing me here. I love it."

"We should thank Gabriel and the Foundation."

"Maybe, but after your hard work you've done... your research brought us here."

"True. We will see where else my research can take us," Joe said withholding the rest of his secret.

Joe fell with Mary onto the bed kissing each other. After a few moments, a knock at the front door interrupted them.

Mary stood from the bed to answer. Sami returned holding a chilled, glass plate with green, red, yellow, and purple fruit. The sweetness lifted off the plate. Mary took the plate as Sami reminded them to call if they needed anything.

Sami left. Joe and Mary were alone.

Joe looked out the glass doors to the beach, while Mary ate the fruit, most she had never before seen. Joe smiled. He was at peace.

This has to be the most beautiful place on Earth.

"Okay, they are settled into their room," Sami said into his cell phone.

Sami sat in the golf cart looking at an iPad in his lap. A video feed of Joe and Mary played from within the bungalow. Sami watched as Mary sat the fruit plate on a table beside the bed before slipping off her shirt. Her bare chest pressed into Joe's back.

"I'll let you know if there are any problems, Mr. Gabriel."

PRESENT - MAURITIUS
JANUARY 31, 2016
1,685 DAYS PRIOR TO IMPACT

A DAY OF BLUE SKIES devoid of clouds basking in the summer, Southern Hemisphere sun, Mauritius may as well have been a world far removed from Long Island. Crystal-clear, turquoise water surrounded the island peninsula of the resort.

A snorkeler's paradise lies within a coral reef five-hundred-feet offshore creating a calm lagoon, which encircled the island. Warm, tropical breezes pushed through the coconut palm trees swaying in the afternoon sun.

Joe and Mary enjoyed a secluded stretch of beach within the expansive resort. The spa effects of the golden, powdered sand provided warmth under their feet leaving the water carrying their dripping masks.

Sami greeted them as they returned to their bamboo beach chairs under a thatched-roof umbrella. "Good afternoon. Hope you are having a great day?" Sami asked.

"An absolutely wonderful day," Mary said as she smiled at Sami.

"I wanted to check if you needed anything... a drink by any chance?"

"Yeah, I'll have a beer, please," Joe said as he applied sunblock across Mary's upper back.

"And, you, Mrs. Bishop?"

"Uh... um... just some water, please."

"Anything to eat?"

"Could you bring more of the fruit you brought to the room yesterday?" Joe asked as the white lotion disappeared into Mary's skin. "Would you like some too, Sweetie?"

"No, only water for me. I'm still paying the price for drinking too much on our flight."

"Okay. One beer, one water, and fruit... I'll be back in a few minutes." Sami left. Spits of sand flew to them from Sami's bare feet as he trudged through the beach back to the main building.

Joe's legs straddled across the beach chair. His feet planted deep into the warm sand. As he finished applying the sunblock to his face, he wrapped his arms around Mary sitting in front of him on the same chair.

She tilted her head back kissing his lips and leaned into him. Joe supported her in his arms as he leaned back into the chair. The swaying palms behind them balanced the sound of the lapping waves before them.

"It's so relaxing here, isn't it?" Joe said. His heartbeat slowed to a pace not experienced in years.

"Yeah, it's like we're lost in paradise."

"No kidding, it's like we're sitting in the middle of a postcard, isn't it?" Joe said squeezing his Mary against him.

"I know we will have to leave, but I could stay here, forever."

Wow, this will be the last time we see the ocean?

The thought transfixed his mind to the unspoken secret he still had to tell Mary.

"Me, too… hey, I've got an idea… let's run away and stay here," Joe said. Part of him was serious; the other revealing the true reason they were in Mauritius.

"I'll go anywhere with you, Honey," Mary said as she rubbed the inside portion of his legs wrapped around her on the chair.

23 - DECEPTION

PRESENT - MAURITIUS
FEBRUARY 2, 2016
1,683 DAYS PRIOR TO IMPACT

PARADISE IS WONDERFUL. Beauty and astonishing views are everywhere. Cares are gone, melted away under the bright sunshine. Real life seems another world away; time is in slow motion.

Morning number three in Mauritius had arrived as the sun rose over the breaking waves in the distance across the lagoon. Mary had risen early to walk the beach, no longer having ill-effects from the overindulgence on the flight.

Joe took advantage of the rising sun to explore the lush, aromatic gardens on the grounds in the morning light. A purple dragonfly hovered above the lily pads in the pond ahead. Its flight was hypnotic. Joe was alone with his thoughts.

This waiting to leave is killing me.

"Pretty neat, isn't it?"

Joe recognized the familiar voice behind him. "Gabriel, it's about time you showed up."

"Joe, I'm sure you've been having a relaxing time and Sami has been taking great care of you, both."

"Oh, we have, and Sami's been great. But, that's not what I'm talking about… when are you telling me how to tell Mary? I'm tired of keeping this from her."

"We are getting closer. Trust me."

"Trust you? Hell, that's all I've got at this point."

Joe and Gabriel continued down the pathway through the botanical garden. Gabriel said, "Actually, I came to find you. I wanted to tell you about an excursion we've planned."

"An excursion?"

"Yes, it is a day-trip for you and Mary along with six others who are going to Salvation."

"Six others? So, eight of us are leaving?"

"Yes, plus three crew members… so, you finally will meet some of the others. And, since you will spend the rest of your lives together, we wanted to send you all on this trip to begin building relationships."

"A team-building trip?"

"Well, yes… we can call it that. You will learn more about the others… where they are from… "

Joe stopped walking. Gabriel had his full attention.

"But, the same rule applies as before… I am telling you and the others not to talk about Salvation. We are confident these conversations will not happen. No one knows whom among you knows what."

"Don't you think the real team-building starts by letting us talk with each other? About what we've experienced… or about what our roles will be at Salvation?"

"All those conversations will come soon enough. There are others like you with a partner who knows nothing about what is happening. You do not want Mary to find out this way. Trust me, I have seen it happen before."

The pathway twisted through the botanical garden ending at the main pool area. A free table by the poolside bar welcomed them.

Joe blocked out the scenic beauty of his surroundings. "So, others are bringing their wives too?" Joe asked.

"Wives, husbands, partners… some are single."

Two beers arrived at their table. The staff of the resort knows all the preferences of its guests from months of observations by Eden.

Joe and Gabriel reached for their beers at the same time. Gabriel lifted his glass toward Joe. Over the clinking glasses, Gabriel said, "Cheers."

"Cheers," Joe said in return.

The humid, morning air sent condensation droplets racing down the ice-cold glasses. Beads of water dripped from the bottom of each to the table.

They chugged their beers like long-lost fraternity brothers reunited after years apart. Joe slammed his empty glass on the table.

"Ah... that's good stuff." Joe wiped his lips with the back of his hand and watched Gabriel. "When do I tell Mary?"

Gabriel finished his beer. "I promise, after your flight, I will give you the instructions."

"Flight? I assumed this trip was happening here on the island."

"Actually, on Thursday morning, you all will board a van. We will take everyone to the local airfield where you fly out to Reunion Island nearby. There, you will spend the day."

"And, we couldn't do this here?"

"It is an easy hike through the jungle there to a lake with two waterfalls. You think it is beautiful, here?"

Joe spun his head around taking in his surroundings. He forced a grin as the ocean emerged from his Gabriel-focused blinders.

"Wait until you see this little place. Sami will give you more details this afternoon about the arrangements."

"Gabriel, you have to understand why it's been killing me keeping this secret from her, don't you?" Joe motioned to the bartender for another round. "Hell, I've not even asked if are you married or have a girlfriend, and what in the hell do they think you do?"

Gabriel leaned backward. A slight wrinkle appeared in the middle of his flawless forehead. He paused for a moment before responding to Joe.

"I was in a relationship before I got into this work."

"And, what happened to her? Why aren't y'all together now?"

The bartender brought them another beer as Gabriel stood. "Well, she was a he... He and I were from the same small town in Iowa. As you can imagine... we had to leave home to be together..."

Gabriel stepped to the edge of the bar's platform overlooking the pool. Joe watched as Gabriel turned away. Gabriel's normal perfect posture slumped.

"We moved to Los Angeles and were happy together. Then, the Foundation recruited me to join... and like you, they told me not to tell Jason anything."

"So, you must have told him or left him because he doesn't sound like he's in the picture anymore?"

"One night, we were down at Venice Beach watching the sunset... and... I couldn't take it any longer and told him."

"And, what happened? That's when he left you?"

Gabriel faced Joe. "The next day, when I got home, he was gone... his closet was empty... and, I've not heard from him since."

"Why do you think he left?"

"It's obvious, isn't it? He thought I was crazy... our lives were already crazy enough... and... that was just too much for him to take."

Confidence had left Gabriel's voice. He rejoined Joe at the table.

"To be honest, I realized I was foolish to tell him."

"Foolish? What part? The part about a manufacturing Moon-base supporting the construction of a Martian facility. A place where the human race will escape... that part, you mean?"

"Yeah... *that part*." Gabriel pounded the second beer in seconds. As Gabriel slammed the table with his empty glass, the momentary slip of his posture had straightened. The wrinkle on his forehead vanished.

"Okay, I have to tell the others about the trip." Gabriel stood and followed the stone pathway between the bar and pool. He stopped and said to Joe, "I will see you after your flight. Then, I will help prepare you to tell Mary."

"Fine. I'll need all the help I can get... I'm trusting your experience here with others on how to do this."

"Well, have fun Thursday," Gabriel said, as he left the bar area. Joe remained behind enjoying his beer, and the next one, and another.

Gabriel walked around the pool to the thatched-roof building. Once out of Joe's view, Gabriel reached into his front pants' pocket pulling out a black, leather wallet.

The well-worn leather opened. Between various currencies of cash, Gabriel slipped into his hand a small two-inch-by-two-inch picture. A young Gabriel was arm-in-arm with an equally attractive young guy with black hair.

Gabriel slumped his posture again staring at the picture. After a few moments, he slipped the picture back into his wallet and straightened himself. He walked down the pathway from the building. A purple dragonfly buzzed behind him.

Gabriel opened the door of the spa and walked inside. Two young women, each wearing nothing but a white cotton robe, stepped out of a steamy sauna.

"Pretty neat, isn't it?"

PRESENT - MAURITIUS, 9:11 A.M.
FEBRUARY 4, 2016
1,681 DAYS PRIOR TO IMPACT

AFTER BREAKFAST, Joe and Mary waited in the open-air lobby of the thatched-roof building in front of the resort as Sami had instructed. Another gorgeous day was before them.

"I'm actually happy to see other people. It's been kinda strange being so isolated here," Mary said.

Two attractive women entered the lobby area where Joe and Mary waited. From their looks and the way they carried themselves, Joe guessed they were in their early twenties. One was blonde, the other brunette.

"Isn't it so beautiful here? Hi, my name is Joanie, and *this* is my sister, Heather," the blonde woman said.

Joe is usually first to do the introductions, but Mary was quick to shake their hands. "Hi, I'm Mary, and *this* is my husband, Joseph."

"Nice to meet you," Joe said smiling at the young women.

They look too young to be scientists.

"Can you believe how like awesome it is here?" Heather said, "I still can't believe how like lucky we are."

The two sisters walked to the pond area behind where Joe and Mary stood. A large, orange fish swimming around the lily pads captured their attention.

"So, where are y'all from?" Mary asked.

Heather spun around to Mary. "Oh, I love your accent. We're like from Santa Monica."

Joanie joined Heather in giving Mary her attention. "So, how did you two win this trip?" Joanie asked.

"Win this trip?" Joe asked as Mary grabbed his hand.

"Yeah, like how did you like win? This guy like approached us on the beach, and he asked us like some questions—"

"Those questions were hard, too," Heather said interrupting her sister.

"Hells yeah they were," Joanie said as she took her sister's hand, "he gave us two tickets to come here."

Joe stood quiet, unsure what to make of what the two sisters were telling them.

What the hell? Why would you leave to go to an island with some stranger?

"So, y'all trusted this guy?" Mary asked.

"Honey, we're approached all the time back home with men giving us things," Joanie said.

Heather continued almost as if she knew what her sister would say next. "Yeah, and when that limo arrived the next day, we were like, yep we're going."

"Hello, how are you all doing?" a man's voice from the front of the lobby area said. "Gabriel said this is where we were to meet for our trip."

Joe introduced himself with Mary followed by the two sisters. "So, where are you from?" Joe asked.

The man introduced himself as Gary, who appeared about the same age as Joe. "I'm from Seattle."

"What line of work are you in, Gary?" Joe asked.

Please don't tell me you won a competition.

"Me, oh... I work as a systems engineer at Boeing on the communications and electrical systems for new jets the company designs."

Okay, that's more like it. So, you're like me and know what's really going on here.

"That's cool," Joe said.

"And, I've worked as a private consultant part-time. That's when the Eden Foundation approached me to help with some engineering designs."

"So, you're like my husband then, where the Foundation sent you here as a reward for your work?"

"Sure... uh... exactly," Gary said as he stuttered and lifted one eyebrow making eye contact with Joe.

Is that a hint, Gary?

The two sisters became bored with the conversation and stepped back over to watch the fish. Gary asked, "So, Joseph, what is it you do?"

Joe explained his work in genetic research and his promising developments in finding cures for various cancers. During the conversation, Joe and Gary could only hope the other could read their true thoughts. Both struggled with the real knowledge of what is happening.

After a few moments had passed, the group of strangers saw Gabriel walking through the open-air hallway from the swimming pool. Three people followed him, all chatting together. They approached Joe's group.

"Good morning, everyone. I hope you are all excited about our little adventure today?" Gabriel said. He followed by introducing the three people with him, including the others.

With Gabriel was Chantal, an African woman from Uganda, who looked to be in her early thirties. Chantal is in the food nutrition industry. She had developed a unique system for delivering nutrients to foods grown in drought-stricken areas of Africa.

Next, Gabriel introduced Mr. Lin Wu from Shanghai. Wu had developed nano-structures with the ability to travel to specific cells within the human body to administer specialized medication.

And, the last person Gabriel introduced was Heinrich Dieter from Austria. At over six-feet-tall, Heinrich was a chiseled statue of a man. His muscular features erupted through his shorts and tank-top.

"Heinrich is the world-record holder in the decathlon," Gabriel said. The sisters gave their full attention to Heinrich's introduction.

After Gabriel had provided the background of the sisters, Gary, Joe and Mary; the group introductions were complete.

"Well, good news," Gabriel said, "I have cleared my schedule. So, I will join everyone today for the trip."

His announcement made Joanie giggle as she gave a flirtatious smile to Gabriel. Her sister seemed not to mind Joanie's obvious advances as Heather rubbed Heinrich's biceps with her frisky hands.

"Okay, our ride is here. Let us head to the airport shall we."

All eight, including Gabriel, got inside a parked, black mini-van. They left following the same two-lane road everyone had taken earlier when they had arrived.

Idle conversations continued between the strangers. Gabriel and the driver held their own, private discussion.

Mary, sitting beside Joe, turned to chat with the two sisters, who sat behind them. Joe stared out of the window at the passing scenery. New questions filled his mind.

Who knows the real reason we're here? Obviously, the lady from Africa and the guy from China. Oh, and Gary from Seattle... we all seem like people needed at Salvation... but the Austrian and the sisters?

Joe's questions were short-lived. After fifteen minutes, the mini-van had arrived at a small, grass-covered airfield. A plane sat at the end of the grass runway with two propellers, one on either side of the cabin. What caught everyone's attention were the combination wheels and water skis for ground or sea landings.

As the mini-van parked beside the plane, Gabriel said, "Okay, everyone. We are here."

The lone mountain hid the airfield surrounded by a thick forest of coconut palm trees. During World War II, the Allies had built the airfield. Today, it serves the locals, separate from the international airport on the north-end of the island.

Gabriel and his guests stepped inside the plane. The pilot greeted everyone and instructed them to put on their headsets after fastening their seat belts.

The headset allowed Gabriel to speak to everyone during the flight. He planned to explain different things about the location and history of the area.

Everyone was ready. The plane bounced down the flat, grassy runway. Palm trees lining the airfield approached fast as they climbed clearing the treetops.

The plane flew in front of the lone mountain and crossed over the turquoise lagoon encircling the island. A chorus of *ooh's* and *ah's* accompanied the view of colorful corals through the pristine, clear waters. The plane continued its westward ascent to a cruising altitude.

Gabriel's voice came over the headsets. "I will pass around small bottles of water. Please drink these because we want to make sure everyone stays well-hydrated today."

Gabriel passed through the cabin water bottles with tiny, black labels with the resort's red triangle logo. Yet, another hot-and-humid day easily persuaded everyone to drink.

"We will be *there* in about thirty minutes," Gabriel said through the headsets.

Gabriel left his microphone open allowing the passengers to overhear the conversations in the cockpit. "Looks like clouds are building up," the pilot said.

The headsets went silent. Joe looked through the cockpit and saw billowing cumulous nimbus clouds ahead. The clouds seemed to appear out of nowhere on the horizon.

To this point, the flight had remained smooth as if they were floating above the ocean. After everyone had overheard what the pilot had told Gabriel, the plane vibrated up-and-down.

Clouds grew taller and menacing frightening away the sun as the light disappeared. The plane bounced off one cloud to the other as the pilot did his best holding the flight steady.

Gabriel's voice appeared again through the headsets. "Looks like we're experiencing some turbulence here. Make sure your seatbelts are tight and hold on."

The once, bright sunshine turned into a scary purple-greenish hue. Before, the plane had flown through the maze of billowing clouds, but no longer.

Clouds caved in their pathway through the sky. Flashes of lightning danced around them. Each flash brought a round of screams from the passengers. Mary clutched her nails deep into Joe's bare leg beside her.

Gabriel's microphone remained open. The pilot said, "Sir, I don't know if I can handle... the plane... is... May Day, May Day.... this is *Foxtrot-Alpha-Kilo-Echo*. We are at position—"

The headsets fell silent. All the passengers held onto the seats and windows. They braced themselves to keep from slamming against the seats. Everyone looked around at each other. Their faces etched with the sheer terror of what was happening.

Mary pressed herself as close to Joe as possible with a white-knuckle death-grip on his arm. The growing pressure snapped Joe from his frighten trance.

What the hell is happening? All this shit I've gone through keeping this secret, and we're going to die in a plane crash?

Joe sensed the growing panic coming from Gabriel and the pilot. The plane nose-dived. A sudden tip forward caused a loud scream to erupt from everyone, including Joe.

The screams eclipsed the noise of the plane's engines and roaring thunder. Joe grabbed Mary as tight as he could and yelled, "I love you."

She responded the same. The plane leaped in a violent motion upward as if it had come to the bottom of a roller-coaster.

With a sudden, quick-change in direction, Joe saw Mary's face look as if she was falling inside of a tunnel. The surrounding area grew darker-and-darker. He watched as her eyes opened-and-closed as slow as his.

They both passed out at the same time. Complete darkness filled their eyes. Silence entered the cabin. Their grip on each other loosened as they slumped together.

The other five passengers joined them in a similar, peaceful slumber in their seats. The plane bounced performing a roller-coaster ride through the storm clouds.

Through the headsets inside the frantic plane came Gabriel's voice. "Okay, pull up now. We are clear. They are all out."

"Yes, sir," the pilot said. He pulled back on the flight controls causing the plane to thrust its way through the sudden storm.

The pilot reached down on the console and turned off the flight-locator beacon. Moments had passed as the plane floated as calm as before emerging from the black, cloud tops

"Okay, take us to the ship," Gabriel said.

The pilot turned the plane. They flew in the opposite direction across the Indian Ocean for hours. The cabin remained quiet with its passengers asleep in their seats unaware they were safe.

24-SAFETY

DARKNESS. Joe had lost consciousness for several hours.

Light. It flickered inside his closed eyelids as he slowly opened them, his vision blurry. Joe felt padding and paper underneath him in a mysterious room.

Uneasiness overcame Joe. The table rocked back-and-forth feeling as if he was playing on a large swing.

What in the hell?

The motion was constant but gentle. Joe's eyes blinked faster clearing his vision. He lay on a hospital bed inside of a gray, dim-lit room.

Joe forced his torso up and swung his legs across the edge of the bed. He scanned around the room. It was empty. A single wooden chair sat in the corner. On the opposite wall from him was a large mirror.

Where... where am I?

His tongue moved inside his mouth; the dryness of his throat as coarse as cotton balls.

Moisture filled his lips. Joe stretched trying to shake-off what reminded him of the worst hangover he had ever experienced after Charlie's bachelor party many years prior.

What happened?

Not moving his body, the bed continued rocking. Joe lowered his head stretching out his neck, and in an instant, one name came to him.

Mary?

"Mary!" he shouted.

As he prepared to stand from the table, the gray door of the room opened. A bright light from the other side of the door surrounded Joe.

Through the light, the figure of Gabriel appeared. Gabriel entered the room closing the door behind him.

"Gabriel?"

Joe tried to stand. His legs were too weak as Gabriel rushed to his bedside preventing him from falling.

"What the hell happened? I remember the storm coming out of nowhere... and... the plane was..."

"Joe, everything is okay."

"Mary, where's Mary?"

"She's okay. We have her resting in another room."

Joe pushed himself back onto the bed as Gabriel backed away to give him space. "Where the hell are we?"

"It's part of the departure plan for Salvation," Gabriel said.

"Part of the plan... what plan? Where the hell is Mary?"

Gabriel sat in the chair. "Joe, we are on a boat. We are going to our launch site on a tiny island two-thousand miles southeast of Mauritius."

"A boat? ... What about the plane... the storm?"

Gabriel placed his elbows on the armrest and balled his hands into a double-fist in front of his face. "Yes, the excursion... the plane ride to Reunion Island... that was a decoy."

"A decoy for what?"

"Like I told you, Salvation will do everything possible to protect its secret. With the passengers on board your plane leaving to go to Salvation... co-workers... friends... family... everyone will look for you."

Joe shook his head. His brain could not comprehend what Gabriel was saying.

"And, we can't have them asking questions. So, to them, you all died in a plane crash."

By this time, blood rushed through Joe's legs, boiling in his heart pounding through his chest.

Joe pushed himself off the table and rushed to the door. The door handle did not open as it locked automatically behind Gabriel when he entered.

"Mary!" Joe shouted banging his fist against the door.

"Joe, relax... she's fine. Trust me."

"Trust you? Trust you? I'm tired of trusting you," Joe said as he turned from the door and approached Gabriel. Before Gabriel could stand, Joe grabbed Gabriel's arms pinning his body back against the chair.

Gabriel attempted to free himself. In a rushed voice, Gabriel said, "Don't you see. If they find the debris of the plane and no bodies, they will presume everyone is dead. No one will continue to look for you or ask questions.... Let me go!"

Gabriel freed his left arm. This gave him the leverage to push Joe's weakened body away.

"No more games. No more secrecy. Where the hell is Mary?"

Joe paced the room until ending up leaning his backside against the padded table.

"Everyone was safe the entire time of the flight. We got the weather forecast telling us it would turn rough. This was when we executed our plan."

Joe resisted an urge to charge at Gabriel.

"The water I handed out during our flight... it contained a drug to make everyone unconscious so we could bring you here."

Joe sat in disbelief as Gabriel continued. "The record will show you all departed a flight from Mauritius, a storm developed, our pilot sent a distress call, and the plane crashed into the ocean."

Joe's body relaxed. Gabriel's words made strange sense.

"But, once the pilot radioed for help, he turned off the tracking beacon and flew out of the storm. Two hours later, we made our water landing and boarded this ship. Tomorrow, we will arrive at our launch site."

"But... um... why the hell go through all that shit, when we all knew we were leaving for Salvation, soon?"

"Just how willing would you have been to take part in faking your death? Are you sure everyone on board the flight knew what was in store for them about Salvation? It had to be believable... it had to seem real."

Joe looked at the ceiling in disbelief on what he was hearing. "But, what about the plane? If it brought us to this ship, where's the debris coming from?"

"We flew the plane back by remote control to the coordinates of the storm. It flew at a low altitude avoiding any radar. Once it got to the area where we encountered the storm, we crashed it."

Joe forced his stare direct to Gabriel. His eyes became small-and-narrow. His focus burned through Gabriel.

"Where... in... the... hell... is... Mary?" Joe asked.

4:04 P.M.

DARKNESS. Mary's last memory onboard the plane as it entered the fast-developing storm.

Light. The false sensation of the plane moving up-and-down jolted her eyes wide-open. As Mary awoke, plastic padding of a bed stuck to her arms.

Uneasiness overcame her. The bed swayed back-and-forth under her. She took several quick breaths attempting to wake herself from her stupor.

Mary pushed herself up. The paper, protective layer under her crackled with each move.

As Mary regained her strength, she swung her legs off the bed sitting on its edge. A dim-lit window was before her.

She studied the vision in the window, her eyes still groggy. As an image of a person came into her focus, the door of her room opened. A bright light from the hallway surrounded her.

"Mary, are you okay?" a man asked as he walked through the light.

"Uh… yes…. what the hell happened, Gabriel?"

Gabriel rushed to Mary as she sat. He grabbed her shoulders.

"You're okay. Everyone is safe," Gabriel said.

"That… that was not supposed to happen," Mary said as she shook her head clearing her thoughts.

"It was the only way we could safely get everyone here and fake your deaths." Gabriel smiled as he made eye contact with her.

"Well, you should have at least warned me ahead of time this was the plan." Mary straightened up on the bed allowing Gabriel to step away from her.

"So, we're headed to the launch site? And, Joe's okay, right?"

"Yes. We're on our way, and he's fine."

"I'm sure he is worried about me and where am I?"

"We'll bring him to you soon. But, first, we have to go over our next steps."

"Joe still has to tell me about going to Salvation. I was sure as hell you would have told Joe to let me in on the secret before we even came to Mauritius."

"Mary, we went over this before… about your reaction… so, whether we told you back in Long Island, in the air to Mauritius, at the resort… it doesn't matter now."

"Doesn't matter to you, but I've got to do a convincing acting job here. And, y'all sure as hell made this worse by him having to explain the faked plane crash."

"Maybe so, but we had to make it look to the rest of the world everyone on the plane died. And, if Joe would have told you about Salvation, would you have even been able to go on a supposed trip with him?"

Mary sat in silence. She thought about the scenario Gabriel had explained.

"Okay... I see your point. Whatever. I'm finally happy to get to this point as I've been waiting for a very long time."

"You have held up your end of the bargain perfectly, Mary."

Her eyes widened as the figure of Joe became clear in the window behind Gabriel.

As she pointed to the window, Mary said, "Joe's waking up, now."

Gabriel turned his head and saw into the room where Joe lay as he awoke.

"Collect your thoughts about how you will react tonight when Joe tells you. Someone will come get you in a few moments to take you to another room, and I'll bring him to you."

Mary replied, "Collect my thoughts... that's all I've been rehearsing to myself."

The door closed. She watched as Gabriel entered the room where Joe attempted to sit up on the edge of his bed. Joe called out Gabriel's name.

Mary stood from her table and walked over to the window. It was a one-way mirror preventing Joe from seeing her on the other side. A smile came upon Mary's face when Joe yelled out her name.

"Joseph, don't worry... I'm right here, Honey," she said in a soft voice. Her left palm pressed against the window as her right hand caressed the diamond, heart-shaped pendant around her neck.

"I'm here."

JUNE 11, 1997
PASADENA, TEXAS - GRADUATION DAY

THE BACKFIRE OF THE pickup truck startled Mary as it lunged forward from the stoplight a block away from the high school. Her adopted father, Bob Warner, sat behind the steering wheel with a proud smile. His daughter is graduating tonight from high school.

"I'm so proud of you, Mary."

"Thanks," she replied in a sarcastic tone waving through the front windshield to her friend in the car ahead.

"So, what are you and Joseph doing after graduation?"

"We're going out somewhere," Mary said as they drove into the football stadium parking lot.

"Look, I'm sorry about our fight this morning... it's just... it..."

"You were asking way too many personal questions about us. You're always getting into my personal space. Always asking me about Joe and his grandma... if I want to go live with him in New York, then I will."

Bob tightened his grip on the steering wheel. His lips pursed together holding back his comments to prevent restarting their earlier fight.

"Can you let me out here? Joe's right there," Mary said.

"Okay. I'll see you later. I love you, Mary."

Bob stopped the pickup truck long enough for her to get out without responding to him. As Bob drove through the parking lot, Mary was in his rearview mirror talking with Joseph and another friend.

The parking lot accommodates ten thousand cars on any Friday night during the Texas football season. A free spot was available beside the entrance to the stadium. Bob placed his handicap sign on his rearview mirror from behind his visor and parked.

The stadium crowd was a challenge to push through for Bob. Beads of sweat rolled down his back in the unbearable summer afternoon. The glaring sun lowered behind the tall pine treetops surrounding the stadium.

Bob found the perfect seat open for him at mid-field, four rows from the top. A terrific vantage point of the ceremony.

Tears filled Bob's eyes as he sat alone among the crowd on the aluminum bleachers. Memories of his daughter flashed before him. Bob remembered their first meeting when Mary was a little girl at the children's home. The good and bad times brought an unfamiliar emotion over him.

I can't believe how attached I've come to that girl.

To hold back the tears, Bob lowered his head into his hands.

One day... she'll understand why I did what I did. They will convince her...

Bob lifted his head and scanned across the football field. Clouds thickened on the horizon in front of the setting sun.

I need a drink so bad... they better live up to their end of the deal... they promised to protect her as long as I reported-in on the Bishops... they promised-

A familiar voice behind Bob broke his thoughts. "Well, hey Bob. I bet Mary is so excited."

Liz stood beside him on the bleacher steps. Bob rose and gave her a tremendous bear hug.

His bloodshot eyes usually a sign Bob had been on a bender. But, the fresh tears in the corner of his eyes signaled otherwise to Liz tonight.

"I can't believe my little girl is finally graduating," Bob said.

"I know. Isn't it something? Joseph's been so excited the past couple of days."

"I mean... she's ah, she's..." Bob said stuttering.

"Yeah, I bet she's excited too," Liz said confirming what Bob had attempted to convey.

"No, she's leaving me." Bob slid over as far as he could allowing Liz room to squeeze onto the end of the metal bleacher. "We had a big ol' fight this morning, and uh, she says she's moving to New York with Joseph."

Liz did a double-take at the surprising news, while Bob stared straight ahead. "Really? That's news to me," she said. "I'm sure Mary didn't mean she would go live with Joseph, just to visit."

No, Liz, she meant it. In fact, I want her to because she can watch Joseph from New York that way.

"I know Mary and me, we don't always get along. But, I love that girl."

"Awe and Mary loves you too," she said. Liz placed her arm around Bob's shoulders comforting him. "Plus, as long as I'm alive those two ain't living together unless they're married."

Her warm smile provided relief. Bob made eye-contact with her. "Liz, what say you and me... uh, maybe, we can go have dinner one night?"

JULY 27, 1989
PASADENA, TEXAS

FRIENDS AND FAMILY had stopped by after the funeral to pay their respects filling Rachel's house. The funeral had been a wonderful remembrance of Joseph's mother.

Cancer had taken her life at a young age, leaving behind ten-year-old Joseph, now an orphan. His care was now in the hands of Rachel's mother-in-law, Liz.

Bob Warner had been friends with Rachel and her husband, Jacob, for many years. After Jacob's death, Rachel often had frequented his hardware store needing his help around her house. Rachel's untimely death had shocked Bob as he had been paying significant attention to her in recent years.

During the wake, Bob stood alone in the living room. His new foster child, Mary, sat with Joseph in front of the television.

The discussions in the room went unnoticed to Bob. His memories of Rachel played in his mind while sadness overcame him for the current situation facing her son, Joseph.

Bob was unsure if his emotion came from losing someone he had feelings for, or from losing the money he was being paid.

After Jacob's death, a man had approached Bob in his hardware store. The man claimed to be a concerned friend of Jacob's. Bob had agreed with the man to look after Rachel and her family.

The man had a request, which surprised him. Bob had to call the man each week providing an update on the happenings at the Bishop's house. By complying to this request, Bob received a payment each month. One final stipulation for the payment was Bob had to keep his weekly updates a secret from everyone.

Two-hundred dollars for each call convinced Bob to accept the man's offer. Of course, it may have also been the pity Bob had for the man since the man was in a wheelchair.

As time had passed, guilt grew inside Bob concerning his spying on Rachel and his reporting to the mystery man in a wheelchair. Years had passed since Bob had last met the man in person.

One year before Rachel's death, the man in the wheelchair visited Bob again in his store. This time the man had a new request: to monitor Joseph and report back.

Laughter from Joseph and Mary brought a smile to Bob in the living room.

It seems odd to spy on a ten-year-old.

The man had explained to Bob how much money the State of Texas gave foster parents turning Bob's greedy wheels. Bob knew he could get closer to Joseph through a friendship developed by a foster child. It meant more money from the State plus an increase in his payment from the man in the wheelchair.

Bob remembered what it was like visiting the St. Anthony's Home for Children in Houston. How his heart ached with all the young boys and girls without parents.

A social worker at the home recommended to Bob a little boy to foster. But, after a month of coming home each night finding something broken, the boy had to leave.

When Bob met a quiet, little girl named Mary, happiness replaced his guilty conscious from his earlier failure with the boy. Bob had always loved the name Mary and was happy to give fostering another try.

The first time Bob spoke to Mary she seemed so gentle and soft-spoken. The memory of his first meeting made him smile as Bob watched Mary with Joseph on the floor in Rachel's house.

"Yes!" came a scream in unison from the two kids at the television.

The screaming jolted Bob out of his trance-like state. He saw Liz walking over to them.

Great, I better take her home. I don't want her to cause Joseph to get into any kinda trouble.

Bob stood beside Liz at the television. He heard Joseph say, "We actually did it. We stepped out on the Moon."

"Liz, it was such a beautiful service," Bob said.

"Thanks, Minister Greene gave a lovely service," Liz replied.

Bob knelt behind the children. "Joseph, I'm so sorry about your mama." Bob paused. "If you ever need anything, you let us know, Son."

Joseph shook his head to acknowledge he understood Bob, his gaze never left the television.

"Well, Mary, we probably should be going," Bob said as he took her cheese-caked hand.

"Mary, thank you for coming. I hope to see you at church," Liz said as she bent over to Mary.

"Thanks," Mary said in a soft voice. Mary smiled as she walked away with Bob.

As Liz was about to kneel beside Joseph to talk to him, Mary came back over to them. She stood beside Joseph.

A smudge of yellow-powered cheese stuck in the corner of her mouth as she placed her arms around Joseph's shoulders. "Sorry again about your mama."

Mary left with Bob as he took her hand leaving Rachel's house to his pickup truck.

"What did you and Joseph talk about?" Bob asked.

"Oh... um... we both love macaroni-and-cheese... and the Moon landing."

"Anything else? Anything about his grandma or anything?"

"Uh-uh." Mary mumbled her response while eating a sugar cookie she had picked up before they had left the house.

The pickup truck continued through the neighborhood. Bob's sadness faded away.

I think I've found the perfect foster kid to monitor Joseph...

25-Confessions

PRESENT - Somewhere in the southern Indian
Ocean, 6:30 p.m.
February 4, 2016
1,681 Days Prior to Impact

SILENCE FILLED the gray room on the boat. Gabriel had left Joe alone to prepare for his long-awaited opportunity to tell Mary everything.

Gabriel's advice to Joe was to be honest. To preface what Joe told Mary by saying he only had her best interests in mind by keeping this a secret from her.

Gabriel prepared Joe for how upset Mary may be. To keep expressing to her over-and-over, he understands why she is angry. It is only good news Joe is telling her. But, no matter how well Joe had prepared, knots churned in his stomach at how she would accept the secret he had kept from her.

I've never kept secrets from her before... How will she ever trust me again? I hope she understands why I did this?

A quick knock at the door interrupted his thoughts. The bright light from the hallway once again flooded into his room. Gabriel stood in the opened doorway holding a red folder.

"Joe, it's time."

Great... well, here I go.

Joe stood from his chair and followed Gabriel out into the hallway. Together, they walked down a corridor within the ship. They drifted side-to-side in unison as the ship rocked through the open waters of the southern Indian Ocean.

"I have already checked on her to make sure she is okay and told her you were fine. I explained the plane went down and we are now onboard a rescue ship," Gabriel said as they weaved down the rocking corridor.

"And... um... how did she take that?"

"Once she knew you were okay, she seemed calm with the news... it could be she is in shock, though."

"And, you don't think what I'm about to tell her will be too much?"

"Start from the beginning, but remember the advice I gave you. Let her know you had her best interest in mind. We basically forced you not to tell her."

Gabriel stopped in front of a door. He gave Joe the red notebook with all the details of Salvation. With a head nod, Joe was ready before knocking on the door.

Gabriel pushed the door open. Joe saw Mary over Gabriel's shoulder. Joe and Mary made eye contact. She stood from her chair running to Joe, who pushed his way into the room by Gabriel. Their immediate embrace and kiss were Gabriel's cue to leave, closing the door.

She pulled her head back from Joe. "Can you believe this? When I woke up and couldn't find you... I... I was—"

Joe interrupted Mary holding her tight at his waist. "When I woke and didn't see you, I almost lost it."

"Our plane crashed. Talk about a story to tell everyone when we go home," Mary said.

When we go home...

"Mary, let's sit down. We need to talk."

Joe led Mary back to the chair she had been sitting. He slid another chair to Mary sitting facing her; their knees touched.

Her hands were in his. A wealth of emotion overcame him.

"Oh, my God, Joseph, what is it?"

"Well, uh… I… I've got to tell you some things. But, first, I want you to know I only did this to protect you. To make sure we will be okay in the future."

Joe could feel her hands tensing up inside his. Mary said, "Joseph… you're scaring me… it can't be that bad?"

Joe took a deep breath. The words he had wanted to say to her for months were about to reveal his secret. "I… wanted to tell you as soon as they told me, but *they* gave me strict instructions not to."

"*They?* They, who?"

"Gabriel, and the Eden Foundation he works for."

"Told you not to tell me *what*, exactly?"

Mary heard Joe's breathing as he released a deep sigh. The heavy breath carried the literal weight of the world.

"Remember back when I flew out to Colorado?"

"Yeah, in September? That's where you met Gabriel and gave your presentation… right?"

"Yes and no… True, I met Gabriel. We talked about my research, but I never presented my work. He shared a secret with me. I didn't believe it at all until I reviewed it myself, and he showed me pictures and the videos."

Mary leaned to Joe. "Pictures and videos about your research?"

"No… he told me about this object they discovered in Space back in the 1950s."

A perplexed look overcame Mary. She leaned back into her chair. "What? What kind of object?"

"To be exact, it's a small planet that's bigger than the Moon, but smaller than Earth."

"Um… o… kay? What does that even have to do with you?"

Joe pulled Mary close as he spoke. The words he was about to say, he had only said out-loud to one other person before. Charlie.

"It will collide with Earth in 2020. The Eden Foundation that Gabriel represents has a plan to save the human race."

Don't tell her about Mars yet…

Mary wrangled her arm, freeing one of her hands and placing it along the side of his head. "Oh, you poor thing. You must have hit your head during the crash."

Joe grabbed her wrist. "No, Mary. I'm completely aware of what I am saying here. Back in September, they told me a planet will destroy Earth by colliding with us in 2020."

Mary tensed her body against her chair.

"The reason they contacted me was because of their plan to continue human civilization. My research will contribute in the future by finding a cure for cancer and other diseases."

Mary sat in silence, unsure of what to do or say. Seconds had passed. Joe delivered the information, which she already had known. Guilt crept upon her, not for already knowing the information, but for her secret of monitoring Joe the past twenty years.

Gabriel had made a promise to Mary many years before. Through her cooperation, Salvation would save them both.

As Joe explained what would happen to Earth in 2020, for a moment, Mary debated with herself to confess everything to him.

But, he will never forgive me... He doesn't know I've known this whole time... He's not aware I've been reporting into Gabriel since we were in college.

Her memories of Gabriel broke the silence in the room. As Joe continued revealing the secret, Mary retraced in her mind how she became associated with Gabriel... with the Eden Foundation.

SEPTEMBER 9, 2001
PARIS, FRANCE

MARY STROLLED DOWN the *Champs-Élysées* in amazement. She had seen these fancy stores only in magazines and in the movies.

Today, Mary visited the Parisian shops by herself. Joe had left her in their hotel room to go to his interview dinner with *Sauvage* Enterprises. Still getting over her jet lag from yesterday's flight from JFK, Mary wanted to see Paris rather than sleep the day away.

Halfway down the grand avenue, full of its shops and restaurants, Mary rested on a bench. People-watching, as everyone passed by was one of her favorite things to do.

Within a minute of sitting alone, a man approached her. "Mind if I sit down?"

"Sure." Mary admired his expensive suit and his lack of a French accent. "Do you live in Paris?"

"Yes. Why do you ask?"

"Well, I asked because I don't see many tourists wearing suits, and your English is perfect."

He laughed. "Yeah, that's funny. People often ask me where I'm from. When I tell them *Paris*, they usually say something like what you asked. Then, I tell them I'm originally from Iowa."

Mary laughed flipping her hair back across her shoulders. She found him to be funny and charming.

"Hi, my name is Mary."

She extended her hand. The young man shook hers.

"Well, hi Mary.... my name is Gabe, short for Gabriel."

Minutes had passed. Silence sat between them after their introductions.

"Hey, what do you say, we grab a bite to eat? My treat. We can go to that café *over there*. They have the best coffee around," Gabriel said pointing down the block.

Wow, it's like you're reading my mind because I'm hungry.

"I have a boyfriend. He's actually here for an interview."

"I thought I'd ask because I work with a bunch of Parisians. And, it would be great to have lunch with a fellow American. Plus, we're right here on a busy street, so no worries I'm some crazy guy or something."

Gabriel flashed a playful smile. His invitation was innocent enough. Gabriel figured Mary was hungry since he had followed her from the hotel all morning.

After a cautious pause, Mary answered, "Well... um... I don't think I should." Awkwardness overcame her after rejecting his offer.

"Mary, I must confess something to you?"

Oh, great... here comes the pickup line.

"Yes?"

"Does my voice sound familiar?"

"Familiar, how? It sounds nice."

"No, familiar… like we've talked before?"

Okay, this is new… I've not heard this one before.

"Um… I can't say it is?"

"What about the phone number you call each week to provide an update about what Joseph is doing?"

Mary froze at Gabriel's question.

How does he know about—

"The number you've been calling since your dad Bob asked you to do so," Gabriel said interrupting her thoughts.

"That's *you* I've been speaking to this whole time? My dad told me to call some number and answer their questions."

"I know… for you to receive a monthly insurance benefit after his death."

"We needed the money. So, I did it and never told Joe about calling and giving out our personal information."

Joe won't understand why I did this…

"Yes, Mary. You've been speaking to me this entire time," Gabriel said, trying his best not to frighten her away from the bench.

"I don't understand. Why are you *here*, now? How did you know where to find me?"

"The number you've been calling these past years routes to my office *here* in Paris. When I knew you would be here, I wanted to meet you in person."

The urge to bolt from the bench consumed Mary. "What is the real reason I have been calling and telling you about us?"

"I can imagine you've not enjoyed keeping secrets from Joseph, but it's for his and your protection." Gabriel saw a look of concern from her.

"When you visited your dad in the hospital a couple years ago, he told you he had been doing this for years. It was a promise to Joseph's father. Your dad and Jacob, they were best friends. And, when Jacob died, Bob was crushed."

"But, I don't see what this has to do with me or my dad calling you each week?"

"Think of our firm as a protection agency. Bob hired us to monitor Joseph and his family."

"A protection agency... *protection* from what?"

"Let's just say if there are ever any financial or legal issues, our firm steps in without you being aware and takes care of things. That was in the past. But, in the future, we will continue doing the same for you both."

"I don't understand. I've never heard of a service like that, let alone how much it would cost?"

"Your dad paid for our services in-full before he died as a type of insurance policy. He wanted to make sure you and Joseph were taken care of..."

Taken care of, huh. The bastard sure had a funny way of showing it when he was alive?

"Bob felt guilty for not being that great of a father to you."

"Huh," Mary grunted.

"But, there's one condition to continue with this service, you must continue to keep this a secret from Joseph or anyone else. If we find out, then we can no longer provide our services."

"How do I even know you've been providing any service before?"

"Remember the night this past June after Joseph's college graduation? That night you both left a party. Joseph had too much to drink and hit a parked car."

"Um... yeah." Mary could not believe Gabriel knew the details as the police finding out still frightened her.

"And, you remember calling us that week to report where you had been that weekend?"

"Uh-huh."

"Our team intercepted the police report on that incident. Come to find out, you both had left the scene of an accident. You had to have been scared you would get caught by eyewitnesses?"

Mary shook her head in disbelief to confirm what Gabriel was saying.

"Well, the police never called, did they?" Gabriel asked.

"Um… no."

How did you know?

"Or, you would not want to tell Joseph how he got this opportunity in Paris… arranged by our firm, would you?"

Mary became angry hearing his last comment. "What do you mean, *your firm* got him *this* interview? His grades and work in college speak for themselves."

"Yes, they do. But, a job interview out-of-the-blue… to a company he didn't even apply… in Paris?"

Mary realized what Gabriel was saying. "Joe would be devastated if he didn't get this opportunity on his own."

"Or, would he be devastated knowing his girlfriend had been contacting us each week to report things to us about his activity?"

Mary squirmed as she sat listening.

"Or, would he be devastated knowing your dad had been doing the same reporting about his mother, Rachel, when she was alive?"

Mary sat dumbfounded. She could not think of a comeback to his statements.

"Stop! Stop it! You've made your point. No one knew of *that* accident. Joe and I never spoke again about it. And, Joe cannot find out how he got this interview or the fact I've been sharing our information with you."

"See, we only have your best interests in mind. It's all thanks to your adoptive father… even this wonderful opportunity Joseph's interviewing for, now."

Motionless Mary remained.

"So… where do we go from here?" Mary asked unsure what to do, and why Gabriel was meeting with her now in person.

"Mary, I could have continued our conversations over the phone. But, I got the sense you were getting close to telling him."

"Um… uh."

"For our services to work, they must remain secret. So, you cannot tell him or anyone else. Continue calling the number. Now, you understand who we are and what we are all about. You can even give us more details of problems you're having, and we will take care of it. It's as simple as that."

People passed by as they remained sitting on the bench. Mary so wanted to run away and hide among the crowd forgetting this conversation. Gabriel had forced Mary to rationalize her thoughts about what was happening.

If he gets this job in Paris, we may need Gabriel's help here? Hell, what's the worst that can happen? It's not like I'm telling them deep, dark secrets about us… but, how can I keep this a secret from Joe?

"And, Mary, trust me. There will come a day where I will tell you everything about our firm. Who knows… we may even end up saving both your lives someday?" Gabriel said.

PRESENT - SOMEWHERE IN THE SOUTHERN INDIAN OCEAN, 6:54 P.M.
FEBRUARY 4, 2016
1,681 DAYS PRIOR TO IMPACT

MARY FACED a stark reality. Her thoughts of how she met Gabriel vanished. Joe sat before her in tears.

Honey, it's okay… I know everything… don't worry.

"What the hell, Joseph? We need a doctor to check out your head," Mary said. She freed her hands placing them on either side of his face. "I don't *feel* any lumps."

Joe pushed her hands away in frustration, stood and walked to the table where he had placed the red notebook. With a heavy sigh, he sat again in front of her and opened the pages on her lap.

"See *this* black dot *here?*" Joe asked pointing to a photograph taken in 1957.

"Uh-huh."

He turned the page and pointed. "Now, *this* dot *here*… it's bigger?" He flipped back-and-forth between the two pages. "The second photograph is from 1965." He turned through the next several pages. "Mary... look... *the dot*... gets bigger."

"So?"

"The impact when it happens in 2020 will destroy the Earth. No one else in the world knows about this except for those involved with the Eden Foundation."

"But, if you have *these* pictures, what stops others from seeing the same thing in the sky?"

"Gabriel explained the Foundation hacks into all the observatories preventing other discoveries of this object. The telescopes can't scan this area of the sky."

"And, Gabriel... he gave you *this*... in Colorado?"

"Yes. And, he gave me all the data, how long they've been tracking it, its composition.... everything."

"And, you believe it... this information isn't fake?"

"At first... I couldn't... I didn't want to believe it... it's not possible that a planet could destroy Earth... it's all too crazy."

Joe lowered his head onto the red notebook opened on her lap. Mary sat in stunned silence, unsure what to say next or how to react.

"But... I examined their calculations and asked to see it. At the facility in Colorado, they had one of those large telescopes. And, I saw *this* for myself. Everything is true, Mary."

Should I be upset now or wait? I should still think he's hit his head. I need a reason to get angry with him.

"Did you ask what the government has done to stop it?" she asked.

Joe was explaining the calculations of the planet's orbit in excruciating detail. Her question brought him back to reality. The most unbelievable part of the secret was yet to be revealed.

"Well, that's just it. They've tried. They've sent rockets with nuclear weapons attempting to break it up or knock it off course. But, it's too big and dense, and moving too fast... all the attempts failed."

"And, the Public wasn't aware of these launches?" Mary asked in a sarcastic tone hiding the information she had known.

"How many times have we watched the news? There's always a report of a military launch with a secret payload."

Mary listened planning her next statements.

"Or, the space shuttle releases a top-secret satellite into orbit. All those were missions to destroy it. Even the astronauts involved didn't know what was happening... the Foundation controlled everything."

"You sound like one of those conspiracy theory guys on the Internet or something." Mary took his hand into hers. "You don't believe this, do you?" she asked.

"Uh... yes... I do, now."

"So, what are you saying? *This thing* will hit Earth in 2020... What happens when it does?"

"Well, the asteroid that killed the dinosaurs, they think it was only six miles in diameter."

"Only six miles? That sounds big."

"Six miles is big, but not compared to what's coming in a few years. The Moon is 2,100 miles across. Earth is 8,000 miles... *this black dot here*... is 4,000 miles in diameter."

Mary sat in disbelief. Gabriel had shared some of the information to her before, but not all the exact details. Salvation to her was a remote island where Gabriel had promised they would be safe.

"This means the impact will kill everything on Earth in an instant. If it's a direct hit as the calculations show... it will cause Earth to explode."

Mary pushed the notebook off her lap onto the floor. Its pages raced across the tiles. She stood rushing to the door.

"Joseph, that's crazy. Gabriel has some explaining to do if he's the one who gave you *that* and filled your head with this shit."

The locked door surprised Mary. She banged against it with both palms yelling, "Gabriel! Gabriel!"

"Mary... I asked him to lock the door. We didn't want you to run out until I explained everything to you."

"What the hell, there's more?" Mary's response came with one last simultaneous slam against the door.

Joe leaned over from his chair and scooped up the reports from the floor. He held in the air the last pages.

"Mary, but there's good news. The Foundation selected us to go *here* because of my research. *This* is where we will live."

Joe pointed to pages of pictures, some at least twenty-years old, while others were from a few months ago. The pictures showed living spaces, dormitory rooms, gym equipment, and laboratories.

Mary turned from the door and approached Joe. They were the same pictures Gabriel had shared with her before persuading her to continue in her monitoring role.

Gabriel had promised Mary she had a place in Salvation. The details of how large this planet is and its destruction of Earth were both absent in his explanations. Mary had thought Salvation was where the boat was taking them on its present course.

"What... where were *those* taken, and how is *that* going to protect us?"

"Mary, *this* is Project Salvation. When they discovered the planet and realized it would destroy Earth, the government developed this complex."

"The government? What government?"

"Well, I call it that. I don't think the Eden Foundation belongs to any formal governmental agency."

"This agency, are they American?"

"Gabriel told me there is no distinction between countries. The people who discovered this object attempted to inform our government. No one believed them."

"Why not? The pictures? The data?"

"We have these high-resolution pictures and sophisticated computer models now. Back in the '50s, it was only a few pictures of black dots and handwritten, mathematical calculations."

"If no one believed them then, how did this Salvation place even develop?"

Joe held the notebook on his lap. "I've been struggling with this question, too. I mean, the money and resources that had to go into developing Salvation are unbelievable. But, I guess someone with power believed them?"

"A lot of money? I don't know about that because it looks like pictures from college as far as the dorms and labs go," Mary said. "If the Earth explodes, where is Salvation? How will it save us?"

"Ah... Mary, this is so hard for me to tell you."

"That's okay; I'm not even sure I believe you."

"Well, if you haven't believed me, yet, you're not going to now. *These pictures*... they come from Project Salvation... and... uh... that's on Mars, Sweetie."

Mary studied the pictures trying to comprehend what Joe had told her. "Mars?... as in the planet, Mars?"

"Yes... and, I didn't believe it either when Gabriel told me."

"Mars!" Mary yelled with a pale-faced stare. "You want me to believe a planet will kill everything on Earth, let alone destroy it, five years from now. And, we're escaping to Mars?"

Gabriel, you didn't tell me this, you son-of-a-bitch.

"Uh-huh, I know how crazy it sounds, Mary, but please—"

"Do you? Do you? I don't think you do, Joseph... and, *this* secret you've been keeping from me since Colorado?" Her hot breath rolled toward him from across the small room.

"Um... yes... Gabriel told me not to tell anyone."

"Not to tell. Last time I checked, I'm your wife, not Gabriel."

Joe approached her. Mary pushed his hands away turning around taking a deep breath.

"Where *are* we? This is a joke, right? Ha ha ha, you've got me, Joseph."

He tried to calm her. "Mary, I wish *this* was a joke."

"No, just stop," she yelled as he attempted to place his arms across her shoulders. "Stop, let go of me." Mary slapped his hands away.

"Mary? Come on; I know it's upsetting."

"I don't think you do... my husband sounds like a mad man... the world is going to end... we're escaping to Mars... what the hell?"

Mary backed herself toward the door while making eye contact with Joe on the other side of the room. She was unsure if she knew this man, whom she had known since they were ten-years-old.

When her back hit the locked door, tears filled both eyes. She repeated to herself in a low voice, "It can't be... it can't be..."

Her emotions were unexpected. Gabriel had informed Mary everything Joe was telling her... except for Salvation being on Mars.

Mary had rehearsed her planned reactions with Gabriel. But, real emotions escaped from her as Joe explained what was happening. The release due to years of pent-up guilt for being in contact with Gabriel. All this time not knowing the full truth behind his intentions.

For months, Mary had kept the secret of Salvation from Joe. Gabriel had promised them safety. This promise coupled with her guilt of monitoring Joe forced her to comply with Gabriel's demands.

While Joe felt the burden of his guilt leave him, Mary's guilt became crippling. She knew she could never tell Joe what she had done.

NOVEMBER 25, 2015
STONY BROOK, NEW YORK

GROCERY SHOPPING the day before Thanksgiving can be a contact sport. Mary faced this task this morning by agreeing at the last-minute to cook a holiday dinner.

Since Charlie's funeral, the past month had been terrible for Joe and Mary. Gone was their larger-than-life friend, and gone too were Becky and her girls.

Joe and Mary hoped a Thanksgiving dinner would help put their sadness behind them. It was their chance to start anew.

If inside the grocery store is a circus, then the outside parking lot is a zoo. Mary drove around the lot three times attempting to find any open spot.

On her last loop around, she saw a car backing out of a space at the far end. Mary sped through the parking lot exchanging menacing looks at the people she passed.

Thank God, there's a place.

She parked and turned off the ignition. The light rain pelted the windshield as the noise from the engine fell silent.

To her sudden fright, her passenger-side door opened. A man in a long, black raincoat with a black fedora got into her car.

The collar of the coat covered his face while the hat hid the top of his head. Mary reached for the mace bottle affixed on her key chain, ready to defend herself.

"Mary! Mary! It's me... Gabriel," the man said as he pulled the black fedora and his collar off his head and face.

"Gabriel? What the hell?" Mary said. The mace can rocked back-and-forth from her fingers.

"Hey, Mary, there's no need for *that*," Gabriel said taking the mace from her.

"Why are you *here*? You scared the shit out of me."

"I thought I'd check-in with you since you have not called me in weeks."

"Huh... I haven't felt like calling. It's been a pretty, shitty time, here."

"I heard about your friend, Charlie, and I'm so, so sorry for your loss."

Rain fell heavier on the windshield, tapping on the roof of the car. The rain drowned out their conversation causing them to speak louder.

"Great. It's raining... Gabriel, I don't have time for this. I need to go inside for groceries. I promise to start calling again next week." Mary had hoped her response would be acceptable enough for him to leave.

"Mary, that's fine, but I'm *here* because I need your help." Protected under his coat, he pulled out a red notebook and turned its pages. "I need to share a secret with you and explain the real reason you've been contacting us."

Mary sat with a bewildered look. She had been calling and reporting to Gabriel for so long; it had become automatic for her. Each call was fairly generic. Gabriel's basic questions related to their activities during the past week. To her, she was living up to her end of the deal... checking in with him in return for payment and supposed protection.

"I need to confess something else to you... I am the person Joe flew to Colorado to meet... what I am about to share with you is the same information I shared with him."

"You met Joe? If he already knows about you, then why the hell do I need to keep doing this?"

"This is entirely different, and to be honest, I'm worried about him."

"Worried? Why?"

"Mary, let me assure you I have only yours and his best interests in mind here. Trust me; you'll be thankful you're both going to be a part of Salvation."

The Eden Foundation has kept Project Salvation in secrecy for decades. Here, in the front seat of her car in a crowded parking lot, Gabriel was about to share everything with her… almost everything.

As Gabriel opened the red notebook on his lap and slid it closer to her, the rain fell even harder. The running water down the windows created a veil of secrecy ensuring their privacy.

"Mary, do you see this black dot *here* in this picture…"

26-ARRIVAL

PRESENT - SOMEWHERE IN THE SOUTHERN INDIAN OCEAN, 8:15 P.M.
FEBRUARY 4, 2016
1,681 DAYS PRIOR TO IMPACT

CRYING FILLED the small, gray room on the boat as Mary sat on the floor, her back against the door. Tears streamed down her face. Joe crawled and sat beside her.

"Mary, it's okay," he said rubbing the back of her shoulders.

"I knew, Joe."

"You knew what?"

"I... uh... I... knew you were keeping something from me."

"Honey, I didn't want to keep *this* from you. It's been the hardest thing I've ever had to do."

Mary leaned forward, burying her head into his shoulder crying. The stress building inside her for years had grown worse since Thanksgiving.

I can never tell him what I've done.

"So... so... *this* is really happening, huh?" Mary said, Joe's shirt muffling her face.

Joe rubbed her back. The more he tried to comfort Mary, the more he felt his emotions build inside him. In an instant, Joe cried. His body trembled against hers.

Everything they had known… everyone they had met… will be gone. Anticipated fear encroached upon them cowering in the corner of the room by the door. The reality of traveling to Salvation… to Mars hit them as they held each other, both sobbing.

"I think I'm going to be sick," Mary said, pulling away from him and crawling to her knees.

"It will be okay, Sweetie," Joe said trying to reassure her.

"No, really, I'm gonna throw up—" Those were her last words Mary said as she reached for a trash can behind them.

Joe leaned over to her making sure she was all right. The door clicked open. Gabriel entered the room.

"Can I bring you anything?" Gabriel asked.

"Please, some water," a frail voice from Mary said buried in the trash can.

Gabriel left returning moments later with a glass of water.

"Sorry to see how the news has affected you, Mary. Like I'm sure Joe told you, it was me who gave him the order to keep Salvation a secret. It was for your protection."

Gabriel took the empty glass from her. "We wanted to give Joe plenty of time to prepare to bring his research to Salvation. I know it's hard to understand why we did not tell you before, but over time you'll come to understand, why."

The water brought her immediate relief. "I guess it was too much to hear, and I…"

"No need to explain or worry about it," Gabriel said reassuring Mary everything was okay.

Joe helped her to her feet walking back to the two chairs in the opposite corner of the room. Mary flipped through the red notebook and said, "So, when do we leave?"

Gabriel smiled and stepped closer to them. "Well, good news. We leave Sunday. Tomorrow morning, we arrive at the island where we will launch from."

"Sunday? What? No training or preparation for the flight?" Joe asked.

"We'll spend the day tomorrow going over the flight plans and preparation. You'll get the instructions for what to do onboard." Joe and Mary stood with surprised faces.

"Only one day of training?" Joe said holding Mary's hands.

"Guys, you're just passengers on board. There's nothing for you to prepare in flying there. Our flights have become routine for us over the years, like flying an airplane. We'll explain what to expect and how to maneuver around the ship."

"Ship?" Mary asked.

Gabriel laughed. "Yes, a ship. This isn't like one of those science-fiction movies you've seen. We can't teleport you there. You're not onboard the Enterprise. Nothing like that. The inside looks more like the International Space Station you've seen on TV."

"Where they're floating around inside?" Mary asked.

"Yes. I'm sure it is amazing to learn we have been building structures on the Moon and sending them to Mars. But, we still have been unable to create a gravitational system for inside the ship."

"What about lasers?" Mary said joking to lighten the atmosphere in the room.

"Lasers... actually, Eden worked for the longest time in developing them. Our hopes were we could build one strong enough to deflect the planet coming toward Earth."

"And?" Mary's feeble voice asked.

"Well, the good news for us is in doing this laser research, we developed a way to use them as a propulsion system. What once took six months to travel to Mars, now with this photonic propulsion system, you'll get there in three weeks."

Gabriel stood in the doorway to leave. "Let me make you a promise. Tomorrow, we will wake at six o'clock for breakfast onboard this boat. We'll arrive at our island by eight o'clock."

He had their full attention.

"Once there, we will go over the details with you, and the others you met this morning. But, for now, try to get some rest. Your bedroom is next door."

"*The others* are coming too?" Mary said, looking stunned at Joe.

"Yeah... uh... I didn't know about them until this morning," Joe said.

Mary stood and hugged Gabriel before he left. "Thank you," she said.

"For what?" Gabriel asked still trapped in her embrace.

"For saving us from the end."

Mary turned her head to Gabriel's left ear during her hug. She whispered, "You could have told me the whole truth."

Gabriel pulled away smiling at her. "See you both in the morning."

PRESENT - SOMEWHERE IN THE SOUTHERN INDIAN OCEAN, 7:32 A.M.
FEBRUARY 5, 2016
1,680 DAYS PRIOR TO IMPACT

THE AIR GREW COLD as the boat continued on its journey to the most southern depths of the Indian Ocean. While it was the middle of summer in the Southern Hemisphere, their approach was not far from Antarctica. They were traveling to the edge of the world.

As eight new strangers finished their breakfast, their fate shared a common bond. Still unsure of what others knew for certain, all eight sat in quiet reflection in the dining room. Gabriel had spent the past night with each telling them their own story about what had and will happen.

Even Joe and Mary with their contentious discussions last night ate in silence. The passengers devoured the eggs and bacon. No one had eaten since yesterday's breakfast. While everyone was finishing, Gabriel walked into the dining room.

"Good morning, everyone. Today is the day. We'll be arriving soon. If you would come with me to the top deck, we can see our island coming in view."

The passengers filed out of the dining room passing Gabriel. Joe and Mary were last in line.

"Good morning, Mary, how are you feeling? You look pale."

"I've been better. Between not sleeping and being seasick, I'm okay." Mary staggered by him holding the back of Joe's shoulders.

"Up the stairs and through the door," Gabriel said instructing everyone ahead.

At the top of the stairs, Heinrich pushed open the door. The rush of cold wind cascaded down the steps to the rest of his new friends.

One-by-one, they made their way through the door and onto the boat's observation deck. Gabriel followed last passing everyone as he came through the door.

"Come, over *here*... you'll get a great view," Gabriel said leading everyone around the deck to the port side.

As they swayed across the bow of the ship, the wind smacked them in the face with its Antarctic furor. Cold and howling, the wind blew until Gabriel led them behind a Plexiglas wall on the deck meant to block the wind.

"*There* she is... our island straight ahead."

Gabriel pointed toward the front of the boat. A small island appeared through the low-hanging clouds on the horizon.

The island was devoid of any trees or greenery. Calm, gray water reflecting the overcast sky surrounded a flat outcropping of sand and rocks. An uninviting sight lay ahead.

Several small buildings emerged as the boat sailed closer to the island. The most noticeable features were five, large rockets positioned across the island pointed upward.

"*That one,* on the far left... that is the one you will take."

"What about the other rockets?" Gary asked, standing beside the two sisters huddled together in a state of shock about what was happening.

"They're for the other teams arriving throughout next week."

"*Others,* so there's more than just us?" Heather asked as she hugged her sister Joanie tighter. The sisters shivered in the icy wind.

"Oh, yes. One of these takes off every few days. Each takes eight to ten people at a time."

"So, this has been the launch location?" Joe asked.

"Yes. We're so remote down here at the bottom of the world; we've been launching since the '70s."

Once the boat was secure against the dock, Gabriel led everyone to the back. A crewmember placed a platform across the gap to the dock to allow the passengers to disembark.

The weathered wood of the dock creaked under their feet as everyone walked to shore. Even seagulls dared not venture this far south. It was eerily quiet.

Decades of rockets blasting off from the island had caused no birds to make their habitat here. The gray sky mirrored the eerie silence as they walked to the nearby buildings.

"These rockets are amazing in their design. We can blast them off from Earth, and *that module on top* ejects from the rocket."

Everyone lifted their head to the sky as Gabriel spoke.

"The module with the crew inside continues to Mars, while we pilot the rocket back to land on its platform. We reuse the rockets. And, this technology has saved a tremendous amount of time and money for the Foundation."

"Have you seen them take off, before?" Gary asked being the first one of the group to step on shore. With his flight engineering background, Gary was full of questions about how they functioned.

"Yes, I have seen these in action dozens of times. Just as I have been recruiting and working with you, I have done the same with others. And, I will continue doing so afterward."

Gabriel walked ahead of everyone as they followed inside the first building. Gabriel opened the door. Several staff members in dark-blue lab suits greeted the anxious passengers.

"Everyone, these people will help prepare you over the next few days until you leave on Sunday. We have one person assigned to each of you, and they will tend to your needs," Gabriel said.

Among the group of staff members, a woman stepped up onto a platform so everyone could see her.

"Good morning. My name is Amy. I will be your pilot on Sunday. Assisting me are my two crew members, Alison and Antwan." Her co-pilots waved hello to the group.

"I know you all are both excited and scared, but trust me. You're in good hands. This will be my twentieth flight to Salvation."

Twentieth flight... oh my, this is crazy. Joe thought to himself, squeezing Mary's hand.

"After you're fitted into your flight suits, you will join me *over there* at our simulator. And, that's where we will show you what to expect inside the ship as we take off to Salvation." Amy pointed behind her to a mock-up of the passenger module like the one affixed to the top of each rocket.

"Okay, now, your assigned staff member will find you and begin the next process. They'll be happy to answer your questions. And, we look forward to seeing you again this afternoon." Amy waved to everyone while stepping off the platform.

The once talkative group from yesterday morning, now stood in shocked silence; the moment too surreal.

Two staff members held up a flight suit to show as an example to the new passengers. A lightweight, gray fabric made up the suit. Within the fabric were thin, red and black lines spiraling across from head-to-toe.

A staff member spoke. "Good morning, my name is Huang Chin, and we will help you get fitted for your flight suits with *these machines.*"

Huang stood beside a seven-foot tall cylindrical booth with clear windows. He demonstrated what was about to happen.

"Each of you will step inside and hold your arms straight above your head *like this.* For thirty seconds, lasers will scan and measure your body. You then will step out."

Huang walked to a machine beside the measuring booth. "*Over here* in this machine, we inject a polymer through dozens of jet nozzles. Similar to a 3D printer, the machine creates your bio-suit which will be an exact fit to your body."

Mary gazed around the inside of the building. Her nerves still had not calmed as a swarm of butterflies churned in her stomach.

"We insert a shape-memory alloy made from nickel-titanium. This forms the crisscross lines *you see here.* They act as smart zippers within the suits tightening you up across your entire body. This creates pressure."

The science amazed Gary. "So, we won't be wearing those big astronaut suits?" he asked.

"No. In fact, the pressure of the smart zippers replicates the atmospheric pressure you experience here on Earth."

A thick Austrian accent echoed over the crowd as Heinrich asked, "We stand in there, naked?"

Over the group's nervous laughter, Huang answered. "When we start this, we'll have curtains set-up. You must take off your clothes before stepping inside so we can get exact measurements."

Mary squeezed Joe's hand, always a signal to him she was nervous. Joe whispered in Mary's ear, "I love you." Her grip loosened.

Over the next several minutes, each of the eight entered behind the curtain one at a time. Slipping off their clothes, they stepped into the glass, cylindrical measuring device.

For Mary's turn, she pulled Joe behind the curtain with her. "It's okay, Sweetie. I'm right here." This seemed to reassure her as she took off her clothes and gave them to him.

Mary stepped inside the machine. The cold, metal floor sent a shock through her naked body.

"Okay, now raise your arms and stand as still as possible," the technician said.

"Do I breathe, while I'm in here?"

"Yes, just breathe normally, but close your eyes," the technician said.

A checkered, red beam of light appeared on her feet. The laser grid inched its way up her ankles and her thighs. It produced no heat or sensation on her body as it continued up her torso, ending at the tips of her out-stretched fingers above her head.

"Okay, we're good. You can step out now," the technician said to her relief.

No sooner than Mary stepped out of the measurement chamber, Joe helped her put back on her clothes. After Joe had given Mary back her shoes, the technician said to Joe, "Okay, you're next."

With a shy gulp, Joe slipped out of his clothes and sat them on the floor beside Mary. Joe entered the measurement chamber. The metal plate under his bare feet jolted the nerve-endings through his legs. Joe followed the same instructions lifting his arms above his head closing his eyes. The laser grid appeared inched its way up his body.

I can't believe this is happening… I wonder how tight this will be?

"Okay, that's it," the technician said. Joe stepped out of the chamber to put back on his clothes.

Joe had never felt more naked in his life…

LAUNCH SITE, 12:45 P.M.

THE EIGHT PASSENGERS finished their lunch sandwiches prepared by the staff. It was time for the next demonstration.

"If I could have everyone's attention *over here*," Amy said as she waved her arms. She led them to the mock-up module on the opposite side of the building.

"Please go on inside… I want to show you guys how you'll be living for the next three weeks."

The sisters, Joanie and Heather, went inside first followed by the engineer, Gary. The food nutritionist Chantal was next. Joe and Mary walked ahead of the bio-medical engineer, Lin Wu, and the decathlete, Heinrich.

"The module you're in is a replica of what you saw on top of the rockets when you walked into the building this morning. Basically, *this* is where you will spend your time during our flight." Amy guided everyone through the module.

"You'll wear your suits at all times."

"How do we go to the bathroom?" Chantal asked.

Amy took them to the toilet area inside the module. She demonstrated the steps needed.

"Press *this button* to open the door. Inside, you slip over your waist *this belt* and press *this button* where the belt connects to the wall. This activates and loosens the smart zippers in your suit. You pull *this tab* on the side to open the bottom half of your suit."

Everyone watched as Amy gave instructions.

"Do your business *there*, close the lid and press *this button* above the toilet. Pull the bottom back up into place and slip the belt again around your waist, press *this second button* to tighten the smart zippers."

"Can we try it before we actually need to use it?" Chantal asked.

"Trust me. You'll get the hang of it. There will be plenty of time tomorrow to test it in your suits."

Amy led the group back to the entrance of the module. Eight chairs sat around the cylindrical module with the seat-backs against the wall. Each faced into the center of the module.

"These chairs around, *here*," Amy said pointing around the perimeter, "*these* will be both your seats and your sleeping quarters."

Amy sat in the chair explaining how to fasten the restraints and to work the seat. She showed them the buttons to press, causing the seat to recline flat forming a bed.

Another button operated a clear, flexible glass, which rose on either side. The glass rounded upward and met above the center of the seat.

"In the full bed position, the seat transforms into a hyperbaric chamber. You will be in a 100%, pure-oxygen environment. The atmospheric pressure will be one-half what it is at sea level on Earth."

"Do you understand any of this?" Joanie whispered in Heather's ear.

"No, but, I'm like going to do what Gary does."

"This pressure serves two purposes. First, you will sleep well inside the chamber. Second, it minimizes your muscle and bone loss from the three weeks in a zero-gravity environment."

"Will we be flying through this thing like I've seen in the movies?" Heinrich asked as he sat in one of the seats.

Amy replied, "Yes, and no. Once we're out of Earth's gravitational pull, you'll sense weightlessness. But, our module rotates as we travel to Salvation."

Heinrich rubbed his hands across the fabric of the seat.

"This rotation creates a centrifugal force which will give you some sensation of gravity. It won't be the same as here on Earth. But, you'll feel like half the weight you do now."

Gary held his stomach and said with a nervous laugh, "Half of my current weight? Well, that's the best news I've heard all day."

A similar nervous laugh from the group followed.

"What about eating?" Heinrich asked as his chiseled muscular features demanded a daily, large amount of protein.

"We have nutrient-rich foods and drinks on the ship. I will not lie to you, though, it could taste better. But, it serves its purpose," Amy said, walking over to show how to heat the food onboard.

"The food is pre-packaged in vacuum-sealed bags." Amy held a clear, square bag with a brown square piece of food inside into the air.

Rubberized tubing hung from a wall panel with many knobs and controls on it. "What you do is take *this tube*, and press it into the bag on *this end*. Then, we use controls on *this panel* to electrically heat the contents inside."

"It takes four minutes, and it's done. The cooking automatically stops, and you pull out the tube. Once *that's* out of the way, open the bag and enjoy." Amy passed around the bag of food and a small plastic fork.

Joe sampled the fiesta chicken meal. As he tried the food, he said, "Not too bad."

Mary took the bag and attempted to eat it. "I'll eat *that* when I have to," she said, passing the bag of food to her right to Chantal.

Amy and her flight crew spent the rest of the time on Friday and Saturday going over the living quarters inside the module. She outlined the module's safety procedures during takeoff, the flight, and landing.

To the surprise of everyone, no medical testing occurred. As part of the ongoing monitoring of each passenger, the Eden Foundation already had everyone's medical records assuring safe travel for all.

With the training the passengers received, there were no jokes. Everyone remained serious in their crash-course preparation. They are leaving in two days.

For Joe, his excitement grew. The weight the secret had created had vanished.

For Mary, her nerves grew tense with the uncertainty of what was to come. However, unlike Joe, her burden remained.

For both Mary and Joseph, their adventure was only about to begin...

27-Launch

NO ONE HAD SLEPT overnight. The anticipation of blasting off into space for a three-week long journey to Mars had made it impossible.

Morning came early to the group of eight passengers. They were preparing to leave home... to leave Earth, in only a few short hours.

The building, which they had spent the past two days, was full of pre-flight checks. The flight crew reviewed their flight-prep plans. Technicians performed their final inspections of the rocket and modules.

As the eight passengers assembled in the meeting area of the building, this was the first time each had seen everyone in their flight suits. The compression from the fabric created a flattering, form-figure for each person.

Even Gary, with his potbelly, seemed to be extra svelte in appearance. For Heinrich, he was having difficulty hiding his excitement in his suit as he admired the curvaceous sisters in theirs.

To say his farewells to everyone before they left, Gabriel met them one last time inside the building. "Wow, you all look great."

Everyone was unsure if Gabriel was sincere or faking his excitement.

"I wanted to say it has been my honor getting to know you. Some of you, we've worked together for a very long time... others only the past few weeks."

All the passengers looked around at each other as Gabriel spoke.

"But you each bring something special to Salvation. And, I'm proud to know I played a part in recruiting you all to ensure the survival of the human race."

Gabriel's speech fell on deaf ears. Shock overcame everyone. The moment surreal... this was about to happen. Everything they had known was getting ready to change forever.

A voice came over the speakers inside the building. "Please proceed to the platform as we will prepare for the final countdown to launch."

With the announcement, each person filed by Gabriel, shaking his hand. As Joe and Mary passed, Joe gave Gabriel a firm handshake, while Mary gave him a tremendous bear hug.

"I feel like I've known you for several years... are you sure there's no way for you to come to Salvation?" Mary asked Gabriel to the surprise of Joe.

"Mary, I'll miss you too. But, like I've told you all before, I've accepted my role. My joy is recruiting those who have gone before you, and those coming after you."

Mary smiled at Gabriel.

"And, don't worry... in my time remaining here, I'll live pretty damn well."

After shaking everyone's hand, Gabriel led them to an elevator. The platform to the module entrance is seventy meters up.

As the elevator doors closed, Gabriel disappeared from their view. The eight passengers stood inside, alone together.

They ascended to the platform. The elevator stopped. An open-air platform awaited them as the doors opened. A technician greeted them and pointed the way inside the living module atop the rocket.

One-by-one, each passenger entered. The upside-down orientation and the curvature of the module meant most had to climb into their seats. Joe and Mary sat beside each other opposite from the entry door.

The technicians secured each person in their seats. Air escaped from the locks inside the helmet as a technician fastened it to the flight suit for each passenger.

A shock-absorbent plastic housing protects the top, sides, and back of the head with a bullet-proof-glass face shield. At both ears, noise-canceling microphones and speakers allow for crystal-clear communication inside the helmet.

From the viewpoint of the person inside, a holographic image projects onto the glass for video communication. A miniature, high-definition camera points to their face inside their helmet.

A new set of technicians entered the living module. Their task is to connect various monitoring sensors to the outside the passengers' flight suits.

During the flight, the flight crew monitors the passengers' vital signs to Salvation. This ensures the Foundation's precious cargo remains safe and secure.

The technicians worked to complete their tasks. Joe and Mary held hands across the space between their seats. The fabric of their gloves prevented them to feel each other.

In the flight module linked above the living module, Amy, and her crew, went through their pre-flight checklists. The flight crew comprised Captain Amy, her co-captain Alison, and her navigator Antwan. Besides navigation, Antwan monitored the passengers' vitals during the flight.

Sensor readings came online as the technicians connected each passenger. Antwan checked the first sensor's readings, which appeared on his computer from Gary, followed by Lin Wu.

Each passenger's previously collected records provided a baseline. As the reading appeared, Antwan compared them against the baseline.

All the readings so far, appear to be within the acceptable tolerance levels. This is surprising considering none are trained astronauts and they are about to experience blast-off.

Every reading was normal... until Antwan read the vitals coming from the last person the technicians had connected.

"Uh... Flight Control, I am reading an anomaly in the readings from Passenger Seven. Can you please send a technician back inside? Have them double-check the sensor hookups," Antwan said into the microphone inside his helmet.

"Everything okay over there, 'Twan?" Amy asked.

"Something didn't seem right with one reading. I'm sure it's an improper connection to the suit."

The eight passengers sat secured in their seats. Each scanned around at their fellow travelers.

Two technicians re-entered the module. They started with Gary to double-check his sensor connections followed by the other passengers.

Joe and Mary held hands while turning their heads to the other. They could not hear anything.

The flight crew only activates the microphones inside the helmets once out of the Earth's atmosphere. This prevents all the voices coming over everyone's speakers at the same time. This forced Joe and Mary to mouth simple words to each other.

The technicians finished checking the sensors connected to Heinrich's suit. Next, they checked Joe's, pressing each sensor ensuring a proper connection within the suit. The technicians checked Mary last before exiting the module.

"All connections are confirmed properly in place," a technician said via the speakers inside Antwan's helmet.

"Roger. Thank you," Antwan said through his microphone.

Antwan continued through his pre-flight checklist, re-starting his review of everyone's vital signs. Passenger One is within tolerance to her baseline readings, as were the others. Antwan stopped again at Passenger Seven as he saw the same anomaly as before.

"Captain, uh... you need to see *this*. I'm getting the same readings."

"Roger. Push the readings to my screen."

Amy pressed a small button on the side of her helmet. The readings from Antwan appeared as an image inside her face shield. She reviewed the readings from Passenger Seven.

"Antwan, am I seeing what I think I see here?"

"Yes, Captain, I believe so."

"Hold on," Amy said as she turned on the intercom microphone inside Passenger Seven's helmet.

"Mary, this is Amy. I need you to check something out for me."

"Um… okay," Mary said startled to hear the Captain's voice in her helmet.

"Your suit… nothing feels loose anywhere does it?"

She let go of Joe's hand and moved her arms and legs in her seat. "Um… no. It fits tight, but I can still move my arms and legs with no problems."

"Do you see the sensor pad in the center of your chest?"

"Um… yeah. It's clear and round?"

"Yes, that's it. Use your hand and press down on it to make sure it's tight against the suit?"

Mary followed Amy's instructions and pressed against the clear, plastic disc on her chest. The wireless sensor was secure.

"I pressed down as hard as I could on it… is everything okay?"

Several, silent seconds had passed.

"Yes… uh… yes, Mary, everything's okay," Amy said through Mary's speakers.

Joe waved at Mary to get her attention. He mouthed the words, *Every… thing… okay?*

Mary mouthed in return, *I… guess?*

"Captain, what should we do?" Antwan asked.

Amy reached in front of her, turning on the microphone to the Flight Command Center. As with the past flights of his recruits to Salvation, Gabriel sat inside the center to watch.

"Flight Command…. we have a problem with Passenger Seven," Amy said into her microphone.

"Go ahead, Captain?"

"Passenger Seven appears to be experiencing an anomaly. We've double-checked the sensors, but we're still getting the same readings."

"What anomaly are you incurring? Over."

"Passenger Seven seems to have a problem in her heartbeat readings," Amy said.

Gabriel overhead the conversation with the Captain. He leaned over the shoulder of a technician in the Command Center as he confirmed the readings.

"Can this be right, Captain?" Gabriel asked into the technician's microphone.

"Sir, we've checked the sensors, and this is showing the correct readings."

"Hold on, Captain. We'll check with Salvation Command to determine how they wish to proceed." Gabriel's voice cracked as he spoke.

"Roger."

LAUNCH SITE, 1:19 P.M.

THE FLIGHT CREW atop the rocket on Launch Pad Number One continued with their pre-flight checks. However, all three became distracted for their concern with Mary, Passenger Seven.

"Go ahead, Gabriel; this is Salvation Command. Over," a voice said through the speaker system inside the Flight Command Center.

"We are sending you the vital readings from Passenger Seven. We have confirmed that they are correct and need to know how you wish to proceed."

Given the distance between Earth and Mars, a time delay exists between return radio responses. Due to the elliptical orbits of both planets, at their closest point, the time delay is three minutes. At their farthest, the delay is twenty-two.

Fifteen minutes later, a different voice came over the speaker system in the Flight Command Center. This voice was deeper, more authoritarian. It was the voice of the Leader at Salvation.

"Gabriel, continue with the flight as scheduled. We will make the proper arrangements on our side to take care of her upon arrival."

Receiving his orders direct from the Leader himself, Gabriel reached for the technician's microphone. "Captain. Gabriel here."

"Go ahead, Gabriel."

"Amy, we spoke with Salvation Command. You are instructed to continue with the mission. Take them to Salvation."

"Say again, Gabriel?"

"Take them to Salvation, Captain. You have your orders." His voice was stern.

"Yes… yes, Sir."

Antwan shook his head in disbelief at what he heard. "Captain, but we've never—"

"Antwan, we have our orders."

On the computer terminal in front of Antwan, he switched to Mary's heart readings. He made a manual entry into his computer. The anomaly required an update to her baseline information.

Antwan typed: *Passenger Seven - heartbeat at 85-bpm & heartbeat number 2 at 107-bpm.*

LAUNCH SITE, 2:01 P.M.

THE PASSENGERS SAT secure in their seats. Each experienced an elevated heartbeat with the anticipation for lift-off.

For five months, this moment had been a fantasy for Joe. Now, he faced the surreal reality of sitting upside-down, seventy meters in the air on top of a rocket.

Why the hell did we have to board so early if all we will do is sit here?

A video played inside the helmets on their face shields to help calm everyone during the flight crew's final pre-checks. The same image of a man appeared to the passengers.

The man wore a form-fitted suit like those of the passengers, making him look muscular. His salt-and-pepper hair provided the indication of his advanced age. To Joe and Mary, his face seemed familiar, but neither could place where they may have seen him.

Inside their helmets, passengers heard the man as he spoke, except for Mary. Her audio did not work as she only saw the man's lips move.

"Hello. Welcome to Salvation. You are about to depart on a life-changing adventure... not only for you... but for all mankind."

As the video played, Joe and Mary continued to hold hands across the space between their seats. They faced each other, focused on the man speaking.

Mary mouthed the words, *I... can't... hear... anything.* Joe did not notice Mary as the man held his full attention.

"Soon, you will arrive *here* to Salvation. You each will play an important role to ensure humanity lives on. I am sure when we approached you to join; it seemed unbelievable. But, based on your actions on Earth, we have chosen you to join us."

Mary's hand squeezed Joe's through their gloves. Joe shook her hand to get her attention from the video as Joe understood her nervous signal.

She glanced at Joe. He mouthed, *Mary... I love you... it... is... okay.*

Her smile was bright within her dark-tinted face shield. Her grip loosened reassuring Joe, Mary was fine. If only someone could reassure Joe.

The man in the video continued. "When you arrive here in less than a month, I will personally greet you, then. But, let me be first, now, and introduce myself..."

Joe's attention became laser-focused on the man filling Joe's field of vision. Finally, a sense of peace overcame Joe by putting a face behind the mystery eluding him who was in control at Salvation.

"... I am the leader here at Salvation. Everything that happens here comes through me. My name is Jacob, and I am pleased to meet you." The leader smiled a wicked grin. "I will see you all very soon."

With his introduction, the image of the man disappeared from everyone's screen. The flight crew still had deactivated all the microphones inside the passengers' helmets. Blast-off is less than a minute away.

With the image gone, Mary closed her eyes. She whispered a prayer to herself.

Mary felt Joe's hand tremble like hers did earlier. She opened her eyes and focused on Joe's face inside his helmet. Mary had not remembered a time his hand had shaken from nerves before.

Joe was visibly agitated by the introduction of the man. He squirmed in his seat attempting to get loose from his restraints. With less than thirty-seconds until blast-off, the Captain locked everyone in place as a safety measure.

With his free hand, Joe tapped the side and top of his helmet in a failed attempt to activate his microphone. Mary knew Joe was not okay. She squeezed his hand hard until he calmed down and focused his attention on her.

Inside the living module, the walls and seats roared vibrating underneath them. The seventy-meter-tall rocket came to life. Engines fired. The sound was incredible.

However, inside the passengers' helmets, everything was quiet. The noise-canceling speakers block-out ninety-five percent of all ambient sound.

A strange, calm silence enveloped their heads. In contrast, horrific sounds surrounded their bodies coming three-hundred feet below.

Joe and Mary made eye contact. Joe attempted to mouth something to Mary.

Mary tried to understand what Joe was saying. The violent vibrations and knowing what was about to happen prevented her.

An electronic countdown played over the speakers in everyone's helmet: *twenty-seconds... nineteen... eighteen...*

With each passing second counting down in reverse, everyone's heartbeat skyrocketed. The two heartbeats beating within Mary did as well.

Seventeen... sixteen... fifteen...

Joe never wavered. He continued mouthing the same words over-and-over to Mary. It was impossible for Mary to understand. Her seat vibrated side-to-side as if a large giant was outside shaking them like a toy.

Eleven... ten... nine...

Mary mouthed back to Joe in frustration. *What?*

Five… four… three…

"Mary, please understand what I'm trying to say…" Joe said out-loud inside his helmet. No one could hear him.

Two… one….

The vibration turned violent smacking everyone in their seats. Their bodies became three times their normal body weight due to the gravitational forces of lift-off.

Mary gave up trying to understand Joe. She closed her eyes so tight she saw her red blood veins within her eyelids. Inside her helmet, a constant guttural scream emerged from deep within her lungs; heard by no one.

All eight passengers' heads bounced and bobbed as the rocket climbed. Joe closed his eyes. He displaced the shear reality of what was happening by replaying the man's voice introducing himself in his mind.

Jacob… Jacob… Jacob Bishop?

The rocket continued its climb. The blue skies of Earth darkened into black space.

A savage jolt ricocheted throughout the living module. The rocket below them ejected the connected modules forward to Salvation.

A strange silence and calm filled the inside of the living module considering the mayhem of the last-minute. Joe and Mary resumed their focus onto each other.

Joe continued to mouth words Mary did not understand. The only thing Mary heard was silence.

What appeared as silence to Mary was quite the contrary. Inside Joe's helmet, he no longer just mouthed the words… he screamed them.

"He is my father! He is my father!"

End of Book One

EPILOGUE

"DR. BISHOP, THE NEXT SAMPLES are complete. How should we proceed?"

"Send the results to my computer."

Joe stood at his corner workstation in Wing B of Salvation Station 4 reviewing the numbers from the lab staffer. He compared the latest data-set to the previous fifteen samples.

"Not again," Joe rubbed his hand against his forehead, "I can't figure out what is happening."

The lab staffer stood next to Joe. "Dr. Bishop, I followed the new testing protocol you established. Do you think we should perform the next test on the latest patient?"

Joe paced the lab. Light steps long had replaced his once heavy gait on Earth. The latest testing protocol required the magnetic floor, meant to provide a sense of gravity within the Salvation compound, turned off within the laboratory. An unknown source of the anomalies in Joe's samples had frustrated him for weeks.

"Let me think about it. I'll review the past sample runs when I get back from my meeting with the Leader."

Joe grunted as he returned to his workstation to collect his reports. *Why is the decay rate speeding up in the cell samples?*

"While you're gone, Doctor, I will cleanup the sample stations."

"Okay, I'll be back in an hour. We can set-up the next test then."

Halfway across the lab, Joe stopped as a ten-year-old girl stood in his entranceway. Her short, auburn hair contrasted against her light-green eyes, her mother's eyes. Joe smiled.

"Emma, why aren't you in class?" Joe asked taking the girl by her hand. "You know you are not allowed out of the children's wing."

"I know, but I'm so lonely, there." Emma wrapped her arms around Joe's legs. "Plus, I was with Grandpa."

Joe knelt beside Emma. "Do you know what's today?"

Emma smiled. "It's Mommy's birthday, Daddy."

He hugged his daughter. "Yes, you're right."

"Can we visit her, today?"

Joe sighed feeling heaviness in his chest. "Let me take you back to your area. After my meeting with Grandpa, I'll come to get you, and we will go visit Mommy."

Emma kissed Joe's cheek. "I love you, Daddy."

"I love you too, my little Emma."

Joe stood and held Emma's hand exiting his lab. As they approached a translucent door, Joe pressed his left hand flat against a small, glass panel on the wall. A red light scanned his palm turning green as the door opened.

Joe and Emma stepped inside as Emma placed her hand on the glass panel beside the door on the wall. Red letters scrolled across the top of the panel. *Emmanuel Bishop.* Emma recorded her attendance.

The children's wing can accommodate up to one-hundred children younger than thirteen for classes during the day. Emma hugged Joe and joined the thirty-two others, who were left remaining.

"I'll be back in about an hour. I love you."

"Love you, too, Daddy."

The translucent door swished closed as Joe exited. The notes in his hand shuffled as he fumbled the folder. Joe stopped and reviewed his last handwritten comments. The top sheet inside listed the latest numbers of sick children.

Three more this week… So far, Emma seems healthy, but she's not been sick a day in her life… What's causing this?

Joe stacked his notes neatly together inside the folder and exited the children's wing. His feet fell firm against the floor walking on the magnetic floor following the way to the Leader's wing located in Salvation Station 1. Masterpieces of artwork adorned the hallway from the *Mona Lisa* to a plethora of works by Monet.

Joe stopped in front a translucent door pausing before placing his hand on the glass panel to gain entry.

Emma wants to visit you, today. Joe held his hand against his chest. *Happy Birthday, Sweetie. I love you.*

He rubbed a blue-and-white diamond pendant affixed to a platinum necklace under his bio-suit, while gazing at the *Waterlilies* painting on the wall.

Mary, I miss you.

2,416 DAYS AFTER IMPACT
APRIL 24, 2027 (EARTH DATE)

ABOUT THE AUTHOR

CHAD JOSEY is an engineering project manager by day and a writer by night. Originally from North Carolina, Chad resides in New Jersey after living and working four years in Germany.

Chad attended North Carolina State University obtaining his Industrial Engineering degree. Upon graduation, Chad pursued his MBA from Queen's University of Charlotte.

Chad has traveled to sixty-two countries documenting his travels and his American Expat life with his wife and their dog at his travel website WorldThruOurEyes.com. Chad weaves his travel experiences and professional life into his writing.

The Salvation Trilogy:
Book One: *SECRET SALVATION*
Book Two: *SALVATION CONSPIRACY*
Book Three: *PROMISE OF SALVATION*

Please consider leaving a review at AMAZON and GOODREADS to share your impression of **SECRET SALVATION** with other potential readers.

Follow Chad on social media and his website for updates:

Website: https://chadjosey.com

Facebook: https://www.facebook.com/AuthorChadJosey/

Twitter: https://twitter.com/chadjosey

Pinterest: https://www.pinterest.com/chadjosey

www.ingramcontent.com/pod-product-compliance
Lightning Source LLC
Chambersburg PA
CBHW030553020726
47494CB00005B/1594